THREE NOVELS
BY SAMUEL BECKETT

Works by Samuel Beckett published by Grove Press

THREE NOVELS
BY SAMUEL BECKETT

MOLLOY

MALONE DIES

THE UNNAMABLE

GROVE PRESS
NEW YORK

Published simultaneously in Canada
Printed in the United States of America

Library of Congress Catalog Card Number 59-13886
ISBN 0-8021-5091-8

Grove Press
841 Broadway
New York, NY 10003

06 07 20 19 18 17 16 15 14 13

MOLLOY

**Translated from the French by
Patrick Bowles
in collaboration with the author**

I

I am in my mother's room. It's I who live there now. I don't know how I got there. Perhaps in an ambulance, certainly a vehicle of some kind. I was helped. I'd never have got there alone. There's this man who comes every week. Perhaps I got there thanks to him. He says not. He gives me money and takes away the pages. So many pages, so much money. Yes, I work now, a little like I used to, except that I don't know how to work any more. That doesn't matter apparently. What I'd like now is to speak of the things that are left, say my goodbyes, finish dying. They don't want that. Yes, there is more than one, apparently. But it's always the same one that comes. You'll do that later, he says. Good. The truth is I haven't much will left. When he comes for the fresh pages he brings back the previous week's. They are marked with signs I don't understand. Anyway I don't read them. When I've done nothing he gives me nothing, he scolds me. Yet I don't work for money. For what then? I don't know. The truth is I don't know much. For example my mother's death. Was she already dead when I came? Or did she only die later? I mean enough to bury. I don't know. Perhaps they haven't buried her yet. In any case I have her room. I sleep in her bed. I piss and shit in her pot. I have taken her place. I must resemble her more and more. All I need now is a son. Perhaps I have one somewhere. But I think not. He would be old now, nearly as old as myself. It was a little chambermaid. It wasn't true love. The true love was in another. We'll come to that. Her name? I've forgotten it again. It seems to me sometimes that I even knew my son, that I helped him. Then I tell myself it's impossible. It's impossible I could ever have helped anyone. I've forgotten how to spell too, and half the words. That doesn't matter appar-

ently. Good. He's a queer one the one who comes to see me.
He comes every Sunday apparently. The other days he isn't
free. He's always thirsty. It was he told me I'd begun all
wrong, that I should have begun differently. He must be
right. I began at the beginning, like an old ballocks, can you
imagine that? Here's my beginning. Because they're keeping
it apparently. I took a lot of trouble with it. Here it is. It
gave me a lot of trouble. It was the beginning, do you understand? Whereas now it's nearly the end. Is what I do now any
better? I don't know. That's beside the point. Here's my beginning. It must mean something, or they wouldn't keep it.
Here it is.

This time, then once more I think, then perhaps a last
time, then I think it'll be over, with that world too. Premoni-
tion of the last but one but one. All grows dim. A little more
and you'll go blind. It's in the head. It doesn't work any
more, it says, I don't work any more. You go dumb as well
and sounds fade. The threshhold scarcely crossed that's how
it is. It's the head. It must have had enough. So that you say,
I'll manage this time, then perhaps once more, then perhaps
a last time, then nothing more. You are hard set to formu-
late this thought, for it is one, in a sense. Then you try to
pay attention, to consider with attention all those dim things,
saying to yourself, laboriously, It's my fault. Fault? That
was the word. But what fault? It's not goodbye, and what
magic in those dim things to which it will be time enough,
when next they pass, to say goodbye. For you must say goodbye, it would be madness not to say goodbye, when the time
comes. If you think of the forms and light of other days it
is without regret. But you seldom think of them, with what
would you think of them? I don't know. People pass too,
hard to distinguish from yourself. That is discouraging. So
I saw A and C going slowly towards each other, unconscious
of what they were doing. It was on a road remarkably bare,
I mean without hedges or ditches or any kind of edge, in the
country, for cows were chewing in enormous fields, lying and
standing, in the evening silence. Perhaps I'm inventing a
little, perhaps embellishing, but on the whole that's the way
it was. They chew, swallow, then after a short pause effort-
lessly bring up the next mouthful. A neck muscle stirs and
the jaws begin to grind again. But perhaps I'm remembering

things. The road, hard and white, seared the tender pastures, rose and fell at the whim of hills and hollows. The town was not far. It was two men, unmistakably, one small and one tall. They had left the town, first one, then the other, and then the first, weary or remembering a duty, had retraced his steps. The air was sharp for they wore greatcoats. They looked alike, but no more than others do. At first a wide space lay between them. They couldn't have seen each other, even had they raised their heads and looked about, because of this wide space, and then because of the undulating land, which caused the road to be in waves, not high, but high enough, high enough. But the moment came when together they went down into the same trough and in this trough finally met. To say they knew each other, no, nothing warrants it. But perhaps at the sound of their steps, or warned by some obscure instinct, they raised their heads and observed each other, for a good fifteen paces, before they stopped, breast to breast. Yes, they did not pass each other by, but halted, face to face, as in the country, of an evening, on a deserted road, two wayfaring strangers will, without there being anything extraordinary about it. But they knew each other perhaps. Now in any case they do, now I think they will know each other, greet each other, even in the depths of the town. They turned towards the sea, which, far in the east, beyond the fields, loomed high in the waning sky, and exchanged a few words. Then each went on his way. Each went on his way, A back towards the town, C on by-ways he seemed hardly to know, or not at all, for he went with uncertain step and often stopped to look about him, like someone trying to fix landmarks in his mind, for one day perhaps he may have to retrace his steps, you never know. The treacherous hills where fearfully he ventured were no doubt only known to him from afar, seen perhaps from his bedroom window or from the summit of a monument which, one black day, having nothing in particular to do and turning to height for solace, he had paid his few coppers to climb, slower and slower, up the winding stones. From there he must have seen it all, the plain, the sea, and then these self-same hills, that some call mountains, indigo in places in the evening light, their serried ranges crowding to the skyline, cloven with hidden valleys that the eye divines from sudden

shifts of colour and then from other signs for which there
are no words, nor even thoughts. But all are not divined,
even from that height, and often where only one escarpment
is discerned, and one crest, in reality there are two, two
escarpments, two crests, riven by a valley. But now he knows
these hills, that is to say he knows them better, and if ever
again he sees them from afar it will be I think with other
eyes, and not only that but the within, all that inner space
one never sees, the brain and heart and other caverns where
thought and feeling dance their sabbath, all that too quite
differently disposed. He looks old and it is a sorry sight to see
him solitary after so many years, so many days and nights
unthinkingly given to that rumour rising at birth and even
earlier, What shall I do? What shall I do? now low, a murmur, now precise as the headwaiter's And to follow? and
often rising to a scream. And in the end, or almost, to be
abroad alone, by unknown ways, in the gathering night, with
a stick. It was a stout stick, he used it to thrust himself onward, or as a defence, when the time came, against dogs
and marauders. Yes, night was gathering, but the man was
innocent, greatly innocent, he had nothing to fear, though
he went in fear, he had nothing to fear, there was nothing
they could do to him, or very little. But he can't have known
it. I wouldn't know myself, if I thought about it. Yes, he
saw himself threatened, his body threatened, his reason threatened, and perhaps he was, perhaps they were, in spite of his
innocence. What business has innocence here? What relation
to the innumerable spirits of darkness? It's not clear. It
seemed to me he wore a cocked hat. I remember being struck
by it, as I wouldn't have been for example by a cap or by a
bowler. I watched him recede, overtaken (myself) by his
anxiety, at least by an anxiety which was not necessarily his,
but of which as it were he partook. Who knows if it wasn't
my own anxiety overtaking him. He hadn't seen me. I was
perched higher than the road's highest point and flattened what
is more against a rock the same colour as myself, that is grey.
The rock he probably saw. He gazed around as if to engrave
the landmarks on his memory and must have seen the rock
in the shadow of which I crouched like Belaqua, or Sordello,
I forget. But a man, a fortiori myself, isn't exactly a landmark, because. I mean if by some strange chance he were to

pass that way again, after a long lapse of time, vanquished,
or to look for some lost thing, or to destroy something, his
eyes would search out the rock, not the haphazard in its
shadow of that unstable fugitive thing, still living flesh. No,
he certainly didn't see me, for the reasons I've given and then
because he was in no humour for that, that evening, no humour for the living, but rather for all that doesn't stir, or
stirs so slowly that a child would scorn it, let alone an old
man. However that may be, I mean whether he saw me or
whether he didn't, I repeat I watched him recede, at grips
(myself) with the temptation to get up and follow him, perhaps even to catch up with him one day, so as to know him
better, be myself less lonely. But in spite of my soul's leap
out to him, at the end of its elastic, I saw him only darkly,
because of the dark and then because of the terrain, in the
folds of which he disappeared from time to time, to re-emerge
further on, but most of all I think because of other things
calling me and towards which too one after the other my soul
was straining, wildly. I mean of course the fields, whitening
under the dew, and the animals, ceasing from wandering and
settling for the night, and the sea, of which nothing, and the
sharpening line of crests, and the sky where without seeing
them I felt the first stars tremble, and my hand on my knee
and above all the other wayfarer, A or C, I don't remember,
going resignedly home. Yes, towards my hand also, which
my knee felt tremble and of which my eyes saw the wrist
only, the heavily veined back, the pallid rows of knuckles.
But that is not, I mean my hand, what I wish to speak of
now, everything in due course, but A or C returning to the
town he had just left. But after all what was there particularly
urban in his aspect? He was bare-headed, wore sand-shoes,
smoked a cigar. He moved with a kind of loitering indolence
which rightly or wrongly seemed to me expressive. But all that
proved nothing, refuted nothing. Perhaps he had come from
afar, from the other end of the island even, and was approaching the town for the first time or returning to it after a long
absence. A little dog followed him, a pomeranian I think, but
I don't think so. I wasn't sure at the time and I'm still not
sure, though I've hardly thought about it. The little dog followed wretchedly, after the fashion of pomeranians, stopping,
turning in slow circles, giving up and then, a little further on,

beginning all over again. Constipation is a sign of good health
in pomeranians. At a given moment, pre-established if you
like, I don't much mind, the gentleman turned back, took the
little creature in his arms, drew the cigar from his lips and
buried his face in the orange fleece, for it was a gentleman,
that was obvious. Yes, it was an orange pomeranian, the less
I think of it the more certain I am. And yet. But would he
have come from afar, bare-headed, in sand-shoes, smoking
a cigar, followed by a pomeranian? Did he not seem rather
to have issued from the ramparts, after a good dinner, to
take his dog and himself for a walk, like so many citizens,
dreaming and farting, when the weather is fine? But was not
perhaps in reality the cigar a cutty, and were not the sand-
shoes boots, hobnailed, dust-whitened, and what prevented
the dog from being one of those stray dogs that you pick up
and take in your arms, from compassion or because you have
long been straying with no other company than the endless
roads, sands, shingle, bogs and heather, than this nature
answerable to another court, than at long intervals the fellow-
convict you long to stop, embrace, suck, suckle and whom
you pass by, with hostile eyes, for fear of his familiarities?
Until the day when, your endurance gone, in this world for
you without arms, you catch up in yours the first mangy
cur you meet, carry it the time needed for it to love you and
you it, then throw it away. Perhaps he had come to that, in
spite of appearances. He disappeared, his head on his chest,
the smoking object in his hand. Let me try and explain. From
things about to disappear I turn away in time. To watch
them out of sight, no, I can't do it. It was in this sense he
disappeared. Looking away I thought of him, saying, He is
dwindling, dwindling. I knew what I meant. I knew I could
catch him, lame as I was. I had only to want to. And yet
no, for I did want to. To get up, to get down on the road,
to set off hobbling in pursuit of him, to hail him, what could
be easier? He hears my cries, turns, waits for me. I am up
against him, up against the dog, gasping, between my crutches.
He is a little frightened of me, a little sorry for me, I disgust
him not a little. I am not a pretty sight, I don't smell good.
What is it I want? Ah that tone I know, compounded of
pity, of fear, of disgust. I want to see the dog, see the man,
at close quarters, know what smokes, inspect the shoes, find

out other things. He is kind, tells me of this and that and other things, whence he comes, whither he goes. I believe him, I know it's my only chance to—my only chance, I believe all I'm told, I've disbelieved only too much in my long life, now I swallow everything, greedily. What I need now is stories, it took me a long time to know that, and I'm not sure of it. There I am then, informed as to certain things, knowing certain things about him, things I didn't know, things I had craved to know, things I had never thought of. What rigmarole. I am even capable of having learnt what his profession is, I who am so interested in professions. And to think I try my best not to talk about myself. In a moment I shall talk about the cows, about the sky, if I can. There I am then, he leaves me, he's in a hurry. He didn't seem to be in a hurry, he was loitering, I've already said so, but after three minutes of me he is in a hurry, he has to hurry. I believe him. And once again I am I will not say alone, no, that's not like me, but, how shall I say, I don't know, restored to myself, no, I never left myself, free, yes, I don't know what that means but it's the word I mean to use, free to do what, to do nothing, to know, but what, the laws of the mind perhaps, of my mind, that for example water rises in proportion as it drowns you and that you would do better, at least no worse, to obliterate texts than to blacken margins, to fill in the holes of words till all is blank and flat and the whole ghastly business looks like what is, senseless, speechless, issueless misery. So I doubtless did better, at least no worse, not to stir from my observation post. But instead of observing I had the weakness to return in spirit to the other, the man with the stick. Then the murmurs began again. To restore silence is the role of objects. I said, Who knows if he hasn't simply come out to take the air, relax, stretch his legs, cool his brain by stamping the blood down to his feet, so as to make sure of a good night, a joyous awakening, an enchanted morrow. Was he carrying so much as a scrip? But the way of walking, the anxious looks, the club, could these be reconciled with one's conception of what is called a little turn? But the hat, a town hat, an old-fashioned town hat, which the least gust would carry far away. Unless it was attached under the chin, by means of a string or an elastic. I took off my hat and looked at it. It is fastened, it has always been fastened, to my buttonhole,

always the same buttonhole, at all seasons by a long lace. I
am still alive then. That may come in useful. The hand that
held the hat I thrust as far as possible from me and moved
in an arc, to and fro. As I did so, I watched the lapel of my
greatcoat and saw it open and close. I understand now why
I never wore a flower in my buttonhole, though it was large
enough to hold a whole nosegay. My buttonhole was set aside
for my hat. It was my hat that I beflowered. But it is neither
of my hat nor of my greatcoat that I hope to speak at present, it would be premature. Doubtless I shall speak of them
later, when the time comes to draw up the inventory of my
goods and possessions. Unless I lose them between now and
then. But even lost they will have their place, in the inventory
of my possessions. But I am easy in my mind, I shall not lose
them. Nor my crutches, I shall not lose my crutches either.
But I shall perhaps one day throw them away. I must have
been on the top, or on the slopes, of some considerable eminence, for otherwise how could I have seen, so far away, so
near at hand, so far beneath, so many things, fixed and moving. But what was an eminence doing in this land with hardly
a ripple? And I, what was I doing there, and why come?
These are things that we shall try and discover. But these are
things we must not take seriously. There is a little of everything, apparently, in nature, and freaks are common. And I
am perhaps confusing several different occasions, and different times, deep down, and deep down is my dwelling, oh not
deepest down, somewhere between the mud and the scum.
And perhaps it was A one day at one place, then C
another at another, then a third the rock and I, and so on
for the other components, the cows, the sky, the sea, the
mountains. I can't believe it. No, I will not lie, I can easily
conceive it. No matter, no matter, let us go on, as if all arose
from one and the same weariness, on and on heaping up
and up, until there is no room, no light, for any more. What
is certain is that the man with the stick did not pass by
again that night, because I would have heard him, if he had.
I don't say I would have seen him, I say I would have heard
him. I sleep little and that little by day. Oh not systematically,
in my life without end I have dabbled with every kind of
sleep, but at the time now coming back to me I took my doze
in the daytime and, what is more, in the morning. Let me

hear nothing of the moon, in my night there is no moon, and
if it happens that I speak of the stars it is by mistake. Now
of all the noises that night not one was of those heavy uncertain steps, or of that club with which he sometimes smote
the earth until it quaked. How agreeable it is to be confirmed,
after a more or less long period of vacillation, in one's first
impressions. Perhaps that is what tempers the pangs of death.
Not that I was so conclusively, I mean confirmed, in my
first impressions with regard to—wait—C. For the wagons
and carts which a little before dawn went thundering by, on
their way to market with fruit, eggs, butter and perhaps
cheese, in one of these perhaps he would have been found,
overcome by fatigue or discouragement, perhaps even dead.
Or he might have gone back to the town by another way
too far away for me to hear its sounds, or by little paths
through the fields, crushing the silent grass, pounding the
silent ground. And so at last I came out of that distant night,
divided between the murmurs of my little world, its dutiful
confusions, and those so different (so different?) of all that
between two suns abides and passes away. Never once a
human voice. But the cows, when the peasants passed, crying
in vain to be milked. A and C I never saw again. But perhaps
I shall see them again. But shall I be able to recognize them?
And am I sure I never saw them again? And what do I mean
by seeing and seeing again? An instant of silence, as when
the conductor taps on his stand, raises his arms, before the
unanswerable clamour. Smoke, sticks, flesh, hair, at evening,
afar, flung about the craving for a fellow. I know how to
summon these rags to cover my shame. I wonder what that
means. But I shall not always be in need. But talking of the
craving for a fellow let me observe that having waked between eleven o'clock and midday (I heard the angelus, recalling the incarnation, shortly after) I resolved to go and see
my mother. I needed, before I could resolve to go and see
that woman, reasons of an urgent nature, and with such
reasons, since I did not know what to do, or where to go, it
was child's play for me, the play of an only child, to fill my
mind until it was rid of all other preoccupation and I seized
with a trembling at the mere idea of being hindered from
going there, I mean to my mother, there and then. So I got
up, adjusted my crutches and went down to the road, where

I found my bicycle (I didn't know I had one) in the same
place I must have left it. Which enables me to remark that,
crippled though I was, I was no mean cyclist, at that period.
This is how I went about it. I fastened my crutches to the
cross-bar, one on either side, I propped the foot of my stiff
leg (I forget which, now they're both stiff) on the projecting
front axle, and I pedalled with the other. It was a chainless
bicycle, with a free-wheel, if such a bicycle exists. Dear bicycle, I shall not call you bike, you were green, like so many
of your generation, I don't know why. It is a pleasure to meet
it again. To describe it at length would be a pleasure. It had
a little red horn instead of the bell fashionable in your days.
To blow this horn was for me a real pleasure, almost a vice.
I will go further and declare that if I were obliged to record,
in a roll of honour, those activities which in the course of my
interminable existence have given me only a mild pain in the
balls, the blowing of a rubber horn—toot!—would figure
among the first. And when I had to part from my bicycle I
took off the horn and kept it about me. I believe I have it
still, somewhere, and if I blow it no more it is because it has
gone dumb. Even motor-cars have no horns nowadays, as I
understand the thing, or rarely. When I see one, through the
lowered window of a stationary car, I often stop and blow
it. This should all be re-written in the pluperfect. What a
rest to speak of bicycles and horns. Unfortunately it is not
of them I have to speak, but of her who brought me into
the world, through the hole in her arse if my memory is
correct. First taste of the shit. So I shall only add that every
hundred yards or so I stopped to rest my legs, the good one as
well as the bad, and not only my legs, not only my legs. I
didn't properly speaking get down off the machine, I remained
astride it, my feet on the ground, my arms on the handlebars, my head on my arms, and I waited until I felt better.
But before I leave this earthly paradise, suspended between
the mountains and the sea, sheltered from certain winds and
exposed to all that Auster vents, in the way of scents and
langours, on this accursed country, it would ill become me
not to mention the awful cries of the corncrakes that run
in the corn, in the meadows, all the short summer night long,
dinning their rattles. And this enables me, what is more, to
know when that unreal journey began, the second last but

one of a form fading among fading forms, and which I here declare without further ado to have begun in the second or third week of June, at the moment that is to say most painful of all when over what is called our hemisphere the sun is at its pitilessmost and the arctic radiance comes pissing on our midnights. It is then the corncrakes are heard. My mother never refused to see me, that is she never refused to receive me, for it was many a long day since she had seen anything at all. I shall try and speak calmly. We were so old, she and I, she had had me so young, that we were like a couple of old cronies, sexless, unrelated, with the same memories, the same rancours, the same expectations. She never called me son, fortunately, I couldn't have borne it, but Dan, I don't know why, my name is not Dan. Dan was my father's name perhaps, yes, perhaps she took me for my father. I took her for my mother and she took me for my father. Dan, you remember the day I saved the swallow. Dan, you remember the day you buried the ring. I remembered, I remembered, I mean I knew more or less what she was talking about, and if I hadn't always taken part personally in the scenes she evoked, it was just as if I had. I called her Mag, when I had to call her something. And I called her Mag because for me, without my knowing why, the letter g abolished the syllable Ma, and as it were spat on it, better than any other letter would have done. And at the same time I satisfied a deep and doubtless unacknowledged need, the need to have a Ma, that is a mother, and to proclaim it, audibly. For before you say mag you say ma, inevitably. And da, in my part of the world, means father. Besides for me the question did not arise, at the period I'm worming into now, I mean the question of whether to call her Ma, Mag or the Countess Caca, she having for countless years been as deaf as a post. I think she was quite incontinent, both of faeces and water, but a kind of prudishness made us avoid the subject when we met, and I could never be certain of it. In any case it can't have amounted to much, a few niggardly wetted goat-droppings every two or three days. The room smelt of ammonia, oh not merely of ammonia, but of ammonia, ammonia. She knew it was me, by my smell. Her shrunken hairy old face lit up, she was happy to smell me. She jabbered away with a rattle of dentures and most

of the time didn't realize what she was saying. Anyone but
myself would have been lost in this clattering gabble, which
can only have stopped during her brief instants of uncon-
sciousness. In any case I didn't come to listen to her. I got
into communication with her by knocking on her skull. One
knock meant yes, two no, three I don't know, four money,
five goodbye. I was hard put to ram this code into her ruined
and frantic understanding, but I did it, in the end. That she
should confuse yes, no, I don't know and goodbye, was all
the same to me, I confused them myself. But that she should
associate the four knocks with anything but money was
something to be avoided at all costs. During the period of
training therefore, at the same time as I administered the
four knocks on her skull, I stuck a bank-note under her nose
or in her mouth. In the innocence of my heart! For she
seemed to have lost, if not absolutely all notion of mensura-
tion, at least the faculty of counting beyond two. It was too
far for her, yes, the distance was too great, from one to four.
By the time she came to the fourth knock she imagined she
was only at the second, the first two having been erased
from her memory as completely as if they had never been
felt, though I don't quite see how something never felt can
be erased from the memory, and yet it is á common occur-
rence. She must have thought I was saying no to her all the
time, whereas nothing was further from my purpose. Enlightened by these considerations I looked for and finally
found a more effective means of putting the idea of money
into her head. This consisted in replacing the four knocks
of my index-knuckle by one or more (according to my needs)
thumps of the fist, on her skull. That she understood. In any
case I didn't come for money. I took her money, but I didn't
come for that. My mother. I don't think too harshly of her.
I know she did all she could not to have me, except of course the
one thing, and if she never succeeded in getting me unstuck,
it was fate that ear-marked me for less compassionate sewers.
But it was well-meant and that's enough for me. No it is not
enough for me, but I give her credit, though she is my
mother, for what she tried to do for me. And I forgive her
for having jostled me a little in the first months and spoiled
the only endurable, just endurable, period of my enormous
history. And I also give her credit for not having done it

again, thanks to me, or for having stopped in time, when she did. And if ever I'm reduced to looking for a meaning to my life, you never can tell, it's in that old mess I'll stick my nose to begin with, the mess of that poor old uniparous whore and myself the last of my foul brood, neither man nor beast. I should add, before I get down to the facts, you'd swear they were facts, of that distant summer afternoon, that with this deaf blind impotent mad old woman, who called me Dan and whom I called Mag, and with her alone, I— no, I can't say it. That is to say I could say it but I won't say it, yes, I could say it easily, because it wouldn't be true. What did I see of her? A head always, the hands sometimes, the arms rarely. A head always. Veiled with hair, wrinkles, filth, slobber. A head that darkened the air. Not that seeing matters, but it's something to go on with. It was I who took the key from under the pillow, who took the money out of the drawer, who put the key back under the pillow. But I didn't come for money. I think there was a woman who came each week. Once I touched with my lips, vaguely, hastily, that little grey wizened pear. Pah. Did that please her? I don't know. Her babble stopped for a second, then began again. Perhaps she said to herself, Pah. I smelt a terrible smell. It must have come from the bowels. Odour of antiquity. Oh I'm not criticizing her, I don't diffuse the perfumes of Araby myself. Shall I describe the room? No. I shall have occasion to do so later perhaps. When I seek refuge there, bet to the world, all shame drunk, my prick in my rectum, who knows. Good. Now that we know where we're going, let's go there. It's so nice to know where you're going, in the early stages. It almost rids you of the wish to go there. I was distraught, who am so seldom distraught, from what should I be distraught, and as to my motions even more uncertain than usual. The night must have tired me, at least weakened me, and the sun, hoisting itself higher and higher in the east, had poisoned me, while I slept. I ought to have put the bulk of the rock between it and me before closing my eyes. I confuse east and west, the poles too, I invert them readily. I was out of sorts. They are deep, my sorts, a deep ditch, and I am not often out of them. That's why I mention it. Nevertheless I covered several miles and found myself under the ramparts. There I dismounted in compliance with the

regulations. Yes, cyclists entering and leaving town are required by the police to dismount, cars to go into bottom gear
and horsedrawn vehicles to slow down to a walk. The reason
for this regulation is I think this, that the ways into and of
course out of this town are narrow and darkened by enormous vaults, without exception. It is a good rule and I
observe it religiously, in spite of the difficulty I have in
advancing on my crutches pushing my bicycle at the same
time. I managed somehow. Being ingenious. Thus we cleared
these difficult straits, my bicycle and I, together. But a little
further on I heard myself hailed. I raised my head and saw
a policeman. Elliptically speaking, for it was only later, by
way of induction, or deduction, I forget which, that I knew
what it was. What are you doing there? he said. I'm used
to that question, I understood it immediately. Resting, I said.
Resting, he said. Resting, I said. Will you answer my question?
he cried. So it always is when I'm reduced to confabulation,
I honestly believe I have answered the question I am asked
and in reality I do nothing of the kind. I won't reconstruct
the conversation in all its meanderings. It ended in my understanding that my way of resting, my attitude when at rest,
astride my bicycle, my arms on the handlebars, my head
on my arms, was a violation of I don't know what, public
order, public decency. Modestly I pointed to my crutches
and ventured one or two noises regarding my infirmity, which
obliged me to rest as I could, rather than as I should. But
there are not two laws, that was the next thing I thought I
understood, not two laws, one for the healthy, another for
the sick, but one only to which all must bow, rich and poor,
young and old, happy and sad. He was eloquent. I pointed
out that I was not sad. That was a mistake. Your papers, he
said, I knew it a moment later. Not at all, I said, not at
all. Your papers! he cried. Ah my papers. Now the only
papers I carry with me are bits of newspaper to wipe myself, you understand, when I have a stool. Oh I don't say
I wipe myself every time I have a stool, no, but I like to be
in a position to do so, if I have to. Nothing strange about
that, it seems to me. In a panic I took this paper from my
pocket and thrust it under his nose. The weather was fine.
We took the little side streets, quiet, sunlit, I springing along
between my crutches, he pushing my bicycle, with the tips of

his white-gloved fingers. I wasn't—I didn't feel unhappy.
I stopped a moment, I made so bold, to lift my hand and
touch the crown of my hat. It was scorching. I felt the faces
turning to look after us, calm faces and joyful faces, faces
of men, of women and of children. I seemed to hear, at a
certain moment, a distant music. I stopped, the better to listen.
Go on, he said. Listen, I said. Get on, he said. I wasn't
allowed to listen to the music. It might have drawn a crowd.
He gave me a shove. I had been touched, oh not my skin,
but none the less my skin had felt it, it had felt a man's
hard fist, through its coverings. While still putting my best
foot foremost I gave myself up to that golden moment, as
if I had been someone else. It was the hour of rest, the
forenoon's toil ended, the afternoon's to come. The wisest
perhaps, lying in the squares or sitting on their door-steps,
were savouring its languid ending, forgetful of recent cares,
indifferent to those at hand. Others on the contrary were
using it to hatch their plans, their heads in their hands. Was
there one among them to put himself in my place, to feel
how removed I was then from him I seemed to be, and in that
remove what strain, as of hawsers about to snap? It's possible. Yes, I was straining towards those spurious deeps,
their lying promise of gravity and peace, from all my old
poisons I struggled towards them, safely bound. Under the
blue sky, under the watchful gaze. Forgetful of my mother,
set free from the act, merged in this alien hour, saying,
Respite, respite. At the police station I was haled before a
very strange official. Dressed in plain-clothes, in his shirt-
sleeves, he was sprawling in an arm-chair, his feet on his
desk, a straw hat on his head and protruding from his mouth
a thin flexible object I could not identify. I had time to
become aware of these details before he dismissed me. He
listened to his subordinate's report and then began to inter-
rogate me in a tone which, from the point of view of civility,
left increasingly to be desired, in my opinion. Between his
questions and my answers, I mean those deserving of consideration, the intervals were more or less long and turbu-
lent. I am so little used to being asked anything that when
I am asked something I take some time to know what. And
the mistake I make then is this, that instead of quietly
reflecting on what I have just heard, and heard distinctly,

not being hard of hearing, in spite of all I have heard, I
hasten to answer blindly, fearing perhaps lest my silence
fan their anger to fury. I am full of fear, I have gone in
fear all my life, in fear of blows. Insults, abuse, these I can
easily bear, but I could never get used to blows. It's strange.
Even spits still pain me. But they have only to be a little
gentle. I mean refrain from hitting me, and I seldom fail
to give satisfaction, in the long run. Now the sergeant, content to threaten me with a cylindrical ruler, was little by
little rewarded for his pains by the discovery that I had no
papers in the sense this word had a sense for him, nor any
occupation, nor any domicile, that my surname escaped
me for the moment and that I was on my way to my mother,
whose charity kept me dying. As to her address, I was in
the dark, but knew how to get there, even in the dark. The
district? By the shambles your honour, for from my mother's
room, through the closed windows, I had heard, stilling her
chatter, the bellowing of the cattle, that violent raucous
tremulous bellowing not of the pastures but of the towns,
their shambles and cattle-markets. Yes, after all, I had perhaps gone too far in saying that my mother lived near the
shambles, it could equally well have been the cattle-market,
near which she lived. Never mind, said the sergeant, it's
the same district. I took advantage of the silence which followed these kind words to turn towards the window, blindly
or nearly, for I had closed my eyes, proffering to that bland-
ness of blue and gold my face and neck alone, and my mind
empty too, or nearly, for I must have been wondering if I
did not feel like sitting down, after such a long time standing, and remembering what I had learnt in that connexion,
namely that the sitting posture was not for me any more,
because of my short stiff leg, and that there were only two
postures for me any more, the vertical, drooping between
my crutches, sleeping on my feet, and the horizontal, down
on the ground. And yet the desire to sit down came upon
me from time to time, back upon me from a vanished world.
And I did not always resist it, forewarned though I was.
Yes, my mind felt it surely, this tiny sediment, incomprehensibly stirring like grit at the bottom of a puddle, while
on my face and great big Adam's apple the air of summer
weighed and the splendid summer sky. And suddenly I re-

membered my name, Molloy. My name is Molloy, I cried,
all of a sudden, now I remember. Nothing compelled me to
give this information, but I gave it, hoping to please I
suppose. They let me keep my hat on, I don't know why. Is
it your mother's name? said the sergeant, it must have been
a sergeant. Molloy, I cried, my name is Molloy. Is that
your mother's name? said the sergeant. What? I said. Your
name is Molloy, said the sergeant. Yes, I said, now I remember. And your mother? said the sergeant. I didn't follow. Is your mother's name Molloy too? said the sergeant.
I thought it over. Your mother, said the sergeant, is your
mother's—Let me think! I cried. At least I imagine that's
how it was. Take your time, said the sergeant. Was mother's
name Molloy? Very likely. Her name must be Molloy too,
I said. They took me away, to the guardroom I suppose, and
there I was told to sit down. I must have tried to explain.
I won't go into it. I obtained permission, if not to lie down
on a bench, at least to remain standing, propped against
the wall. The room was dark and full of people hastening
to and fro, malefactors, policemen, lawyers, priests and
journalists I suppose. All that made a dark, dark forms
crowding in a dark place. They paid no attention to me and
I repaid the compliment. Then how could I know they were
paying no attention to me, and how could I repay the compliment, since they were paying no attention to me? I don't
know. I knew it and I did it, that's all I know. But suddenly
a woman rose up before me, a big fat woman dressed in
black, or rather in mauve. I still wonder today if it wasn't
the social worker. She was holding out to me, on an odd
saucer, a mug full of a greyish concoction which must have
been green tea with saccharine and powdered milk. Nor
was that all, for between mug and saucer a thick slab of
dry bread was precariously lodged, so that I began to say,
in a kind of anguish, It's going to fall, it's going to fall,
as if it mattered whether it fell or not. A moment later I
myself was holding, in my trembling hands, this little pile
of tottering disparates, in which the hard, the liquid and
the soft were joined, without understanding how the transfer had been effected. Let me tell you this, when social
workers offer you, free, gratis and for nothing, something to
hinder you from swooning, which with them is an obsession,

it is useless to recoil, they will pursue you to the ends of the earth, the vomitory in their hands. The Salvation Army is no better. Against the charitable gesture there is no defence, that I know of. You sink your head, you put out your hands all trembling and twined together and you say, Thank you, thank you lady, thank you kind lady. To him who has nothing it is forbidden not to relish filth. The liquid over-flowed, the mug rocked with a noise of chattering teeth, not mine, I had none, and the sodden bread sagged more and more. Until, panic-stricken, I flung it all far from me. I did not let it fall, no, but with a convulsive thrust of both my hands I threw it to the ground, where it smashed to smithereens, or against the wall, far from me, with all my strength. I will not tell what followed, for I am weary of this place, I want to go. It was late afternoon when they told me I could go. I was advised to behave better in future. Conscious of my wrongs, knowing now the reasons for my arrest, alive to my irregular situation as revealed by the enquiry, I was surprised to find myself so soon at freedom once again, if that is what it was, unpenalised. Had I, without my knowledge, a friend at court? Had I, without knowing it, favourably impressed the sergeant? Had they succeeded in finding my mother and obtaining from her, or from the neighbours, partial confirmation of my statements? Were they of the opinion that it was useless to prosecute me? To apply the letter of the law to a creature like me is not an easy matter. It can be done, but reason is against it. It is better to leave things to the police. I don't know. If it is unlawful to be without papers, why did they not insist on my getting them. Because that costs money and I had none? But in that case could they not have appropriated my bicycle? Probably not, without a court order. All that is incomprehensible. What is certain is this, that I never rested in that way again, my feet obscenely resting on the earth, my arms on the handlebars and on my arms my head, rocking and abandoned. It is indeed a deplorable sight, a deplorable example, for the people, who so need to be encouraged, in their bitter toil, and to have before their eyes manifestations of strength only, of courage and of joy, without which they might collapse, at the end of the day, and roll on the ground. I have only to be told what

good behaviour is and I am well-behaved, within the limits of
my physical possibilities. And so I have never ceased to
improve, from this point of view, for I—I used to be
intelligent and quick. And as far as good-will is concerned,
I had it to overflowing, the exasperated good-will of the
overanxious. So that my repertory of permitted attitudes
has never ceased to grow, from my first steps until my last,
executed last year. And if I have always behaved like a
pig, the fault lies not with me but with my superiors, who
corrected me only on points of detail instead of showing
me the essence of the system, after the manner of the great
English schools, and the guiding principles of good man-
ners, and how to proceed, without going wrong, from the
former to the latter, and how to trace back to its ultimate
source a given comportment. For that would have allowed
me, before parading in public certain habits such as the
finger in the nose, the scratching of the balls, digital emunc-
tion and the peripatetic piss, to refer them to the first rules
of a reasoned theory. On this subject I had only negative
and empirical notions, which means that I was in the dark,
most of the time, and all the more completely as a lifetime
of observations had left me doubting the possibility of
systematic decorum, even within a limited area. But it
is only since I have ceased to live that I think of these
things and the other things. It is in the tranquillity of decomposition that I remember the long confused emotion
which was my life, and that I judge it, as it is said that
God will judge me, and with no less impertinence. To
decompose is to live too, I know, I know, don't torment me, but
one sometimes forgets. And of that life too I shall tell you
perhaps one day, the day I know that when I thought I
knew I was merely existing and that passion without form
or stations will have devoured me down to the rotting flesh
itself and that when I know that I know nothing, am only
crying out as I have always cried out, more or less piercingly,
more or less openly. Let me cry out then, it's said to be
good for you. Yes, let me cry out, this time, then another
time perhaps, then perhaps a last time. Cry out that the
declining sun fell full on the white wall of the barracks.
It was like being in China. A confused shadow was cast.
It was I and my bicycle. I began to play, gesticulating,

waving my hat, moving my bicycle to and fro before me, blowing the horn, watching the wall. They were watching me through the bars, I felt their eyes upon me. The police-man on guard at the door told me to go away. He needn't have, I was calm again. The shadow in the end is no better than the substance. I asked the man to help me, to have pity on me. He didn't understand. I thought of the food I had refused. I took a pebble from my pocket and sucked it. It was smooth, from having been sucked so long, by me, and beaten by the storm. A little pebble in your mouth, round and smooth, appeases, soothes, makes you forget your hunger, forget your thirst. The man came towards me, angered by my slowness. Him too they were watching, through the windows. Somewhere someone laughed. Inside me too someone was laughing. I took my sick leg in my hands and passed it over the frame. I went. I had forgotten where I was going. I stopped to think. It is difficult to think riding, for me. When I try and think riding I lose my balance and fall. I speak in the present tense, it is so easy to speak in the present tense, when speaking of the past. It is the mythological present, don't mind it. I was already settling in my raglimp stasis when I remembered it wasn't done. I went on my way, that way of which I knew nothing, qua way, which was nothing more than a surface, bright or dark, smooth or rough, and always dear to me, in spite of all, and the dear sound of that which goes and is gone, with a brief dust, when the weather is dry. There I am then, before I knew I had left the town, on the canal-bank. The canal goes through the town, I know I know, there are even two. But then these hedges, these fields? Don't torment yourself, Molloy. Suddenly I see, it was my right leg the stiff one, then. Toiling towards me along the tow-path I saw a team of little grey donkeys, on the far bank, and I heard angry cries and dull blows. I got down. I put my foot to the ground the better to see the approaching barge, so gently approaching that the water was unruffled. It was a cargo of nails and timber, on its way to some carpenter I suppose. My eyes caught a donkey's eyes, they fell to his little feet, their brave fastidious tread. The boat-man rested his elbow on his knee, his head on his hand. He had a long white beard. Every three or four puffs, without taking his pipe from his mouth, he spat into the water. I could not see his eyes. The horizon was burning with sulphur and phosphorus, it was there I was bound. At last I got right down, hobbled down to the ditch and lay down, beside my bicycle. I lay at full stretch, with outspread arms. The white hawthorn stooped towards me, unfortunately I don't like the smell of hawthorn. In the ditch the grass was thick and high, I took off my hat and pressed about my face the long leafy stalks. Then I could smell the earth, the smell of the earth was in the grass that my hands wove round my face till I was blinded. I ate a little too, a little grass. It came back to my mind, from nowhere, as a moment before my name, that I had set out to see my mother, at the beginning of this ending day. My reasons? I had forgotten them. But I knew them, I must have known them, I had only to find them again and I would sweep, with the clipped wings of necessity, to my mother. Yes, it's all easy when you know why, a mere matter of magic. Yes, the whole thing is to know what saint to implore, any fool can implore him. For the particulars, if you are interested in particulars, there is no need to despair, you may scrabble on the right door, in the right way, in the end. It's for the whole there seems to be no spell. Perhaps there is no whole, before you're dead. An opiate for the life of the dead, that should be easy. What am I waiting for then, to exorcize mine? It's coming, it's coming. I hear from here the howl resolving all, even if it is not mine. Meanwhile there's no use knowing you are gone, you are not, you are writhing yet, the hair is growing, the nails are growing, the entrails emptying, all the morticians are dead. Someone has drawn the blinds, you perhaps. Not the faintest sound. Where are the famous flies? Yes, there is no denying it, any longer, it is not you who are dead, but all the others. So you get up and go to your mother, who thinks she is alive. That's my impression. But now I shall have to get myself out of this ditch. How joyfully I would vanish there, sinking deeper and deeper under the rains. No doubt I'll come back some day, here, or to a similar slough, I can trust my feet for that, as no doubt some day I'll meet again the sergeant and his merry men. And if, too changed to know it is they, I do not say it is they, make no mistake, it will be

they, though changed. For to contrive a being, a place, I
nearly said an hour, but I would not hurt anyone's feelings,
and then to use them no more, that would be, how shall I
say, I don't know. Not to want to say, not to know what
you want to say, not to be able to say what you think
you want to say, and never to stop saying, or hardly ever,
that is the thing to keep in mind, even in the heat of composition. That night was not like the other night, if it
had been I would have known. For when I try and think
of that night, on the canal-bank, I find nothing, no night
properly speaking, nothing but Molloy in the ditch, and
perfect silence, and behind my closed lids the little night
and its little lights, faint at first, then flaming and extinguished, now ravening, now fed, as fire by filth and
martyrs. I say that night, but there was more than one
perhaps. The lie, the lie, to lying thought. But I find the
morning, a morning, and the sun already high, and the little
sleep I had then, according to my custom, and space with
its sounds again, and the shepherd watching me sleep and
under whose eyes I opened my eyes. Beside him a panting
dog, watching me too, but less closely than his master, for
from time to time he stopped watching me to gnaw at his
flesh, furiously, where the ticks were in him I suppose. Did
he take me for a black sheep entangled in the brambles and
was he waiting for an order from his master to drag me
out? I don't think so. I don't smell like a sheep, I wish I
smelt like a sheep, or a buck-goat. When I wake I see
the first things quite clearly, the first things that offer, and
I understand them, when they are not too difficult. Then
in my eyes and in my head a fine rain begins to fall, as
from a rose, highly important. So I knew at once it was a
shepherd and his dog I had before me, above me rather,
for they had not left the path. And I identified the bleating
too, without any trouble, the anxious bleating of the sheep,
missing the dog at their heels. It is then too that the meaning of words is least obscure to me, so that I said, with
tranquil assurance, Where are you taking them, to the
fields or to the shambles? I must have completely lost my
sense of direction, as if direction had anything to do with
the matter. For even if he was going towards the town,
what prevented him from skirting it, or from leaving it

again by another gate, on his way to new pastures, and if
he was going away from it that meant nothing either, for
slaughter-houses are not confined to towns, no, they are
everywhere, the country is full of them, every butcher has
his slaughter-house and the right to slaughter, according to
his lights. But whether it was he didn't understand, or didn't
want to reply, he didn't reply, but went on his way without
a word, without a word for me I mean, for he spoke to
his dog who listened attentively, cocking his ears. I got
to my knees, no, that doesn't work, I got up and watched
the little procession recede. I heard the shepherd whistle,
and I saw him flourishing his crook, and the dog bustling
about the herd, which but for him would no doubt have
fallen into the canal. All that through a glittering dust, and
soon through that mist too which rises in me every day
and veils the world from me and veils me from myself. The
bleating grew faint, because the sheep were less anxious, or
because they were further away, or because my hearing
was worse than a moment before, which would surprise me,
for my hearing is still very good, scarcely blunted coming
up to dawn, and if I sometimes hear nothing for hours on
end it is for reasons of which I know nothing, or because
about me all goes really silent, from time to time, whereas
for the righteous the tumult of the world never stops. That
then is how that second day began, unless it was the third, or
the fourth, and it was a bad beginning, because it left me
with persisting doubts, as to the destination of those sheep,
among which there were lambs, and often wondering if
they had safely reached some commonage or fallen, their
skulls shattered, their thin legs crumpling, first to their
knees, then over on their fleecy sides, under the pole-axe,
though that is not the way they slaughter sheep, but with
a knife, so that they bleed to death. But there is much
to be said too for these little doubts. Good God, what a
land of breeders, you see quadrupeds everywhere. And it's
not over yet, there are still horses and goats, to mention
only them, I feel them watching out for me, to get in my
path. I have no need of that. But I did not lose sight of
my immediate goal, which was to get to my mother as
quickly as possible, and standing in the ditch I summoned
to my aid the good reasons I had for going there, without

a moment's delay. And though there were many things I could do without thinking, not knowing what I was going to do until it was done, and not even then, going to my mother was not one of them. My feet, you see, never took me to my mother unless they received a definite order to do so. The glorious, the truly glorious weather would have gladdened any other heart than mine. But I have no reason to be gladdened by the sun and I take good care not to be. The Aegean, thirsting for heat and light, him I killed, he killed himself, early on, in me. The pale gloom of rainy days was better fitted to my taste, no, that's not it, to my humour, no, that's not it either, I had neither taste nor humour, I lost them early on. Perhaps what I mean is that the pale gloom, etc., hid me better, without its being on that account particularly pleasing to me. Chameleon in spite of himself, there you have Molloy, viewed from a certain angle. And in winter, under my greatcoat, I wrapped myself in swathes of newspaper, and did not shed them until the earth awoke, for good, in April. The Times Literary Supplement was admirably adapted to this purpose, of a neverfailing toughness and impermeability. Even farts made no impression on it. I can't help it, gas escapes from my fundament on the least pretext, it's hard not to mention it now and then, however great my distaste. One day I counted them. Three hundred and fifteen farts in nineteen hours, or an average of over sixteen farts an hour. After all it's not excessive. Four farts every fifteen minutes. It's nothing. Not even one fart every four minutes. It's unbelievable. Damn it, I hardly fart at all, I should never have mentioned it. Extraordinary how mathematics help you to know yourself. In any case this whole question of climate left me cold, I could stomach any mess. So I will only add that the mornings were often sunny, in that part of the world, until ten o'clock or coming up to eleven, and that then the sky darkened and the rain fell, fell till evening. Then the sun came out and went down, the drenched earth sparkled an instant, then went out, bereft of light. There I am then back in the saddle, in my numbed heart a prick of misgiving, like one dying of cancer obliged to consult his dentist. For I did not know if it was the right road. All roads were right for me, a wrong road was an event, for me. But when I was on my way to my mother only one road was right, the one that led to her, or one of those that led to her, for all did not lead to her. I did not know if I was on one of those right roads and that disturbed me, like all recall to life. Judge then of my relief when I saw, ahead of me, the familiar ramparts loom. I passed beyond them, into a district I did not know. And yet I knew the town well, for I was born there and had never succeeded in putting between it and me more than ten or fifteen miles, such was its grasp on me, I don't know why. So that I came near to wondering if I was in the right town, where I first saw the murk of day and which still harboured my mother, somewhere or other, or if I had not stumbled, as a result of a wrong turn, on a town whose very name I did not know. For my native town was the only one I knew, having never set foot in any other. But I had read with care, while I still could read, accounts of travellers more fortunate than my-self, telling of other towns as beautiful as mine, and even more beautiful, though with a different beauty. And now it was a name I sought, in my memory, the name of the only town it had been given me to know, with the intention, as soon as I had found it, of stopping, and saying to a passer-by, doffing my hat, I beg your pardon, Sir, this *is* X, is it not?, X being the name of my town. And this name that I sought, I felt sure that it began with a B or with a P, but in spite of this clue, or perhaps because of its falsity, the other letters continued to escape me. I had been living so far from words so long, you understand, that it was enough for me to see my town, since we're talking of my town, to be unable, you understand. It's too difficult to say, for me. And even my sense of identity was wrapped in a namelessness often hard to penetrate, as we have just seen I think. And so on for all the other things which made merry with my senses. Yes, even then, when already all was fading, waves and particles, there could be no things but nameless things, no names but thing-less names. I say that now, but after all what do I know now about then, now when the icy words hail down upon me, the icy meanings, and the world dies too, foully named. All I know is what the words know, and the dead things, and that makes a handsome little sum, with a beginning, a middle and an end as in the well-built phrase and the long sonata of the dead. And truly it little matters what I say, this, this or that or any other thing. Saying is inventing. Wrong, very rightly wrong. You invent nothing, you think you are inventing, you think you are escaping, and all you do is stammer out your lesson, the remnants of a pensum one day got by heart and long forgotten, life without tears, as it is wept. To hell with it anyway. Where was I. Unable to remember the name of my town I resolved to stop by the kerb, to wait for a passer-by with a friendly and intelligent air and then to whip off my hat and say, with my smile, I beg your pardon Sir, excuse me Sir, what is the name of this town, if you please? For the word once let fall I would know if it was the right word the one I was seeking, in my memory, or another, and so where I stood. This resolution, actually formed as I rode along, was never to be carried out an absurd mishap prevented it. Yes, my resolutions were remarkable in this, that they were no sooner formed than something always happened to prevent their execution. That must be why I am even less resolute now than then, just as then I was even less so than I once had been. But to tell the truth (to tell the truth!) I have never been particularly resolute, I mean given to resolutions, but rather inclined to plunge headlong into the shit, without knowing who was shitting against whom or on which side I had the better chance of skulking with success. But from this leaning too I derived scant satisfaction and if I have never quite got rid of it it is not for want of trying. The fact is, it seems, that the most you can hope is to be a little less, in the end, the creature you were in the beginning, and the middle. For I had hardly perfected my plan, in my head, when my bicycle ran over a dog, as subsequently appeared, and fell to the pavement, docile at its mistress's heels. Precautions are like resolutions, to be taken with precaution. The lady must have thought she had left nothing to chance, so far as the safety of her dog was concerned, whereas in reality she was setting the whole system of nature at naught, no less surely than I myself with my insane demands for more light. But instead of grovelling in my turn, invoking my great age and infirmities, I made things worse by trying to run away. I was soon overtaken, by a bloodthirsty mob of both sexes and all ages, for I caught a glimpse of white beards and little almost angelfaces, and they were preparing to tear me to pieces when the lady intervened. She said in effect, she

told me so later on and I believed her, Leave this poor old
man alone. He has killed Teddy, I grant you that, Teddy
whom I loved like my own child, but it is not so serious as
it seems, for as it happens I was taking him to the veterinary
surgeon, to have him put out of his misery. For Teddy was
old, blind, deaf, crippled with rheumatism and perpetually
incontinent, night and day, indoors and out of doors. Thanks
then to this poor old man I have been spared a painful task,
not to mention the expense which I am ill able to afford,
having no other means of support than the pension of my
dear departed, fallen in defense of a country that called itself
his and from which in his lifetime he never derived the
smallest benefit, but only insults and vexations. The crowd
was beginning to disperse, the danger was past, but the lady
in her stride. You may say, she said, that he did wrong to
run away, that he should have explained, asked to be forgiven.
Granted. But it is clear he has not all his wits about him, that
he is beside himself, for reasons of which we know nothing
and which might put us all to shame, if we did know them.
I even wonder if he knows what he has done. There emanated
such tedium from this droning voice that I was making ready
to move on when the unavoidable police constable rose up
before me. He brought down heavily on my handlebars his
big red hairy paw, I noticed it myself, and had it appears
with the lady the following conversation. Is this the man
who ran over your dog, Madam? He is, sergeant, and what
of it? No, I can't record this fatuous colloquy. So I will
merely observe that finally in his turn the constable too dispersed, the word is not too strong, grumbling and growling,
followed by the last idlers who had given up all hope of
my coming to a bad end. But he turned back and said, Remove
that dog. Free at last to go I began to do so. But the lady,
a Mrs. Loy, I might as well say it now and be done with
it, or Lousse, I forget, Christian name something like Sophie,
held me back, by the tail of my coat, and said, assuming the
words were the same when I heard them as when first spoken,
Sir, I need you. And seeing I suppose from my expression,
which frequently betrays me, that she had made herself understood, she must have said, If he understands that he can
understand anything. And she was not mistaken, for after
some time I found myself in possession of certain ideas or

points of view which could only have come to me from
her, namely that having killed her dog I was morally obliged
to help her carry it home and bury it, that she did not wish
to prosecute me for what I had done, but that it was not
always possible to do as one did not wish, that she found me
likeable enough in spite of my hideous appearance and would
be happy to hold out to me a helping hand, and so on, I've
forgotten the half of it. Ah yes, I too needed her, it seemed.
She needed me to help her get rid of her dog, and I needed
her, I've forgotten for what. She must have told me, for
that was an insinuation I could not decently pass over in
silence as I had the rest, and I made no bones about telling
her I needed neither her nor anyone else, which was perhaps
a slight exaggeration, for I must have needed my mother,
otherwise why this frenzy of wanting to get to her? That is
one of the many reasons why I avoid speaking as much as
possible. For I always say either too much or too little, which
is a terrible thing for a man with a passion for truth like mine.
And I shall not abandon this subject, to which I shall probably
never have occasion to return, with such a storm blowing
up, without making this curious observation, that it often
happened to me, before I gave up speaking for good, to think
I had said too little when in fact I had said too much and
in fact to have said too little when I thought I had said too
much. I mean that on reflexion, in the long run rather, my
verbal profusion turned out to be penury, and inversely.
So time sometimes turns the tables. In other words, or perhaps another thing, whatever I said it was never enough and
always too much. Yes, I was never silent, whatever I said I
was never silent. Divine analysis that conduces thus to knowledge of yourself, and of your fellow-men, if you happen to
have any. For to say I needed no one was not to say too much,
but an infinitesimal part of what I should have said, could
not have said, should never have said. Need of my mother!
No, there were no words for the want of need in which I
was perishing. So that she, I mean Sophie, must have told me
the reasons why I needed her, since I had dared to disagree.
And perhaps if I took the trouble I might find them again, but
trouble, many thanks, some other time. And now enough
of this boulevard, it must have been a boulevard, of all these
righteous ones, these guardians of the peace, all these feet

and hands, stamping, clutching, clenched in vain, these bawling mouths that never bawl out of season, this sky beginning to drip, enough of being abroad, trapped, visible. Someone was poking the dog, with a malacca. The dog was uniformly yellow, a mongrel I suppose, or a pedigree, I can never tell the difference. His death must have hurt him less than my fall me. And he at least was dead. We slung him across the saddle and set off like an army in retreat, helping each other I suppose, to keep the corpse from falling, to keep the bicycle moving, to keep ourselves moving, through the jeering crowd. The house where Sophie—no, I can't call her that any more, I'll try calling her Lousse, without the Mrs—the house where Lousse lived was not far away. Oh it was not nearby either, I had my bellyful by the time I got there. That is to say I didn't have it really. You think you have your bellyful but you seldom have it really. It was because I knew I was there that I had my bellyful, a mile more to go and I would only have had my bellyful an hour later. Human nature. Marvellous thing. The house where Lousse lived. Must I describe it? I don't think so. I won't, that's all I know, for the moment. Perhaps later on, if I get to know it. And Lousse? Must I describe her? I suppose so. Let's first bury the dog. It was she dug the hole, under a tree. You always bury your dog under a tree, I don't know why. But I have my suspicions. It was she dug the hole because I couldn't, though I was the gentleman, because of my leg. That is to say I could have dug with a trowel, but not with a spade. For when you dig a grave one leg supports the weight of the body while the other, flexing and unflexing, drives the spade into the earth. Now my sick leg, I forget which, it's immaterial here, was in a condition neither to dig, because it was rigid, nor alone to support me, because it would have collapsed. I had so to speak only one leg at my disposal, I was virtually onelegged, and I would have been happier, livelier, amputated at the groin. And if they had removed a few testicles into the bargain I wouldn't have objected. For from such testicles as mine, dangling at mid-thigh at the end of a meagre cord, there was nothing more to be squeezed, not a drop. So that non che la speme il desiderio, and I longed to see them gone, from the old stand where they bore false witness, for and against, in the lifelong charge against me. For if they accused me of having made a balls of it, of me, of them, they thanked me for it too, from the depths of their rotten bag, the right lower than the left, or inversely, I forget, decaying circus clowns. And, worse still, they got in my way when I tried to walk, when I tried to sit down, as if my sick leg was not enough, and when I rode my bicycle they bounced up and down. So the best thing for me would have been for them to go, and I would have seen to it myself, with a knife or secateurs, but for my terror of physical pain and festered wounds, so that I shook. Yes, all my life I have gone in terror of festered wounds, I who never festered, I was so acid. My life, my life, now I speak of it as of something over, now as of a joke which still goes on, and it is neither, for at the same time it is over and it goes on, and is there any tense for that? Watch wound and buried by the watchmaker, before he died, whose ruined works will one day speak of God, to the worms. But these cullions, I must be attached to them after all, cherish them as others do their scars, or the family album. In any case it wasn't their fault I couldn't dig, but my leg's. It was Lousse dug the hole while I held the dog in my arms. He was heavy already and cold, but he had not yet begun to stink. He smelt bad, if you like, but bad like an old dog, not like a dead dog. He too had dug holes, perhaps at this very spot. We buried him as he was, no box or wrapping of any kind, like a Carthusian monk, but with his collar and lead. It was she put him in the hole, though I was the gentleman. For I cannot stoop, neither can I kneel, because of my infirmity, and if ever I stoop, forgetting who I am, or kneel, make no mistake, it will not be me, but another. To throw him in the hole was all I could have done, and I would have done it gladly. And yet I did not do it. All the things you would do gladly, oh without enthusiasm, but gladly, all the things there seems no reason for your not doing, and that you do not do! Can it be we are not free? It might be worth looking into. But what was my contribution to this burial? It was she dug the hole, put in the dog, filled up the hole. On the whole I was a mere spectator, I contributed my presence. As if it had been my own burial. And it was. It was a larch. It is the only tree I can identify, with certainty. Funny she should have chosen, to bury her dog beneath, the only tree I can identify, with certainty. The sea-green needles are like silk and speckled, it always seemed to me, with little red, how shall I say, with little red specks. The dog had ticks in his ears, I have an eye for such things, they were buried with him. When she had finished her grave she handed me the spade and began to muse, or brood. I thought she was going to cry, it was the thing to do, but on the contrary she laughed. It was perhaps her way of crying. Or perhaps I was mistaken and she was really crying, with the noise of laughter. Tears and laughter, they are so much Gaelic to me. She would see him no more, her Teddy she had loved like an only child. I wonder why, since she had obviously made up her mind to bury the dog at home, she had not asked the vet to call and destroy the brute on the premises. Was she really on her way to the vet at the moment her path crossed mine? Or had she said so solely in order to attenuate my guilt? Private calls are naturally more expensive. She ushered me into the drawing-room and gave me food and drink, good things without a doubt. Unfortunately I didn't much care for good things to eat. But I quite liked getting drunk. If she lived in embarrassed circumstances there was no sign of it. That kind of embarrassment I feel at once. Seeing how painful the sitting posture was for me she fetched a chair for my stiff leg. Without ceasing to ply me with delicacies she kept up a chatter of which I did not understand the hundredth part. With her own hand she took off my hat, and carried it away, to hang it up somewhere, on a hat-rack I suppose, and seemed surprised when the lace pulled her up in her stride. She had a parrot, very pretty, all the most approved colours. I understood him better than his mistress. I don't mean I understood him better than she understood him, I mean I understood him better than I understood her. He exclaimed from time to time, Fuck the son of a bitch, fuck the son of a bitch. He must have belonged to an American sailor, before he belonged to Lousse. Pets often change masters. He didn't say much else. No, I'm wrong, he also said, Putain de merde! He must have belonged to a French sailor before he belonged to the American sailor. Putain de merde! Unless he had hit on it alone, it wouldn't surprise me. Lousse tried to make him say, Pretty Polly! I think it was too late. He listened, his head on one side, pondered, then said, Fuck the son of a bitch.

It was clear he was doing his best. Him too one day she would bury. In his cage probably. Me too, if I had stayed, she would have buried. If I had her address I'd write to her, to come and bury me. I fell asleep. I woke up in a bed, in my skin. They had carried their impertinence to the point of washing me, to judge by the smell I gave off, no longer gave off. I went to the door. Locked. To the window. Barred. It was not yet quite dark. What is there left to try when you have tried the door and the window? The chimney perhaps. I looked for my clothes. I found a light switch and switched it on. No result. What a story! All that left me cold, or nearly. I found my crutches, against an easy chair. It may seem strange that I was able to go through the motions I have described without their help. I find it strange. You don't remember immediately who you are, when you wake. On a chair I found a white chamber pot with a roll of toilet-paper in it. Nothing was being left to chance. I recount these moments with a certain minuteness, it is a relief from what I feel coming. I set a pouffe against the easy chair, sat down in the latter and on the former laid my stiff leg. The room was chock-full of pouffes and easy chairs, they thronged all about me, in the gloom. There were also occasional tables, footstools, tallboys, etc., in abundance. Strange feeling of congestion that the night dispersed, though it lit the chandelier, which I had left turned on. My beard was missing, when I felt for it with anguished hand. They had shaved me, they had shorn me of my scant beard. How had my sleep withstood such liberties? My sleep as a rule so uneasy. To this question I found a number of replies. But I did not know which of them was right. Perhaps they were all wrong. My beard grows properly only on my chin and dewlap. Where the pretty bristles grow on other faces, on mine there are none. But such as it was they had docked my beard. Perhaps they had dyed it too, I had no proof they had not. I thought I was naked, in the easy chair, but I finally realized I was wearing a nightdress, very flimsy. If they had come and told me I was to be sacrificed at sunrise I would not have been taken aback. How foolish one can be. It seemed to me too that I had been perfumed, lavender perhaps. I said, If only your poor mother could see you now. I am no enemy of the commonplace. She seemed far away, my mother, far away from me, and yet I was a little closer to her than the night before, if my reckoning was accurate. But was it? If I was in the right town, I had made progress. But was I? If on the other hand I was in the wrong town, from which my mother would necessarily be absent, then I had lost ground. I must have fallen asleep, for all of a sudden there was the moon, a huge moon framed in the window. Two bars divided it in three segments, of which the middle remained constant, while little by little the right gained what the left lost. For the moon was moving from left to right, or the room was moving from right to left, or both together perhaps, or both were moving from left to right, but the room not so fast as the moon, or from right to left, but the moon not so fast as the room. But can one speak of right and left in such circumstances? That movements of an extreme complexity were taking place seemed certain, and yet what a simple thing it seemed, that vast yellow light sailing slowly behind my bars and which little by little the dense wall devoured, and finally eclipsed. And now its tranquil course was written on the walls, a radiance scored with shadow, then a brief quivering of leaves, if they were leaves, then that too went out, leaving me in the dark. How difficult it is to speak of the moon and not lose one's head, the witless moon. It must be her arse she shows us always. Yes, I once took an interest in astronomy, I don't deny it. Then it was geology that killed a few years for me. The next pain in the balls was anthropology and the other disciplines, such as psychiatry, that are connected with it, disconnected, then connected again, according to the latest discoveries. What I liked in anthropology was its inexhaustible faculty of negation, its relentless definition of man, as though he were no better than God, in terms of what he is not. But my ideas on this subject were always horribly confused, for my knowledge of men was scant and the meaning of being beyond me. Oh I've tried everything. In the end it was magic that had the honour of my ruins, and still today, when I walk there, I find its vestiges. But mostly they are a place with neither plan nor bounds and of which I understand nothing, not even of what it is made, still less into what. And the thing in ruins. I don't know what it is, what it was, nor whether it is not less a question of ruins than the indestructible chaos of timeless things, if that is the right expression. It is in any case a place devoid of mystery, deserted by magic, because devoid of mystery. And if I do not go there gladly, I go perhaps more gladly there than anywhere else, astonished and at peace, I nearly said as in a dream, but no, no. But it is not the kind of place where you go, but where you find yourself, sometimes, not knowing how, and which you cannot leave at will, and where you find yourself without any pleasure, but with more perhaps than in those places you can escape from, by making an effort, places full of mystery, full of the familiar mysteries. I listen and the voice is of a world collapsing endlessly, a frozen world, under a faint untroubled sky, enough to see by, yes, and frozen too. And I hear it murmur that all wilts and yields, as if loaded down, but here there are no loads, and the ground too, unfit for loads, and the light too, down towards an end it seems can never come. For what possible end to these wastes where true light never was, nor any upright thing, nor any true foundation, but only these leaning things, forever lapsing and crumbling away, beneath a sky without memory of morning or hope of night. These things, what things, come from where, made of what? And it says that here nothing stirs, has never stirred, will never stir, except myself, who do not stir either, when I am there, but see and am seen. Yes, a world at an end, in spite of appearances, its end brought it forth, ending it began, is it clear enough? And I too am at an end, when I am there, my eyes close, my sufferings cease and I end, I wither as the living can not. And if I went on listening to that far whisper, silent long since and which I still hear, I would learn still more, about this. But I will listen no longer, for the time being, to that far whisper, for I do not like it, I fear it. But it is not a sound like the other sounds, that you listen to, when you choose, and can sometimes silence, by going away or stopping your ears, no, but it is a sound which begins to rustle in your head, without your knowing how, or why. It's with your head you hear it, not your ears, you can't stop it, but it stops itself, when it chooses. It makes no difference therefore whether I listen to it or not, I shall hear it always, no thunder can deliver me, until it stops. But nothing compels me to speak of it, when it doesn't suit me. And it doesn't suit me, at the moment. No, what suits me, at the moment, is to be

done with this business of the moon which was left unfinished,
by me, for me. And if I get done with it less successfully than
if I had all my wits about me, I shall none the less get done
with it, as best I can, at least I think so. That moon then, all
things considered, filled me suddenly with amaze, with surprise, perhaps better. Yes, I was considering it, after my
fashion, with indifference, seeing it again, in a way, in my
head, when a great fright came suddenly upon me. And deem-
ing this deserved to be looked into I looked into it and
quickly made the following discovery, among others, but I
confine myself to the following, that this moon which had
just sailed gallant and full past my window had appeared
to me the night before, or the night before that, yes, more
likely, all young and slender, on her back, a shaving. And
then I had said, Now I see, he has waited for the new moon
before launching forth on unknown ways, leading south.
And then a little later, Perhaps I should go to mother tomorrow. For all things hang together, by the operation of the
Holy Ghost, as the saying is. And if I failed to mention
this detail in its proper place, it is because you cannot mention everything in its proper place, you must choose, between
the things not worth mentioning and those even less so. For
if you set out to mention everything you would never be
done, and that's what counts, to be done, to have done. Oh I
know, even when you mention only a few of the things there
are, you do not get done either, I know, I know. But it's
a change of muck. And if all muck is the same muck that
doesn't matter, it's good to have a change of muck, to move
from one heap to another a little further on, from time to
time, fluttering you might say, like a butterfly, as if you were
ephemeral. And if you are wrong, and you are wrong, I
mean when you record circumstances better left unspoken,
and leave unspoken others, rightly, if you like, but how shall
I say, for no good reason, yes, rightly, but for no good reason,
as for example that new moon, it is often in good faith,
excellent faith. Had there then elapsed, between that night
on the mountain, that night when I saw A and C and then
made up my mind to go and see my mother, and this other
night, more time than I had thought, namely fourteen full
days, or nearly? And if so, what had happened to those fourteen days, or nearly, and where had they flown? And what

possible chance was there of finding a place for them, no
matter what their burden, in the so rigorous chain of events
I had just undergone? Was it not wiser to suppose either that
the moon seen two nights before, far from being new as I
had thought, was on the eve of being full, or else that the
moon seen from Lousse's house, far from being full, as it
had appeared to me, was in fact merely entering on its first
quarter, or else finally that here I had to do with two moons,
as far from the new as from the full and so alike in outline
that the naked eye could hardly tell between them, and that
whatever was at variance with these hypotheses was so much
smoke and delusion. It was at all events with the aid of these
considerations that I grew calm again and was restored, in the
face of nature's pranks, to my old ataraxy, for what it was
worth. And it came back also to my mind, as sleep stole over
it again, that my nights were moonless and the moon foreign,
to my nights, so that I had never seen, drifting past the
window, carrying me back to other nights, other moons, this
moon I had just seen, I had forgotten who I was (excusably)
and spoken of myself as I would have of another, if I had
been compelled to speak of another. Yes it sometimes happens
and will sometimes happen again that I forget who I am
and strut before my eyes, like a stranger. Then I see the sky
different from what it is and the earth too takes on false
colours. It looks like rest, it is not, I vanish happy in that
alien light, which must have once been mine, I am willing to
believe it, then the anguish of return, I won't say where, I
can't, to absence perhaps, you must return, that's all I know,
it's misery to stay, misery to go. The next day I demanded my
clothes. The valet went to find out. He came back with the news
they had been burnt. I continued my inspection of the room. It
was at first sight a perfect cube. Through the lofty window
I saw boughs. They rocked gently, but not all the time,
shaken now and then by sudden spasms. I noticed the chandelier was burning. My clothes, I said, my crutches, forgetting my crutches were there, against the chair. He left
me alone again, leaving the door open. Through the door I
saw a big window, bigger than the door which it overlapped
entirely, and opaque. The valet came back with the news
my clothes had been sent to the dyers, to have the shine
taken off. He held my crutches, which should have seemed

strange to me, but seemed natural to me, on the contrary. I
took hold of one and began to strike the pieces of furniture
with it, not very hard, just hard enough to overturn them,
without breaking them. They were fewer than in the night.
To tell the truth I pushed them rather than struck them, I
thrust at them, I lunged, and that is not pushing either, but
it's more like pushing than striking. But recalling who I was
I soon threw away my crutch and came to a standstill in the
middle of the room, determined to stop asking for things,
to stop pretending to be angry. For to want my clothes, and
I thought I wanted them, was no reason for pretending to be
angry, when they were refused. And alone once more I
resumed my inspection of the room and was on the point
of endowing it with other properties when the valet came
back with the news my clothes had been sent for and I would
have them soon. Then he began to straighten the tables and
chairs I had overturned and to put them back into place,
dusting them as he did so with a feather duster which suddenly appeared in his hand. And so I began to help him
as best I could, by way of proving that I bore no grudge
against anyone. And though I could not do much, because
of my stiff leg, yet I did what I could, that is to say I
took each object as he straightened it and proceeded with
excruciating meticulousness to restore it to its proper place,
stepping back with raised arms the better to assess the result
and then springing forward to effect minute improvements.
And with the tail of my nightdress as with a duster I petulantly
flicked them one by one. But of this little game too I soon
wearied and suddenly stood stock still in the middle of the
room. But seeing him ready to go I took a step forward and
said, My bicycle. And I said it again, and again, the same
words, until he appeared to understand. I don't know to
what race he belonged, he was so tiny and ageless, assuredly
not to mine. He was an oriental perhaps, a vague oriental,
a child of the Rising Sun. He wore white trousers, a white
shirt and a yellow waist-coat, like a chamois he was, with
brass buttons and sandals. It is not often that I take
cognizance so clearly of the clothes that people wear and
I am happy to give you the benefit of it. The reason for that
was perhaps this, that all morning the talk had been of clothes,
of mine. And perhaps I had been saying, to myself, words

to this effect, Look at him, peaceful in his own clothes, and look at me, floating about inside another man's nightdress, another woman's probably, for it was pink and transparent and adorned with ribands and frills and lace. Whereas the moon, I saw the room but darkly, at each fresh inspection it seemed changed, and that is known as seeing darkly, in the present state of our knowledge. The boughs themselves seemed to shift, as though endowed with an orbital velocity of their own, and in the big frosted window the door was no longer inscribed, but had slightly shifted to the right, or to the left, I forget, so that there now appeared within its frame a panel of white wall, on which I succeeded in casting faint shadows when I moved. But that there were natural causes to all these things I am willing to concede, for the resources of nature are infinite apparently. It was I who was not natural enough to enter into that order of things, and appreciate its niceties. But I was used to seeing the sun rise in the south, used to not knowing where I was going, what I was leaving, what was going with me, all things turning and twisting confusedly about me. It is difficult, is it not, to go to one's mother with things in such a state, more difficult than to the Lousses of this world, or to its police-stations, or to the other places that are waiting for me, I know. But the valet having brought my clothes, in a paper which he unwrapped in front of me, I saw that my hat was not among them, so that I said, My hat. And when he finally understood what I wanted he went away and came back a little later with my hat. Nothing was missing then except the lace to fasten my hat to my buttonhole, but that was something I could not hope to make him understand, and so I did not mention it. An old lace, you can always find an old lace, no lace lasts for ever, the way clothes do, real clothes. As for the bicycle, I had hopes that it was waiting for me somewhere below stairs, perhaps even before the front door, ready to carry me away from these horrible scenes. And I did not see what good it would do to ask for it again, to submit him and myself to this fresh ordeal, when it could be avoided. These considerations crossed my mind with a certain rapidity. Now with regard to the pockets, four in all, of my clothes, I verified their contents in front of the valet and discovered that certain things were missing.

My sucking-stone in particular was no longer there. But
sucking-stones abound on our beaches, when you know where
to look for them, and I deemed it wiser to say nothing about
it, all the more so as he would have been capable, after an
hour's argument, of going and fetching me from the garden
a completely unsuckable stone. This was a decision too which
I took almost instantaneously. But of the other objects which
had disappeared why speak, since I did not know exactly
what they were. And perhaps they had been taken from me
at the police-station, without my knowing it, or scattered and
lost, when I fell, or at some other time, or thrown away,
for I would sometimes throw away all I had about me, in a
burst of irritation. So why speak of them? I resolved nevertheless to declare loudly that a knife was missing, a noble
knife, and I did so to such effect that I soon received a very fine
vegetable knife, so-called stainless, but it didn't take me long
to stain it, and which opened and shut into the bargain,
unlike all the vegetable knives I had ever known, and which
had a safety catch, highly dangerous as soon appeared and
the cause of innumerable cuts, all over my fingers caught
between the handle of so-called genuine Irish horn and the
blade red with rust and so blunted that it was less a matter
of cuts than of contusions. And if I deal at such length with
this knife it is because I have it somewhere still I think,
among my possessions, and because having dealt with it here
at such length I shall not have to deal with it again, when
the moment comes, if it ever comes, to draw up the list of
my possessions, and that will be a relief, a welcome relief,
when that moment comes, I know. For it is natural I should
dilate at lesser length on what I lost than on what I could
not lose, that goes without saying. And if I do not always
appear to observe this principle it is because it escapes me,
from time to time, and vanishes, as utterly as if I had never
educed it. Mad words, no matter. For I no longer know
what I am doing, nor why, those are things I understand less
and less, I don't deny it, for why deny it, and to whom, to
you, to whom nothing is denied? And then doing fills me
with such a, I don't know, impossible to express, for me,
now, after so long, yes, that I don't stop to enquire in virtue
of what principle. And all the less so as whatever I do, that
is to say whatever I say, it will always as it were be the

same thing, yes, as it were. And if I speak of principles, when there are none, I can't help it, there must be some somewhere. And if always doing the same thing as it were is not the same as observing the same principle, I can't help it either. And then how can you know whether you are observing it or not? And how can you want to know? No, all that is not worth while, not worth while bothering about, and yet you do bother about it, your sense of values gone. And the things that are worth while you do not bother about, you let them be, for the same reason, or wisely, knowing that all these questions of worth and value have nothing to do with you, who don't know what you're doing, nor why, and must go on not knowing it, on pain of, I wonder what, yes, I wonder. For anything worse than what I do, without knowing what, or why, I have never been able to conceive, and that doesn't surprise me, for I never tried. For had I been able to conceive something worse than what I had I would have known no peace until I got it, if I know anything about myself. And what I have, what I am, is enough, was always enough for me, and as far as my dear little sweet little future is concerned I have no qualms, I have a good time coming. So I put on my clothes, having first made sure they had not been tampered with that is to say I put on my trousers, my greatcoat, my hat and my boots. My boots. They came up to where my calves would have been if I had had calves, and partly they buttoned, or would have buttoned, if they had had buttons, and partly they laced, and I have them still, I think, somewhere. Then I took my crutches and left the room. The whole day had gone in this tomfoolery and it was dusk again. Going down the stairs I inspected the window I had seen through the door. It lit the staircase with its wild tawny light. Lousse was in the garden, fussing around the grave. She was sowing grass on it, as if grass wouldn't have sown itself on it. She was taking advantage of the cool of evening. Seeing me, she came warmly towards me and gave me food and drink. I ate and drank standing, casting about me in search of my bicycle. She talked and talked. Soon sated, I began the search for my bicycle. She followed me. In the end I found it, half buried in a soft bush. I threw aside my crutches and took it in my hands, by the saddle and the handlebars, intending

to wheel it a little, back and forth, before getting on and
leaving for ever this accursed place. But I pushed and pulled
in vain, the wheels would not turn. It was as though the
brakes were jammed, and heaven knows they were not,
for my bicycle had no brakes. And suddenly overcome by
a great weariness, in spite of the dying day when I always
felt most alive, I threw the bicycle back in the bush and
lay down on the ground, on the grass, careless of the dew,
I never feared the dew. It was then that Lousse, taking advantage of my weakness, squatted down beside me and began
to make me propositions, to which I must confess I listened,
absent-mindedly, I had nothing else to do, I could do nothing
else, and doubtless she had poisoned my beer with something
intended to mollify me, to mollify Molloy, with the result
that I was nothing more than a lump of melting wax, so
to speak. And from these propositions, which she enunciated
slowly and distinctly, repeating each clause several times, I
finally elicited the following, or gist. I could not prevent her
having a weakness for me, neither could she. I would live in
her home, as though it were my own. I would have plenty
to eat and drink, to smoke too if I smoked, for nothing, and
my remaining days would glide away without a care. I
would as it were take the place of the dog I had killed, as
it for her had taken the place of a child. I would help in
the garden, in the house, when I wished, if I wished. I would
not go out on the street, for once out I would never find
my way in again. I would adopt the rhythm of life which
best suited me, getting up, going to bed and taking my meals
at whatsoever hours I pleased. If I did not choose to be
clean, to wear nice clothes, to wash and so on, I need not.
She would be grieved, but what was her grief, compared
to my grief? All she asked was to feel me near her, with
her, and the right to contemplate from time to time this
extraordinary body both at rest and in motion. Every now
and then I interrupted her, to ask what town I was in. But
either because she did not understand me, or because she
preferred to leave me in ignorance, she did not reply to my
question, but went on with her soliloquy, reiterating tire-
lessly each new proposition, then expounding further, slowly,
gently, the benefits for both of us if I would make my
home with her. Till nothing was left but this monotonous

voice, in the deepening night and the smell of the damp earth and of a strongly scented flower which at the time I could not identify, but which later I identified as spike-lavender. There were beds of it everywhere, in this garden, for Lousse loved spike, she must have told me herself, otherwise I would not have known, she loved it above all other herbs and flowers, because of its smell, and then also because of its spikes, and its colour. And if I had not lost my sense of smell the smell of lavender would always make me think of Lousse, in accordance with the well-known mechanism of association. And she gathered this lavender when it bloomed I presume, left it to dry and then made it up into lavender-bags that she put in her cupboards to perfume her handkerchiefs, her underclothing and house-linen. But none the less from time to time I heard the chiming of the hours, from the clocks and belfries, chiming out longer and longer, then suddenly briefly, then longer and longer again. This will give some idea of the time she took to cozen me, of her patience and physical endurance, for all the time she was squatting or kneeling beside me, whereas I was stretched out at my ease on the grass, now on my back, now on my stomach, now on one side, now on the other. And all the time she never stopped talking, whereas I only opened my mouth to ask, at long intervals, more and more feebly, what town we were in. And sure of her victory at last, or simply feeling she had done all she could and that further insistence was useless, she got up and went away, I don't know where, for I stayed where I was, with regret, mild regret. For in me there have always been two fools, among others, one asking nothing better than to stay where he is and the other imagining that life might be slightly less horrible a little further on. So that I was never disappointed, so to speak, whatever I did, in this domain. And these inseparable fools I indulged turn about, that they might understand their foolishness. And that night there was no question of moon, nor any other light, but it was a night of listening, a night given to the faint soughing and sighing stirring at night in little pleasure gardens, the shy sabbath of leaves and petals and the air that eddies there as it does not in other places, where there is less constraint, and as it does not during the day, when there is more vigilance, and then something else that is not clear, being neither the air nor what it moves, perhaps the far unchanging noise the earth makes and which other noises cover, but not for long. For they do not account for that noise you hear when you really listen, when all seems hushed. And there was another noise, that of my life become the life of this garden as it rode the earth of deeps and wildernesses. Yes, there were times when I forgot not only who I was, but that I was, forgot to be. Then I was no longer that sealed jar to which I owed my being so well preserved, but a wall gave way and I filled with roots and tame stems for example, stakes long since dead and ready for burning, the recess of night and the imminence of dawn, and then the labour of the planet rolling eager into winter, winter would rid it of these contemptible scabs. Or of that winter I was the precarious calm, the thaw of the snows which make no difference and all the horrors of it all all over again. But that did not happen to me often, mostly I stayed in my jar which knew neither seasons nor gardens. And a good thing too. But in there you have to be careful, ask yourself questions, as for example whether you still are, and if no when it stopped, and if yes how long it will still go on, anything at all to keep you from losing the thread of the dream. For my part I willingly asked myself questions, one after the other, just for the sake of looking at them. No, not willingly, wisely, so that I might believe I was still there. And yet it means nothing to me to be still there. I called that thinking. I thought almost without stopping, I did not dare stop. Perhaps that was the cause of my innocence. It was a little the worse for wear, a little threadbare perhaps, but I was glad to have it, yes, I suppose. Thanks I suppose, as the urchin said when I picked up his marble, I don't know why, I didn't have to, and I suppose he would have preferred to pick it up himself. Or perhaps it wasn't to be picked up. And the effort it cost me, with my stiff leg. The words engraved themselves for ever on my memory, perhaps because I understood them at once, a thing I didn't often do. Not that I was hard of hearing, for I had quite a sensitive ear, and sounds unencumbered with precise meaning were registered perhaps better by me than by most. What was it then? A defect of the understanding perhaps, which only began to vibrate on repeated solicitations, or which did vibrate, if you like, but at a lower frequency, or a higher, than that of ratiocination, if such a thing is conceivable, and such a thing is conceivable, since I conceive it. Yes, the words I heard, and heard distinctly, having quite a sensitive ear, were heard a first time, then a second, and often even a third, as pure sounds, free of all meaning, and this is probably one of the reasons why conversation was unspeakably painful to me. And the words I uttered myself, and which must nearly always have gone with an effort of the intelligence, were often to me as the buzzing of an insect. And this is perhaps one of the reasons I was so untalkative, I mean this trouble I had in understanding not only what others said to me but also what I said to them. It is true that in the end, by dint of patience, we made ourselves understood, but understood with regard to what, I ask of you, and to what purpose? And to the noises of nature too, and of the works of men, I re-acted I think in my own way and without desire of enlightenment. And my eye too, the seeing one, must have been ill-connected with the spider, for I found it hard to name what was mirrored there, often quite distinctly. And without going so far as to say that I saw the world upside down (that would have been too easy) it is certain I saw it in a way inordinately formal, though I was far from being an aesthete, or an artist. And of my two eyes only one functioning more or less correctly, I misjudged the distance separating me from the other world, and often I stretched out my hand for what was far beyond my reach, and often I knocked against obstacles scarcely visible on the horizon. But I was like that even when I had my two eyes, it seems to me, but perhaps not, for it is long since that era of my life, and my recollection of it is more than imperfect. And now I come to think of it, my attempts at taste and smell were scarcely more fortunate, I smelt and tasted without knowing exactly what, nor whether it was good, nor whether it was bad, and seldom twice running the same thing. I would have been I think an excellent husband, incapable of wearying of my wife and committing adultery only from absent-mind-edness. Now as to telling you why I stayed a good while with Lousse, no, I cannot. That is to say I could I suppose, if I took the trouble. But why should I? In order to estab-lish beyond all question that I could not do otherwise? For

that is the conclusion I would come to, fatally. I who had
loved the image of old Geulincx, dead young, who left me
free, on the black boat of Ulysses, to crawl towards the East,
along the deck. That is a great measure of freedom, for him
who has not the pioneering spirit. And from the poop, poring
upon the wave, a sadly rejoicing slave, I follow with my eyes
the proud and futile wake. Which, as it bears me from no
fatherland away, bears me onward to no shipwreck. A good
while then with Lousse. It's vague, a good while, a few
months perhaps, a year perhaps. I know it was warm again
the day I left, but that meant nothing, in my part of the
world, where it seemed to be warm or cold or merely mild
at any moment of the year and where the days did not run
gently up and down, no, not gently. Perhaps things have
changed since. So all I know is that it was much the same
weather when I left as when I came, so far as I was capable
of knowing what the weather was. And I had been under
the weather so long, under all weathers, that I could tell
quite well between them, my body could tell between them
and seemed even to have its likes, its dislikes. I think I
stayed in several rooms one after the other, or alternately,
I don't know. In my head there are several windows, that
I do know, but perhaps it is always the same one, open
variously on the parading universe. The house was fixed,
that is perhaps what I mean by these different rooms. House
and garden were fixed, thanks to some unknown mechanism
of compensation, and I, when I stayed still, as I did most
of the time, was fixed too, and when I moved, from place
to place, it was very slowly, as in a cage out of time, as the
saying is, in the jargon of the schools, and out of space
too to be sure. For to be out of one and not out of the other
was for cleverer than me, who was not clever, but foolish.
But I may be quite wrong. And these different windows that
open in my head, when I grope again among those days,
really existed perhaps and perhaps do still, in spite of my
being no longer there, I mean there looking at them, opening
them and shutting them, or crouched in a corner of the
room marvelling at the things they framed. But I will not
dwell on this episode, so ludicrously brief when you think
of it and so poor in substance. For I helped neither in the
house nor the garden and knew nothing of what work was

going forward, day and night, nothing save the sounds that
came to me, dull sounds and sharp ones too, and then often
the roar of air being vigorously churned, it seemed to me,
and which perhaps was nothing more than the sound of
burning. I preferred the garden to the house, to judge by
the long hours I spent there, for I spent there the greater
part of the day and of the night, whether it was wet or
whether it was fine. Men were always busy there, working
at I know not what. For the garden seemed hardly to change,
from day to day, apart from the tiny changes due to the
customary cycle of birth, life and death. And in the midst
of those men I drifted like a dead leaf on springs, or else
I lay down on the ground, and then they stepped gingerly
over me as though I had been a bed of rare flowers. Yes,
it was doubtless in order to preserve the garden from apparent change that they laboured at it thus. My bicycle
had disappeared again. Sometimes I felt the wish to look
for it again, to find it again and find out what was wrong
with it or even go for a little ride on the walks and paths
connecting the different parts of the garden. But instead
of trying to satisfy this wish I stayed where I was looking
at it, if I may say so, looking at it as it shrivelled up and
finally disappeared, like the famous fatal skin, only much
quicker. For there seem to be two ways of behaving in the
presence of wishes, the active and the contemplative, and
though they both give the same result it was the latter I
preferred, matter of temperament I presume. The garden
was surrounded with a high wall, its top bristling with
broken glass like fins. But what must have been absolutely
unexpected was this, that this wall was broken by a wicket-
gate giving free access to the road, for it was never locked,
of that I was all but convinced, having opened and closed
it without the least trouble on more than one occasion, both
by day and by night, and seen it used by others than myself,
for the purpose as well of entrance as of exit. I would stick
out my nose, then hastily call it in again. A few further
remarks. Never did I see a woman within these precincts, and
by precincts I do not merely mean the garden, as I probably
should, but the house too, but only men, with the obvious
exception of Lousse. What I saw and did not see did not
matter much admittedly, but I mention it all the same. Lousse

herself I saw but little, she seldom showed herself, to me, out of tact perhaps, fearing to alarm me. But I think she spied on me a great deal, hiding behind the bushes, or the curtains, or skulking in the shadows of a first-floor room, with a spy-glass perhaps. For had she not said she desired above all to see me, both coming and going and rooted to the spot. And to get a good view you need the keyhole, the little chink among the leaves, and so on, whatever prevents you from being seen and from seeing more than a little at a time. No? I don't know. Yes, she inspected me, little by little, and even in my very going to bed, my sleeping and my getting up, the mornings that I went to bed. For in this matter I remained faithful to my custom, which was to sleep in the morning, when I slept at all. For it sometimes happened that I did not sleep at all, for several days, without feeling at all the worse for it. For my waking was a kind of sleeping. And I did not always sleep in the same place, but now I slept in the garden, which was large, and now I slept in the house, which was large too, really extremely spacious. And this uncertainty as to the hour and place of my sleeping must have entranced her, I imagine, and made the time pass pleasantly. But it is useless to dwell on this period of my life. If I go on long enough calling that my life I'll end up by believing it. It's the principle of advertising. This period of my life. It reminds me, when I think of it, of air in a water-pipe. So I will only add that this woman went on giving me slow poison, slipping I know not what poisons into the drink she gave me, or into the food she gave me, or both, or one day one, the next the other. That is a grave charge to bring and I do not bring it lightly. And I bring it without ill-feeling, yes, I accuse her without ill-feeling of having drugged my food and drink with noxious and insipid powders and potions. But even sipid they would have made no difference, I would have swallowed it all down with the same whole-heartedness. That celebrated whiff of almonds for example would never have taken away my appetite. My appetite! What a subject. For conversation. I had hardly any. I ate like a thrush. But the little I did eat I devoured with a voracity usually attributed to heavy eaters, and wrongly, for heavy eaters as a rule eat ponderously and with method, that follows from the very notion of heavy eating. Whereas

I flung myself at the mess, gulped down the half or the quarter of it in two mouthfuls without chewing (with what would I have chewed?), then pushed it from me with loathing. One would have thought I ate to live! Similarly I would engulf five or six mugs of beer with one swig, then drink nothing for a week. What do you expect, one is what one is, partly at least. Nothing or little to be done. Now as to the substances she insinuated thus into my various systems, I could not say whether they were stimulants or whether they were not rather depressants. The truth is, coenaesthetically speaking of course, I felt more or less the same as usual, that is to say, if I may give myself away, so terror-stricken that I was virtually bereft of feeling, not to say of consciousness, and drowned in a deep and merciful torpor shot with brief abominable gleams, I give you my word. Against such harmony of what avail the miserable molys of Lousse, administered in infinitesimal doses probably, to draw the pleasure out. Not that they remained entirely without effect, no, that would be an exaggeration. For from time to time I caught myself making a little bound in the air, two or three feet off the ground at least, at least, I who never bounded. It looked like levitation. And it happened too, less surprisingly, when I was walking, or even propped up against something, that I suddenly collapsed, like a puppet when its strings are dropped, and lay long where I fell, literally boneless. Yes, that struck me as less strange, for I was used to collapsing thus, but with this difference, that I felt it coming, and prepared myself accordingly, as an epileptic does when he feels the fit coming. I mean that knowing I was going to fall I lay down, or I wedged myself where I stood so firmly that nothing short of an earthquake could have dislodged me, and I waited. But these were precautions I did not always take, preferring the fall to the trouble of having to lie down or stand fast. Whereas the falls I suffered when with Lousse did not give me a chance to circumvent them. But all the same they surprised me less, they were more in keeping with me, than the little bounds. For even as a child I do not remember ever having bounded, neither rage nor pain ever made me bound, even as a child, however ill-qualified I am to speak of that time. Now with regard to my food, it seems to me I ate it as, when and where it best

suited me. I never had to call for it. It was brought to me,
wherever I happened to be, on a tray. I can still see the
tray, almost at will, it was round, with a low rim, to keep
the things from falling off, and coated with red lacquer,
cracking here and there. It was small too, as became a tray
having to hold a single dish and one slab of bread. For the
little I ate I crammed into my mouth with my hands, and
the bottles I drank from the bottle were brought to me
separately, in a basket. But this basket made no impression
on me, good or bad, and I could not tell you what it was
like. And many a time, having strayed for one reason or
another from the place where the meal had been brought
to me, I couldn't find it again, when I felt the desire to
eat. Then I searched high and low, often with success, being
fairly familiar with the places where I was likely to have
been, but often too in vain. Or I did not search at all, preferring hunger and thirst to the trouble of having to search
without being sure of finding, or of having to ask for another tray to be brought, and another basket, or the same,
to the place where I was. It was then I regretted my sucking-
stone. And when I talk of preferring, for example, or regretting, it must not be supposed that I opted for the least evil,
and adopted it, for that would be wrong. But not knowing
exactly what I was doing or avoiding, I did it and avoided
it all unsuspecting that one day, much later, I would have
to go back over all these acts and omissions, dimmed and
mellowed by age, and drag them into the eudemonistic slop.
But I must say that with Lousse my health got no worse,
or scarcely. By which I mean that what was already wrong
with me got worse and worse, little by little, as was only
to be expected. But there was kindled no new seat of suffering or infection, except of course those arising from the
spread of existing plethoras and deficiences. But I may very
well be wrong. For of the disorders to come, as for example
the loss of the toes of my left foot, no, I am wrong, my
right foot, who can say exactly when on my helpless clay
the fatal seeds were sown. So all I can say, and I do my
best to say no more, is that during my stay with Lousse no
more new symptoms appeared, of a pathological nature, I
mean nothing new or strange, nothing I could not have foreseen if I could have, nothing at all comparable to the sudden

loss of half my toes. For that is something I could never have
foreseen and the meaning of which I have never fathomed,
I mean its connexion with my other discomforts, from my
ignorance of medical matters, I suppose. For all things run
together, in the body's long madness, I feel it. But it is
useless to drag out this chapter of my, how shall I say, my
existence, for it has no sense, to my mind. It is a dug at
which I tug in vain, it yields nothing but wind and spatter.
So I will confine myself to the following brief additional
remarks, and the first of which is this, that Lousse was a
woman of an extraordinary flatness, physically speaking of
course, to such a point that I am still wondering this evening, in the comparative silence of my last abode, if she
was not a man rather or at least an androgyne. She had a
somewhat hairy face, or am I imagining it, in the interests
of the narrative? The poor woman, I saw her so little, so
little looked at her. And was not her voice suspiciously deep?
So she appears to me today. Don't be tormenting yourself,
Molloy, man or woman, what does it matter? But I cannot
help asking myself the following question. Could a woman
have stopped me as I swept towards mother? Probably. Better
still, was such an encounter possible, I mean between me
and a woman? Now men, I have rubbed up against a few
men in my time, but women? Oh well, I may as well confess it now, yes, I once rubbed up against one. I don't mean
my mother, I did more than rub up against her. And if you
don't mind we'll leave my mother out of all this. But another
who might have been my mother, and even I think my grand-
mother, if chance had not willed otherwise. Listen to him
now talking about chance. It was she made me acquainted
with love. She went by the peaceful name of Ruth I think,
but I can't say for certain. Perhaps the name was Edith.
She had a hole between her legs, oh not the bunghole I
had always imagined, but a slit, and in this I put, or rather
she put, my so-called virile member, not without difficulty,
and I toiled and moiled until I discharged or gave up trying
or was begged by her to stop. A mug's game in my opinion
and tiring on top of that, in the long run. But I lent myself
to it with a good enough grace, knowing it was love, for
she had told me so. She bent over the couch, because of
her rheumatism, and in I went from behind. It was the

only position she could bear, because of her lumbago. It
seemed all right to me, for I had seen dogs, and I was
astonished when she confided that you could go about it
differently. I wonder what she meant exactly. Perhaps after
all she put me in her rectum. A matter of complete indifference to me, I needn't tell you. But is it true love, in the
rectum? That's what bothers me sometimes. Have 1 never
known true love, after all? She too was an eminently flat
woman and she moved with short stiff steps, leaning on an
ebony stick. Perhaps she too was a man, yet another of
them. But in that case surely our testicles would have col-
lided, while we writhed. Perhaps she held hers tight in her
hand, on purpose to avoid it. She favoured voluminous
tempestuous shifts and petticoats and other undergarments
whose names I forget. They welled up all frothing and
swishing and then, congress achieved, broke over us in slow
cascades. And all I could see was her taut yellow nape which
every now and then I set my teeth in, forgetting I had none,
such is the power of instinct. We met in a rubbish dump,
unlike any other, and yet they are all alike, rubbish dumps.
I don't know what she was doing there. I was limply poking
about in the garbage saying probably, for at that age I must
still have been capable of general ideas, This is life. She
had no time to lose, I had nothing to lose, I would have
made love with a goat, to know what love was. She had
a dainty flat, no, not dainty, it made you want to lie down
in a corner and never get up again. I liked it. It was full
of dainty furniture, under our desperate strokes the couch
moved forward on its castors, the whole place fell about our
ears, it was pandemonium. Our commerce was not without
tenderness, with trembling hands she cut my toe-nails and
I rubbed her rump with winter cream. This idyll was of
short duration. Poor Edith, I hastened her end perhaps.
Anyway it was she who started it, in the rubbish dump,
when she laid her hand upon my fly. More precisely, I was
bent double over a heap of muck, in the hope of finding
something to disgust me for ever with eating, when she,
undertaking me from behind, thrust her stick between my
legs and began to titillate my privates. She gave me money
after each session, to me who would have consented to
know love, and probe it to the bottom, without charge. But

she was an idealist. I would have preferred it seems to
me an orifice less arid and roomy, that would have given
me a higher opinion of love it seems to me. However. Twixt
finger and thumb tis heaven in comparison. But love is no
doubt above such base contingencies. And not when you are
comfortable, but when your frantic member casts about for
a rubbing-place, and the unction of a little mucous mem-
brane, and meeting with none does not beat in retreat, but
retains its tumefaction, it is then no doubt that true love
comes to pass, and wings away, high above the tight fit and
the loose. And when you add a little pedicure and massage,
having nothing to do with the instant of bliss strictly speaking,
then I feel no further doubt is justified, in this connexion.
The other thing that bothers me, in this connexion, is the
indifference with which I learnt of her death, one black night
I was crawling towards her, an indifference softened indeed
by the pain of losing a source of revenue. She died taking
a warm tub, as her custom was before receiving me. It
limbered her up. When I think she might have expired in
my arms! The tub overturned and the dirty water spilt all
over the floor and down on top of the lodger below, who
gave the alarm. Well, well, I didn't think I knew this story
so well. She must have been a woman after all, if she hadn't
been it would have got around in the neighbourhood. It is
true they were extraordinarily reserved, in my part of the
world, about everything connected with sexual matters. But
things have perhaps changed since my time. And it is quite
possible that the fact of having found a man when they
should have found a woman was immediately repressed and
forgotten, by the few unfortunate enough to know about
it. As it is quite possible that everybody knew about it,
and spoke about it, with the sole exception of myself. But
there is one thing that torments me, when I delve into all
this, and that is to know whether all my life has been devoid
of love or whether I really met with it, in Ruth. What I do
know for certain is that I never sought to repeat the experience, having I suppose the intuition that it had been unique
and perfect, of its kind, achieved and inimitable, and that
it behoved me to preserve its memory, pure of all pastiche,
in my heart, even if it meant my resorting from time to time
to the alleged joys of so-called self-abuse. Don't talk to me

about the chambermaid, I should never have mentioned her, she was long before, I was sick, perhaps there was no chambermaid, ever, in my life. Molloy, or life without a chambermaid. All of which goes to demonstrate that the fact of having met Lousse and even frequented her, in a way, proved nothing as to her sex. And I am quite willing to go on thinking of her as an old woman, widowed and withered, and of Ruth as another, for she too used to speak of her defunct husband and of his inability to satisfy her legitimate cravings. And there are days, like this evening, when my memory confuses them and I am tempted to think of them as one and the same old hag, flattened and crazed by life. And God forgive me, to tell you the horrible truth, my mother's image sometimes mingles with theirs, which is literally unendurable, like being crucified, I don't know why and I don't want to. But I left Lousse at last, one warm airless night, without saying goodbye, as I might at least have done, and without her trying to hold me back, except perhaps by spells. But she must have seen me go, get up, take my crutches and go away, springing on them through the air. And she must have seen the wicket close behind me, for it closed by itself, with the help of a spring, and known me gone, for ever. For she knew the way I had of going to the wicket and peeping out, then quickly drawing back. And she did not try and hold me back but she went and sat down on her dog's grave, perhaps, which was mine too in a way, and which by the way she had not sown with grass, as I had thought, but with all kinds of little many-coloured flowers and herbacious plants, selected I imagine in such a way that when some went out others lit up. I left her my bicycle which I had taken a dislike to, suspecting it to be the vehicle of some malignant agency and perhaps the cause of my recent misfortunes. But all the same I would have taken it with me if I had known where it was and that it was in running order. But I did not. And I was afraid, if I tried to find out, of wearing out the small voice saying, Get out of here, Molloy, take your crutches and get out of here and which I had taken so long to understand, for I had been hearing it for a long time. And perhaps I understood it all wrong, but I understood it and that was the novelty. And it seemed to me I was not necessarily going

for good and that I might come back one day, by devious
winding ways, to the place I was leaving. And perhaps my
course is not yet fully run. Outside in the road the wind
was blowing, it was another world. Not knowing where I
was nor consequently what way I ought to go I went with
the wind. And when, well slung between my crutches, I took
off, then I felt it helping me, that little wind blowing from
what quarter I could not tell. And don't come talking at
me of the stars, they look all the same to me, yes, I cannot
read the stars, in spite of my astronomical studies. But I
entered the first shelter I came to and stayed there till dawn,
for I knew I was bound to be stopped by the first policeman
and asked what I was doing, a question to which I have never
been able to find the correct reply. But it cannot have been
a real shelter and I did not stay till dawn, for a man came
in soon after me and drove me out. And yet there was
room for two. I think he was a kind of nightwatchman, a
man of some kind certainly, he must have been employed
to watch over some kind of public works, digging I suppose.
I see a brazier. There must have been a touch of autumn
in the air, as the saying is. I therefore moved on and en-
sconced myself on a flight of stairs, in a mean lodging-house,
because there was no door or it didn't shut, I don't know.
Long before dawn this lodging-house began to empty. People
came down the stairs, men and women. I glued myself
against the wall. They paid no heed to me, nobody interfered
with me. In the end I too went away, when I deemed it
prudent, and wandered about the town in search of a familiar
monument, so that I might say, I am in my town, after all,
I have been there all the time. The town was waking, doors
opening and shutting, soon the noise would be deafening.
But espying a narrow alley between two high buildings I
looked about me, then slipped into it. Little windows over-
looked it, on either side, on every floor, facing one another.
Lavatory lights I suppose. There are things from time to
time, in spite of everything, that impose themselves on the
understanding with the force of axioms, for unknown reasons. There was no way out of the alley, it was not so
much an alley as a blind alley. At the end there were two
recesses, no, that's not the word, opposite each other,
littered with miscellaneous rubbish and with excrements, of

dogs and masters, some dry and odorless, others still moist.
Ah those papers never to be read again, perhaps never read.
Here lovers must have lain at night and exchanged their
vows. I entered one of the alcoves, wrong again, and leaned
against the wall. I would have preferred to lie down and there
was no proof that I would not. But for the moment I was
content to lean against the wall, my feet far from the wall,
on the verge of slipping, but I had other props, the tips of
my crutches. But a few minutes later I crossed the alley
into the other chapel, that's the word, where I felt I might
feel better, and settled myself in the same hypotenusal posture. And at first I did actually seem to feel a little better,
but little by little I acquired the conviction that such was
not the case. A fine rain was falling and I took off my hat
to give my skull the benefit of it, my skull all cracked and
furrowed and on fire, on fire. But I also took it off because
it was digging into my neck, because of the thrust of the
wall. So I had two good reasons for taking it off and they
were none too many, neither alone would ever have prevailed I feel. I threw it from me with a careless lavish gesture and back it came, at the end of its string or lace,
and after a few throes came to rest against my side. At last
I began to think, that is to say to listen harder. Little chance
of my being found there, I was in peace for as long as I
could endure peace. For the space of an instant I considered settling down there, making it my lair and sanctuary,
for the space of an instant. I took the vegetable knife from
my pocket and set about opening my wrist. But pain soon
got the better of me. First I cried out, then I gave up, closed
the knife and put it back in my pocket. I wasn't particularly
disappointed, in my heart of hearts I had not hoped for anything better. So much for that. And backsliding has always
depressed me, but life seems made up of backsliding, and
death itself must be a kind of backsliding, I wouldn't be
surprised. Did I say the wind had fallen? A fine rain falling,
somehow that seems to exclude all idea of wind. My knees
are enormous, I have just caught a glimpse of them, when I
got up for a second. My two legs are as stiff as a life-
sentence and yet I sometimes get up. What can you expect?
Thus from time to time I shall recall my present existence
compared to which this is a nursery tale. But only from time

to time, so that it may be said, if necessary, whenever necessary, Is it possible that thing is still alive? Or again, Oh it's
only a diary, it'll soon be over. That my knees are enormous,
that I still get up from time to time, there are things that
do not seem at first sight to signify anything in particular.
I record them all the more willingly. In the end I left the
impasse, where half-standing half-lying I may have had a
little sleep, my little morning sleep, and I set off, believe it
or not, towards the sun, why not, the wind having fallen. Or
rather towards the least gloomy quarter of the heavens which
a vast cloud was shrouding from the zenith to the skylines.
It was from this cloud the above rain was falling. See how
things hang together. And as to making up my mind which
quarter of the heaven was the least gloomy, it was no easy
matter. For at first sight the heavens seemed uniformly
gloomy. But by taking a little pains, for there were moments
in my life when I took a little pains, I obtained a result, that
is to say I came to a decision, in this matter. So I was able
to continue on my way, saying, I am going towards the sun,
that is to say in theory towards the East, or perhaps the
South-East, for I am no longer with Lousse, but out in the
heart again of the pre-established harmony, which makes
so sweet a music, which is so sweet a music, for one who
has an ear for music. People were hastening angrily to and
fro, most of them, some in the shelter of the umbrella,
others in that perhaps a little less effective of the rainproof
coat. A few had taken refuge under trees and archways.
And among those who, more courageous or less delicate,
came and went, and among those who had stopped, to avoid
getting wet, many a one must have said, They are right,
I am wrong, meaning by they the category to which he
did not belong, or so I imagine. As many a one too must
have said, I am right, they are wrong, while continuing to
storm against the foul weather that was the occasion of
his superiority. But at the sight of a young old man of
wretched aspect, shivering all alone in a narrow doorway,
I suddenly remembered the project conceived the day of
my encounter with Lousse and her dog and which this encounter had prevented me from carrying out. So I went
and stood beside him, with the air I hoped of one who
says, Here's a clever fellow, let me follow his example. But

before I should make my little speech, which I wished to
seem spontaneous and so did not make at once, he went
out into the rain and away. For this speech was one liable, in
virtue of its content, if not to offend at least to astonish.
And that was why it was important to deliver it at the right
moment and in the right tone. I apologize for these details, in
a moment we'll go faster, much faster. And then perhaps
relapse again into a wealth of filthy circumstance. But
which in its turn again will give way to vast frescoes, dashed
off with loathing. Homo mensura can't do without staffage.
There I am then in my turn alone, in the doorway. I could
not hope for anyone to come and stand beside me, and
yet it was a possibility I did not exclude. That's a fairly
good caricature of my state of mind at that instant. Net
result, I stayed where I was. I had stolen from Lousse a
little silver, oh nothing much, massive teaspoons for the
most part, and other small objects whose utility I did not
grasp but which seemed as if they might have some value.
Among these latter there was one which haunts me still,
from time to time. It consisted of two crosses, joined, at
their points of intersection, by a bar, and resembled a tiny
sawing-horse, with this difference however, that the crosses
of the true sawing-horse are not perfect crosses, but truncated
at the top, whereas the crosses of the little object I am
referring to were perfect, that is to say composed each of
two identical V's, one upper with its opening above, like
all V's for that matter, and the other lower with its opening
below, or more precisely of four rigorously identical V's,
the two I have just named and then two more, one on the
right hand, the other on the left, having their openings on
the right and left respectively. But perhaps it is out of place
to speak here of right and left, of upper and lower. For this
little object did not seem to have any base properly so-called,
but stood with equal stability on any one of its four bases,
and without any change of appearance, which is not true of
the sawing-horse. This strange instrument I think I still
have somewhere, for I could never bring myself to sell it,
even in my worst need, for I could never understand what
possible purpose it could serve, nor even contrive the faintest
hypothesis on the subject. And from time to time I took it
from my pocket and gazed upon it, with an astonished and

affectionate gaze, if I had not been incapable of affection. But for a certain time I think it inspired me with a kind of veneration, for there was no doubt in my mind that it was not an object of virtu, but that it had a most specific function always to be hidden from me. I could therefore puzzle over it endlessly without the least risk. For to know nothing is nothing, not to want to know anything likewise, but to be beyond knowing anything, to know you are beyond knowing anything, that is when peace enters in, to the soul of the incurious seeker. It is then the true division begins, of twenty-two by seven for example, and the pages fill with the true ciphers at last. But I would rather not affirm anything on this subject. What does seem undeniable to me on the contrary is this, that giving in to the evidence, to a very strong probability rather, I felt the shelter of the doorway and began levering myself forward, swinging slowly through the sullen air. There is rapture, or there should be, in the motion crutches give. It is a series of little flights, skimming the ground. You take off, you land, through the thronging sound in wind and limb, who have to fasten one foot to the ground before they dare lift up the other. And even their most joyous hastening is less aerial than my hobble. But these are reasonings, based on analysis. And though my mind was still taken up with my mother, and with the desire to know if I was near her, it was gradually less so, perhaps because of the silver in my pockets, but I think not, and then too because these were ancient cares and the mind cannot always brood on the same cares, but needs fresh cares from time to time, so as to revert with renewed vigor, when the time comes, to ancient cares. But can one speak here of fresh and ancient cares? I think not. But it would be hard for me to prove it. What I can assert, without fear of—without fear, is that I gradually lost interest in knowing, among other things, what town I was in and if I should soon find my mother and settle the matter between us. And even the nature of that matter grew dim, for me, without however vanishing completely. For it was no small matter and I was bent on it. All my life, I think, I had been bent on it. Yes, so far as I was capable of being bent on anything all a lifetime long, and what a lifetime, I had been bent on settling this matter between my mother

and me, but had not succeeded. And while saying to myself
that time was running out, and that soon it would be too late,
was perhaps too late already, to settle the matter in question,
I felt myself drifting towards other cares, other phantoms.
And far more than to know what town I was in, my haste was
now to leave it, even were it the right one, where my mother
had waited so long and perhaps was waiting still. And it
seemed to me that if I kept on in a straight line I was bound
to leave it, sooner or later. So I set myself to this as best
I could, making allowance for the drift to the right of the
feeble light that was my guide. And my pertinacity was such
that I did indeed come to the ramparts as night was falling,
having described a good quarter of a circle, through bad
navigation. It is true I stopped many times, to rest, but not
for long, for I felt harried, wrongly perhaps. But in the
country there is another justice, other judges, at first. And
having cleared the ramparts I had to confess the sky was
clearing, prior to its winding in the other shroud, night. Yes,
the great cloud was ravelling, discovering here and there a
pale and dying sky, and the sun, already down, was manifest in the living tongue of fire darting towards the zenith,
falling and darting again, ever more pale and languid, and
doomed no sooner lit to be extinguished. This phenomenon,
if I remember rightly, was characteristic of my region. Things
are perhaps different today. Though I fail to see, never having left my region, what right I have to speak of its char-
acteristics. No, I never escaped, and even the limits of my
region were unknown to me. But I felt they were far away.
But this feeling was based on nothing serious, it was a
simple feeling. For if my region had ended no further than
my feet could carry me, surely I would have left it changing slowly. For regions do not suddenly end, as far as I
know, but gradually merge into one another. And I never
noticed anything of the kind, but however far I went, and
in no matter what direction, it was always the same sky,
always the same earth, precisely, day after day and night after
night. On the other hand, if it is true that regions gradually
merge into one another, and this remains to be proved, then
I may well have left mine many times, thinking I was still
within it. But I preferred to abide by my simple feeling and
its voice that said, Molloy, your region is vast, you have

never left it and you never shall. And wheresoever you
wander, within its distant limits, things will always be the
same, precisely. It would thus appear, if this is so, that my
movements owed nothing to the places they caused to
vanish, but were due to something else, to the buckled wheel
that carried me, in unforeseeable jerks, from fatigue to rest,
and inversely, for example. But now I do not wander any
more, anywhere any more, and indeed I scarcely stir at all,
and yet nothing is changed. And the confines of my room,
of my bed, of my body, are as remote from me as were those
of my region, in the days of my splendour. And the cycle
continues, joltingly, of flight and bivouac, in an Egypt without bounds, without infant, without mother. And when I
see my hands, on the sheet, which they love to floccillate
already, they are not mine, less than ever mine, I have no
arms, they are a couple, they play with the sheet, love-play
perhaps, trying to get up perhaps, one on top of the other.
But it doesn't last, I bring them back, little by little, towards
me, it's resting time. And with my feet it's the same, sometimes, when I see them at the foot of the bed, one with toes,
the other without. And that is more deserving of mention.
For my legs, corresponding here to my arms of a moment
ago, are both stiff now and very sore, and I shouldn't be
able to forget them as I can my arms, which are more or
less sound and well. And yet I do forget them and I watch
the couple as they watch each other, a great way off. But
my feet are not like my hands, I do not bring them back
to me, when they become my feet again, for I cannot, but
they stay there, far from me, but not so far as before. End
of the recall. But you'd think that once well clear of the
town, and having turned round to look at it, what there was
to see of it, you'd think that then I should have realized
whether it was really my town or not. But no, I looked at
it in vain, and perhaps unquestioningly, and simply to give
the gods a chance, by turning round. Perhaps I only made
a show of looking at it. I didn't feel I missed my bicycle,
no, not really, I didn't mind going on my way the way I said,
swinging low in the dark over the earth, along the little
empty country roads. And I said there was little likelihood
of my being molested and that it was more likely I should
molest them, if they saw me. Morning is the time to hide.

They wake up, hale and hearty, their tongues hanging out for order, beauty and justice, baying for their due. Yes, from eight or nine till noon is the dangerous time. But towards noon things quiet down, the most implacable are sated, they go home, it might have been better but they've done a good job, there have been a few survivors but they'll give no more trouble, each man counts his rats. It may begin again in the early afternoon, after the banquet, the celebrations, the congratulations, the orations, but it's nothing compared to the morning, mere fun. Coming up to four or five of course there is the night-shift, the watchmen, beginning to bestir themselves. But already the day is over, the shadows lengthen, the walls multiply, you hug the walls, bowed down like a good boy, oozing with obsequiousness, having nothing to hide, hiding from mere terror, looking neither right nor left, hiding but not provocatively, ready to come out, to smile, to listen, to crawl, nauseating but not pestilent, less rat than toad. Then the true night, perilous too but sweet to him who knows it, who can open to it like the flower to the sun, who himself is night, day and night. No there is not much to be said for the night either, but compared to the day there is much to be said for it, and notably compared to the morning there is everything to be said for it. For the night purge is in the hands of technicians, for the most part. They do nothing else, the bulk of the population have no part in it, preferring their warm beds, all things considered. Day is the time for lynching, for sleep is sacred, and especially in the morning, between breakfast and lunch. My first care then, after a few miles in the desert dawn, was to look for a place to sleep, for sleep too is a kind of protection, strange as it may seem. For sleep, if it excites the lust to capture, seems to appease the lust to kill, there and then and bloodily, any hunter will tell you that. For the monster on the move, or on the watch, lurking in his lair, there is no mercy, whereas he taken unawares, in his sleep, may sometimes get the benefit of milder feelings, which deflect the barrel, sheathe the kris. For the hunter is weak at heart and sentimental, overflowing with repressed treasures of gentleness and compassion. And it is thanks to this sweet sleep of terror or exhaustion that many a foul beast, and worthy of extermination, can live on till he dies

in the peace and quiet of our zoological gardens, broken
only by the innocent laughter, the knowing laughter, of
children and their elders, on Sundays and Bank Holidays.
And I for my part have always preferred slavery to death,
I mean being put to death. For death is a condition I have
never been able to conceive to my satisfaction and which
therefore cannot go down in the ledger of weal and woe.
Whereas my notions on being put to death inspired me with
confidence, rightly or wrongly, and I felt I was entitled to
act on them, in certain emergencies. Oh they weren't notions
like yours, they were notions like mine, all spasm, sweat
and trembling, without an atom of common sense or lucidity.
But they were the best I had. Yes, the confusion of my ideas
on the subject of death was such that I sometimes wondered,
believe me or not, if it wasn't a state of being even worse
than life. So I found it natural not to rush into it and,
when I forgot myself to the point of trying, to stop in time.
It's my only excuse. So I crawled into some hole somewhere
I suppose and waited, half sleeping, half sighing, groaning
and laughing, or feeling my body, to see if anything had
changed, for the morning frenzy to abate. Then I resumed
my spirals. And as to saying what became of me, and where
I went, in the months and perhaps the years that followed,
no. For I weary of these inventions and others beckon to
me. But in order to blacken a few more pages may I say
I spent some time at the seaside, without incident. There are
people the sea doesn't suit, who prefer the mountains or
the plain. Personally I feel no worse there than anywhere
else. Much of my life has ebbed away before this shivering
expanse, to the sound of the waves in storm and calm,
and the claws of the surf. Before, no, more than before,
one with, spread on the sand, or in a cave. In the sand
I was in my element, letting it trickle between my fingers,
scooping holes that I filled in a moment later or that filled
themselves in, flinging it in the air by handfuls, rolling in
it. And in the cave, lit by the beacons at night, I knew
what to do in order to be no worse off than elsewhere. And
that my land went no further, in one direction at least, did
not displease me. And to feel there was one direction at
least in which I could go no further, without first getting
wet, then drowned, was a blessing. For I have always said,

First learn to walk, then you can take swimming lessons. But don't imagine my region ended at the coast, that would be a grave mistake. For it was this sea too, its reefs and distant islands, and its hidden depths. And I too once went forth on it, in a sort of oarless skiff, but I paddled with an old bit of driftwood. And I sometimes wonder if I ever came back, from that voyage. For if I see myself putting to sea, and the long hours without landfall, I do not see the return, the tossing on the breakers, and I do not hear the frail keel grating on the shore. I took advantage of being at the seaside to lay in a store of sucking-stones. They were pebbles but I call them stones. Yes, on this occasion I laid in a considerable store. I distributed them equally among my four pockets, and sucked them turn and turn about. This raised a problem which I first solved in the following way. I had say sixteen stones, four in each of my four pockets these being the two pockets of my trousers and the two pockets of my greatcoat. Taking a stone from the right pocket of my greatcoat, and putting it in my mouth, I replaced it in the right pocket of my greatcoat by a stone from the right pocket of my trousers, which I replaced by a stone from the left pocket of my trousers, which I replaced by a stone from the left pocket of my greatcoat, which I replaced by the stone which was in my mouth, as soon as I had finished sucking it. Thus there were still four stones in each of my four pockets, but not quite the same stones. And when the desire to suck took hold of me again, I drew again on the right pocket of my greatcoat, certain of not taking the same stone as the last time. And while I sucked it I rearranged the other stones in the way I have just described. And so on. But this solution did not satisfy me fully. For it did not escape me that, by an extraordinary hazard, the four stones circulating thus might always be the same four. In which case, far from sucking the sixteen stones turn and turn about, I was really only sucking four, always the same, turn and turn about. But I shuffled them well in my pockets, before I began to suck, and again, while I sucked, before transferring them, in the hope of obtaining a more general circulation of the stones from pocket to pocket. But this was only a makeshift that could not long content a man like me. So I began to

look for something else. And the first thing I hit upon was
that I might do better to transfer the stones four by four,
instead of one by one, that is to say, during the sucking, to
take the three stones remaining in the right pocket of my
greatcoat and replace them by the four in the right pocket
of my trousers, and these by the four in the left pocket of
my trousers, and these by the four in the left pocket of
my greatcoat, and finally these by the three from the right
pocket of my greatcoat, plus the one, as soon as I had
finished sucking it, which was in my mouth. Yes, it seemed
to me at first that by so doing I would arrive at a better
result. But on further reflection I had to change my mind
and confess that the circulation of the stones four by four
came to exactly the same thing as their circulation one by
one. For if I was certain of finding each time, in the right
pocket of my greatcoat, four stones totally different from
their immediate predecessors, the possibility nevertheless
remained of my always chancing on the same stone, within
each group of four, and consequently of my sucking, not the
sixteen turn and turn about as I wished, but in fact four
only, always the same, turn and turn about. So I had to
seek elsewhere than in the mode of circulation. For no matter how I caused the stones to circulate, I always ran the
same risk. It was obvious that by increasing the number
of my pockets I was bound to increase my chances of en-
joying my stones in the way I planned, that is to say one
after the other until their number was exhausted. Had I
had eight pockets, for example, instead of the four I did
have, then even the most diabolical hazard could not have
prevented me from sucking at least eight of my sixteen
stones, turn and turn about. The truth is I should have
needed sixteen pockets in order to be quite easy in my mind.
And for a long time I could see no other conclusion than this,
that short of having sixteen pockets, each with its stone, I
could never reach the goal I had set myself, short of an
extraordinary hazard. And if at a pitch I could double the
number of my pockets, were it only by dividing each pocket
in two, with the help of a few safety-pins let us say, to
quadruple them seemed to be more than I could manage.
And I did not feel inclined to take all that trouble for a
half-measure. For I was beginning to lose all sense of measure,

after all this wrestling and wrangling, and to say, All or
nothing. And if I was tempted for an instant to establish
a more equitable proportion between my stones and my
pockets, by reducing the former to the number of the latter,
it was only for an instant. For it would have been an admission of defeat. And sitting on the shore, before the sea,
the sixteen stones spread out before my eyes, I gazed at
them in anger and perplexity. For just as I had difficulty
in sitting on a chair, or in an arm-chair, because of my stiff
leg you understand, so I had none in sitting on the ground,
because of my stiff leg, for it was about this time that my
good leg, good in the sense that it was not stiff, began to
stiffen. I needed a prop under the ham you understand, and
even under the whole length of the leg, the prop of the
earth. And while I gazed thus at my stones, revolving interminable martingales all equally defective, and crushing
handfuls of sand, so that the sand ran through my fingers
and fell back on the strand, yes, while thus I lulled my mind
and part of my body, one day suddenly it dawned on the
former, dimly, that I might perhaps achieve my purpose
without increasing the number of my pockets, or reducing
the number of my stones, but simply by sacrificing the
principle of trim. The meaning of this illumination, which
suddenly began to sing within me, like a verse of Isaiah,
or of Jeremiah, I did not penetrate at once, and notably the
word trim, which I had never met with, in this sense, long
remained obscure. Finally I seemed to grasp that this word
trim could not here mean anything else, anything better,
than the distribution of the sixteen stones in four groups
of four, one group in each pocket, and that it was my refusal
to consider any distribution other than this that had vitiated
my calculations until then and rendered the problem literally
insoluble. And it was on the basis of this interpretation,
whether right or wrong, that I finally reached a solution,
inelegant assuredly, but sound, sound. Now I am willing
to believe, indeed I firmly believe, that other solutions to
this problem might have been found, and indeed may still
be found, no less sound, but much more elegant, than the
one I shall now describe, if I can. And I believe too that
had I been a little more insistent, a little more resistant, I
could have found them myself. But I was tired, but I

was tired, and I contented myself ingloriously with the
first solution that was a solution, to this problem. But not
to go over the heartbreaking stages through which I passed
before I came to it, here it is, in all its hideousness. All
(all!) that was necessary was to put for example, to begin
with, six stones in the right pocket of my greatcoat, or
supply-pocket, five in the right pocket of my trousers, and
five in the left pocket of my trousers, that makes the lot,
twice five ten plus six sixteen, and none, for none remained,
in the left pocket of my greatcoat, which for the time being
remained empty, empty of stones that is, for its usual
contents remained, as well as occasional objects. For where
do you think I hid my vegetable knife, my silver, my horn
and the other things that I have not yet named, perhaps
shall never name. Good. Now I can begin to suck. Watch
me closely. I take a stone from the right pocket of my
greatcoat, suck it, stop sucking it, put it in the left pocket
of my greatcoat, the one empty (of stones). I take a second
stone from the right pocket of my greatcoat, suck it, put
it in the left pocket of my greatcoat. And so on until the
right pocket of my greatcoat is empty (apart from its usual
and casual contents) and the six stones I have just sucked,
one after the other, are all in the left pocket of my greatcoat.
Pausing then, and concentrating, so as not to make a balls
of it, I transfer to the right pocket of my greatcoat, in which
there are no stones left, the five stones in the right pocket
of my trousers, which I replace by the five stones in the left
pocket of my trousers, which I replace by the six stones in
the left pocket of my greatcoat. At this stage then the left
pocket of my greatcoat is again empty of stones, while the
right pocket of my greatcoat is again supplied, and in the
right way, that is to say with other stones than those I
have just sucked. These other stones I then begin to suck,
one after the other, and to transfer as I go along to the
left pocket of my greatcoat, being absolutely certain, as
far as one can be in an affair of this kind, that I am not
sucking the same stones as a moment before, but others.
And when the right pocket of my greatcoat is again empty
(of stones), and the five I have just sucked are all without
exception in the left pocket of my greatcoat, then I proceed
to the same redistribution as a moment before, or a similar

redistribution, that is to say I transfer to the right pocket of my greatcoat, now again available, the five stones in the right pocket of my trousers, which I replace by the six stones in the left pocket of my trousers, which I replace by the five stones in the left pocket of my greatcoat. And there I am ready to begin again. Do I have to go on? No, for it is clear that after the next series, of sucks and transfers, I shall be back where I started, that is to say with the first six stones back in the supply-pocket, the next five in the right pocket of my stinking old trousers and finally the last five in left pocket of same, and my sixteen stones will have been sucked once at least in impeccable succession, not one sucked twice, not one left unsucked. It is true that the next time I could scarcely hope to suck my stones in the same order as the first time and that the first, seventh and twelfth for example of the first cycle might very well be the sixth, eleventh and sixteenth respectively of the second, if the worst came to the worst. But that was a drawback I could not avoid. And if in the cycles taken together utter confusion was bound to reign, at least within each cycle taken separately I could be easy in my mind, at least as easy as one can be, in a proceeding of this kind. For in order for each cycle to be identical, as to the succession of stones in my mouth, and God knows I had set my heart on it, the only means were numbered stones or sixteen pockets. And rather than make twelve more pockets or number my stones, I preferred to make the best of the comparative peace of mind I enjoyed within each cycle taken separately. For it was not enough to number the stones, but I would have had to remember, every time I put a stone in my mouth, the number I needed and look for it in my pocket. Which would have put me off stone for ever, in a very short time. For I would never have been sure of not making a mistake, unless of course I had kept a kind of register, in which to tick off the stones one by one, as I sucked them. And of this I believed myself incapable. No, the only perfect solution would have been the sixteen pockets, symmetrically disposed, each one with its stone. Then I would have needed neither to number nor to think, but merely, as I sucked a given stone, to move on the fifteen others, each to the next pocket, a delicate business admittedly, but within my power, and

to call always on the same pocket when I felt like a suck.
This would have freed me from all anxiety, not only within
each cycle taken separately, but also for the sum of all cycles,
though they went on forever. But however imperfect my
own solution was, I was pleased at having found it all alone,
yes, quite pleased. And if it was perhaps less sound than I
had thought in the first flush of discovery, its inelegance
never diminished. And it was above all inelegant in this,
to my mind, that the uneven distribution was painful to
me, bodily. It is true that a kind of equilibrium was reached,
at a given moment, in the early stages of each cycle, namely
after the third suck and before the fourth, but it did not
last long, and the rest of the time I felt the weight of the
stones dragging me now to one side, now to the other. So
it was something more than a principle I abandoned, when
I abandoned the equal distribution, it was a bodily need. But
to suck the stones in the way I have described, not haphazard, but with method, was also I think a bodily need.
Here then were two incompatible bodily needs, at logger-
heads. Such things happen. But deep down I didn't give a
tinker's curse about being off my balance, dragged to the
right hand and the left, backwards and forwards. And deep
down it was all the same to me whether I sucked a different
stone each time or always the same stone, until the end
of time. For they all tasted exactly the same. And if I had
collected sixteen, it was not in order to ballast myself in
such and such a way, or to suck them turn about, but
simply to have a little store, so as never to be without. But
deep down I didn't give a fiddler's curse about being without,
when they were all gone they would be all gone, I wouldn't
be any the worse off, or hardly any. And the solution to
which I rallied in the end was to throw away all the stones
but one, which I kept now in one pocket, now in another,
and which of course I soon lost, or threw away, or gave away,
or swallowed. It was a wild part of the coast. I don't remember having been seriously molested. The black speck I was, in
the great pale stretch of sand, who could wish it harm?
Some came near, to see what it was, whether it wasn't
something of value from a wreck, washed up by the storm.
But when they saw the jetsam was alive, decently if wretchedly clothed, they turned away. Old women and young ones,

yes, too, come to gather wood, came and stared, in the early days. But they were always the same and it was in vain I moved from one place to another, in the end they all knew what I was and kept their distance. I think one of them one day, detaching herself from her companions, came and offered me something to eat and that I looked at her in silence, until she went away. Yes, it seems to me some such incident occurred about this time. But perhaps I am thinking of another stay, at an earlier time, for this will be my last, my last but one, or two, there is never a last, by the sea. However that may be I see a young woman coming towards me and stopping from time to time to look back at her companions. Huddled together like sheep they watch her recede, urging her on, and laughing no doubt, I seem to hear laughter, far away. Then it is her back I see, as she goes away, now it is towards me she looks back, but without stopping. But perhaps I am merging two times in one, and two women, one coming towards me, shyly, urged on by the cries and laughter of her companions, and the other going away from me, unhesitatingly. For those who came towards me I saw coming from afar, most of the time, that is one of the advantages of the seaside. Black specks in the distance I saw them coming, I could follow all their manoeuvres, saying, It's getting smaller, or, it's getting bigger. Yes, to be taken unawares was so to speak impossible, for I turned often towards the land too. Let me tell you something, my sight was better at the seaside! Yes, ranging far and wide over these vast flats, where nothing lay, nothing stood, my good eye saw more clearly and there were even days when the bad one too had to look away. And not only did I see more clearly, but I had less difficulty in saddling with a name the rare things I saw. These are some of the advantages and disadvantages of the seaside. Or perhaps it was I who was changing, why not? And in the morning, in my cave, and even sometimes at night, when the storm raged, I felt reasonably secure from the elements and mankind. But there too there is a price to pay. In your box, in your caves, there too there is a price to pay. And which you pay willingly, for a time, but which you cannot go on paying forever. For you cannot go on buying the same thing forever, with your little pittance. And unfor-

tunately there are other needs than that of rotting in peace,
it's not the word, I mean of course my mother whose image,
blunted for some time past, was beginning now to harrow
me again. So I went back inland, for my town was not
strictly speaking on the sea, whatever may have been said
to the contrary. And to get to it you had to go inland, I at
least knew of no other way. For between my town and the
sea there was a kind of swamp which, as far back as I
can remember, and some of my memories have their roots
deep in the immediate past, there was always talk of
draining, by means of canals I suppose, or of transforming
into a vast port and docks, or into a city on piles for the
workers, in a word of redeeming somehow or other. And
with the same stone they would have killed the scandal, at
the gates of their metropolis, of a stinking steaming swamp
in which an incalculable number of human lives were yearly
engulfed, the statistics escape me for the moment and
doubtless always will, so complete is my indifference to this
aspect of the question. It is true they actually began to work
and that work is still going on in certain areas in the teeth
of adversity, setbacks, epidemics and the apathy of the Public
Works Department, far from me to deny it. But from this
to proclaiming that the sea came lapping at the ramparts
of my town, there was a far cry. And I for my part will
never lend myself to such a perversion (of the truth), until
such time as I am compelled or find it convenient to do so.
And I knew this swamp a little, having risked my life in it,
cautiously, on several occasions, at a period of my life
richer in illusions than the one I am trying to patch together
here, I mean richer in certain illusions, in others poorer. So
there was no way of coming at my town directly, by sea,
but you had to disembark well to the north or the south and
take to the roads, just imagine that, for they had never
heard of Watt, just imagine that too. And now my progress,
slow and painful at all times, was more so than ever, because of my short stiff leg, the same which I thought had
long been as stiff as a leg could be, but damn the bit of
it, for it was growing stiffer than ever, a thing I would
not have thought possible, and at the same time shorter
every day, but above all because of the other leg, supple
hitherto and now growing rapidly stiff in its turn but not
yet shortening, unhappily. For when the two legs shorten

at the same time, and at the same speed, then all is not
lost, no. But when one shortens, and the other not, then you
begin to be worried. Oh not that I was exactly worried,
but it was a nuisance, yes, a nuisance. For I didn't know
which foot to land on, when I came down. Let us try and
get this dilemma clear. Follow me carefully. The stiff leg hurt
me, admittedly, I mean the old stiff leg, and it was the
other which I normally used as a pivot, or prop. But now
this latter, as a result of its stiffening I suppose, and the
ensuing commotion among nerves and sinews, was beginning
to hurt me even more than the other. What a story, God send
I don't make a balls of it. For the old pain, do you follow
me, I had got used to it, in a way, yes, in a kind of way.
Whereas to the new pain, though of the same family exactly,
I had not yet had time to adjust myself. Nor should it be
forgotten that having one bad leg plus another more or less
good, I was able to nurse the former exclusively, with the
help of my crutches. But I no longer had this resource! For
I no longer had one bad leg plus another more or less good,
but now both were equally bad. And the worse, to my
mind, was that which till now had been good, at least com-
paratively good, and whose change for the worse I had not
yet got used to. So in a way, if you like, I had still one
bad leg and one good, or rather less bad, with this difference
however, that the less bad now was the less good of heretofore. It was therefore on the old bad leg that I often longed
to lean, between one crutch-stroke and the next. For while
still extremely sensitive, it was less so than the other, or it
was equally so, if you like, but it did not seem so, to me,
because of its seniority. But I couldn't! What? Lean on it.
For it was shortening, don't forget, whereas the other,
though stiffening, was not yet shortening, or so far behind
its fellow that to all intents and purposes, I'm lost, no matter.
If I could even have bent it, at the knee, or even at the hip,
I could have made it seem as short as the other, long enough
to land on the true short one, before taking off again. But
I couldn't. What? Bend it. For how could I bend it, when
it was stiff? I was therefore compelled to work the same
old leg as heretofore, in spite of its having become, at least
as far as the pain was concerned, the worse of the two and
the more in need of nursing. Sometimes to be sure, when

I was lucky enough to chance on a road conveniently cambered, or by taking advantage of a not too deep ditch or any other breach of surface, I managed to lengthen my short leg, for a short time. But it had done no work for so long that it did not know how to go about it. And I think a pile of dishes would have better supported me than it, which had so well supported me, when I was a tiny tot. And another factor of disequilibrium was here involved, I mean when I thus made the best of the lie of the land, I mean my crutches, which would have needed to be unequal, one short and one long, if I was to remain vertical. No? I don't know. In any case the ways I went were for the most part little forest paths, that's understandable, where differences of level, though abounding, were too confused and too erratic to be of any help to me. But did it make such a difference after all, as far as the pain was concerned, whether my leg was free to rest or whether it had to work? I think not. For the suffering of the leg at rest was constant and monotonous. Whereas the leg condemned to the increase of pain inflicted by work knew the decrease of pain dispensed by work suspended, the space of an instant. But I am human, I fancy, and my progress suffered, from this state of affairs, and from the slow and painful progress it had always been, whatever may have been said to the contrary, was changed, saving your presence, to a veritable calvary, with no limit to its stations and no hope of crucifixion, though I say it myself, and no Simon, and reduced me to frequent halts. Yes, my progress reduced me to stopping more and more often, it was the only way to progress, to stop. And though it is no part of my tottering intentions to treat here in full, as they deserve, these brief moments of the immemorial expiation, I shall nevertheless deal with them briefly, out of the goodness of my heart, so that my story, so clear till now, may not end in darkness, the darkness of these towering forests, these giant fronds, where I hobble, listen, fall, rise, listen and hobble on, wondering sometimes, need I say, if I shall ever see again the hated light, at least unloved, stretched palely between the last boles, and my mother, to settle with her, and if I would not do better, at least just as well, to hang myself from a bough, with a liane. For frankly light meant nothing to me now, and my mother could scarcely be waiting for me still, after so long. And my leg, my legs. But the thought of suicide had little hold on me, I don't know why, I thought I did, but I see I don't. The idea of strangulation in particular, however tempting, I always overcame, after a short struggle. And between you and me there was never anything wrong with my respiratory tracts, apart of course from the agonies intrinsic to that system. Yes, I could count the days when I could neither breathe in the blessed air with its life-giving oxygen nor, when I had breathed it in, breathe out the bloody stuff, I could have counted them. Ah yes, my asthma, how often I was tempted to put an end to it, by cutting my throat. But I never succumbed. The noise betrayed me, I turned purple. It came on mostly at night, fortunately, or unfortunately, I could never make up my mind. For if sudden changes of colour matter less at night, the least unusual noise is then more noticeable, because of the silence of the night. But these were mere crises, and what are crises compared to all that never stops, knows neither ebb nor flow, its surface leaden above infernal depths. Not a word, not a word against the crises that seized me, wrung me, and finally threw me away, mercifully, safe from help. And I wrapped my head in my coat, to stifle the obscene noise of choking, or I disguised it as a fit of coughing, universally accepted and approved and whose only disadvantage is this, that it is liable to let you in for pity. And this is perhaps the moment to observe, better late than never, that when I speak of my progress being slowed down, consequent on the defection of my good leg, I express only an infinitesimal part of the truth. For the truth is I had other weak points, here and there, and they too were growing weaker and weaker, as was only to be expected. But what was not to be expected was the speed at which their weakness had increased since my departure from the seaside. For as long as I had remained at the seaside my weak points, while admittedly increasing in weakness, as was only to be expected, only increased imperceptibly, in weakness I mean. So that I would have hesitated to exclaim, with my finger up my arsehole for example, Jesus-Christ, it's much worse than yesterday, I can hardly believe it is the same hole. I apologize for having to revert to this lewd orifice, 'tis my muse will have it so. Perhaps it is less to

be thought of as the eyesore he called by its name than as
the symbol of those passed over in silence, a distinction due
perhaps to its centrality and its air of being a link between
me and the other excrement. We underestimate this little
hole, it seems to me, we call it the arsehole and affect to
despise it. But is it not rather the true portal of our being
and the celebrated mouth no more than the kitchen-door.
Nothing goes in, or so little, that is not rejected on the spot,
or very nearly. Almost everything revolts it that comes from
without and what comes from within does not seem to receive a very warm welcome either. Are not these significant
facts. Time will tell. But I shall do my utmost none the less
to keep it in the background, in the future. And that will
be easy, for the future is by no means uncertain, the unspeakable future. And when it comes to neglecting funda-
mentals, I think I have nothing to learn, and indeed I confuse them with accidentals. But to return to my weak points,
let me say again that at the seaside they had developed
normally, yes, I had noticed nothing abnormal. Either because I did not pay enough attention to them, absorbed as
I was in the metamorphosis of my excellent leg, or because
there was in fact nothing special to report, in this connexion.
But I had hardly left the shore, harried by the dread of
waking one fine day, far from my mother, with my two
legs as stiff as my crutches, when they suddenly began to
gallop, my weak points did, and their weakness became
literally the weakness of death, with all the disadvantages
that this entails, when they are not vital points. I fix at this
period the dastardly desertion of my toes, so to speak in
the thick of the fray. You may object that this is covered
by the business of my legs, that it has no importance, since
in any case I could not put to the ground the foot in question. Quite, quite. But do you as much as know what foot
we're talking about? No. Nor I. Wait till I think. But you
are right, that wasn't a weak point properly speaking, I
mean my toes, I thought they were in excellent fettle, apart
from a few corns, bunions, ingrowing nails and a tendency
to cramp. No, my true weak points were elsewhere. And
if I do not draw up here and now the impressive list of them
it is because I shall never draw it up. No, I shall never draw
it up, yes, perhaps I shall. And then I should be sorry to

give a wrong idea of my health which, if it was not exactly rude, to the extent of my bursting with it, was at bottom of an incredible robustness. For otherwise how could I have reached the enormous age I have reached. Thanks to moral qualities? Hygienic habits? Fresh air? Starvation? Lack of sleep? Solitude? Persecution? The long silent screams (dangerous to scream)? The daily longing for the earth to swallow me up? Come come. Fate is rancorous, but not to that extent. Look at Mammy. What rid me of her, in end? I sometimes wonder. Perhaps they buried her alive, it wouldn't surprise me. Ah the old bitch, a nice dose she gave me, she and her lousy unconquerable genes. Bristling with boils ever since I was a brat, a fat lot of good that ever did me. The heart beats, and what a beat. That my ureters —no, not a word on that subject. And the capsules. And the bladder. And the urethra. And the glans. Santa Maria. I give you my word, I cannot piss, my word of honour, as a gentleman. But my prepuce, sat verbum, oozes urine, day and night, at least I think it's urine, it smells of kidney. What's all this, I thought I had lost the sense of smell. Can one speak of pissing, under these conditions? Rubbish! My sweat too, and God knows I sweat, has a queer smell. I think it's in my dribble as well, and heaven knows I dribble. How I eliminate, to be sure, uremia will never be the death of me. Me too they would bury alive, in despair, if there was any justice in the world. And this list of my weak points I shall never draw up, for the fear of its finishing me, I shall perhaps, one day, when the time comes for the inventory of my goods and chattels. For that day, if it ever dawns, I shall be less afraid, of being finished, than I am today. For today, if I do not feel precisely at the beginning of my career, I have not the presumption either to think I am near the end. So I husband my strength, for the spurt. For to be unable to spurt, when the hour strikes, no, you might as well give up. But it is forbidden to give up and even to stop an instant. So I wait, jogging along, for the bell to say, Molloy, one last effort, it's the end. That's how I reason, with the help of images little suited to my situation. And I can't shake off the feeling, I don't know why, that the day will come for me to say what is left of all I had. But I must first wait, to be sure there is nothing more I can acquire, or lose, or throw away, or give way. Then I can say, without fear of error, what is left, in the end, of my possessions. For it will be the end. And between now and then I may get poorer, or richer, oh not to the extent of being any better off or any worse off, but sufficiently to preclude me from announcing, here and now, what is left of all I had, for I have not yet had all. But I can make no sense of this presentiment, and that I understand is very often the case with the best presentiments, that you can make no sense of them. So perhaps it is a true presentiment, apt to be borne out. But can any more sense be made of false presentiments? I think so, yes, I think that all that is false may more readily be reduced, to notions clear and distinct, distinct from all other notions. But I may be wrong. But I was not given to presentiments, but to sentiments sweet and simple, to episentiments rather, if I may venture to say so. For I knew in advance, which made all presentiment superfluous. I will even go further (what can I lose?), I knew only in advance, for when the time came I knew no longer, you may have noticed it, or only when I made a superhuman effort, and when the time was past I no longer knew either, I regained my ignorance. And all that taken together, if that is possible, should serve to explain many things, and notably my astonishing old age, still green in places, assuming the state of my health, in spite of all I have said about it, is insufficient to account for it. Simple supposition, committing me to nothing. But I was saying that if my progress, at this stage was becoming more and more slow and painful, this was not due solely to my legs, but also to innumerable so-called weak points, having nothing to do with my legs. Unless one is to suppose, gratuitously, that they and my legs were part of the same syndrome, which in that case would have been of a diabolical complexity. The fact is, and I deplore it, but it is too late now to do anything about it, that I have laid too much stress on my legs, throughout these wanderings, to the detriment of the rest. For I was no ordinary cripple, far from it, and there were days when my legs were the best part of me; with the exception of the brain capable of forming such a judgement. I was therefore obliged to stop more and more often, I shall never weary of repeating it, and to lie down, in defiance of the rules, now prone, now

supine, now on one side, now on the other, and as much
as possible with the feet higher than the head, to dislodge
the clots. And to lie with the feet higher than the head, when
your legs are stiff, is no easy matter. But don't worry, I
did it. When my comfort was at stake there was no trouble
I would not go to. The forest was all about me and the
boughs, twining together at a prodigious height, compared
to mine, sheltered me from the light and the elements. Some
days I advanced no more than thirty or forty paces, I give
you my oath. To say I stumbled in impenetrable darkness, no,
I cannot. I stumbled, but the darkness was not impenetrable.
For there reigned a kind of blue gloom, more than sufficient
for my visual needs. I was astonished this gloom was not
green, rather than blue, but I saw it blue and perhaps it was.
The red of the sun, mingling with the green of the leaves,
gave a blue result, that is how I reasoned. But from time
to time. From time to time. What tenderness in these little
words, what savagery. But from time to time I came on a
kind of crossroads, you know, a star, or circus, of the kind
to be found in even the most unexplored of forests. And
turning then methodically to face the radiating paths in
turn, hoping for I know not what, I described a complete
circle, or less than a circle, or more than a circle, so great
was the resemblance between them. Here the gloom was not
so thick and I made haste to leave it. I don't like gloom
to lighten, there's something shady about it. I had a certain
number of encounters in this forest, naturally, where does
one not, but nothing to signify. I notably encountered a charcoal-burner. I might have loved him, I think, if I had been
seventy years younger. But it's not certain. For then he too
would have been younger by as much, oh not quite as much,
but much younger. I never really had much love to spare,
but all the same I had my little quota, when I was small,
and it went to the old men, when it could. And I even
think I had time to love one or two, or not with true love,
no, nothing like the old woman, I've lost her name again,
Rose, no, anyway you see who I mean, but all the same,
how shall I say, tenderly, as those on the brink of a better
earth. Ah I was a precocious child, and then I was a precocious man. Now they all give me the shits, the ripe, the
unripe and the rotting from the bough. He was all over me,

begging me to share his hut, believe it or not. A total
stranger. Sick with solitude probably. I say charcoal-burner,
but I really don't know. I see smoke somewhere. That's
something that never escapes me, smoke. A long dialogue
ensued, interspersed with groans. I could not ask him the
way to my town, the name of which escaped me still. I
asked him the way to the nearest town, I found the necessary
words, and accents. He did not know. He was born in the
forest probably and had spent his whole life there. I asked
him to show me the nearest way out of the forest. I grew
eloquent. His reply was exceedingly confused. Either I didn't
understand a word he said, or he didn't understand a word
I said, or he knew nothing, or he wanted to keep me near
him. It was towards this fourth hypothesis that in all modesty
I leaned, for when I made to go, he held me back by the
sleeve. So I smartly freed a crutch and dealt him a good dint
on the skull. That calmed him. The dirty old brute. I got
up and went on. But I hadn't gone more than a few paces,
and for me at this time a few paces meant something, when
I turned and went back to where he lay, to examine him.
Seeing he had not ceased to breathe I contented myself with
giving him a few warm kicks in the ribs, with my heels. This
is how I went about it. I carefully chose the most favourable
position, a few paces from the body, with my back of
course turned to it. Then, nicely balanced on my crutches,
I began to swing, backwards, forwards, feet pressed together,
or rather legs pressed together, for how could I press my
feet together, with my legs in the state they were? But how
could I press my legs together, in the state they were? I
pressed them together, that's all I can tell you. Take it or
leave it. Or I didn't press them together. What can that
possibly matter? I swung, that's all that matters, in an ever-
widening arc, until I decided the moment had come and
launched myself forward with all my strength and consequently, a moment later, backward, which gave the desired result. Where did I get this access of vigour? From
my weakness perhaps. The shock knocked me down. Naturally. I came a cropper. You can't have everything, I've often
noticed it. I rested a moment, then got up, picked up my
crutches, took up my position on the other side of the body
and applied myself with method to the same exercise. I

always had a mania for symmetry. But I must have aimed
a little low and one of my heels sank in something soft.
However. For if I had missed the ribs, with that heel, I
had no doubt landed in the kidney, oh not hard enough to
burst it, no, I fancy not. People imagine, because you are
old, poor, crippled, terrified, that you can't stand up for yourself, and generally speaking that is so. But given favourable
conditions, a feeble and awkward assailant, in your own
class what, and a lonely place, and you have a good chance of
showing what stuff you are made of. And it is doubtless in
order to revive interest in this possibility, too often forgotten,
that I have delayed over an incident of no interest in itself,
like all that has a moral. But did I at least eat, from time
to time? Perforce, perforce, roots, berries, sometimes a little
mulberry, a mushroom from time to time, trembling, knowing nothing about mushrooms. What else, ah yes, carobs, so
dear to goats. In a word whatever I could find, forests abound
in good things. And having heard, or more probably read
somewhere, in the days when I thought I would be well
advised to educate myself, or amuse myself, or stupefy
myself, or kill time, that when a man in a forest thinks
he is going forward in a straight line, in reality he is going
in a circle, I did my best to go in a circle, hoping in this
way to go in a straight line. For I stopped being half-witted
and became sly, whenever I took the trouble. And my head
was a storehouse of useful knowledge. And if I did not
go in a rigorously straight line, with my system of going
in a circle, at least I did not go in a circle, and that was
something. And by going on doing this, day after day, and
night after night, I looked forward to getting out of the
forest, some day. For my region was not all forest, far from
it. But there were plains too, mountains and sea, and some
towns and villages, connected by highways and byways. And I
was all the more convinced that I would get out of the forest
some day as I had already got out of it, more than once, and
I knew how difficult it was not to do again what you have done
before. But things had been rather different then. And yet I
did not despair of seeing the light tremble, some day, through
the still boughs, the strange light of the plain, its pale wild
eddies, through the bronze-still boughs, which no breath ever
stirred. But it was a day I dreaded too. So that I was sure it

would come sooner or later. For it was not bad being in the forest, I could imagine worse, and I could have stayed there till I died, unrepining, yes, without pining for the light and the plain and the other amenities of my region. For I knew them well, the amenities of my region, and I considered that the forest was no worse. And it was not only no worse, to my mind, but it was better, in this sense, that I was there. That is a strange way, is it not, of looking at things. Perhaps less strange than it seems. For being in the forest a place neither worse nor better than the others, and being free to stay there, was it not natural I should think highly of it, not because of what it was, but because I was there. For I was there. And being there I did not have to go there, and that was not to be despised, seeing the state of my legs and my body in general. That is all I wished to say, and if I did not say it at the outset it is simply that something was against it. But I could not, stay in the forest I mean, I was not free to. That is to say I could have, physically nothing could have been easier, but I was not purely physical, I lacked something, and I would have had the feeling, if I had stayed in the forest, of going against an imperative, at least I had that impression. But perhaps I was mistaken, perhaps I would have been better advised to stay in the forest, perhaps I could have stayed there, without remorse, without the painful impression of committing a fault, almost a sin. For I have greatly sinned, at all times, greatly sinned against my prompters. And if I cannot decently be proud of this I see no reason either to be sorry. But imperatives are a little different, and I have always been inclined to submit to them, I don't know why. For they never led me anywhere, but tore me from places where, if all was not well, all was no worse than anywhere else, and then went silent, leaving me stranded. So I knew my imperatives well, and yet I submitted to them. It had become a habit. It is true they nearly all bore on the same question, that of my relations with my mother, and on the importance of bringing as soon as possible some light to bear on these and even on the kind of light that should be brought to bear and the most effective means of doing so. Yes, these imperatives were quite explicit and even detailed until, having set me in motion at last, they began to falter, then went silent, leaving me there like a fool who neither knows where he is going nor why he is going there. And they nearly all bore, as I may have said already, on the same painful and thorny question. And I do not think I could mention even one having a different purport. And the one enjoining me then to leave the forest without delay was in no way different from those I was used to, as to its meaning. For in its framing I thought I noticed something new. For after the usual blarney there followed this solemn warning, Perhaps it is already too late. It was in Latin, nimis sero, I think that's Latin. Charming things, hypothetical imperatives. But if I had never succeeded in liquidating this matter of my mother, the fault must not be imputed solely to that voice which deserted me, prematurely. It was partly to blame, that's all it can be reproached with. For the outer world opposed my succeeding too, with its wiles, I have given some examples. And even if the voice could have harried me to the very scene of action, even then I might well have succeeded no better, because of the other obstacles barring my way. And in this command which faltered, then died, it was hard not to hear the unspoken entreaty, Don't do it, Molloy. In forever reminding me thus of my duty was its purpose to show me the folly of it? Perhaps. Fortunately it did no more than stress, the better to mock if you like, an innate velleity. And of myself, all my life, I think I had been going to my mother, with the purpose of establishing our relations on a less precarious footing. And when I was with her, and I often succeeded, I left her without having done anything. And when I was no longer with her I was again on my way to her, hoping to do better the next time. And when I appeared to give up and to busy myself with something else, or with nothing at all any more, in reality I was hatching my plans and seeking the way to her house. This is taking a queer turn. So even without this so-called imperative I impugn, it would have been difficult for me to stay in the forest, since I was forced to assume my mother was not there. And yet it might have been better for me to try and stay. But I also said, Yet a little while, at the rate things are going, and I won't be able to move, but will have to stay, where I happen to be unless someone comes and carries me. Oh I did not say it in such limpid language.

And when I say I said, etc., all I mean is that I knew
confusedly things were so, without knowing exactly what
it was all about. And every time I say, I said this, or I said
that, or speak of a voice saying, far away inside me, Molloy,
and then a fine phrase more or less clear and simple, or
find myself compelled to attribute to others intelligible words,
or hear my own voice uttering to others more or less articulate sounds, I am merely complying with the convention that
demands you either lie or hold your peace. For what really
happened was quite different. And I did not say, Yet a little
while, at the rate things are going, etc., but that resembled
perhaps what I would have said, if I had been able. In reality
I said nothing at all, but I heard a murmur, something gone
wrong with the silence, and I pricked up my ears, like an
animal I imagine, which gives a start and pretends to be
dead. And then sometimes there arose within me, confusedly,
a kind of consciousness, which I express by saying, I said,
etc., or, Don't do it Molloy, or, Is that your mother's name?
said the sergeant, I quote from memory. Or which I express without sinking to the level of oratio recta, but by
means of other figures quite as deceitful, as for example, It
seemed to me that, etc., or, I had the impression that, etc.,
for it seemed to me nothing at all, and I had no impression
of any kind, but simply somewhere something had changed,
so that I too had to change, or the world too had to change,
in order for nothing to be changed. And it was these little
adjustments, as between Galileo's vessels, that I can only
express by saying, I feared that, or, I hoped that, or, Is that
your mother's name? said the sergeant, for example, and
that I might doubtless have expressed otherwise and better,
if I had gone to the trouble. And so I shall perhaps some
day when I have less horror of trouble than today. But I
think not. So I said, Yet a little while, at the rate things
are going, and I won't be able to move, but will have to stay,
where I happen to be, unless some kind person comes and
carries me. For my marches got shorter and shorter and
my halts in consequence more and more frequent and I may
add prolonged. For the notion of the long halt does not
necessarily follow from that of the short march, nor that
of the frequent halt either, when you come to think of it,
unless you give frequent a meaning it does not possess, and

I could never bring myself to do a thing like that. And it seemed to me all the more important to get out of this forest with all possible speed as I would very soon be powerless to get out of anything whatsoever, were it but a bower. It was winter, it must have been winter, and not only many trees had lost their leaves, but these lost leaves had gone all black and spongy and my crutches sank into them, in places right up to the fork. Strange to say I felt no colder than usual. Perhaps it was only autumn. But I was never very sensitive to changes of temperature. And the gloom, if it seemed less blue than before, was as thick as ever. Which made me say in the end, It is less blue because there is less green, but it is no less thick thanks to the leaden winter sky. Then something about the black dripping from the black boughs, something in that line. The black slush of leaves slowed me down even more. But leaves or no leaves I would have abandoned erect motion, that of man. And I still remember the day when, flat on my face by way of rest, in defiance of the rules, I suddenly cried, striking my brow, Christ, there's crawling, I never thought of that. But could I crawl, with my legs in such a state, and my trunk? And my head. But before I go on, a word about the forest murmurs. It was in vain I listened, I could hear nothing of the kind. But rather, with much goodwill and a little imagination, at long intervals a distant gong. A horn goes well with the forest, you expect it. It is the huntsman. But a gong! Even a tom-tom, at a pinch, would not have shocked me. But a gong! It was mortifying, to have been looking forward to the celebrated murmurs if to nothing else, and to succeed only in hearing, at long intervals, in the far distance, a gong. For a moment I dared hope it was only my heart, still beating. But only for a moment. For it does not beat, not my heart, I'd have to refer you to hydraulics for the squelch that old pump makes. To the leaves too I listened, before their fall, attentively in vain. They made no sound, motionless and rigid, like brass, have I said that before? So much for the forest murmurs. From time to time I blew my horn, through the cloth of my pocket. Its hoot was fainter every time. I had taken it off my bicycle. When? I don't know. And now, let us have done. Flat on my belly, using my crutches like grapnels,

I plunged them ahead of me into the undergrowth, and when
I felt they had a hold, I pulled myself forward, with an
effort of the wrists. For my wrists were still quite strong,
fortunately, in spite of my decrepitude, though all swollen
and racked by a kind of chronic arthritis probably. That
then briefly is how I went about it. The advantage of this
mode of locomotion compared to others, I mean those I have
tried, is this, that when you want to rest you stop and rest,
without further ado. For standing there is no rest, nor
sitting either. And there are men who move about sitting,
and even kneeling, hauling themselves to right and left,
forward and backward, with the help of hooks. But he who
moves in this way, crawling on his belly, like a reptile, no
sooner comes to rest than he begins to rest, and even the
very movement is a kind of rest, compared to other movements, I mean those that have worn me out. And in this
way I moved onward in the forest, slowly, but with a certain
regularity, and I covered my fifteen paces, day in, day out,
without killing myself. And I even crawled on my back,
plunging my crutches blindly behind me into the thickets,
and with the black boughs for sky to my closing eyes. I was
on my way to mother. And from time to time I said, Mother,
to encourage me I suppose. I kept losing my hat, the lace
had broken long ago, until in a fit of temper I banged it
down on my skull with such violence that I couldn't get
it off again. And if I had met any lady friends, if I had had
any lady friends, I would have been powerless to salute them
correctly. But there was always present to my mind, which
was still working, if laboriously, the need to turn, to keep
on turning, and every three or four jerks I altered course,
which permitted me to describe, if not a circle, at least
a great polygon, perfection is not of this world, and to
hope that I was going forward in a straight line, in spite
of everything, day and night, towards my mother. And true
enough the day came when the forest ended and I saw the
light, the light of the plain, exactly as I had foreseen. But I
did not see it from afar, trembling beyond the harsh trunks,
as I had foreseen, but suddenly I was in it, I opened my
eyes and saw I had arrived. And the reason for that was
probably this, that for some time past I had not opened
my eyes, or seldom. And even my little changes of course

were made blindly, in the dark. The forest ended in a ditch,
I don't know why, and it was in this ditch that I became
aware of what had happened to me. I suppose it was the
fall into the ditch that opened my eyes, for why would they
have opened otherwise? I looked at the plain rolling away
as far as the eye could see. No, not quite so far as that.
For my eyes having got used to the light I fancied I saw,
faintly outlined against the horizon, the towers and steeples
of a town, which of course I could not assume was mine,
on such slight evidence. It is true the plain seemed familiar,
but in my region all the plains looked alike, when you knew
one you knew them all. In any case, whether it was my town
or not, whether somewhere under that faint haze my mother
panted on or whether she poisoned the air a hundred miles
away, were ludicrously idle questions for a man in my position, though of undeniable interest on the plane of pure
knowledge. For how could I drag myself over that vast
moor, where my crutches would fumble in vain. Rolling
perhaps. And then? Would they let me roll on to my mother's
door? Fortunately for me at this painful juncture, which
I had vaguely foreseen, but not in all its bitterness, I heard
a voice telling me not to fret, that help was coming. Literally.
These words struck it is not too much to say as clearly
on my ear, and on my understanding, as the urchin's thanks
I suppose when I stooped and picked up his marble. Don't
fret Molloy, we're coming. Well, I suppose you have to
try everything once, succour included, to get a complete
picture of the resources of their planet. I lapsed down to
the bottom of the ditch. It must have been spring, a morning
in spring. I thought I heard birds, skylarks perhaps. I had not
heard a bird for a long time. How was it I had not heard
any in the forest? Nor seen any. It had not seemed strange
to me. Had I heard any at the seaside? Mews? I could not
remember. I remembered the corn-crakes. The two travellers
came back to my memory. One had a club. I had forgotten
them. I saw the sheep again. Or so I say now. I did not
fret, other scenes of my life came back to me. There seemed
to be rain, then sunshine, turn about. Real spring weather.
I longed to go back into the forest. Oh not a real longing.
Molloy could stay, where he happened to be.

II

It is midnight. The rain is beating on the windows. I am calm. All is sleeping. Nevertheless I get up and go to my desk. I can't sleep. My lamp sheds a soft and steady light. I have trimmed it. It will last till morning. I hear the eagle-owl. What a terrible battle-cry! Once I listened to it unmoved. My son is sleeping. Let him sleep. The night will come when he too, unable to sleep, will get up and go to to his desk. I shall be forgotten.

My report will be long. Perhaps I shall not finish it. My name is Moran, Jacques. That is the name I am known by. I am done for. My son too. All unsuspecting. He must think he's on the threshold of life, of real life. He's right there. His name is Jacques, like mine. This cannot lead to confusion.

I remember the day I received the order to see about Molloy. It was a Sunday in summer. I was sitting in my little garden, in a wicker chair, a black book closed on my knees. It must have been about eleven o'clock, still too early to go to church. I was savouring the day of rest, while deploring the importance attached to it, in certain parishes. To work, even to play on Sunday, was not of necessity reprehensible, in my opinion. It all depended on the state of mind of him who worked, or played, and on the nature of his work, of his play, in my opinion. I was reflecting with satisfaction on this, that this slightly libertarian view was gaining ground, even among the clergy, more and more disposed to admit that the sabbath, so long as you go to mass and contribute to the collection, may be considered a day like any other, in certain respects. This did not affect me personally, I've always loved doing nothing. And I would gladly have rested on weekdays too, if I could have afforded it. Not that I was positively lazy. It was something else. Seeing something done which I could have done better myself, if I had wished, and which I did do better whenever I put my mind to it, I had the impression of discharging a function to which no form of activity could have exalted me. But this was a joy in which, during the week, I could seldom indulge.

The weather was fine. I watched absently the coming and going of my bees. I heard on the gravel the scampering steps of my son, caught up in I know not what fantasy of flight and pursuit. I called to him not to dirty himself. He did not answer.

All was still. Not a breath. From my neighbours' chimneys the smoke rose straight and blue. None but tranquil sounds, the clicking of mallet and ball, a rake on pebbles, a distant lawn-mower, the bell of my beloved church. And birds of course, blackbird and thrush, their song sadly dying, vanquished by the heat, and leaving dawn's high boughs for the bushes' gloom. Contentedly I inhaled the scent of my lemon-verbena.

In such surroundings slipped away my last moments of peace and happiness.

A man came into the garden and walked swiftly towards me. I knew him well. Now I have no insuperable objection to a neighbour's dropping in, on a Sunday to pay his respects, if he feels the need, though I much prefer to see nobody. But this man was not a neighbour. Our dealings were strictly of a business nature and he had journeyed from afar, on purpose to disturb me. So I was disposed to receive him frostily enough, all the more so as he had the impertinence to come straight to where I was sitting, under my Beauty of Bath. With people who took this liberty I had no patience. If they wished to speak to me they had only to ring at the door of my house. Martha had her instructions. I thought I was hidden from anybody coming into my grounds and following the short path which led from the garden-gate to the front door, and in fact I must have been. But at the noise of the gate being slammed I turned angrily and saw, blurred by the leaves, this high mass bearing down on me, across the lawn. I neither got up nor invited him to sit down. He stopped in front of me and we stared at each other in silence. He was dressed in his heavy, sombre Sunday best, and at this my displeasure knew no bounds. This gross external observance, while the soul exults in its rags, has always appeared to me an abomination. I watched the enormous feet crushing my daisies. I would gladly have driven him away, with a knout. Unfortunately it was not he who

mattered. Sit down, I said, mollified by the reflection that
after all he was only acting his part of go-between. Yes,
suddenly I had pity on him, pity on myself. He sat down
and mopped his forehead. I caught a glimpse of my son
spying on us from behind a bush. My son was thirteen or
fourteen at the time. He was big and strong for his age.
His intelligence seemed at times little short of average. My
son, in fact. I called him and ordered him to go and fetch
some beer. Peeping and prying were part of my profession.
My son imitated me instinctively. He returned after a remarkably short interval with two glasses and a quart bottle
of beer. He uncorked the bottle and served us. He was very
fond of uncorking bottles. I told him to go and wash himself,
to straighten his clothes, in a word to get ready to appear in
public, for it would soon be time for mass. He can stay, said
Gaber. I don't wish him to stay, I said. And turning to my
son I told him again to go and get ready. If there was one
thing displeased me, at that time, it was being late for the
last mass. Please yourself, said Gaber. Jacques went away
grumbling with his finger in his mouth, a detestable and
unhygienic habit, but preferable all things considered to that
of the finger in the nose, in my opinion. If putting his finger
in his mouth prevented my son from putting it in his nose,
or elsewhere, he was right to do it, in a sense.

Here are your instructions, said Gaber. He took a notebook from his pocket and began to read. Every now and
then he closed the notebook, taking care to leave his finger
as a marker, and indulged in comments and observations
of which I had no need, for I knew my business. When at
last he had finished I told him the job did not interest me
and that the chief would do better to call on another agent.
He wants it to be you, God knows why, said Gaber. I presume he told you why, I said, scenting flattery for which I
had a weakness. He said, replied Gaber, that no one could
do it but you. This was more or less what I wanted to hear.
And yet, I said, the affair seems childishly simple. Gaber
began bitterly to inveigh against our employer, who had
made him get up in the middle of the night, just as he was
getting into position to make love to his wife. For this kind
of nonsense, he added. And he said he had confidence in
no one but me? I said. He doesn't know what he says, said

Gaber. He added, Nor what he does. He wiped the lining
of his bowler, peering inside as if in search of something.
In that case it's hard for me to refuse, I said, knowing
perfectly well that in any case it was impossible for me to
refuse. Refuse! But we agents often amused ourselves with
grumbling among ourselves and giving ourselves the airs
of free men. You leave today, said Gaber. Today! I cried,
but he's out of his mind! Your son goes with you, said
Gaber. I said no more. Gaber buttoned his notebook and
put it back in his pocket, which he also buttoned. He stood
up, rubbing his hands over his chest. I could do with another
beer, he said. Go to the kitchen, I said, the maid will serve
you. Goodbye, Moran, he said.

It was too late for mass. I did not need to consult my
watch to know, I could feel mass had begun without me.
I who never missed mass, to have missed it on that Sunday
of all Sundays! When I so needed it! To buck me up. I decided to ask for a private communion, in the course of the
afternoon. I would go without lunch. Father Ambrose was
always very kind and accommodating.

I called Jacques. Without result. I said, Seeing me still
in conference he has gone to mass alone. This explanation
turned out subsequently to be the correct one. But I added,
He might have come and seen me, before leaving. I liked
thinking in monologue and then my lips moved visibly. But
no doubt he was afraid of disturbing me and of being
reprimanded. For I was sometimes inclined to go too far
when I reprimanded my son, who was consequently a little
afraid of me. I myself had never been sufficiently chastened.
Oh I had not been spoiled either, merely neglected. Whence
bad habits ingrained beyond remedy and of which even
the most meticulous piety has never been able to break me.
I hoped to spare my son this misfortune, by giving him a
good clout from time to time, together with my reasons for
doing so. Then I said, Is he barefaced enough to tell me,
on his return, that he has been to mass if he has not, if
for example he has merely run off to join his little friends,
behind the slaughter-house? And I determined to get the
truth out of Father Ambrose, on this subject. For it was
imperative my son should not imagine he was capable of
lying to me with impunity. And if Father Ambrose could

not enlighten me, I would apply to the verger, whose vigilance
it was inconceivable that the presence of my son at twelve
o'clock mass had escaped. For I knew for a fact that the
verger had a list of the faithful and that, from his place
beside the font, he ticked us off when it came to the absolution. It is only fair to say that Father Ambrose knew nothing
of these manoeuvers, yes, anything in the nature of surveillance
was hateful to the good Father Ambrose. And he would
have sent the verger flying about his business if he had
suspected him of such a work of supererogation. It must
have been for his own edification that the verger kept this
register, with such assiduity. Admittedly I knew only what
went on at the last mass, having no experience personally
of the other offices, for the good reason that I never went
within a mile of them. But I had heard it said that they
were the occasion of exactly the same supervision, at the
hands either of the verger himself or, when his duties called
him elsewhere, of one of his sons. A strange parish whose
flock knew more than its pastor of a circumstance which
seemed rather in his province than in theirs.

Such were my thoughts as I waited for my son to come
back and Gaber, whom I had not yet heard leave, to go.
And tonight I find it strange I could have thought of such
things, I mean my son, my lack of breeding, Father Ambrose,
Verger Joly with his register, at such a time. Had I not
something better to do, after what I had just heard? The
fact is I had not yet begun to take the matter seriously.
And I am all the more surprised as such light-mindedness
was not like me. Or was it in order to win a few more
moments of peace that I instinctively avoided giving my
mind to it? Even if, as set forth in Gaber's report, the affair
had seemed unworthy of me, the chief's insistence on having
me, me Moran, rather than anybody else, ought to have
warned me that it was no ordinary one. And instead of bringing to bear upon it without delay all the resources of my
mind and of my experience, I sat dreaming of my breed's
infirmities and the singularities of those about me. And yet
the poison was already acting on me, the poison I had just
been given. I stirred restlessly in my arm-chair, ran my
hands over my face, crossed and uncrossed my legs, and
so on. The colour and weight of the world were changing
already, soon I would have to admit I was anxious.

I remembered with annoyance the lager I had just absorbed. Would I be granted the body of Christ after a pint of Wallenstein? And if I said nothing? Have you come fasting, my son? He would not ask. But God would know, sooner or later. Perhaps he would pardon me. But would the eucharist produce the same effect, taken on top of beer, however light? I could always try. What was the teaching of the Church on the matter? What if I were about to commit sacrilege? I decided to suck a few peppermints on the way to the presbytery.

I got up and went to the kitchen. I asked if Jacques was back. I haven't seen him, said Martha. She seemed in bad humour. And the man? I said. What man? she said. The man who came for a glass of beer, I said. No one came for anything, said Martha. By the way, I said, unperturbed apparently, I shall not eat lunch today. She asked if I were ill. For I was naturally a rather heavy eater. And my Sunday midday meal especially I always liked extremely copious. It smelt good in the kitchen. I shall lunch a little later today, that's all, I said. Martha looked at me furiously. Say four o'clock, I said. In that wizened, grey skull what raging and rampaging then, I knew. You will not go out today, I said coldly, I regret. She flung herself at her pots and pans, dumb with anger. You will keep all that hot for me, I said, as best you can. And knowing her capable of poisoning me I added, You can have the whole day off tomorrow, if that is any good to you.

I left her and went out on the road. So Gaber had gone without his beer. And yet he had wanted it badly. It was a good brand, Wallenstein. I stood there on the watch for Jacques. Coming from church he would appear on my right, on my left if he came from the slaughter-house. A neighbour passed. A free-thinker. Well well, he said, no worship today? He knew my habits, my Sunday habits I mean. Everyone knew them and the chief perhaps better than any, in spite of his remoteness. You look as if you had seen a ghost, said the neighbour. Worse than that, I said, you. I went in, at my back the dutifully hideous smile. I could see him running to his concubine with the news. You know that poor bastard Moran, you should have heard me, I had him leppin! Couldn't speak! Took to his heels!

Jacques came back soon afterwards. No trace of frolic.

He said he had been to church alone. I asked him a few
pertinent questions concerning the march of the ceremony.
His answers were plausible. I told him to wash his hands
and sit down to his lunch. I went back to the kitchen. I did
nothing but go to and fro. You may dish up, I said. She
had wept. I peered into the pots. Irish stew. A nourishing
and economical dish, if a little indigestible. All honour to
the land it has brought before the world. I shall sit down
at four o'clock, I said. I did not need to add sharp. I liked
punctuality, all those whom my roof sheltered had to like
it too. I went up to my room. And there, stretched on my
bed, the curtains drawn, I made my first attempt to grasp
the Molloy affair.

My concern at first was only with its immediate vexations
and the preparations they demanded of me. The kernel of
the affair I continued to shirk. I felt a great confusion coming over me.

Should I set out on my autocycle? This was the question
with which I began. I had a methodical mind and never
set out on a mission without prolonged reflection as to the
best way of setting out. It was the first problem to solve,
at the outset of each enquiry, and I never moved until I
had solved it, to my satisfaction. Sometimes I took my
autocycle, sometimes the train, sometimes the motor-coach,
just as sometimes too I left on foot, or on my bicycle, silently,
in the night. For when you are beset with enemies, as I
am, you cannot leave on your autocycle, even in the night,
without being noticed, unless you employ it as an ordinary
bicycle, which is absurd. But if I was in the habit of first
settling this delicate question of transport, it was never
without having, if not fully sifted, at least taken into account
the factors on which it depended. For how can you decide
on the way of setting out if you do not first know where
you are going, or at least with what purpose you are going
there? But in the present case I was tackling the problem
of transport with no other preparation than the languid
cognizance I had taken of Gaber's report. I would be able
to recover the minutest details of this report when I wished.
But I had not yet troubled to do so, I had avoided doing
so, saying, The affair is banal. To try and solve the problem
of transport under such conditions was madness. Yet that
was what I was doing. I was losing my head already.

I liked leaving on my autocycle, I was partial to this
way of getting about. And in my ignorance of the reasons
against it I decided to leave on my autocycle. Thus was
inscribed, on the threshold of the Molloy affair, the fatal
pleasure principle.

The sun's beams shone through the rift in the curtains
and made visible the sabbath of the motes. I concluded from
this that the weather was still fine and rejoiced. When you
leave on your autocycle fine weather is to be preferred. I
was wrong, the weather was fine no longer, the sky was
clouding over, soon it would rain. But for the moment the
sun was still shining. It was on this that I went, with inconceivable levity, having nothing else to go on.

Next I attacked, according to my custom, the capital
question of the effects to take with me. And on this subject
too I should have come to a quite otiose decision, but for
my son, who burst in wanting to know if he might go out.
I controlled myself. He was wiping his mouth with the
back of his hand, a thing I do not like to see. But there
are nastier gestures, I speak from experience.

Out? I said. Where? Out! Vagueness I abhor. I was
beginning to feel hungry. To the Elms, he replied. So we call
our little public park. And yet there is not an elm to be
seen in it, I have been told. What for? I said. To go over
my botany, he replied. There were times I suspected my
son of deceit. This was one. I would almost have preferred
him to say, For a walk, or, To look at the tarts. The trouble
was he knew far more than I, about botany. Otherwise I
could have set him a few teasers, on his return. Personally
I just liked plants in all innocence and simplicity. I even
saw in them at times a superfetatory proof of the existence
of God. Go, I said, but be back at half-past four, I want to
talk to you. Yes papa, he said. Yes papa! Ah!

I slept a little. Faster, faster. Passing the church, something made me stop. I looked at the door, baroque, very
fine. I found it hideous. I hastened on to the presbytery.
The Father is sleeping, said the servant. I can wait, I said.
Is it urgent? she said. Yes and no, I said. She showed me
into the sitting-room, bare and bleak, dreadful. Father Ambrose came in, rubbing his eyes. I disturb you, Father, I
said. He clicked his tongue against the roof of his mouth,
protestingly. I shall not describe our attitudes, characteristic

his of him, mine of me. He offered me a cigar which I
accepted with good grace and put in my pocket, between
my fountain-pen and my propelling-pencil. He flattered himself, Father Ambrose, with being a man of the world and
knowing its ways, he who never smoked. And everyone
said he was most broad. I asked him if he had noticed my
son at the last mass. Certainly, he said, we even spoke together. I must have looked surprised. Yes, he said, not seeing
you at your place, in the front row, I feared you were ill.
So I called for the dear child, who reassured me. A most
untimely visitor, I said, whom I could not shake off in time.
So your son explained to me, he said. He added, But let us
sit down, we have no train to catch. He laughed and sat down,
hitching up his heavy cassock. May I offer you a little glass
of something? he said. I was in a quandary. Had Jacques
let slip an allusion to the lager. He was quite capable of it.
I came to ask you a favour, I said. Granted, he said. We
observed each other. It's this, I said, Sunday for me without
the Body and Blood is like—. He raised his hand. Above
all no profane comparisons, he said. Perhaps he was thinking of the kiss without a moustache or beef without mustard.
I dislike being interrupted. I sulked. Say no more, he said, a
wink is as good as a nod, you want communion. I bowed
my head. It's a little unusual, he said. I wondered if he
had fed. I knew he was given to prolonged fasts, by way
of mortification certainly, and then because his doctor advised it. Thus he killed two birds with one stone. Not a word
to a soul, he said, let it remain between us and—. He broke
off, raising a finger, and his eyes, to the ceiling. Heavens,
he said, what is that stain? I looked in turn at the ceiling.
Damp, I said. Tut tut, he said, how annoying. The words
tut tut seemed to me the maddest I had heard. There are
times, he said, when one feels like weeping. He got up.
I'll go and get my kit, he said. He called that his kit. Alone,
my hands clasped until it seemed my knuckles would crack,
I asked the Lord for guidance. Without result. That was
some consolation. As for Father Ambrose, in view of his
alacrity to fetch his kit, it seemed evident to me he suspected
nothing. Or did it amuse him to see how far I would go?
Or did it tickle him to have me commit a sin? I summarized
the situation briefly as follows. If knowing I have beer taken
he gives me the sacrament, his sin, if sin there be, is as great

as mine. I was therefore risking little. He came back with
a kind of portable pyx, opened it and dispatched me without
an instant's hesitation. I rose and thanked him warmly. Pah!
he said, it's nothing. Now we can talk.

I had nothing else to say to him. All I wanted was to
return home as quickly as possible and stuff myself with
stew. My soul appeased, I was ravenous. But being slightly
in advance of my schedule I resigned myself to allowing
him eight minutes. They seemed endless. He informed me
that Mrs Clement, the chemist's wife and herself a highly
qualified chemist, had fallen, in her laboratory, from the
top of a ladder, and broken the neck—. The neck! I cried.
Of her femur, he said, can't you let me finish. He added
that it was bound to happen. And I, not to be outdone, told
him how worried I was about my hens, particularly my grey
hen, which would neither brood nor lay and for the past
month and more had done nothing but sit with her arse in
the dust, from morning to night. Like Job, haha, he said.
I too said haha. What a joy it is to laugh, from time to time,
he said. Is it not? I said. It is peculiar to man, he said. So
I have noticed, I said. A brief silence ensued. What do you
feed her on? he said. Corn chiefly, I said. Cooked or raw?
he said. Both, I said. I added that she ate nothing any more.
Nothing! he cried. Next to nothing, I said. Animals never
laugh, he said. It takes us to find that funny, I said. What?
he said. It takes us to find that funny, I said loudly. He
mused. Christ never laughed either, he said, so far as we
know. He looked at me. Can you wonder? I said. There
it is, he said. He smiled sadly. She has not the pip, I hope,
he said. I said she had not, certainly not, anything he liked,
but not the pip. He meditated. Have you tried bicarbonate?
he said. I beg your pardon? I said. Bicarbonate of soda, he
said, have you tried it? Why no, I said. Try it! he cried,
flushing with pleasure, have her swallow a few dessert-
spoonfuls, several times a day, for a few months. You'll
see, you won't know her. A powder? I said. Bless my heart
to be sure, he said. Many thanks, I said, I'll begin today.
Such a fine hen, he said, such a good layer. Or rather
tomorrow, I said. I had forgotten the chemist was closed.
Except in case of emergency. And now that little cordial,
he said. I declined.

This interview with Father Ambrose left me with a pain-

ful impression. He was still the same dear man, and yet not.
I seemed to have surprised, on his face, a lack, how shall
I say, a lack of nobility. The host, it is only fair to say,
was lying heavy on my stomach. And as I made my way
home I felt like one who, having swallowed a pain-killer,
is first astonished, then indignant, on obtaining no relief. And
I was almost ready to suspect Father Ambrose, alive to my
excesses of the forenoon, of having fobbed me off with
unconsecrated bread. Or of mental reservation as he pro-
nounced the magic words. And it was in vile humour that
I arrived home, in the pelting rain.

The stew was a great disappointment. Where are the
onions? I cried. Gone to nothing, replied Martha. I rushed
into the kitchen, to look for the onions I suspected her of
having removed from the pot, because she knew how much
I liked them. I even rummaged in the bin. Nothing. She
watched me mockingly.

I went up to my room again, drew back the curtains on
a calamitous sky and lay down. I could not understand
what was happening to me. I found it painful at that period
not to understand. I tried to pull myself together. In vain.
I might have known. My life was running out, I knew not
through what breach. I succeeded however in dozing off,
which is not so easy, when pain is speculative. And I was
marvelling, in that half-sleep, at my half sleeping, when my
son came in, without knocking. Now if there is one thing
I abhor, it is someone coming into my room, without knocking. I might just happen to be masturbating, before my cheval
glass. Father with yawning fly and starting eyes, toiling to
scatter on the ground his joyless seed, that was no sight for
a small boy. Harshly I recalled him to the proprieties. He
protested he had knocked twice. If you had knocked a
hundred times, I replied, it would not give you the right to
come in without being invited. But, he said. But what? I
said. You told me to be here at half-past four, he said. There
is something, I said, more important in life than punctuality,
and that is decorum. Repeat. In that disdainful mouth my
phrase put me to shame. He was soaked. What have you
been looking at? I said. The liliaceae, papa, he answered. The
liliaceae papa! My son had a way of saying papa, when he
wanted to hurt me, that was very special. Now listen to me,

I said. His face took on an expression of anguished attention. We leave this evening, I said in substance, on a journey.
Put on your school suit, the green—. But it's blue, papa,
he said. Blue or green, put it on, I said violently. I went on.
Put in your little knapsack, the one I gave you for your
birthday, your toilet things, one shirt, one pair of socks
and seven pairs of drawers. Do you understand? Which shirt,
papa? he said. It doesn't matter which shirt, I cried, any
shirt! Which shoes am I to wear? he said. You have two
pairs of shoes, I said, one for Sundays and one for weekdays, and you ask me which you are to wear. I sat up. I
want none of your lip, I said.

Thus to my son I gave precise instructions. But were they
the right ones? Would they stand the test of second thoughts?
Would I not be impelled, in a very short time, to cancel
them? I who never changed my mind before my son. The
worst was to be feared.

Where are we going, papa? he said. How often had I
told him not to ask me questions. And where were we going,
in point of fact. Do as you're told, I said. I have an appoint-
ment with Mr Py tomorrow, he said. You'll see him another
day, I said. But I have an ache, he said. There exist other
dentists, I said, Mr Py is not the unique dentist of the
northern hemisphere. I added rashly, We are not going into
the wilderness. But he's a very good dentist, he said. All
dentists are alike, I said. I could have told him to get to
hell out of that with his dentist, but no, I reasoned gently
with him, I spoke with him as with an equal. I could furthermore have pointed out to him that he was lying when he
said he had an ache. He did have an ache, in a bicuspid I
believe, but it was over. Py himself had told me so. I
have dressed the tooth, he said, your son cannot possibly
feel any more pain. I remembered this conversation well.
He has naturally very bad teeth, said Py. Naturally, I said,
what do you mean, naturally? What are you insinuating?
He was born with bad teeth, said Py, and all his life he will
have bad teeth. Naturally I shall do what I can. Meaning,
I was born with the disposition to do all I can, all my life
I shall do all I can, necessarily. Born with bad teeth! As
for me, I was down to my incisors, the nippers.

Is it still raining? I said. My son had drawn a small glass

from his pocket and was examining the inside of his mouth,
prising away his upper lip with his finger. Aaw, he said,
without interrupting his inspection. Stop messing about with
your mouth! I cried. Go to the window and tell me if it's
still raining. He went to the window and told me it was
still raining. Is the sky completely overcast? I said. Yes,
he said. Not the least rift? I said. No, he said. Draw the
curtains, I said. Delicious instants, before one's eyes get
used to the dark. Are you still there? I said. He was still
there. I asked him what he was waiting for to do as I had
told him. If I had been my son I would have left me long
ago. He was not worthy of me, not in the same class at all.
I could not escape this conclusion. Cold comfort that is,
to feel superior to one's son, and hardly sufficient to calm
the remorse of having begotten him. May I bring my stamps?
he said. My son had two albums, a big one for his collection
properly speaking and a small one for the duplicates. I
authorized him to bring the latter. When I can give pleasure,
without doing violence to my principles, I do so gladly. He
withdrew.

I got up and went to the window. I could not keep still.
I passed my head between the curtains. Fine rain, lowering
sky. He had not lied to me. Likely to lift round about eight.
Fine sunset, twilight, night. Waning moon, rising towards
midnight. I rang for Martha and lay down again. We shall
dine at home, I said. She looked at me in astonishment.
Did we not always dine at home? I had not yet told her
we were leaving. I would not tell her till the last moment,
one foot in the stirrup as the saying is. I did not wholly
trust her. I would call her at the last moment and say,
Martha, we're leaving, for one day, two days, three days, a
week, two weeks, God knows, goodbye. It was important
to leave her in the dark. Then why had I called her? She
would have served us dinner in any case, as she did every
day. I had made the mistake of putting myself in her place.
That was understandable. But to tell her we would dine
at home, what a blunder. For she knew it already, thought
she knew, did know. And as a result of this useless reminder she would sense that something was afoot and spy
on us, in the hope of learning what it was. First mistake.
The second, first in time, was my not having enjoined my

son to keep what I had told him to himself. Not that this would have served any purpose. Nevertheless I should have insisted on it, as due to myself. I was floundering. I so sly as a rule. I tried to mend matters, saying, A little later than usual, not before nine. She turned to go, her simple mind already in a turmoil. I am at home to no one, I said. I knew what she would do, she would throw a sack over her shoulders and slip off to the bottom of the garden. There she would call Hannah, the old cook of the Elsner sisters, and they would whisper together for a long time, through the railings. Hannah never went out, she did not like going out. The Elsner sisters were not bad neighbours, as neighbours go. They made a little too much music, that was the only fault I could find with them. If there is one thing gets on my nerves it is music. What I assert, deny, question, in the present, I still can. But mostly I shall use the various tenses of the past. For mostly I do not know, it is perhaps no longer so, it is too soon to know, I simply do not know, perhaps shall never know. I thought a little of the Elsner sisters. Everything remained to be planned and there I was thinking of the Elsner sisters. They had an aberdeen called Zulu. People called it Zulu. Sometimes, when I was in a good humour, I called, Zulu! Little Zulu! and he would come and talk to me, through the railings. But I had to be feeling gay. I don't like animals. It's a strange thing, I don't like men and I don't like animals. As for God, he is beginning to disgust me. Crouching down I would stroke his ears, through the railings, and utter wheedling words. He did not realize he disgusted me. He reared up on his hind legs and pressed his chest against the bars. Then I could see his little black penis ending in a thin wisp of wetted hair. He felt insecure, his hams trembled, his little paws fumbled for purchase, one after the other. I too wobbled, squatting on my heels. With my free hand I held on to the railings. Perhaps I disgusted him too. I found it hard to tear myself away from these vain thoughts.

I wondered, suddenly rebellious, what compelled me to accept this commission. But I had already accepted it. I had given my word. Too late. Honour. It did not take me long to gild my impotence.

But could I not postpone our departure to the following day? Or leave alone? Ah shilly-shally. But we would wait till the very last moment, a little before midnight. This decision is irrevocable, I said. It was justified moreover by the state of the moon.

I did as when I could not sleep. I wandered in my mind, slowly, noting every detail of the labyrinth, its paths as familiar as those of my garden and yet ever new, as empty as the heart could wish or alive with strange encounters. And I heard the distant cymbals, There is still time, still time. But there was not, for I ceased, all vanished and I tried once more to turn my thoughts to the Molloy affair. Unfathomable mind, now beacon, now sea.

The agent and the messenger. We agents never took anything in writing. Gaber was not an agent in the sense I was. Gaber was a messenger. He was therefore entitled to a notebook. A messenger had to be possessed of singular qualities, good messengers were even more rare than good agents. I who was an excellent agent would have made but a sorry messenger. I often regretted it. Gabor was protected in numerous ways. He used a code incomprehensible to all but himself. Each messenger, before being appointed, had to submit his code to the directorate. Gabor understood nothing about the messages he carried. Reflecting on them he arrived at the most extravagantly false conclusions. Yes, it was not enough for him to understand nothing about them, he had also to believe he understood everything about them. This was not all. His memory was so bad that his messages had no existence in his head, but only in his notebook. He had only to close his notebook to become, a moment later, perfectly innocent as to its contents. And when I say that he reflected on his messages and drew conclusions from them, it was not as we would have reflected on them, you and I, the book closed and probably the eyes too, but little by little as he read. And when he raised his head and indulged in his commentaries, it was without losing a second, for if he had lost a second he would have forgotten everything, both text and gloss. I have often wondered if the messengers were not compelled to undergo a surgical operation, to induce in them such a degree of amnesia. But I think not. For otherwise their memory was good enough. And I have heard Gaber speak of his childhood, and of his family, in extremely plausible terms. To be undecipherable to all but oneself, dead without knowing it to the meaning of one's instructions and incapable of remembering them for more than a few seconds, these are capacities rarely united in the same individual. No less however was demanded of our messengers. And that they were more highly esteemed than the agents, whose qualities were sound rather than brilliant, is shown by the fact that they received a weekly wage of eight pounds as against ours of six pounds ten only, these figures being exclusive of bonuses and travelling expenses. And when I speak of agents and of messengers in the plural, it is with no guarantee of truth. For I had never seen any other messenger than Gaber nor any other agent than myself. But I supposed we were not the only ones and Gaber must have supposed the same. For the feeling that we were the only ones of our kind would, I believe, have been more than we could have borne. And it must have appeared natural, to me that each agent had his own particular messenger, and to Gaber that each messenger had his own particular agent. Thus I was able to say to Gaber, Let him give this job to someone else, I don't want it, and Gaber was able to reply, He wants it to be you. And these last words, assuming Gaber had not invented them especially to annoy me, had perhaps been uttered by the chief with the sole purpose of fostering our illusion, if it was one. All this is not very clear.

That we thought of ourselves as members of a vast organization was doubtless also due to the all too human feeling that trouble shared, or is it sorrow, is trouble something, I forget the word. But to me at least, who knew how to listen to the falsetto of reason, it was obvious that we were perhaps alone in doing what we did. Yes, in my moments of lucidity I thought it possible. And, to keep nothing from you, this lucidity was so acute at times that I came even to doubt the existence of Gaber himself. And if I had not hastily sunk back into my darkness I might have gone to the extreme of conjuring away the chief too and regarding myself as solely responsible for my wretched existence. For I knew I was wretched, at six pounds ten a week plus bonuses and expenses. And having made away with Gaber and the chief (one Youdi), could I have denied myself the pleasure of—you know. But I was not made

for the great light that devours, a dim lamp was all I had
been given, and patience without end, to shine it on the
empty shadows. I was a solid in the midst of other solids.

I went down to the kitchen. I did not expect to find
Martha there, but I found her there. She was sitting in her
rocking-chair, in the chimney-corner, rocking herself moodily.
This rocking-chair, she would have you believe, was the
only possession to which she clung and she would not have
parted with it for an empire. It is interesting to note that she
had installed it not in her room, but in the kitchen, in the
chimney-corner. Late to bed and early to rise, it was in
the kitchen that she benefited by it most. The wage-payers
are numerous, and I was one of them, who do not like to
see, in the place set aside for toil, the furniture of reclining
and repose. The servant wishes to rest? Let her retire to
her room. In the kitchen all must be of wood, white and
rigid. I should mention that Martha had insisted, before
entering my service, that I permit her to keep her rocking-
chair in the kitchen. I had refused, indignantly. Then, seeing
she was inflexible, I had yielded. I was too kind-hearted.

My weekly supply of lager, half-a-dozen quart bottles,
was delivered every Saturday. I never touched them until the
next day, for lager must be let to settle after the least
disturbance. Of these six bottles Gaber and I, together,
had emptied one. There should therefore be five left, plus
the remains of a bottle from the previous week. I went into
the pantry. The five bottles were there, corked and sealed,
and one open bottle three-quarters empty. Martha followed
me with her eyes. I left without a word to her and went
upstairs. I did nothing but go to and fro. I went into my
son's room. Sitting at his little desk he was admiring his
stamps, the two albums, large and small, open before him.
On my approach he shut them hastily. I saw at once what
he was up to. But first I said, Have you got your things
ready? He stood up, got his pack and gave it to me. I looked
inside. I put my hand inside and felt through the contents,
staring vacantly before me. Everything was in. I gave it
back to him. What are you doing? I said. Looking at my
stamps he said. You call that looking at your stamps? I
said. Yes papa, he said with unimaginable effrontery. Silence,
you little liar! I cried. Do you know what he was doing?

Transferring to the album of duplicates, from his good
collection properly so-called, certain rare and valuable stamps
which he was in the habit of gloating over daily and could
not bring himself to leave, even for a few days. Show me
your new Timor, the five reis orange, I said. He hesitated.
Show it to me! I cried. I had given it to him myself, it
had cost me a florin. A bargain, at the time. I've put it in
here, he said piteously, picking up the album of duplicates.
That was all I wanted to know, to hear him say rather, for
I knew it already. Very good, I said. I went to the door.
You leave both your albums at home, I said, the small one
as well as the large one. Not a word of reproach, a simple
prophetic present, on the model of those employed by
Youdi. Your son goes with you. I went out. But as with
delicate steps, almost mincing, congratulating myself as usual
on the resilience of my Wilton, I followed the corridor towards
my room, I was struck by a thought which made me go
back to my son's room. He was sitting in the same place,
but in a slightly different attitude, his arms on the table
and his head on his arms. This sight went straight to my
heart, but nevertheless I did my duty. He did not move.
To make assurance doubly sure, I said, we shall put the
albums in the safe, until our return. He still did not move.
Do you hear me? I said. He rose with a bound that knocked
over his chair and uttered the furious words, Do what you
like with them! I never want to see them again! Anger should
be left to cool, in my opinion, crisis to pass, before one
operates. I took the albums and withdrew, without a word.
He had been lacking in respect, but this was not the moment
to have him admit it. Motionless in the corridor I heard
sounds of falling and collision. Another, less master of
himself than I of myself, would have intervened. But it
did not positively displease me that my son should give free
vent to his grief. It purges. Sorrow does more harm when
dumb, to my mind.

The albums under my arm, I returned to my room. I
had spared my son a grave temptation, that of putting in
his pocket his most cherished stamps, in order to gloat on
them, during our journey. Not that his having one or two
stamps about him was reprehensible in itself. But it would
have been an act of disobedience. To look at them he would

have had to hide from his father. And when he had lost
them, as he inevitably would, he would have been driven
to lie, to account for their disappearance. No, if he could
not really bear to be parted from the gems of his collection,
it would have been better for him to take the entire album.
For an album is less readily lost than a stamp. But I was
a better judge than he of what he could and could not.
For I knew what he did not yet know, among other things
that this ordeal would be of profit to him. *Sollst entbehren,*
that was the lesson I desired to impress upon him, while
he was still young and tender. Magic words which I had
never dreamt, until my fifteenth year, could be coupled
together. And should this undertaking make me odious in
his eyes and not only me, but the very idea of fatherhood,
I would pursue it none the less, with everything in my power.
The thought that between my death and his own, ceasing
for an instant from heaping curses on my memory, he
might wonder, in a flash, whether I had not been right, that
was enough for me, that repaid me for all the trouble I
had taken and was still to take. He would answer in the
negative, the first time, and resume his execrations. But the
doubt would be sown. He would go back to it. That was
how I reasoned.

I still had a few hours left before dinner. I decided to make
the most of them. Because after dinner I drowse. I took
off my coat and shoes, opened my trousers and got in
between the sheets. It is lying down, in the warmth, in the
gloom, that I best pierce the outer turmoil's veil, discern
my quarry, sense what course to follow, find peace in another's ludicrous distress. Far from the world, its clamours,
frenzies, bitterness and dingy light, I pass judgement on it
and on those, like me, who are plunged in it beyond recall,
and on him who has need of me to be delivered, who
cannot deliver myself. All is dark, but with that simple
darkness that follows like a balm upon the great dismember-
ings. From their places masses move, stark as laws. Masses
of what? One does not ask. There somewhere man is too,
vast conglomerate of all of nature's kingdoms, as lonely and
as bound. And in that block the prey is lodged and thinks
himself a being apart. Anyone would serve. But I am paid
to seek. I arrive, he comes away. His life has been nothing

but a waiting for this, to see himself preferred, to fancy
himself damned, blessed, to fancy himself everyman, above
all others. Warmth, gloom, smells of my bed, such is the
effect they sometimes have on me. I get up, go out, and
everything is changed. The blood drains from my head, the
noise of things bursting, merging, avoiding one another,
assails me on all sides, my eyes search in vain for two
things alike, each pinpoint of skin screams a different message,
I drown in the spray of phenomena. It is at the mercy of
these sensations, which happily I know to be illusory, that
I have to live and work. It is thanks to them I find myself
a meaning. So he whom a sudden pain awakes. He stiffens,
ceases to breathe, waits, says, It's a bad dream, or, It's a
touch of neuralgia, breathes again, sleeps again, still trembling.
And yet it is not unpleasant, before setting to work, to
steep oneself again in this slow and massive world, where
all things move with the ponderous sullenness of oxen,
patiently through the immemorial ways, and where of course
no investigation would be possible. But on this occasion, I
repeat, on this occasion, my reasons for doing so were I
trust more serious and imputable less to pleasure than to
business. For it was only by transferring it to this atmosphere, how shall I say, of finality without end, why not,
that I could venture to consider the work I had on hand.
For where Molloy could not be, nor Moran either for that
matter, there Moran could bend over Molloy. And though
this examination prove unprofitable and of no utility for
the execution of my orders, I should nevertheless have established a kind of connexion, and one not necessarily false.
For the falsity of the terms does not necessarily imply that
of the relation, so far as I know. And not only this, but I
should have invested my man, from the outset, with the
air of a fabulous being, which something told me could
not fail to help me later on. So I took off my coat and my
shoes, I opened my trousers and I slipped in between the
sheets, with an easy conscience, knowing only too well what
I was doing.

Molloy, or Mollose, was no stranger to me. If I had had
colleagues, I might have suspected I had spoken of him to
them, as of one destined to occupy us, sooner or later. But
I had no colleagues and knew nothing of the circumstances

in which I had learnt of his existence. Perhaps I had invented
him, I mean found him ready made in my head. There is
no doubt one sometimes meets with strangers who are not
entire strangers, through their having played a part in certain cerebral reels. This had never happened to me, I considered myself immune from such experiences, and even
the simple *déjà vu* seemed infinitely beyond my reach. But
it was happening to me then, or I was greatly mistaken.
For who could have spoken to me of Molloy if not myself
and to whom if not to myself could I have spoken of him?
I racked my mind in vain. For in my rare conversations with
men I avoided such subjects. If anyone else had spoken to
me of Molloy I would have requested him to stop and I
myself would not have confided his existence to a living
soul for anything in the world. If I had had colleagues things
would naturally have been different. Among colleagues one
says things which in any other company one keeps to oneself. But I had no colleagues. And perhaps this accounts
for the immense uneasiness I had been feeling ever since
the beginning of this affair. For it is no small matter, for
a grown man thinking he is done with surprises, to see himself the theatre of such ignominy. I had really good cause
to be alarmed.

Mother Molloy, or Mollose, was not completely foreign
to me either, it seemed. But she was much less alive than
her son, who God knows was far from being so. After all
perhaps I knew nothing of mother Molloy, or Mollose, save
in so far as such a son might bear, like a scurf of placenta,
her stamp.

Of these two names, Molloy and Mollose, the second
seemed to me perhaps the more correct. But barely. What
I heard, in my soul I suppose, where the acoustics are so
bad, was a first syllable, Mol, very clear, followed almost
at once by a second, very thick, as though gobbled by the
first, and which might have been oy as it might have been
ose, or one, or even oc. And if I inclined towards ose, it
was doubtless that my mind had a weakness for this ending,
whereas the others left it cold. But since Gaber had said
Molloy, not once but several times, and each time with
equal incisiveness, I was compelled to admit that I too
should have said Molloy and that in saying Mollose I was

at fault. And henceforward, unmindful of my preferences, I shall force myself to say Molloy, like Gaber. That there may have been two different persons involved, one my own Mollose, the other the Molloy of the enquiry, was a thought which did not so much as cross my mind, and if it had I should have driven it away, as one drives away a fly, or a hornet. How little one is at one with oneself, good God. I who prided myself on being a sensible man, cold as crystal and as free from spurious depth.

I knew then about Molloy, without however knowing much about him. I shall say briefly what little I did know about him. I shall also draw attention, in my knowledge of Molloy, to the most striking lacunae.

He had very little room. His time too was limited. He hastened incessantly on, as if in despair, towards extremely close objectives. Now, a prisoner, he hurled himself at I know not what narrow confines, and now, hunted, he sought refuge near the centre.

He panted. He had only to rise up within me for me to be filled with panting.

Even in open country he seemed to be crashing through jungle. He did not so much walk as charge. In spite of this he advanced but slowly. He swayed, to and fro, like a bear.

He rolled his head, uttering incomprehensible words.

He was massive and hulking, to the point of misshapenness. And, without being black, of a dark colour.

He was forever on the move. I had never seen him rest. Occasionally he stopped and glared furiously about him.

This was how he came to me, at long intervals. Then I was nothing but uproar, bulk, rage, suffocation, effort unceasing, frenzied and vain. Just the opposite of myself, in fact. It was a change. And when I saw him disappear, his whole body a vociferation, I was almost sorry.

What it was all about I had not the slightest idea.

I had no clue to his age. As he appeared to me, so I felt he must have always appeared and would continue to appear until the end, an end indeed which I was hard put to imagine. For being unable to conceive what had brought him to such a pass, I was no better able to conceive how, left to his own resources, he could put an end to it. A natural end seemed unlikely to me, I don't know why. But

then my own natural end, and I was resolved to have no
other, would it not at the same time be his? Modest, I had
my doubts. And then again, what end is not natural, are
they not all by the grace of nature, the undeniably good and
the so-called bad? Idle conjectures.

I had no information as to his face. I assumed it was
hirsute, craggy and grimacing. Nothing justified my doing so.

That a man like me, so meticulous and calm in the main,
so patiently turned towards the outer world as towards the
lesser evil, creature of his house, of his garden, of his few
poor possessions, discharging faithfully and ably a revolting
function, reining back his thoughts within the limits of the
calculable so great is his horror of fancy, that a man so contrived, for I was a contrivance, should let himself be haunted
and possessed by chimeras, this ought to have seemed strange
to me and been a warning to me to have a care, in my own
interest. Nothing of the kind. I saw it only as the weakness
of a solitary, a weakness admittedly to be deplored, but
which had to be indulged in if I wished to remain a solitary,
and I did, I clung to that, with as little enthusiasm as to
my hens or to my faith, but no less lucidly. Besides this took
up very little room in the inenarrable contraption I called
my life, jeopardized it as little as my dreams and was as
soon forgotten. Don't wait to be hunted to hide, that was
always my motto. And if I had to tell the story of my life
I should not so much as allude to these apparitions, and
least of all to that of the unfortunate Molloy. For his was
a poor thing, compared to others.

But images of this kind the will cannot revive without
doing them violence. Much of what they had it takes away,
much they never had it foists upon them. And the Molloy
I brought to light, that memorable August Sunday, was
certainly not the true denizen of my dark places, for it was
not his hour. But so far as the essential features were concerned, I was easy in my mind, the likeness was there. And
the discrepancy could have been still greater for all I cared.
For what I was doing I was doing neither for Molloy, who
mattered nothing to me, nor for myself, of whom I despaired,
but on behalf of a cause which, while having need of us
to be accomplished, was in its essence anonymous, and would
subsist, haunting the minds of men, when its miserable artisans

should be no more. It will not be said, I think, that I did
not take my work to heart. But rather, tenderly, Ah those
old craftsmen, their race is extinct and the mould broken.

Two remarks.

Between the Molloy I stalked within me thus and the
true Molloy, after whom I was so soon to be in full cry,
over hill and dale, the resemblance cannot have been great.

I was annexing perhaps already, without my knowing
it, to my private Molloy, elements of the Molloy described
by Gaber.

The fact was there were three, no, four Molloys. He
that inhabited me, my caricature of same, Gaber's and
the man of flesh and blood somewhere awaiting me. To these
I would add Youdi's were it not for Gaber's corpse fidelity
to the letter of his messages. Bad reasoning. For could it
seriously be supposed that Youdi had confided to Gaber
all he knew, or thought he knew (all one to Youdi) about
his protégé? Assuredly not. He had only revealed what he
deemed of relevance for the prompt and proper execution
of his orders. I will therefore add a fifth Molloy, that of
Youdi. But would not this fifth Molloy necessarily coincide
with the fourth, the real one as the saying is, him dogged
by his shadow? I would have given a lot to know. There
were others too, of course. But let us leave it at that, if you
don't mind, the party is big enough. And let us not meddle
either with the question as to how far these five Molloys
were constant and how far subject to variation. For there
was this about Youdi, that he changed his mind with great
facility.

That makes three remarks. I had only anticipated two.

The ice thus broken, I felt equal to facing Gaber's report
and getting down to the official facts. It seemed as if the
enquiry were about to start at last.

It was then that the sound of a gong, struck with violence,
filled the house. True enough, it was nine o'clock. I got up,
adjusted my clothes and hurried down. To give notice that
the soup was in, nay, that it had begun to coagulate, was
always for Martha a little triumph and a great satisfaction.
For as a rule I was at table, my napkin tucked into my collar,
crumbling the bread, fiddling with the cover, playing with
the knife-rest, waiting to be served, a few minutes before

the appointed hour. I attacked the soup. Where is Jacques? I said. She shrugged her shoulders. Detestable slavish gesture. Tell him to come down at once, I said. The soup before me had stopped steaming. Had it ever steamed? She came back. He won't come down, she said. I laid down my spoon. Tell me, Martha, I said, what is this preparation? She named it. Have I had it before? I said. She assured me I had. I then made a joke which pleased me enormously. I laughed so much I began to hiccup. It was lost on Martha who stared at me dazedly. Tell him to come down, I said at last. What? said Martha. I repeated my phrase. She still looked genuinely perplexed. There are three of us in this charming home, I said, you, my son and finally myself. What I said was, Tell him to come down. But he's sick, said Martha. Were he dying, I said, down he must come. Anger led me sometimes to slight excesses of language. I could not regret them. It seemed to me that all language was an excess of language. Naturally I confessed them. I was short of sins.

Jacques was scarlet in the face. Eat your soup, I said, and tell me what you think of it. I'm not hungry, he said. Eat your soup, I said. I saw he would not eat it. What ails you? I said. I don't feel well, he said. What an abominable thing is youth. Try and be more explicit, I said. I was at pains to use this term, a little difficult for juveniles, having explained its meaning and application to him a few days before. So I had high hopes of his telling me he didn't understand. But he was a cunning little fellow, in his way. Martha! I bellowed. She appeared. The sequel, I said. I looked more attentively out of the window. Not only had the rain stopped, that I knew already, but in the west scarves of fine red sheen were mounting in the sky. I felt them rather than saw them, through my little wood. A great joy, it is hardly too much to say, surged over me at the sight of so much beauty, so much promise. I turned away with a sigh, for the joy inspired by beauty is often not unmixed, and saw in front of me what with good reason I had called the sequel. Now what have we here? I said. Usually on Sunday evening we had the cold remains of a fowl, chicken, duck, goose, turkey, I can think of no other fowl, from Saturday evening. I have always had great success with my turkeys, they are a better proposition than ducks, in my

opinion, for rearing purposes. More delicate, possibly, but
more remunerative, for one who knows and caters for their
little ways, who likes them in a word and is liked by them
in return. Shepherd's pie, said Martha. I tasted it, from the
dish. And what have you done with yesterday's bird? I
said. Martha's face took on an expression of triumph. She
was waiting for this question, that was obvious, she was
counting on it. I thought, she said, you ought to eat something hot, before you left. And who told you I was leaving?
I said. She went to the door, a sure sign she was about
to launch a shaft. She could only be insulting when in flight.
I'm not blind, she said. She opened the door. More's the
pity, she said. She closed the door behind her.

I looked at my son. He had his mouth open and his eyes
closed. Was it you blabbed on us? I said. He pretended not
to know what I was talking about. Did you tell Martha
we were leaving? I said. He said he had not. And why not?
I said. I didn't see her, he said brazenly. But she has just
been up to your room, I said. The pie was already made,
he said. At times he was almost worthy of me. But he was
wrong to invoke the pie. But he was still young and in-
experienced and I refrained from humbling him. Try and
tell me, I said, a little more precisely, what it is you feel.
I've a stomach-ache, he said. A stomach-ache! Have you
a temperature I said. I don't know, he said. Find out, I
said. He was looking more and more stupefied. Fortunately
I rather enjoyed dotting my i's. Go and get the minute-
thermometer, I said, out of the second right-hand drawer
of my desk, counting from the top, take your temperature
and bring me the thermometer. I let a few minutes go by
and then, without being asked, repeated slowly, word for
word, this rather long and difficult sentence, which contained no fewer than three or four imperatives. As he went
out, having presumably understood the gist of it, I added
jocosely, You know which mouth to put it in? I was not
averse, in conversation with my son, to jests of doubtful
taste, in the interests of his education. Those whose pungency
he could not fully savour at the time, and they must have
been many, he could reflect on at his leisure or seek in
company with his little friends to interpret as best he might.
Which was in itself an excellent exercise. And at the same

time I inclined his young mind towards that most fruitful
of dispositions, horror of the body and its functions. But I
had turned my phrase badly, mouth was not the word I
should have used. It was while examining the shepherd's pie
more narrowly that I had this afterthought. I lifted the crust
with my spoon and looked inside. I probed it with my fork.
I called Martha and said, His dog wouldn't touch it. I
thought with a smile of my desk which had only six drawers
in all and for all, three on each side of the space where
I put my legs. Since your dinner is uneatable, I said, be good
enough to prepare a packet of sandwiches, with the chicken
you couldn't finish. My son came back at last. That's all
the thanks you get for having a minute-thermometer. He
handed it to me. Did you have time to wipe it? I said.
Seeing me squint at the mercury he went to the door and
switched on the light. How remote Youdi was at that instant.
Sometimes in the winter, coming home harassed and weary
after a day of fruitless errands, I would find my slippers
warming in front of the fire, the uppers turned to the flame.
He had a temperature. There's nothing wrong with you,
I said. May I get up? he said. What for? I said. To lie
down, he said. Was not this the providential hindrance for
which I could not be held responsible? Doubtless, but I
would never dare invoke it. I was not going to expose
myself to thunderbolts which might be fatal, simply because
my son had the gripes. If he fell seriously ill on the way,
it would be another matter. It was not for nothing I had
studied the old testament. Have you shat, my child, I said
gently. I've tried, he said. Do you want to, I said. Yes, he
said. But nothing comes, I said. No, he said. A little wind,
I said. Yes, he said. Suddenly I remembered Father Ambrose's
cigar. I lit it. We'll see what we can do, I said, getting
up. We went upstairs. I gave him an enema, with salt water.
He struggled, but not for long. I withdrew the nozzle. Try
and hold it, I said, don't stay sitting on the pot, lie flat
on your stomach. We were in the bathroom. He lay down on
the tiles, his big fat bottom sticking up. Let it soak well in,
I said. What a day. I looked at the ash on my cigar. It
was firm and blue. I sat down on the edge of the bath. The
porcelain, the mirrors, the chromium, instilled a great
peace within me. At least I suppose it was they. It wasn't

a great peace in any case. I got up, laid down my cigar and
brushed my incisors. I also brushed the back gums. I looked
at myself, puffing out my lips which normally recede into
my mouth. What do I look like? I said. The sight of my
moustache, as always, annoyed me. It wasn't quite right.
It suited me, without a moustache I was inconceivable. But
it ought to have suited me better. A slight change in the
cut would have sufficed. But what change? Was there too
much of it, not enough? Now, I said, without ceasing to inspect myself, get back on the pot and strain. Was it not
rather the colour? A noise as of a waste recalled me to less
elevated preoccupations. He stood up trembling all over.
We bent together over the pot which at length I took by
the handle and tilted from side to side. A few fibrous shreds
floated in the yellow liquid. How can you hope to shit, I
said, when you've nothing in your stomach? He protested
he had had his lunch. You ate nothing, I said. He said no
more. I had scored a hit. You forget we are leaving in an
hour or so, I said. I can't, he said. So that, I pursued, you
will have to eat something. An acute pain shot through my
knee. What's the matter, papa? he said. I let myself fall
on the stool, pulled up the leg of my trousers and examined
my knee, flexing and unflexing it. Quick the iodex, I said.
You're sitting on it, he said. I stood up and the leg of my
trousers fell down over my ankle. This inertia of things is
enough to drive one literally insane. I let out a bellow which
must have been heard by the Elsner sisters. They stop
reading, raise their heads, look at each other, listen. Nothing
more. Just another cry in the night. Two old hands, veined,
ringed, seek each other, clasp. I pulled up the leg of my
trousers again, rolled it in a fury round my thigh, raised
the lid of the stool, took out the iodex and rubbed it into
my knee. The knee is full of little loose bones. Let it soak
well in, said my son. He would pay for that later on. When
I had finished I put everything back in place, rolled down
the leg of my trousers, sat down on the stool again and
listened. Nothing more. Unless you'd like to try a real emetic,
I said, as if nothing had happened. I'm tired, he said. You
go and lie down, I said, I'll bring you something nice and
light in bed, you'll have a little sleep and then we'll leave
together. I drew him to me. What do you say to that? I

said. He said to it, Yes papa. Did he love me then as much
as I loved him? You could never be sure with that little
hypocrite. Be off with you now, I said, cover yourself up
well, I won't be long. I went down to the kitchen, prepared
and set out on my handsome lacquer tray a bowl of hot
milk and a slice of bread and jam. He asked for a report,
he'll get his report. Martha watched me in silence, lolling
in her rocking-chair. Like a Fate who had run out of
thread. I cleaned up everything after me and turned to the
door. May I go to bed? she said. She had waited till I
was standing up, the laden tray in my hands, to ask me
this question. I went out, set down the tray on the chair at
the foot of the stairs and went back to the kitchen. Have
you made the sandwiches? I said. Meanwhile the milk was
getting cold and forming a revolting skin. She had made
them. I'm going to bed, she said. Everyone was going to
bed. You will have to get up in an hour or so, I said, to
lock up. It was for her to decide if it was worth while going
to bed, under these conditions. She asked me how long I
expected to be away. Did she realize I was not setting out
alone? I suppose so. When she went up to tell my son to
come down, even if he had told her nothing, she must
have noticed the knapsack. I have no idea, I said. Then
almost in the same breath, seeing her so old, worse than
old, aging, so sad and solitary in her everlasting corner,
There, there, it won't be long. And I advised her, in terms
for me warm, to have a good rest while I was away and
a good time visiting her friends and receiving them. Stint
neither tea nor sugar, I said, and if by any chance you
should happen to need money, apply to Mr Savory. I
carried this sudden cordiality so far as to shake her by
the hand, which she hastily wiped, as soon as she grasped
my intention, on her apron. When I had finished shaking it,
that flabby red hand, I did not let it go. But I took one
finger between the tips of mine, drew it towards me and
gazed at it. And had I had any tears to shed I should have
shed them then, in torrents, for hours. She must have wondered if I was not on the point of making an attempt on
her virtue. I gave her back her hand, took the sandwiches
and left her.

Martha had been a long time in my service. I was often

away from home. I had never taken leave of her in this way,
but always offhandedly, even when a prolonged absence was
to be feared, which was not the case on this occasion. Sometimes I departed without a word to her.

Before going into my son's room I went into my own. I
still had the cigar in my mouth, but the pretty ash had fallen
off. I reproached myself with this negligence. I dissolved
a sleeping-powder in the milk. He asked for a report, he'll
get his report. I was going out with the tray when my eyes
fell on the two albums lying on my desk. I wondered if
I might not relent, at any rate so far as the album of
duplicates was concerned. A little while ago he had come
here to fetch the thermometer. He had been a long time.
Had he taken advantage of the opportunity to secure some
of his favourite stamps? I had not time to check them all. I
put down the tray and looked for a few stamps at random,
the Togo one mark carmine with the pretty boat, the Nyassa
1901 ten reis, and several others. I was very fond of the
Nyassa. It was green and showed a giraffe grazing off the
top of a palm-tree. They were all there. That proved nothing.
It only proved that those particular stamps were there. I
finally decided that to go back on my decision, freely taken
and clearly stated, would deal a blow to my authority which
it was in no condition to sustain. I did so with sorrow. My
son was already sleeping. I woke him. He ate and drank,
grimacing in disgust. That was all the thanks I got. I waited
until the last drop, the last crumb had disappeared. He
turned to the wall and I tucked him in. I was within a hair's
breadth of kissing him. Neither he nor I had uttered a word.
We had no further need of words, for the time being. Besides my son rarely spoke to me unless I spoke to him.
And when I did so he answered but lamely and as it were
with reluctance. And yet with his little friends, when he
thought I was out of the way, he was incredibly voluble.
That my presence had the effect of dampening this disposition was far from displeasing me. Not one person in a
hundred knows how to be silent and listen, no, nor even
to conceive what such a thing means. Yet only then can
you detect, beyond the fatuous clamour, the silence of which
the universe is made. I desired this advantage for my son.
And that he should hold aloof from those who pride them-

selves on their eagle gaże. I had not struggled, toiled, suffered,
made good, lived like a Hottentot, so that my son should
do the same. I tiptoed out. I quite enjoyed playing my parts
through the bitter end.

Since in this way I shirked the issue, have I to apologize
for saying so? I let fall this suggestion for what it is worth.
And perfunctorily. For in describing this day I am once more
he who suffered it, who crammed it full of futile anxious
life, with no other purpose than his own stultification and
the means of not doing what he had to do. And as then
my thoughts would have none of Molloy, so tonight my
pen. This confession has been preying on my mind for some
time past. To have made it gives me no relief.

I reflected with bitter satisfaction that if my son lay
down and died by the wayside, it would be none of my
doing. To every man his own responsibilities. I know of
some they do not keep awake.

I said, There is something in this house tying my hands.
A man like me cannot forget, in his evasions, what it is he
evades. I went down to the garden and moved about in the
almost total darkness. If I had not known my garden so well
I would have blundered into my shrubberies, or my bee-
hives. My cigar had gone out unnoticed. I shook it and
put it in my pocket, intending to discard it in the ash-tray,
or in the waste-paper basket, later on. But the next day,
far from Turdy, I found it in my pocket and indeed not
without satisfaction. For I was able to get a few more puffs
out of it. To discover the cold cigar between my teeth,
to spit it out, to search for it in the dark, to pick it up,
to wonder what should I do with it, to shake it needlessly
and put it in my pocket, to conjure up the ash-tray and the
waste-paper basket, these were merely the principal stages
of a sequence which I spun out for a quarter of an hour
at least. Others concerned the dog Zulu, the perfumes
sharpened tenfold by the rain and whose sources I amused
myself exploring, in my head and with my hands, a neighbour's light, another's noise, and so on. My son's window
was faintly lit. He liked sleeping with a night-light beside
him. I sometimes felt it was wrong of me to let him humour
this weakness. Until quite recently he could not sleep unless
he had his woolly bear to hug. When he had forgotten the

bear (Baby Jack) I would forbid the night-light. What would I have done that day without my son to distract me? My duty perhaps.

Finding my spirits as low in the garden as in the house, I turned to go in, saying to myself it was one of two things, either my house had nothing to do with the kind of nothingness in the midst of which I stumbled or else the whole of my little property was to blame. To adopt this latter hypothesis was to condone what I had done and, in advance, what I was to do, pending my departure. It brought me a semblance of pardon and a brief moment of factitious freedom. I therefore adopted it.

From a distance the kitchen had seemed to be in darkness. And in a sense it was. But in another sense it was not. For gluing my eyes to the window-pane I discerned a faint reddish glow which could not have come from the oven, for I had no oven, but a simple gas-stove. An oven if you like, but a gas-oven. That is to say there was a real oven too in the kitchen, but out of service. I'm sorry, but there it is, in a house without a gas-oven I would not have felt easy. In the night, interrupting my prowl, I like to go up to a window, lit or unlit, and look into the room, to see what is going on. I cover my face with my hands and peer through my fingers. I have terrified more than one neighbour in this way. He rushes outside, finds no one. For me then from their darkness the darkest rooms emerge, as if still instant with the vanished day or with the light turned out a moment before, for reasons perhaps of which less said the better. But the gloaming in the kitchen was of another kind and came from the night-light with the red chimney which, in Martha's room, adjoining the kitchen, burned eternally at the feet of a little Virgin carved in wood, hanging on the wall. Weary of rocking herself she had gone in and lain down on her bed, leaving the door of her room open so as to miss none of the sounds in the house. But perhaps she had gone to sleep.

I went upstairs again. I stopped at my son's door. I stooped and applied my ear to the keyhole. Some apply the eye, I the ear, to keyholes. I heard nothing, to my great surprise. For my son slept noisily, with open mouth. I took good care not to open the door. For this silence was of a

nature to occupy my mind, for some little time. I went to my
room.

It was then the unheard of sight was to be seen of
Moran making ready to go without knowing where he
was going, having consulted neither map nor timetable,
considered neither itinerary nor halts, heedless of the
weather outlook, with only the vaguest notion of the outfit
he would need, the time the expedition was likely to take,
the money he would require and even the very nature of
the work to be done and consequently the means to be
employed. And yet there I was whistling away while I
stuffed into my haversack a minimum of effects, similar to
those I had recommended to my son. I put on my old pepper-
and-salt shooting-suit with the knee-breeches, stockings to
match and a pair of stout black boots. I bent down, my
hands on my buttocks, and looked at my legs. Knock-kneed
and skeleton thin they made a poor show in this accoutrement, unknown locally I may add. But when I left at night,
for a distant place, I wore it with pleasure, for the sake
of comfort, though I looked a sight. All I needed was a
butterfly-net to have vaguely the air of a country school-
master on convalescent leave. The heavy glittering black boots,
which seemed to implore a pair of navy-blue serge trousers,
gave the finishing blow to this get-up which otherwise might
have appeared, to the uninformed, an example of well-bred
bad taste. On my head, after mature hesitation, I decided
to wear my straw boater, yellowed by the rain. It had lost
its band, which gave it an appearance of inordinate height.
I was tempted to take my black cloak, but finally rejected
it in favour of a heavy massive-handled winter umbrella.
The cloak is a serviceable garment and I had more than
one. It leaves great freedom of movement to the arms and at
the same time conceals them. And there are times when a
cloak is so to speak indispensable. But the umbrella too has
great merits. And if it had been winter, or even autumn,
instead of summer, I might have taken both. I had already
done so, with most gratifying results.

Dressed thus I could hardly hope to pass unseen. I did
not wish to. Conspicuousness is the A B C of my profession.
To call forth feelings of pity and indulgence, to be the butt
of jeers and hilarity, is indispensable. So many vent-holes

in the cask of secrets. On condition you cannot feel, nor
denigrate, nor laugh. This state was mine at will. And then
there was night.

My son could only embarrass me. He was like a thousand
other boys of his age and condition. There is something about
a father that discourages derision. Even grotesque he commands a certain respect. And when he is seen out with his
young hopeful, whose face grows longer and longer and
longer with every step, then no further work is possible.
He is taken for a widower, the gaudiest colours are of no
avail, rather make things worse, he finds himself saddled
with a wife long since deceased, in child-bed as likely as
not. And my antics would be viewed as the harmless effect
of my widowhood, presumed to have unhinged my mind. I
boiled with anger at the thought of him who had shackled me
thus. If he had desired my failure he could not have devised
a better means to it. If I could have reflected with my usual
calm on the work I was required to do, it would perhaps
have seemed of a nature more likely to benefit than to suffer
by the presence of my son. But let us not go back on that.
Perhaps I could pass him off as my assistant, or a mere
nephew. I would forbid him to call me papa, or show me
any sign of affection, in public, if he did not want to get
one of those clouts he so dreaded.

And if I whistled fitfully while revolving these lugubrious
thoughts, I suppose it was because I was happy at heart to
leave my house, my garden, my village, I who usually left
them with regret. Some people whistle for no reason at all.
Not I. And while I came and went in my room, tidying up,
putting back my clothes in the wardrobe and my hats in the
boxes from which I had taken them the better to make my
choice, locking the various drawers, while thus employed I had
the joyful vision of myself far from home, from the familiar
faces, from all my sheet-anchors, sitting on a milestone in
the dark, my legs crossed, one hand on my thigh, my elbow
in that hand, my chin cupped in the other, my eyes fixed
on the earth as on a chessboard, coldly hatching my plans,
for the next day, for the day after, creating time to come.
And then I forgot that my son would be at my side, restless,
plaintive, whining for food, whining for sleep, dirtying his
drawers. I opened the drawer of my night-table and took

out a full tube of morphine tablets, my favourite sedative.

I have a huge bunch of keys, it weighs over a pound. Not a door, not a drawer in my house but the key to it goes with me, wherever I go. I carry them in the righthand pocket of my trousers, of my breeches in this case. A massive chain, attached to my braces, prevents me from losing them. This chain, four or five times longer than necessary, lies, coiled, on the bunch in my pocket. Its weight gives me a list to the right, when I am tired, or when I forget to counteract it, by a muscular effort.

I looked round for the last time, saw that I had neglected certain precautions, rectified this, took up my haversack, I nearly wrote my bagpipes, my boater, my umbrella, I hope I'm not forgetting anything, switched off the light, went out into the passage and locked my door. That at least is clear. Immediately I heard a strangling noise. It was my son, sleeping. I woke him. We haven't a moment to lose, I said. Desperately he clung to his sleep. That was natural. A few hours sleep however deep are not enough for an organism in the first stages of puberty suffering from stomach trouble. And when I began to shake him and help him out of bed pulling him first by the arms, then by the hair, he turned away from me in fury, to the wall, and dug his nails into the mattress. I had to muster all my strength to overcome his resistance. But I had hardly freed him from the bed when he broke from my hold, threw himself down on the floor and rolled about, screaming with anger and defiance. The fun was beginning already. This disgusting exhibition left me no choice but to use my umbrella, holding it by the end with both hands. But a word on the subject of my boater, before I forget. Two holes were bored in the brim, one on either side of course, I had bored them myself, with my little gimlet. And in these holes I had secured the ends of an elastic long enough to pass under my chin, under my jaws rather, but not too long, for it had to hold fast, under my jaws rather. In this way, however great my exertions, my boater stayed in its place, which was on my head. Shame on you, I cried, you ill-bred little pig! I would get angry if I were not careful. And anger is a luxury I cannot afford. For then I go blind, blood veils my eyes and I hear what the great Gustave heard, the benches cracking in the

court of assizes. Oh it is not without scathe that one is
gentle, courteous, reasonable, patient, day after day, year
after year. I threw down my umbrella and ran from the
room. On the stairs I met Martha coming up, capless, di-
sheveled, her clothes in disorder. What's going on? she cried.
I looked at her. She went back to her kitchen. Trembling I
hastened to the shed, seized my axe, went into the yard
and began hacking madly at an old chopping-block that
lay there and on which in winter, tranquilly, I split my logs.
Finally the blade sank into it so deeply that I could not
get it out. The efforts I made to do so brought me, with
exhaustion, calm. I went upstairs again. My son was dressing.
He was crying. Everybody was crying. I helped him put
on his knapsack. I told him not to forget his raincoat. He
began to put it in his knapsack. I told him to carry it over
his arm, for the moment. It was nearly midnight. I picked
up my umbrella. Intact. Get on, I said. He went out of the
room which I paused for a moment to survey, before I
followed him. It was a shambles. The night was fine in my
humble opinion. Scents filled the air. The gravel crunched
under our feet. No, I said, this way. I entered the little wood.
My son floundered behind me, bumping into the trees. He
did not know how to find his way in the dark. He was still
young, the words of reproach died on my lips. I stopped.
Take my hand, I said. I might have said, Give me your hand.
I said, Take my hand. Strange. But the path was too narrow
for us to walk abreast. So I put my hand behind me and my
son grasped it, gratefully I fancied. So we came to the little
wicket-gate. It was locked. I unlocked it and stood aside,
to let my son precede me. I turned back to look at my house.
It was partly hidden by the little wood. The roof's serrated
ridge, the single chimney-stack with its four flues, stood out
faintly against the sky spattered with a few dim stars. I
offered my face to the black mass of fragrant vegetation that
was mine and with which I could do as I pleased and never
be gainsaid. It was full of songbirds, their heads under their
wings, fearing nothing, for they knew me. My trees, my
bushes, my flower-beds, my tiny lawns, I used to think I
loved them. If I sometimes cut a branch, a flower, it was
solely for their good, that they might increase in strength
and happiness. And I never did it without a pang. Indeed

if the truth were known, I did not do it at all. I got Christy
to do it. I grew no vegetables. Not far off was the hen-house.
When I said I had turkeys, and so on, I lied. All I had was
a few hens. My grey hen was there, not on the perch with
the others, but on the ground, in a corner, in the dust, at
the mercy of the rats. The cock no longer sought her out
to tread her angrily. The day was at hand, if she did not
take a turn for the better, when the other hens would join
forces and tear her to pieces, with their beaks and claws.
All was silent. I have an extremely sensitive ear. Yet I
have no ear for music. I could just hear that adorable murmur
of tiny feet, of quivering feathers and feeble, smothered
clucking that hen-houses make at night and that dies down
long before dawn. How often I had listened to it, entranced,
in the evening, saying, Tomorrow I am free. And so I turned
again a last time towards my little all, before I left it, in the
hope of keeping it.

In the lane, having locked the wicket-gate, I said to my
son, Left. I had long since given up going for walks with
my son, though I sometimes longed to do so. The least
outing with him was torture, he lost his way so easily. Yet
when alone he seemed to know all the short cuts. When I sent
him to the grocer's or to Mrs Clement's or even further
afield, on the road to V for grain, he was back in half the
time I would have taken for the journey myself, and without having run. For I did not want my son to be seen caper-
ing in the streets like the little hooligans he frequented on
the sly. No, I wanted him to walk like his father, with little
rapid steps, his head up, his breathing even and economical,
his arms swinging, looking neither to left nor right, apparently
oblivious to everything and in reality missing nothing. But
with me he invariably took the wrong turn, a crossing or
a simple corner was all he needed to stray from the right
road, it of my election. I do not think he did this on purpose. But leaving everything to me he did not heed what
he was doing, or look where he was going, and went on
mechanically plunged in a kind of dream. It was as though
he let himself be sucked in out of sight by every opening
that offered. So that we had got in the habit of taking our
walks separately. And the only walk we regularly took together was that which led us, every Sunday, from home to
church and, mass over, from church to home. Caught up

then in the slow tide of the faithful my son was not alone with me. But he was part of that docile herd going yet again to thank God for his goodness and to implore his mercy and forgiveness, and then returning, their souls made easy, to other gratifications.

I waited for him to come back, then spoke the words calculated to settle this matter once and for all. Get behind me, I said, and keep behind me. This solution had its points, from several points of view. But was he capable of keeping behind me? Would not the time be bound to come when he would raise his head and find himself alone, in a strange place, and when I, waking from my reverie, would turn and find him gone? I toyed briefly with the idea of attaching him to me by means of a long rope, its two ends tied about our waists. There are various ways of attracting attention and I was not sure that this was one of the good ones. And he might have undone his knots in silence and escaped, leaving me to go on my way alone, followed by a long rope trailing in the dust, like a burgess of Calais. Until such time as the rope, catching on some fixed or heavy object, should stop me dead in my stride. We should have needed, not the soft and silent rope, but a chain, which was not to be dreamt of. And yet I did dream of it, for an instant I amused myself dreaming of it, imagining myself in a world less ill contrived and wondering how, having nothing more than a simple chain, without collar or band or gyves or fetters of any kind, I could chain my son to me in such a way as to prevent him from ever shaking me off again. It was a simple problem of toils and knots and I could keep my eye on him and intervene, at the least false movement he might make. But apart from having other parts to play, during this expedition, than those of keeper and sick-nurse, the prospect was more than I could bear of being unable to move a step without having before my eyes my son's little sullen plump body. Come here! I cried. For on hearing me say we were to go to the left he had gone to the left, as if his dearest wish was to infuriate me. Slumped over my umbrella, my head sunk as beneath a malediction, the fingers of my free hand between two slats of the wicket, I no more stirred than if I had been of stone. So he came back a second time. I tell you to keep behind me and you go before me, I said.

It was the summer holidays. His school cap was green

with initials and a boar's head, or a deer's, in gold braid
on the front. It lay plumb on his big blond skull as precise
as a lid on a pot. There is something about this strict sit
of hats and caps that never fails to exasperate me. As for
his raincoat, instead of carrying it folded over his arm, or
flung across his shoulder, as I had told him, he had rolled
it in a ball and was holding it with both hands, on his belly.
There he was before me, his big feet splayed, his knees sag-
ging, his stomach sticking out, his chest sunk, his chin in
the air, his mouth open, in the attitude of a veritable half-
wit. I myself must have looked as if only the support of
my umbrella and the wicket were keeping me from falling.
I managed finally to articulate, Are you capable of following
me? He did not answer. But I seized his thoughts as clearly
as if he had spoken them, namely, And you, are you capable
of leading me? Midnight struck, from the steeple of my
beloved church. It did not matter. I was gone from home.
I sought in my mind, where all I need is to be found, what
treasured possession he was likely to have about him. I
hope, I said, you have not forgotten your scout-knife, we
might need it. This knife comprised, apart from the five
or six indispensable blades, a cork-screw, a tin-opener, a
punch, a screw-driver, a claw, a gouge for removing stones
from hooves and I know not what other futilities besides.
I had given it to him myself, on the occasion of his first
first prize for history and geography, subjects which, at the
school he attended were for obscure reasons regarded as inseparable. The veriest dunce when it came to literature and
the so-called exact sciences, he had no equal for the dates
of battles, revolutions, restorations and other exploits of the
human race, in its slow ascension towards the light, and for
the configuration of frontiers and the heights of mountain
peaks. He deserved his scout-knife. Don't tell me you've
left it behind, I said. Not likely, he said, with pride and
satisfaction, tapping his pocket. Then give it to me, I said.
Naturally he did not answer. Prompt obedience was contrary
to his habits. Give me that knife! I cried. He gave it to me.
What could he do, alone with me in the night that tells no
tales? It was for his own good, to save him from getting
lost. For where a scout's knife is, there will his heart be
also, unless he can afford to buy another, which was not the

case with my son. For he never had any money in his pocket, not needing it. But every penny he received, and he did not receive many, he deposited first in his savings-box, then in the savings-bank, where they were entered in a book that remained in my possession. He would doubtless at that moment with pleasure have cut my throat, with that selfsame knife I was putting so placidly in my pocket. But he was still a little on the young side, my son, a little on the soft side, for the great deeds of vengeance. But time was on his side and he consoled himself perhaps with that thought, foolish though he was. Be that as it may, he kept back his tears, for which I was obliged to him. I straightened myself and laid my hand on his shoulder, saying, Patience, my child, patience. The awful thing in affairs of this kind is that when you have the will you do not have the way, and vice versa. But of that my unfortunate son could as yet have no suspicion, he must have thought that the rage which distorted his features and made him tremble would never leave him till the day he could vent it as it deserved. And not even then. Yes, he must have felt his soul the soul of a pocket Monte Cristo, with whose antics as adumbrated in the Schoolboys' Classics he was needless to say familiar. Then with a good clap on that impotent back I said, Off we go. And off indeed I did go, what is more, and my son drew out behind me. I had left, accompanied by my son, in accordance with instructions received.

I have no intention of relating the various adventures which befell us, me and my son, together and singly, before we came to the Molloy country. It would be tedious. But that is not what stops me. All is tedious, in this relation that is forced upon me. But I shall conduct it in my own way, up to a point. And if it has not the good fortune to give satisfaction, to my employer, if there are passages that give offence to him and to his colleagues, then so much the worse for us all, for them all, for there is no worse for me. That is to say, I have not enough imagination to imagine it. And yet I have more than before. And if I submit to this paltry scrivening which is not of my province, it is for reasons very different from those that might be supposed. I am still obeying orders, if you like, but no longer out of fear. No, I am still afraid, but simply from force of habit. And

the voice I listen to needs no Gaber to make it heard. For
it is within me and exhorts me to continue to the end the
faithful servant I have always been, of a cause that is not
mine, and patiently fulfil in all its bitterness my calamitous
part, as it was my will, when I had a will, that others should.
And this with hatred in my heart, and scorn, of my master
and his designs. Yes, it is rather an ambiguous voice and
not always easy to follow, in its reasonings and decrees. But
I follow it none the less, more or less, I follow it in this
sense, that I know what it means, and in this sense, that I do
what it tells me. And I do not think there are many voices of
which as much may be said. And I feel I shall follow it
from this day forth, no matter what it commands. And
when it ceases, leaving me in doubt and darkness, I shall
wait for it to come back, and do nothing, even though the
whole world, through the channel of its innumerable authorities speaking with one accord, should enjoin upon me this
and that, under pain of unspeakable punishments. But this
evening, this morning, I have drunk a little more than usual
and tomorrow I may be of a different mind. It also tells me,
this voice I am only just beginning to know, that the memory
of this work brought scrupulously to a close will help me
to endure the long anguish of vagrancy and freedom. Does
this mean I shall one day be banished from my house, from
my garden, lose my trees, my lawns, my birds of which
the least is known to me and the way all its own it has
of singing, of flying, of coming up to me or fleeing at my
coming, lose and be banished from the absurd comforts of
my home where all is snug and neat and all those things at
hand without which I could not bear being a man, where
my enemies cannot reach me, which it was my life's work
to build, to adorn, to perfect, to keep? I am too old to lose
all this, and begin again, I am too old! Quiet, Moran, quiet.
No emotion, please.

I was saying I would not relate all the vicissitudes of the
journey from my country to Molloy's, for the simple reason
that I do not intend to. And in writing these lines I know
in what danger I am of offending him whose favour I know
I should court, now more than ever. But I write them
all the same, and with a firm hand weaving inexorably back
and forth and devouring my page with the indifference of a

shuttle. But some I shall relate briefly, because that seems to me desirable, and in order to give some idea of the methods of my full maturity. But before coming to that I shall say what little I knew, on leaving my home, about the Molloy country, so different from my own. For it is one of the features of this penance that I may not pass over what is over and straightway come to the heart of the matter. But that must again be unknown to me which is no longer so and that again fondly believed which then I fondly believed, at my setting out. And if I occasionally break this rule, it is only over details of little importance. And in the main I observe it. And with such zeal that I am far more he who finds than he who tells what he has found, now as then, most of the time, I do not exaggerate. And in the silence of my room, and all over as far as I am concerned, I know scarcely any better where I am going and what awaits me than the night I clung to the wicket, beside my idiot of a son, in the lane. And it would not surprise me if I deviated, in the pages to follow, from the true and exact succession of events. But I do not think even Sisyphus is required to scratch himself, or to groan, or to rejoice, as the fashion is now, always at the same appointed places. And it may even be they are not too particular about the route he takes provided it gets him to his destination safely and on time. And perhaps he thinks each journey is the first. This would keep hope alive, would it not, hellish hope. Whereas to see yourself doing the same thing endlessly over and over again fills you with satisfaction.

By the Molloy country I mean that narrow region whose administrative limits he had never crossed and presumably never would, either because he was forbidden to, or because he had no wish to, or of course because of some extraordinary fortuitous conjunction of circumstances. This region was situated in the north, I mean in relation to mine, less bleak, and comprised a settlement, dignified by some with the name of market-town, by others regarded as no more than a village, and the surrounding country. This market-town, or village, was, I hasten to say, called Bally, and represented, with its dependent lands, a surface area of five or six square miles at the most. In modern countries this is what I think is called a commune, or a canton, I forget,

but there exists with us no abstract and generic term for
such territorial subdivisions. And to express them we have
another system, of singular beauty and simplicity, which
consists in saying Bally (since we are talking of Bally) when
you mean Bally and Ballyba when you mean Bally plus its
domains and Ballybaba when you mean the domains exclusive of Bally itself. I myself for example lived, and come to
think of it still live, in Turdy, hub of Turdyba. And in the
evening, when I went for a stroll, in the country outside
Turdy, to get a breath of fresh air, it was the fresh air
of Turdybaba that I got, and no other.

Ballybaba, in spite of its limited range, could boast of
a certain diversity. Pastures so-called, a little bog-land, a few
copses and, as you neared its confines, undulating and almost
smiling aspects, as if Ballybaba was glad to go no further.

But the principal beauty of this region was a kind of
strangled creek which the slow grey tides emptied and filled,
emptied and filled. And the people came flocking from the
town, unromantic people, to admire this spectacle. Some
said, There is nothing more beautiful than these wet sands.
Others, High tide is the best time to see the creek of Ballyba.
How lovely then that leaden water, you would swear it
was stagnant, if you did not know it was not. And yet others
held it was like an underground lake. But all were agreed,
like the inhabitants of Blackpool, that their town was on the
sea. And they had Bally-on-Sea printed on their notepaper.

The population of Ballyba was small. I confess this thought
gave me great satisfaction. The land did not lend itself to
cultivation. No sooner did a tilth, or a meadow, begin to
be sizeable than it fell foul of a sacred grove or a stretch
of marsh from which nothing could be obtained beyond a
little inferior turf or scraps of bog oak used for making
amulets, paper-knives, napkin-rings, rosaries and other knick-
knacks, Martha's madonna, for example, came from Ballyba.
The pastures, in spite of the torrential rains, were exceedingly meagre and strewn with boulders. Here only quitch-
weed grew in abundance, and a curious bitter blue grass
fatal to cows and horses, though tolerated apparently by the
ass, the goat and the black sheep. What then was the source
of Ballyba's prosperity? I'll tell you. No, I'll tell you nothing.
Nothing.

That then is a part of what I thought I knew about Ballyba when I left home. I wonder if I was not confusing it with some other place.

Some twenty paces from my wicket-gate the lane skirts the graveyard wall. The lane descends, the wall rises, higher and higher. Soon you are faring below the dead. It is there I have my plot in perpetuity. As long as the earth endures that spot is mine, in theory. Sometimes I went and looked at my grave. The stone was up already. It was a simple Latin cross, white. I wanted to have my name put on it, with the here lies and the date of my birth. Then all it would have wanted was the date of my death. They would not let me. Sometimes I smiled, as if I were dead already.

We walked for several days, by sequestered ways. I did not want to be seen on the highways.

The first day I found the butt of Father Ambrose's cigar. Not only had I not thrown it away, in the ash-tray, in the waste-paper basket, but I had put it in my pocket, when changing my suit. That had happened unbeknown to me. I looked at it in astonishment, lit it, took a few puffs, threw it away. This was the outstanding event of the first day.

I showed my son how to use his pocket-compass. This gave him great pleasure. He was behaving well, better than I had hoped. On the third day I gave him back his knife.

The weather was kind. We easily managed our ten miles a day. We slept in the open. Safety first.

I showed my son how to make a shelter out of branches. He was in the scouts, but knew nothing. Yes, he knew how to make a camp fire. At every halt he implored me to let him exercise this talent. I saw no point in doing so.

We lived on tinned food which I sent him to get in the villages. He was that much use to me. We drank the water of the streams.

All these precautions were assuredly useless. One day in a field I saw a farmer I knew. He was coming towards us. I turned immediately, took my son by the arm and led him away in the direction we were coming from. The farmer overtook us, as I had foreseen. Having greeted me, he asked where we were going. It must have been his field. I replied that we were going home. Fortunately we had not yet left it far behind. Then he asked me where we had been.

Perhaps one of his cows had been stolen, or one of his pigs.
Out walking, I said. I'll give you a lift and welcome, he said,
but I won't be leaving till night. Oh how very unfortunate,
I said. If you care to wait, he said, you're very welcome. I
declined with thanks. Fortunately it was not yet midday.
There was nothing strange in not wanting to wait till night.
Well, safe home, he said. We made a wide detour and
turned our faces to the north again.

These precautions were doubtless exaggerated. The right
thing would have been to travel by night and hide during
the day, at least in the early stages. But the weather was
so fine I could not bring myself to do it. My pleasure was
not my sole consideration, but it was a consideration! Such
a thing had never happened to me before, in the course of
my work. And our snail's pace! I cannot have been in a hurry
to arrive.

I gave fitful thought, while basking in the balm of the
warm summer days, to Gaber's instructions. I could not
reconstruct them to my entire satisfaction. In the night, under
the boughs, screened from the charms of nature, I devoted
myself to this problem. The sounds my son made during
his sleep hindered me considerably. Sometimes I went out
of the shelter and walked up and down, in the dark. Or I
sat down with my back against a trunk, drew my feet up
under me, took my legs in my arms and rested my chin
on my knee. Even in this posture I could throw no light
on the matter. What was I looking for exactly? It is hard
to say. I was looking for what was wanting to make Gaber's
statement complete. I felt he must have told me what to
do with Molloy once he was found. My particular duties
never terminated with the running to earth. That would have
been too easy. But I had always to deal with the client in one
way or another, according to instructions. Such operations
took on a multitude of forms, from the most vigorous to
the most discreet. The Yerk affair, which took me nearly
three months to conclude successfully, was over on the
day I succeeded in possessing myself of his tiepin and
destroying it. Establishing contact was the least important
part of my work. I found Yerk on the third day. I was never
required to prove I had succeeded, my word was enough.
Youdi must have had some way of verifying. Sometimes I
was asked for a report.

On another occasion my mission consisted in bringing
the person to a certain place at a certain time. A most
delicate affair, for the person concerned was not a woman.
I have never had to deal with a woman. I regret it. I don't
think Youdi had much interest in them. That reminds me
of the old joke about the female soul. Question, Have women
a soul? Answer, Yes. Question, Why? Answer, In order that
they may be damned. Very witty. Fortunately I had been
allowed considerable license as to the day. The hour was
the important thing, not the date. He came to the appointed
place and there I left him, on some pretext or other. He
was a nice youth, rather sad and silent. I vaguely remember
having invented some story about a woman. Wait, it's coming back. Yes, I told him she had been in love with him for
six months and greatly desired to meet him in some secluded
place. I even gave her name. Quite a well-known actress.
Having brought him to the place appointed by her, it was only
natural I should withdraw, out of delicacy. I can see him
still, looking after me. I fancy he would have liked me for
a friend. I don't know what became of him. I lost interest
in my patients, once I had finished with them. I may even
truthfully say I never saw one of them again, subsequently,
not a single one. No conclusions need be drawn from this.
Oh the stories I could tell you, if I were easy. What a rabble
in my head, what a gallery of moribunds. Murphy, Watt,
Yerk, Mercier and all the others. I would never have believed that—yes, I believe it willingly. Stories, stories. I
have not been able to tell them. I shall not be able to tell
this one.

I could not determine therefore how I was to deal with
Molloy, once I had found him. The directions which Gaber
must certainly have given me with reference to this had gone
clean out of my head. That is what came of wasting the
whole of that Sunday on stupidities. There was no good my
saying, Let me see now, what is the usual thing? There were
no usual things, in my instructions. Admittedly there was
one particular operation that recurred from time to time, but
not often enough to be, with any degree of probability, the
one I was looking for. But even if it had always figured in
my instructions, except on one single occasion, then that
single occasion would have been enough to tie my hands,
I was so scrupulous.

I told myself I had better give it no more thought, that
the first thing to do was to find Molloy, that then I would
devise something, that there was no hurry, that the thing
would come back to me when I least expected it and that
if, having found Molloy, I still did not know what to do
with him, I could always manage to get in touch with Gaber
without Youdi's knowing. I had his address just as he had
mine. I would send him a telegram, How deal with M? To
give me an explicit reply, though in terms if necessary veiled,
was not beyond his powers. But was there a telegraph in
Ballyba? But I also told myself, being only human, that the
longer I took to find Molloy the greater my chances of
remembering what I was to do with him. And we would
have peaceably pursued our way on foot, but for the following incident.

One night, having finally succeeded in falling asleep
beside my son as usual, I woke with a start, feeling as if
I had just been dealt a violent blow. It's all right, I am
not going to tell you a dream properly so called. It was
pitch dark in the shelter. I listened attentively without moving.
I heard nothing save the snoring and gasping of my son.
I was about to conclude as usual that it was just another
bad dream when a fulgurating pain went through my knee.
This then was the explanation of my sudden awakening.
The sensation could indeed well be compared to that of a
blow, such as I fancy a horse's hoof might give. I waited
anxiously for it to recur, motionless and hardly breathing,
and of course sweating. I acted in a word precisely as one
does, if my information was correct, at such a juncture. And
sure enough the pain did recur a few minutes later, but not
so bad as the first time, as the second rather. Or did it
only seem less bad to me because I was expecting it? Or
because I was getting used to it already? I think not. For
it recurred again, several times, and each time less bad than
the time before, and finally subsided altogether so that I
was able to get to sleep again more or less reassured. But
before getting to sleep again I had time to remember that
the pain in question was not altogether new to me. For I
had felt it before, in my bathroom, when giving my son his
enema. But then it had only attacked me once and never
recurred, till now. And I went to sleep again wondering,

by the way of lullaby, whether it had been the same knee
then as the one which had just excruciated me, or the other.
And that is a thing I have never been able to determine.
And my son too, when asked, was incapable of telling me
which of my two knees, I had rubbed in front of him, with
iodex, the night we left. And I went to sleep again a little
reassured, saying, It's a touch of neuralgia brought on by
all the tramping and trudging and the chill damp nights,
and promising myself to procure a packet of thermogene
wool, with the pretty demon on the outside, at the first
opportunity. Such is the rapidity of thought. But there was
more to come. For waking again towards dawn, this time
in consequence of a natural need, and with a mild erection,
to make things more lifelike, I was unable to get up. That
is to say I did get up finally to be sure, I simply had to,
but by dint of what exertions! Unable, unable, it's easy to
talk about being unable, whereas in reality nothing is more
difficult. Because of the will I suppose, which the least op-
position seems to lash into a fury. And this explains no
doubt how it was I despaired at first of ever bending my
leg again and then, a little later, through sheer determination,
did succeed in bending it, slightly. The anchylosis was not
total! I am still talking about my knee. But was it the same
one that had waked me early in the night? I could not have
sworn it was. It was not painful. It simply refused to bend.
The pain, having warned me several times in vain, had no
more to say. That is how I saw it. It would have been impossible for me to kneel, for example, for no matter how
you kneel you must always bend both knees, unless you
adopt an attitude frankly grotesque and impossible to main-
tain for more than a few seconds, I mean with the bad leg
stretched out before you, like a Caucasian dancer. I examined
the bad knee in the light of my torch. It was neither red
nor swollen. I fiddled with the knee-cap. It felt like a
clitoris. All this time my son was puffing like a grampus.
He had no suspicion of what life could do to you. I too
was innocent. But I knew it.

The sky was that horrible colour which heralds dawn.
Things steal back into position for the day, take their stand,
sham dead. I sat down cautiously, and I must say with a
certain curiosity, on the ground. Anyone else would have

tried to sit down as usual, offhandedly. Not I. New as
this new cross was I at once found the most comfortable
way of being crushed. But when you sit down on the ground
you must sit down tailor-wise, or like a foetus, these are
so to speak the only possible positions, for a beginner. So
that I was not long in letting myself fall back flat on my
back. And I was not long either in making the following
addition to the sum of my knowledge, that when of the
innumerable attitudes adopted unthinkingly by the normal
man all are precluded but two or three, then these are
enhanced. I would have sworn just the opposite, but for
this experience. Yes, when you can neither stand nor sit
with comfort, you take refuge in the horizontal, like a child
in its mother's lap. You explore it as never before and find
it possessed of unsuspected delights. In short it becomes
infinite. And if in spite of all you come to tire of it in the
end, you have only to stand up, or indeed sit up, for a few
seconds. Such are the advantages of a local and painless
paralysis. And it would not surprise me if the great classical
paralyses were to offer analogous and perhaps even still more
unspeakable satisfactions. To be literally incapable of motion
at last, that must be something! My mind swoons when I
think of it. And mute into the bargain! And perhaps as
deaf as a post! And who knows as blind as a bat! And as
likely as not your memory a blank! And just enough brain
intact to allow you to exult! And to dread death like a
regeneration.

I considered the problem of what I should do if my
leg did not get better or got worse. I watched, through the
branches, the sky shining. The sky sinks in the morning, this
fact has been insufficiently observed. It stoops, as if to get
a better look. Unless it is the earth that lifts itself up, to be
approved, before it sets out.

I shall not expound my reasoning. I could do so easily, so
easily. Its conclusion made possible the composition of the
following passage.

Did you have a good night? I said, as soon as my son
opened his eyes. I could have waked him, but no, I let
him wake naturally. Finally he told me he did not feel
well. My son's replies were often beside the point. Where
are we, I said, and what is the nearest village? He named

it. I knew it, I had been there, it was a small town, luck
was on our side. I even had a few acquaintances, among its
inhabitants. What day is it? I said. He specified the day without a moment's hesitation. And he had only just regained
consciousness! I told you he had a genius for history and
geography. It was from him I learned that Condom is on
the Baise. Good, I said, off you go now to Hole, it'll take
you—I worked it out—at the most three hours. He stared
at me in astonishment. There, I said, buy a bicycle to fit
you, second-hand for preference. You can go up to five
pounds. I gave him five pounds, in ten-shilling notes. It must
have a very strong carrier, I said, if it isn't very strong get
it changed, for a very strong one. I was trying to be clear.
I asked him if he was pleased. He did not look pleased. I
repeated these instructions and asked him again if he was
pleased. He looked if anything stupefied. A consequence
perhaps of the great joy he felt. Perhaps he could not believe his ears. Do you understand if nothing else? I said.
What a boon it is from time to time, a little real conversation.
Tell me what you are to do, I said. It was the only way of
knowing if he understood. Go to Hole, he said, fifteen miles
away. Fifteen miles! I cried. Yes, he said. All right, I said,
go on. And buy a bicycle, he said. I waited. Silence. A
bicycle! I cried. But there are millions of bicycles in Hole!
What kind of bicycle? He reflected. Second-hand, he said,
at a venture. And if you can't find one second-hand, I
said at last, what will you do? You didn't tell me, he said.
What a restful change it is from time to time, a little dialogue.
How much money did I give you? I said. He counted the
notes. Four pounds ten, he said. Count them again, I said.
He counted them again. Four pounds ten, he said. Give
it to me, I said. He gave me the notes and I counted them.
Four pounds ten. I gave you five, I said. He did not answer,
he let the figures speak for themselves. Had he stolen ten
shillings and hidden them on his person? Empty your pockets,
I said. He began to empty them. It must not be forgotten
that all this time I was lying down. He did not know I
was ill. Besides I was not ill. I looked vaguely at the objects
he was spreading out before me. He took them out of his
pockets one by one, held them up delicately between finger
and thumb, turned them this way and that before my eyes

and laid them finally on the ground beside me. When a
pocket was emptied he pulled out its lining and shook it. Then
a little cloud of dust arose. I was very soon overcome by
the absurdity of this verification. I told him to stop. Perhaps he was hiding the ten shillings up his sleeve, or in his
mouth. I should have had to get up and search him myself,
inch by inch. But then he would have seen I was ill. Not
that I was exactly ill. And why did I not want him to know
I was ill? I don't know. I could have counted the money
I had left. But what use would that have been? Did I even
know the amount I had brought with me? No. To me
too I cheerfully applied the maieutic method. Did I know
how much I had spent? No. Usually I kept the most rigorous
accounts when away on business and was in a position to
justify my expenditure down to the last penny. This time
no. For I was throwing my money away with as little concern as if I had been travelling for my pleasure. Let us
suppose I am wrong, I said, and that I only gave you four
pounds ten. He was calmly picking up the objects littered
on the ground and putting them back in his pockets. How
could he be made to understand? Stop that and listen, I said.
I gave him the notes. Count them, I said. He counted them.
How much? I said. Four pounds ten, he said. Ten what?
I said. Ten shillings, he said. You have four pounds ten
shillings? I said. Yes, he said. It was not true, I had given
him five. You agree, I said. Yes, he said. And why do you
think I have given you all that money? I said. His face
brightened. To buy a bicycle, he said, without hesitation.
Do you imagine a second-hand bicycle costs four pounds ten
shillings? I said. I don't know, he said. I did not know
either. But that was not the point. What did I tell you
exactly? I said. We racked our brains together. Second-
hand for preference, I said finally, that's what I told you.
Ah, he said. I am not giving this duet in full. Just the main
themes. I didn't tell you second-hand, I said, I told you
second-hand for preference. He had started picking up his
things again. Will you stop that, I cried, and pay attention
to what I am saying. He ostentatiously let fall a big ball of
tangled string. The ten shillings were perhaps inside it.
You see no difference between second-hand and second-hand
for preference, I said, do you? I looked at my watch. It

was ten o'clock. I was only making our ideas more confused.
Stop trying to understand. I said, just listen to what I am
going to say, because I shall not say it twice. He came over
to me and knelt down. You would have thought I was about
to breathe my last. Do you know what a new bicycle is?
I said. Yes papa, he said. Very well, I said, if you can't
find a second-hand bicycle buy a new bicycle. I repeat. I
repeated. I who had said I would not repeat. Now tell me
what you are to do, I said. I added, Take your face away,
your breath stinks. I almost added, You don't brush your
teeth and you complain of having abscesses, but I stopped
myself in time. It was not the moment to introduce another
theme. I repeated, Tell me what you are to do. He pondered.
Go to Hole, he said, fifteen miles away—. Don't worry
about the miles, I said. You're in Hole. What for? No, I
can't. Finally he understood. Who is this bicycle for, I said,
Goering? He had not yet grasped that the bicycle was for
him. Admittedly he was nearly my size already. As for the
carrier, I might just as well not have mentioned it. But
in the end he had the whole thing off pat. So much so that
he actually asked me what he was to do if he had not
enough money. Come back here and ask me, I said. I had
naturally foreseen, while reflecting on all these matters before
my son woke, that he might have trouble with people asking
how he came by so much money and he so young. And I
knew what he was to do in that event, namely go and see,
or send for, the police-sergeant, give his name, and say it
was I, Jacques Moran, ostensibly at home in Turdy, who
had sent him to buy a bicycle in Hole. Here obviously two
distinct operations were involved, the first consisting in fore-
seeing the difficulty (before my son woke), the second in
overcoming it (at the news that Hole was the nearest locality).
But there was no question of my conveying instructions of
such complexity. But don't worry, I said, you've enough,
and to spare to buy yourself a good bicycle. I added, And
bring it back here as fast as you can. You had to allow for
everything with my son. He could never have guessed what
to do with the bicycle once he had it. He was capable of
hanging about Hole, under God knows what conditions,
waiting for further instructions. He asked me what was wrong.
I must have winced. I'm sick of the sight of you, I said,

that's what wrong. And I asked him what he was waiting
for. I don't feel well, he said. When he asked me how I
was I said nothing, and when no one asked him anything
he announced he was not feeling well. Are you not pleased,
I said, to have a nice brand-new bicycle, all your own? I
was decidedly set on hearing him say he was pleased. But
I regretted my phrase, it could only add to his confusion.
But perhaps this family chat has lasted long enough. He
left the shelter and when I judged he was at a safe distance
I left it too, painfully. He had gone about twenty paces.
Leaning nonchalantly against a tree-trunk, my good leg
boldly folded across the other, I tried to look light-hearted.
I hailed him. He turned. I waved my hand. He stared at
me an instant, then turned away and went on. I shouted
his name. He turned again. A lamp! I cried. A good lamp!
He did not understand. How could he have understood, at
twenty paces, he who could not understand at one. He came
back towards me. I waved him away, crying, Go on! Go
on! He stopped and stared at me, his head on one side
like a parrot, utterly bewildered apparently. Foolishly I
made to stoop, to pick up a stone or a piece of wood or a
clod, anything in the way of a projectile, and nearly fell.
I reached up above my head, broke off a live bough and
hurled it violently in his direction. He spun round and took
to his heels. Really there were times I could not understand
my son. He must have known he was out of range, even
of a good stone, and yet he took to his heels. Perhaps he
was afraid I would run after him. And indeed, I think there
is something terrifying about the way I run, with my head
flung back, my teeth clenched, my elbows bent to the full
and my knees nearly hitting me in the face. And I have often
caught faster runners than myself thanks to this way of
running. They stop and wait for me, rather than prolong
such a horrible outburst at their heels. As for the lamp,
we did not need a lamp. Later, when the bicycle had taken
its place in my son's life, in the round of his duties and his
innocent games, then a lamp would be indispensable, to light
his way in the night. And no doubt it was in anticipation of
those happy days that I had thought of the lamp and cried
out to my son to buy a good one, that later on his comings
and his goings should not be hemmed about with darkness

and with dangers. And similarly I might have told him to be careful about the bell, to unscrew the little cap and examine it well inside, so as to make sure it was a good bell and in good working order, before concluding the transaction, and to ring it to hear the ring it made. But we would have time enough later on, to see to all these things. And it would be my joy to help my son, when the time came, to fit his bicycle with the best lamps, both front and rear, and the best bell and the best brakes that money could buy.

The day seemed very long. I missed my son! I busied myself as best I could. I ate several times. I took advantage of being alone at last, with no other witness than God, to masturbate. My son must have had the same idea, he must have stopped on the way to masturbate. I hope he enjoyed it more than I did. I circled the shelter several times, thinking the exercise would benefit my knee. I moved at quite a good speed and without much pain, but I soon tired. After ten or eleven steps a great weariness seized hold of my leg, a heaviness rather, and I had to stop. It went away at once and I was able to go on. I took a little morphine. I asked myself certain questions. Why had I not told my son to bring me back something for my leg? Why had I hidden my condition from him? Was I secretly glad that this had happened to me, perhaps even to the point of not wanting to get well? I surrendered myself to the beauties of the scene, I gazed at the trees, the fields, the sky, the birds, and I listened attentively to the sounds, faint and clear, borne to me on the air. For an instant I fancied I heard the silence mentioned, if I am not mistaken, above. Stretched out in the shelter, I brooded on the undertaking in which I was embarked. I tried again to remember what I was to do with Molloy, when I found him. I dragged myself down to the stream. I lay down and looked at my reflection, then I washed my face and hands. I waited for my image to come back, I watched it as it trembled towards an ever increasing likeness. Now and then a drop, falling from my face, shattered it again. I did not see a soul all day. But towards evening I heard a prowling about the shelter. I did not move, and the footsteps died away. But a little later, having left the shelter for some reason or other, I saw a man a few paces off, standing motionless. He had his

back to me. He wore a coat much too heavy for the time
of the year and was leaning on a stick so massive, and so
much thicker at the bottom than at the top, that it seemed
more like a club. He turned and we looked at each other
for some time in silence. That is to say I looked him full
in the face, as I always do, to make people think I am
not afraid, whereas he merely threw me a rapid glance from
time to time, then lowered his eyes, less from timidity apparently than in order quietly to think over what he had
just seen, before adding to it. There was a coldness in his
stare, and a thrust, the like of which I never saw. His face
was pale and noble, I could have done with it. I was thinking
he could not be much over fifty-five when he took off his
hat, held it for a moment in his hand, then put it back on
his head. No resemblance to what is called raising one's hat.
But I thought it advisable to nod. The hat was quite extraordinary, in shape and colour. I shall not attempt to describe
it, it was like none I had ever seen. He had a huge shock
of dirty snow-white hair. I had time, before he squeezed it
in back under his hat, to see the way it swelled up on
his skull. His face was dirty and hairy, yes, pale, noble,
dirty and hairy. He made a curious movement, like a hen
that puffs up its feathers and slowly dwindles till it is smaller
than before. I thought he was going to depart without a
word to me. But suddenly he asked me to give him a piece
of bread. He accompanied this humiliating request with a
fiery look. His accent was that of a foreigner or of one who
had lost the habit of speech. But had I not said already,
with relief, at the mere sight of his back, He's a foreigner.
Would you like a tin of sardines? I said. He asked for bread
and I offered him fish. That is me all over. Bread, he said.
I went into the shelter and took the piece of bread I was
keeping for my son, who would probably be hungry when
he came back. I gave it to him. I expected him to devour
it there and then. But he broke it in two and put the pieces
in his coat-pockets. Do you mind if I look at your stick,
I said. I stretched out my hand. He did not move. I put
my hand on the stick, just under his. I could feel his fingers
gradually letting go. Now it was I who held the stick. Its
lightness astounded me. I put it back in his hand. He threw
me a last look and went. It was almost dark. He walked

with swift uncertain step, often changing his course, dragging the stick like a hindrance. I wished I could have stood there looking after him, and time at a standstill. I wished I could have been in the middle of a desert, under the midday sun, to look after him till he was only a dot, on the edge of the horizon. I stayed out in the air for a long time. Every now and then I listened. But my son did not come. Beginning to feel cold I went back into the shelter and lay down, under my son's raincoat. But beginning to feel sleepy I went out again and lit a big wood-fire, to guide my son towards me. When the fire had kindled I said, Why of course, now I can warm myself! I warmed myself, rubbing my hands together after having held them to the flame and before holding them to it again, and turning my back to the flame and lifting the tail of my coat, and turning as on a spit. And in the end, overcome with heat and weariness, I lay down on the ground near the fire and fell asleep, saying, Perhaps a spark will set fire to my clothes and I wake a living torch. And saying many other things besides, belonging to separate and apparently unconnected trains of thought. But when I woke it was day again and the fire was out. But the embers were still warm. My leg was no better, but it was no worse either. That is to say it was perhaps a little worse, without my being in a condition to realize it, for the simple reason that this leg was becoming a habit, mercifully. But I think not. For at the same time as I listened to my knee, and then submitted it to various tests, I was on my guard against the effects of this habit and tried to discount them. And it was not so much Moran as another, in the secret of Moran's sensations exclusively, who said, No change, Moran, no change. This may seem impossible. I went into the copse to cut myself a stick. But having finally found a suitable branch, I remembered I had no knife. I went back to the shelter, hoping to find my son's knife among the things he had laid on the ground and neglected to pick up. It was not among them. To make up for this I came across my umbrella and said, Why cut myself a stick when I have my umbrella? And I practised walking with the help of my umbrella. And though in this way I moved no faster and no less painfully, at least I did not tire so quickly. And instead of having to stop every ten steps, to rest, I easily

managed fifteen, before having to stop. And even while I
rested my umbrella was a help. For I found that when I
leaned upon it the heaviness in my leg, due probably to a
defect in the bloodstream, disappeared even more quickly
than when I stood supported only by my muscles and the
tree of life. And thus equipped I no longer confined myself
to circling about the shelter, as I had done the previous
day, but I radiated from it in every direction. And I even
gained a little knoll from which I had a better view of the
expanse where my son might suddenly rise into view, at any
moment. And in my mind's eye from time to time I saw
him, bent over the handlebars or standing on the pedals,
drawing near, and I heard him panting and saw written on
the chubby face his joy at being back at last. But at the same
time I kept my eye on the shelter, which drew me with an
extraordinary pull, so that to cut across from the terminus
of one sally to the terminus of the next, and so on, which
would have been convenient, was out of the question. But
each time I had to retrace my steps, the way I had come,
to the shelter, and make sure all was in order, before I
sallied forth again. And I consumed the greater part of this
second day in these vain comings and goings, these vigils
and imaginings, but not all of it. For I also lay down from
time to time in the shelter, which I was beginning to think
of as my little house, to ruminate in peace on certain things,
and notably on my provisions of food which were rapidly
running out, so that after a meal devoured at five o'clock
I was left with only two tins of sardines, a handful of biscuits
and a few apples. But I also tried to remember what I was
to do with Molloy, once I had found him. And on myself
too I pored, on me so changed from what I was. And I
seemed to see myself ageing as swiftly as a day-fly. But
the idea of ageing was not exactly the one which offered itself
to me. And what I saw was more like a crumbling, a frenzied
collapsing of all that had always protected me from all I
was always condemned to be. Or it was like a kind of clawing towards a light and countenance I could not name, that
I had once known and long denied. But what words can
describe this sensation at first all darkness and bulk, with
a noise like the grinding of stones, then suddenly as soft
as water flowing. And then I saw a little globe swaying up

slowly from the depths, through the quiet water, smooth
at first, and scarcely paler than its escorting ripples, then
little by little a face, with holes for the eyes and mouth
and other wounds, and nothing to show if it was a man's
face or a woman's face, a young face or an old face, or
if its calm too was not an effect of the water trembling between it and the light. But I confess I attended but absently
to these poor figures, in which I suppose my sense of disaster
sought to contain itself. And that I did not labour at them
more diligently was a further index of the great changes
I had suffered and of my growing resignation to being dis-
possessed of self. And doubtless I should have gone from
discovery to discovery, concerning myself, if I had persisted.
But at the first faint light, I mean in these wild shadows
gathering about me, dispensed by a vision or by an effort
of thought, at the first light I fled to other cares. And all
had been for nothing. And he who acted thus was a stranger
to me too. For it was not my nature, I mean it was not my
custom, to conduct my calculations simultaneously, but separately and turn about, pushing each one as far as it would
go before turning in desperation to another. Similarly the
missing instructions concerning Molloy, when I felt them
stirring in the depths of my memory, I turned from them
in haste towards other unknowns. And I who a fortnight
before would joyfully have reckoned how long I could survive on the provisions that remained, probably with reference
to the question of calories and vitamins, and established in
my head a series of menus asymptotically approaching nutri-
tional zero, was now content to note feebly that I should soon
be dead of inanition, if I did not succeed in renewing my provisions. So much for the second day. But one incident remains
to be noted, before I go on to the third.

It was evening. I had lit my fire and was watching it
take when I heard myself hailed. The voice, already so near
that I started violently, was that of a man. But after this
one violent start I collected myself and continued to busy
myself with my fire as if nothing had happened, poking it
with a branch I had torn from its tree for the purpose a
little earlier and stripped of its twigs and leaves and even
part of its bark, with my bare nails. I have always loved
skinning branches and laying bare the pretty white glossy

shaft of sapwood. But obscure feelings of love and pity for
the tree held me back most of the time. And I numbered
among my familiars the dragon-tree of Teneriffe that perished at the age of five thousand years, struck by lightning.
It was an example of longevity. The branch was thick and
full of sap and did not burn when I stuck it in the fire.
I held it by the thin end. The crackling of the fire, of the
writhing brands rather, for fire triumphant does not crackle,
but makes an altogether different noise, had permitted the
man to come right up to me, without my knowledge. If there
is one thing infuriates me it is being taken myself by surprise. I continued then, in spite of my spasm of fright, hoping
it had passed unnoticed, to poke the fire as if I were alone.
But at the thump of his hand on my shoulder I had no
choice but to do what anyone else would have done in my
place, and this I achieved by suddenly spinning round in
what I trust was a good imitation of fear and anger. There
I was face to face with a dim man, dim of face and dim
of body, because of the dark. Put it there, he said. But
little by little I formed an idea of the type of individual it
was. And indeed there reigned between his various parts
great harmony and concord, and it could be truly said that
his face was worthy of his body, and vice versa. And if I
could have seen his arse, I do not doubt I should have found
it on a par with the whole. What are you doing in this God-
forsaken place, he said, you unexpected pleasure. And moving aside from the fire which was now burning merrily,
so that its light fell full on the intruder, I could see he was
precisely the kind of pest I had thought he was, without
being sure, because of the dark. Can you tell me, he said.
I shall have to describe him briefly, though such a thing is
contrary to my principles. He was on the small side, but
thick-set. He wore a thick navy-blue suit (double-breasted)
of hideous cut and a pair of outrageously wide black shoes,
with the toe-caps higher than the uppers. This dreadful
shape seems only to occur in black shoes. Do you happen
to know, he said. The fringed extremities of a dark muffler,
seven feet long at least, wound several times round his neck,
hung down his back. He had a narrow-brimmed dark blue
felt hat on his head, with a fish-hook and an artificial fly
stuck in the band, which produced a highly sporting effect.

Do you hear me? he said. But all this was nothing compared
to the face which I regret to say vaguely resembled my
own, less the refinement of course, same little abortive moustache, same little ferrety eyes, same paraphimosis of the
nose, and a thin red mouth that looked as if it was raw
from trying to shit its tongue. Hey you! he said. I turned
back to my fire. It was doing nicely. I threw more wood
on it. Do you hear me talking to you? he said. I went towards
the shelter, he barred my way, emboldened by my limp.
Have you a tongue in your head? he said. I don't know you,
I said. I laughed. I had not intended to be witty. Would you
care to see my card? he said. It would mean nothing to me,
I said. He came closer to me. Get out of my way, I said.
It was his turn to laugh. You refuse to answer? he said. I
made a great effort. What do you want to know? I said.
He must have thought I was weakening. That's more like
it, he said. I called to my aid the image of my son who
might arrive at any moment. I've already told you, he said.
I was trembling all over. Have the goodness to tell me
again, I said. To cut a long story short he wanted to know
if I had seen an old man with a stick pass by. He described
him. Badly. The voice seemed to come to me from afar.
No, I said. What do you mean no? he said. I have seen
no one, I said. And yet he passed this way, he said. I said
nothing. How long have you been here? he said. His body
too grew dim, as if coming asunder. What is your business
here? he said. Are you on night patrol? I said. He thrust
his hand at me. I have an idea I told him once again to get
out of my way. I can still see the hand coming towards me,
pallid, opening and closing. As if self-propelled. I do not
know what happened then. But a little later, perhaps a long
time later, I found him stretched on the ground, his head
in a pulp. I am sorry I cannot indicate more clearly how
this result was obtained, it would have been something worth
reading. But it is not at this late stage of my relation that
I intend to give way to literature. I myself was unscathed,
except for a few scratches I did not discover till the following day. I bent over him. As I did so I realized my leg
was bending normally. He no longer resembled me. I took
him by the ankles and dragged him backwards into the
shelter. His shoes shone with highly polished blacking. He

wore fancy socks. The trousers slid back, disclosing the white hairless legs. His ankles were bony, like my own. My fingers encircled them nearly. He was wearing suspenders, one of which had come undone and was hanging loose. This detail went to my heart. Already my knee was stiffening again. It no longer required to be supple. I went back to the shelter and took my son's raincoat. I went back to the fire and lay down, with the coat over me. I did not get much sleep, but I got some. I listened to the owls. They were not eagle-owls, it was a cry like the whistle of a locomotive. I listened to a nightingale. And to distant corncrakes. If I had heard of other birds that cry and sing at night, I should have listened to them too. I watched the fire dying, my cheek pillowed on my hands. I watched out for the dawn. It was hardly breaking when I got up and went to the shelter. His legs too were on the stiff side, but there was still some play in the hip joints, fortunately. I dragged him into the copse, with frequent rests on the way, but without letting go his legs, so as not to have to stoop again to pick them up. Then I dismantled the shelter and threw the branches over the body. I packed and shouldered the two bags, took the raincoat and the umbrella. In a word I struck camp. But before leaving I consulted with myself to make sure I was forgetting nothing, and without relying on my intelligence alone, for I felt my pockets and looked around me. And it was while feeling my pockets that I discovered something of which my mind had been powerless to inform me, namely that my keys were no longer there. I was not long in finding them, scattered on the ground, the ring having broken. And to tell the truth first I found the chain, then the keys and last the ring, in two pieces. And since it was out of the question, even with the help of my umbrella, to stoop each time to pick up a key, I put down my bags, my umbrella and the coat and lay down flat on my stomach among the keys which in this way I was able to recover without much difficulty. And when a key was beyond my reach I took hold of the grass and dragged myself over to it. And I wiped each key on the grass, before putting it in my pocket, whether it needed wiping or not. And from time to time I raised myself on my hands, to get a better view. And in this way I located a number of keys at some distance from me, and these I

reached by rolling over and over, like a great cylinder. And
finding no more keys, I said, There is no use my counting
them, for I do not know how many there were. And my eyes
resumed their search. But finally I said, Hell to it, I'll do
with those I have. And while looking in this way for my keys I
found an ear which I threw into the copse. And, to my even
greater surprise, I found my straw hat which I thought was
on my head! One of the holes for the elastic had expanded
to the edge of the rim and consequently was no longer a
hole, but a slit. But the other had been spared and the elastic
was still in it. And finally I said, I shall rise now and, from
my full height, run my eyes over this area for the last time.
Which I did. It was then I found the ring, first one piece,
then the other. Then, finding nothing more belonging either
to me or to my son, I shouldered my bags again, jammed the
straw-hat hard down on my skull, folded my son's raincoat
over my arm, caught up the umbrella and went.

But I did not go far. For I soon stopped on the crest of a
rise from where I could survey, without fatigue, the camp-
site and the surrounding country. And I made this curious
observation, that the land from where I was, and even the
clouds in the sky, were so disposed as to lead the eyes gently
to the camp, as in a painting by an old master. I made myself
as comfortable as possible, I got rid of my various burdens
and I ate a whole tin of sardines and one apple. I lay down
flat on my stomach on my son's coat. And now I propped
my elbows on the ground and my jaws between my hands,
which carried my eyes towards the horizon, and now I made
a little cushion of my two hands on the ground and laid my
cheek upon it, five minutes one, five minutes the other, all
the while flat on my stomach. I could have made myself a
pillow of the bags, but I did not, it did not occur to me. The
day passed tranquilly, without incident. And the only thing
that relieved the monotony of this third day was a dog. When
I first saw him he was sniffing about the remains of my fire,
then he went into the copse. But I did not see him come out
again, either because my attention was elsewhere, or because
he went out the other side, having simply as it were gone
straight through it. I mended my hat, that is to say with the
tin-opener I pierced a new hole beside the old one and made
fast the elastic again. And I also mended the ring, twisting the

two pieces together, and I slipped on the keys and made fast the long chain again. And to kill time I asked myself a certain number of questions and tried to answer them. For example.

Question. What had happened to the blue felt hat?
Answer.
Question. Would they not suspect the old man with the stick?
Answer. Very probably.
Question. What were his chances of exonerating himself?
Answer. Slight.
Question. Should I tell my son what had happened?
Answer. No, for then it would be his duty to denounce me.
Question. Would he denounce me?
Answer.
Question. How did I feel?
Answer. Much as usual.
Question. And yet I had changed and was still changing?
Answer. Yes.
Question. And in spite of this I felt much as usual?
Answer. Yes.
Question. How was this to be explained?
Answer.

These questions and others too were separated by more or less prolonged intervals of time not only from one another, but also from the answers appertaining to them. And the answers did not always follow in the order of the questions. But while looking for the answer, or the answers, to a given question, I found the answer, or the answers, to a question I had already asked myself in vain, in the sense that I had not been able to answer it, or I found another question, or other questions, demanding in their turn an immediate answer.

Translating myself now in imagination to the present moment, I declare the foregoing to have been written with a firm and even satisfied hand, and a mind calmer than it had been for a long time. For I shall be far away, before these lines are read, in a place where no one will dream of coming to look for me. And then Youdi will take care of me, he will not let me be punished for a fault committed in the execution of my duty. And they can do nothing to my son, rather they will commiserate with him on having had such

a father, and offers of help and expressions of esteem will
pour in upon him from every side.

So this third day wore away. And about five o'clock I ate
my last tin of sardines and a few biscuits, with a good
appetite. This left me with only a few apples and a few biscuits. But about seven o'clock my son arrived. The sun was
low in the west. I must have dozed a moment, for I did not
see him coming, a speck on the horizon, then rapidly bigger
and bigger, as I had foreseen. But he was already between me
and the camp, making for the latter, when I saw him. A wave
of irritation broke over me, I jumped to my feet and began
to vociferate, brandishing my umbrella. He turned and I
beckoned him to join me, waving the umbrella as if I wanted
to hook something with the handle. I thought for a moment
he was going to defy me and continue on his way to the camp, to
where the camp had been rather, for it was there no more. But
finally he came towards me. He was pushing a bicycle which,
when he had joined me, he let fall with a gesture signifying
he could bear no more. Pick it up, I said, till I look at it. I
had to admit it must once have been quite a good bicycle. I
would gladly describe it, I would gladly write four thousand
words on it alone. And you call that a bicycle? I said. Only
half expecting him to answer me I continued to inspect it. But
there was something so strange in his silence that I looked
up at him. His eyes were starting out of his head. What's
the matter, I said, is my fly open? He let go the bicycle
again. Pick it up, I said. He picked it up. What happened
to you? he said. I had a fall, I said. A fall? he said. Yes, a
fall, I cried, did you never have a fall? I tried to remember
the name of the plant that springs from the ejaculations of
the hanged and shrieks when plucked. How much did you
give for it? I said. Four pounds, he said. Four pounds! I
cried. If he had said two pounds or even thirty shillings I
should have cried, Two pounds! or, Thirty shillings! the same.
They asked four pounds five, he said. Have you the receipt?
I said. He did not know what a receipt was. I described one.
The money I spent on my son's education and he did not know
what a simple receipt was. But I think he knew as well as I.
For when I said to him, Now tell me what a receipt is, he told
me very prettily. I really did not care in the least whether
he had been fooled into paying for the bicycle three or four

times what it was worth or whether on the other hand he had appropriated the best part of the purchase money for his own use. The loss would not be mine. Give me the ten shillings, I said. I spent them, he said. Enough, enough. He began explaining that the first day the shops had been closed, that the second—I said, Enough, enough. I looked at the carrier. It was the best thing about that bicycle. It and the pump. Does it go by any chance? I said. I had a puncture two miles from Hole, he said, I walked the rest of the way. I looked at his shoes. Pump it up, I said. I held the bicycle. I forget which wheel it was. As soon as two things are nearly identical I am lost. The dirty little twister was letting the air escape between the valve and the connexion which he had purposely not screwed tight. Hold the bicycle, I said, and give me the pump. The tyre was soon hard. I looked at my son. He began to protest. I soon put a stop to that. Five minutes later I felt the tyre. It was as hard as ever. I cursed him. He took a bar of chocolate from his pocket and offered it to me. I took it. But instead of eating it, as I longed to, and although I have a horror of waste, I cast it from me, after a moment's hesitation, which I trust my son did not notice. Enough. We went down to the road. It was more like a path. I tried to sit down on the carrier. The foot of my stiff leg tried to sink into the ground, into the grave. I propped myself up on one of the bags. Keep her steady, I said. I was still too low. I added the other. Its bulges dug into my buttocks. The more things resist me the more rabid I get. With time, and nothing but my teeth and nails, I would rage up from the bowels of the earth to its crust, knowing full well I had nothing to gain. And when I had no more teeth, no more nails, I would dig through the rock with my bones. Here then in a few words is the solution I arrived at. First the bags, then my son's raincoat folded in four, all lashed to the carrier and the saddle with my son's bits of string. As for the umbrella, I hooked it round my neck, so as to have both hands free to hold on to my son by the waist, under the armpits rather, for by this time my seat was higher than his. Pedal, I said. He made a despairing effort, I can well believe it. We fell. I felt a sharp pain in my shin. I was all tangled up in the back wheel. Help! I cried. My son helped me up. My stocking was torn and my leg bleeding. Happily it was the sick leg. What would I have

done, with both legs out of action? I would have found a
way. It was even perhaps a blessing in disguise. I was thinking
of phlebotomy of course. Are you all right? I said. Yes, he
said. He would be. With my umbrella I caught him a smart
blow on the hamstrings, gleaming between the leg of his
shorts and his stocking. He cried out. Do you want to kill
us? I said. I'm not strong enough, he said, I'm not strong
enough. The bicycle was all right apparently, the back wheel
slightly buckled perhaps. I at once saw the error I had made.
It was to have settled down in my seat, with my feet clear
of the ground, before we moved off. I reflected. We'll try again,
I said. I can't, he said. Don't try me too far, I said. He straddled
the frame. Start off gently when I tell you, I said. I got up
again behind and settled down in my seat, with my feet clear
of the ground. Good. Wait till I tell you, I said. I let myself
slide to one side till the foot of my good leg touched the
ground. The only weight now on the back wheel was that of
my sick leg, cocked up rigid at an excruciating angle. I dug
my fingers into my son's jacket. Go easy, I said. The wheels
began to turn. I followed, half dragged, half hopping. I
trembled for my testicles which swing a little low. Faster! I
cried. He bore down on the pedals. I bounded up to my place.
The bicycle swayed, righted itself, gained speed. Bravo! I
cried, beside myself with joy. Hurrah! cried my son. How
I loathe that exclamation! I can hardly set it down. He was as
pleased as I, I do believe. His heart was beating under my
hand and yet my hand was far from his heart. Happily it
was downhill. Happily I had mended my hat, or the wind
would have blown it away. Happily the weather was fine and
I no longer alone. Happily, happily.

In this way we came to Ballyba. I shall not tell of the
obstacles we had to surmount, the fiends we had to circumvent, the misdemeanours of the son, the disintegrations of
the father. It was my intention, almost my desire, to tell
of all these things, I rejoiced at the thought that the moment
would come when I might do so. Now the intention is dead,
the moment is come and the desire is gone. My leg was no
better. It was no worse either. The skin had healed. I would
never have got there alone. It was thanks to my son. What?
That I got there. He often complained of his health, his
stomach, his teeth. I gave him some morphine. He looked

worse and worse. When I asked him what was wrong he
could not tell me. We had trouble with the bicycle. But I
patched it up. I would not have got there without my son.
We were a long time getting there. Weeks. We kept losing
our way, taking our time. I still did not know what I was to
do with Molloy, when I found him. I thought no more about
it. I thought about myself, much, as we went along, sitting
behind my son, looking over his head, and in the evening,
when we camped, while he made himself useful, and when
he went away, leaving me alone. For he often went away, to
spy out the life of the land and to buy provisions. I did
practically nothing any more. He took good care of me, I
must say. He was clumsy, stupid, slow, dirty, untruthful,
deceitful, prodigal, unfilial, but he did not abandon me.
I thought much about myself. That is to say I often took
a quick look at myself, closed my eyes, forgot, began again.
We took a long time getting to Ballyba, we even got there
without knowing it. Stop, I said to my son one day. I had
just caught sight of a shepherd I liked the look of. He was
sitting on the ground stroking his dog. A flock of black
shorn sheep strayed about them, unafraid. What a pastoral
land, my God. Leaving my son on the side of the road I
went towards them, across the grass. I often stopped and
rested, leaning on my umbrella. The shepherd watched me
as I came, without getting up. The dog too, without barking.
The sheep too. Yes, little by little, one by one, they turned
and faced me, watching me as I came. Here and there faint
movements of recoil, a tiny foot stamping the ground, betrayed their uneasiness. They did not seem timid, as sheep
go. And my son of course watched me as I went, I felt his
eyes in my back. The silence was absolute. Profound in any
case. All things considered it was a solemn moment. The
weather was divine. It was the close of day. Each time I
stopped I looked about me. I looked at the shepherd, the
sheep, the dog and even at the sky. But when I moved I saw
nothing but the ground and the play of my feet, the good one
springing forward, holding back, setting itself down, waiting
for the other to come up. I came finally to a halt about ten
paces from the shepherd. There was no use going any further.
How I would love to dwell upon him. His dog loved him,
his sheep did not fear him. Soon he would rise, feeling the

falling dew. The fold was far, far, he would see from afar the
light in his cot. Now I was in the midst of the sheep, they
made a circle round me, their eyes converged on me. Perhaps
I was the butcher come to make his choice. I took off my
hat. I saw the dog's eyes following the movement of my hand.
I looked about me again incapable of speech. I did not know
how I would ever be able to break this silence. I was on the
point of turning away without having spoken. Finally I said,
Ballyba, hoping it sounded like a question. The shepherd
drew the pipe from his mouth and pointed the stem at the
ground. I longed to say, Take me with you, I will serve you
faithfully, just for a place to lie and a little food. I had understood, but without seeming to I suppose, for he repeated his
gesture, pointing the stem of his pipe at the ground, several
times. Bally, I said. He raised one hand, it wavered an instant as
if over a map, then stiffened. The pipe still smoked faintly, the
smoke hung blue in the air an instant, then vanished. I looked
in the direction indicated. The dog too. We were all three
turned to the north. The sheep were losing interest in me.
Perhaps they had understood. I heard them straying about
again and grazing. I distinguished at last, at the limit of
the plain, a dim glow, the sum of countless points of light
blurred by the distance, I thought of Juno's milk. It lay
like a faint splash on the sharp dark sweep of the horizon.
I gave thanks for evening that brings out the lights, the
stars in the sky and on earth the brave little lights of men.
By day the shepherd would have raised his pipe in vain,
towards the long clear-cut commissure of earth and sky.
But now I felt the man turning towards me again, and the
dog, and the man drawing on his pipe again, in the hope
it had not gone out. And I knew I was all alone gazing at
that distant glow that would get brighter and brighter, I
knew that too, then suddenly go out. And I did not like the
feeling of being alone, with my son perhaps, no, alone,
spellbound. And I was wondering how to depart without
self-loathing or sadness, or with as little as possible, when
a kind of immense sigh all round me announced it was not
I who was departing, but the flock. I watched them move
away, the man in front, then the sheep, huddled together,
their heads sunk, jostling one another, breaking now and
then into a little trot, snatching blindly without stopping a

last mouthful from the earth, and last of all the dog, jauntily,
waving his long black plumy tail, though there was no one
to witness his contentment, if that is what it was. And so
in perfect order, the shepherd silent and the dog unneeded,
the little flock departed. And so no doubt they would plod
on, until they came to the stable or the fold. And there
the shepherd stands aside to let them pass and he counts
them as they go by, though he knows not one is missing.
Then he turns towards his cottage, the kitchen door is open,
the lamp is burning, he goes in and sits down at the table,
without taking off his hat. But the dog stops at the threshold,
not knowing whether he may go in or whether he must stay
out, all night.

That night I had a violent scene with my son. I do not
remember about what. Wait, it may be important.

No, I don't know. I have had so many scenes with my
son. At the time it must have seemed a scene like any other,
that's all I know.

I must have got the better of it as I always did, thanks to
my infallible technique, and brought him unerringly to a
proper sense of his iniquities. But the next day I realized
my mistake. For waking early I found myself alone, in the
shelter, I who was always the first to wake. And what is
more my instinct told me I had been alone for some considerable time, my breath no longer mingling with the breath
of my son, in the narrow shelter he had erected, under my
supervision. Not that the fact of his having disappeared with
the bicycle, during the night or with the first guilty flush of
dawn, was in itself a matter for grave anxiety. And I would
have found excellent and honourable reasons for this, if
this had been all. Unfortunately he had taken his knapsack
and his raincoat. And there remained nothing in the shelter, nor
outside the shelter, belonging to him absolutely nothing.
And this was not yet all, for he had left with a considerable
sum of money, he who was only entitled to a few pence
from time to time, for his savings-box. For since he had
been in charge of everything, under my supervision of
course, and notably of the shopping, I was obliged to place
a certain reliance on him in the matter of money. And he
always had a far greater sum in his pocket than was strictly
necessary. And in order to make all this sound more likely
I shall add what follows.

1. I desired him to learn double-entry book-keeping and had instructed him in its rudiments.

2. I could no longer be bothered with these wretched trifles which had once been my delight.

3. I had told him to keep an eye out, on his expeditions, for a second bicycle, light and inexpensive. For I was weary of the carrier and I also saw the day approaching when my son would no longer have the strength to pedal for the two of us. And I believed I was capable, more than that, I knew I was capable, with a little practice, of learning to pedal with one leg. And then I would resume my rightful place, I mean in the the van. And my son would follow me. And then the scandal would cease of my son's defying me, and going left when I told him right, or right when I told him left, or straight on when I told him right or left as he had been doing of late, more and more frequently.

That is all I wished to add.

But on examining my pocket-book I found it contained no more than fifteen shillings, which led me to the conclusion that my son had not been content with the sum already in his possession, but had gone through my pockets, before he left, while I slept. And the human breast is so bizarre that my first feeling was of gratitude for his leaving me this little sum, enough to keep me going until help arrived, and I saw in this a kind of delicacy!

I was therefore alone, with my bag, my umbrella (which he might easily have taken too) and fifteen shillings, knowing myself coldly abandoned, with deliberation and no doubt premeditation, in Ballyba it is true, if indeed I was in Ballyba, but still far from Bally. And I remained for several days, I do not know how many, in the place where my son had abandoned me, eating my last provisions (which he might easily have taken too), seeing no living soul, powerless to act, or perhaps strong enough at last to act no more. For I had no illusions, I knew that all was about to end, or to begin again, it little mattered which, and it little mattered how, I had only to wait. And on and off, for fun, and the better to scatter them to the winds, I dallied with the hopes that spring eternal, childish hopes, as for example that my son, his anger spent, would have pity on me and come back to me! Or that Molloy, whose country this was, would come to me, who had not been able to go to him, and grow to be

a friend, and like a father to me, and help me do what I had
to do, so that Youdi would not be angry with me and
would not punish me! Yes, I let them spring within me
and grow in strength, brighten and charm me with a thousand fancies, and then I swept them away, with a great
disgusted sweep of all my being, I swept myself clean of
them and surveyed with satisfaction the void they had
polluted. And in the evening I turned to the lights of Bally,
I watched them shine brighter and brighter, then all go out
together, or nearly all, foul little flickering lights of terrified
men. And I said, To think I might be there now, but for
my misfortune! And with regard to the Obidil, of whom I
have refrained from speaking, until now, and whom I so
longed to see face to face, all I can say with regard to him
is this, that I never saw him, either face to face or darkly,
perhaps there is no such person, that would not greatly surprise me. And at the thought of the punishments Youdi
might inflict upon me I was seized by such a mighty fit of
laughter that I shook, with mighty silent laughter and my
features composed in their wonted sadness and calm. But
my whole body shook, and even my legs, so that I had to
lean against a tree, or against a bush, when the fit came
on me standing, my umbrella being no longer sufficient to
keep me from falling. Strange laughter truly, and no doubt
misnamed, through indolence perhaps, or ignorance. And as
for myself, that unfailing pastime, I must say it was far
now from my thoughts. But there were moments when it
did not seem so far from me, when I seemed to be drawing
towards it as the sands towards the wave, when it crests and
whitens, though I must say this image hardly fitted my situation, which was rather that of the turd waiting for the flush.
And I note here the little beat my heart once missed, in my
home, when a fly, flying low above my ash-tray, raised a
little ash, with the breath of its wings. And I grew gradually
weaker and weaker and more and more content. For several
days I had eaten nothing. I could probably have found
blackberries and mushrooms, but I had no wish for them.
I remained all day stretched out in the shelter, vaguely regretting my son's raincoat, and I crawled out in the evening
to have a good laugh at the lights of Bally. And though suffering a little from wind and cramps in the stomach I felt ex-

traordinarily content, content with myself, almost elated, enchanted with my performance. And I said, I shall soon lose consciousness altogether, it is merely a question of time. But Gaber's arrival put a stop to these frolics.

It was evening. I had just crawled out of the shelter for my evening guffaw and the better to savour my exhaustion. He had already been there for some time. He was sitting on a tree-stump, half asleep. Well Moran, he said. You recognize me? I said. He took out and opened his notebook, licked his finger, turned over the pages till he came to the right page, raised it towards his eyes which at the same time he lowered towards it. I can see nothing, he said. He was dressed as when I had last seen him. My strictures on his Sunday clothes had therefore been unjustified. Unless it was Sunday again. But had I not always seen him dressed in this way? Would you have a match? he said. I did not recognize this far-off voice. Or a torch, he said. He must have seen from my face that I possessed nothing of a luminous nature. He took a small electric torch from his pocket and shone it on his page. He read, Moran, Jacques, home, instanter. He put out his torch, closed his notebook on his finger and looked at me. I can't walk, I said. What? he said. I'm sick, I can't move, I said. I can't hear a word you say, he said. I cried to him that I could not move, that I was sick, that I should have to be carried, that my son had abandoned me, that I could bear no more. He examined me laboriously from head to foot. I executed a few steps leaning on my umbrella to prove to him I could not walk. He opened his notebook again, shone the torch on his page, studied it at length and said, Moran, home, instanter. He closed his notebook, put it back in his pocket, put his lamp back in his pocket, stood up, drew his hands over his chest and announced he was dying of thirst. Not a word on how I was looking. And yet I had not shaved since the day my son brought back the bicycle from Hole, nor combed my hair, nor washed, not to mention all the privations I had suffered and the great inward metamorphoses. Do you recognize me? I cried. Do I recognize you? he said. He reflected. I knew what he was doing, he was searching for the phrase most apt to wound me. Ah Moran, he said, what a man! I was staggering with weakness. If I had dropped dead at his feet he would have said,

Ah poor old Moran, that's him all over. It was getting darker
and darker. I wondered if it was really Gaber. Is he angry?
I said. You wouldn't have a sup of beer by any chance? he
said. I'm asking you if he is angry, I cried. Angry, said
Gaber, don't make me laugh, he keeps rubbing his hands
from morning to night, I can hear them in the outer room.
That means nothing, I said. And chuckling to himself, said
Gaber. He must be angry with me, I said. Do you know
what he told me the other day? said Gaber. Has he changed?
I cried. Changed, said Gaber, no, he hasn't changed, why
would he have changed, he's getting old, that's all, like the
world. You have a queer voice this evening, I said. I do not
think he heard me. Well, he said, drawing his hands once
more over his chest, downwards, I'll be going, if that's all
you have to say to me. He went, without saying goodbye. But
I overtook him, in spite of my loathing for him, in spite of
my weakness and my sick leg, and held him back by the
sleeve. What did he tell you? I said. He stopped. Moran,
he said, you are beginning to give me a serious pain in the
arse. For pity's sake, I said, tell me what he told you. He
gave me a shove. I fell. He had not intended to make me
fall, he did not realize the state I was in, he had only wanted
to push me away. I did not try to get up. I let a roar. He
came and bent over me. He had a walrus moustache, chestnut in colour. I saw it lift, the lips open, and almost at the
same time I heard words of solicitude, at a great distance.
He was not brutal, Gaber, I knew him well. Gaber, I said,
it's not much I'm asking you. I remember this scene well. He
wanted to help me up. I pushed him away. I was all right
where I was. What did he tell you? I said. I don't understand, said Gaber. You were saying a minute ago that he had
told you something, I said, then I cut you short. Short? said
Gaber. Do you know what he told me the other day, I said,
those were your very words. His face lit up. The clod was
just about as quick as my son. He said to me, said Gaber,
Gaber, he said—. Louder! I cried. He said to me, said
Gaber, Gaber, he said, life is a thing of beauty, Gaber, and
a joy for ever. He brought his face nearer mine. A joy for
ever, he said, a thing of beauty, Moran, and a joy for ever.
He smiled. I closed my eyes. Smiles are all very nice in their
own way, very heartening, but at a reasonable distance. I

said, Do you think he meant human life? I listened. Perhaps
he didn't mean human life, I said. I opened my eyes. I was
alone. My hands were full of grass and earth I had torn
up unwittingly, was still tearing up. I was literally uprooting.
I desisted, yes, the second I realized what I had done, what
I was doing, such a nasty thing, I desisted from it, I opened
my hands, they were soon empty.

That night I set out for home. I did not get far. But it
was a start. It is the first step that counts. The second counts
less. Each day saw me advance a little further. That last
sentence is not clear, it does not say what I hoped it would.
I counted at first by tens of steps. I stopped when I could
go no further and I said, Bravo, that makes so many tens,
so many more than yesterday. Then I counted by fifteens, by
twenties and finally by fifties. Yes, in the end I could go
fifty steps before having to stop, for rest, leaning on my
faithful umbrella. In the beginning I must have strayed a
little in Ballyba, if I really was in Ballyba. Then I followed
more or less the same paths we had taken on the way out.
But paths look different, when you go back along them. I
ate, in obedience to the voice of reason, all that nature, the
woods, the fields, the waters had to offer me in the way of
edibles. I finished the morphine.

It was in August, in September at the latest, that I was
ordered home. It was spring when I got there, I will not be
more precise. I had therefore been all winter on the way.

Anyone else would have lain down in the snow, firmly
resolved never to rise again. Not I. I used to think that men
would never get the better of me. I still think I am cleverer
than things. There are men and there are things, to hell
with animals. And with God. When a thing resists me, even
if it is for my own good, it does not resist me long. This
snow, for example. Though to tell the truth it lured me more
than it resisted me. But in a sense it resisted me. That was
enough. I vanquished it, grinding my teeth with joy, it is
quite possible to grind one's incisors. I forged my way
through it, towards what I would have called my ruin if I
could have conceived what I had left to be ruined. Perhaps I have conceived it since, perhaps I have not done con-
ceiving it, it takes time, one is bound to in time, I am bound
to. But on the way home, a prey to the malignancy of man

and nature and my own failing flesh, I could not conceive it.
My knee, allowance made for the dulling effects of habit,
was neither more nor less painful than the first day. The
disease, whatever it was, was dormant! How can such things
be? But to return to the flies, I like to think of those that
hatch out at the beginning of winter, within doors, and die
shortly after. You see them crawling and fluttering in the
warm corners, puny, sluggish, torpid, mute. That is you see
an odd one now and then. They must die very young, without having been able to lay. You sweep them away, you
push them into the dustpan with the brush, without knowing.
That is a strange race of flies. But I was succumbing to
other affections, that is not the word, intestinal for the most
part. I would have described them once, not now, I am
sorry, it would have been worth reading. I shall merely say
that no one else would have surmounted them, without
help. But I! Bent double, my free hand pressed to my belly,
I advanced, and every now and then I let a roar, of triumph
and distress. Certain mosses I consumed must have disagreed
with me. If I once made up my mind not to keep the hang-
man waiting, the bloody flux itself would not stop me, I
would get there on all fours shitting out my entrails and
chanting maledictions. Didn't I tell you it's my brethren that
have done for me.

But I shall not dwell upon this journey home, its furies
and treacheries. And I shall pass over in silence the fiends
in human shape and the phantoms of the dead that tried
to prevent me from getting home, in obedience to Youdi's
command. But one or two words nevertheless, for my own
edification and to prepare my soul to make an end. To begin
with my rare thoughts.

Certain questions of a theological nature preoccupied me
strangely. As for example.

1. What value is to be attached to the theory that Eve
sprang, not from Adam's rib, but from a tumour in the fat
of his leg (arse?)?

2. Did the serpent crawl, or as Comestor affirms, walk
upright?

3. Did Mary conceive through the ear, as Augustine and
Adobard assert?

4. How much longer are we to hang about waiting for
the antichrist?

5. Does it really matter which hand is employed to absterge the podex?

6. What is one to think of the Irish oath sworn by the natives with the right hand on the relics of the saints and the left on the virile member?

7. Does nature observe the sabbath?

8. Is it true that the devils do not feel the pains of hell?

9. The algebraic theology of Craig. What is one to think of this?

10. Is it true that the infant Saint-Roch refused suck on Wednesdays and Fridays?

11. What is one to think of the excommunication of vermin in the sixteenth century?

12. Is one to approve of the Italian cobbler Lovat who, having cut off his testicles, crucified himself?

13. What was God doing with himself before the creation?

14. Might not the beatific vision become a source of boredom, in the long run?

15. Is it true that Judas' torments are suspended on Saturdays?

16. What if the mass for the dead were read over the living?

And I recited the pretty quietist Pater, Our Father who art no more in heaven than on earth or in hell, I neither want nor desire that thy name be hallowed, thou knowest best what suits thee. Etc. The middle and the end are very pretty.

It was in this frivolous and charming world that I took refuge, when my cup ran over.

But I asked myself other questions concerning me perhaps more closely. As for example.

1. Why had I not borrowed a few shillings from Gaber?

2. Why had I obeyed the order to go home?

3. What had become of Molloy?

4. Same question for me.

5. What would become of me?

6. Same question for my son.

7. Was his mother in heaven?

8. Same question for my mother.

9. Would I go to heaven?

10. Would we all meet again in heaven one day, I, my

mother, my son, his mother, Youdi, Gaber, Molloy, his mother, Yerk, Murphy, Watt, Camier and the rest?

11. What had become of my hens, my bees? Was my grey hen still living?

12. Zulu, the Elsner sisters, were they still living?

13. Was Youdi's business address still 8, Acacia Square? What if I wrote to him? What if I went to see him? I would explain to him. What would I explain to him? I would crave his forgiveness. Forgiveness for what?

14. Was not the winter exceptionally severe?

15. How long had I gone now without either confession or communion?

16. What was the name of the martyr who, being in prison, loaded with chains, covered with wounds and vermin, unable to stir, celebrated the consecration on his stomach and gave himself absolution?

17. What would I do until my death? Was there no means of hastening this, without falling into a state of sin?

But before I launch my body properly so-called across these icy, then, with the thaw, muddy solitudes, I wish to say that I often thought of my bees, more often than my hens, and God knows I thought often of my hens. And I thought above all of their dance, for my bees danced, oh not as men dance to amuse themselves, but in a different way. I alone of all mankind knew this, to the best of my belief. I had investigated this phenomenon very fully. The dance was best to be observed among the bees returning to the hive, laden more or less with nectar, and it involved a great variety of figures and rhythms. These evolutions I finally interpreted as a system of signals by means of which the incoming bees, satisfied or dissatisfied with their plunder, informed the outgoing bees in what direction to go, and in what not to go. But the outgoing bees danced too. It was no doubt their way of saying, I understand, or Don't worry about me. But away from the hive, and busily at work, the bees did not dance. Here their watchword seemed to be, Every man for himself, assuming bees to be capable of such notions. The most striking feature of the dance was its very complicated figures, traced in flight, and I had classified a great number of these, with their probable meanings. But there was also the question of the hum, so various in tone

in the vicinity of the hive that this could hardly be an effect
of chance. I first concluded that each figure was reinforced
by means of a hum peculiar to it. But I was forced to
abandon this agreeable hypothesis. For I saw the same figure
(at least what I called the same figure) accompanied by
very different hums. So that I said, The purpose of the
hum is not to emphasize the dance, but on the contrary to
vary it. And the same figure exactly differs in meaning according to the hum that goes with it. And I had collected
and classified a great number of observations on this subject, with gratifying results. But there was to be considered
not only the figure and the hum, but also the height at which
the figure was executed. And I acquired the conviction that
the selfsame figure, accompanied by the selfsame hum, did
not mean at all the same thing at twelve feet from the
ground as it did at six. For the bees did not dance at any
level, haphazard, but there were three or four levels, always
the same, at which they danced. And if I were to tell you
what these levels were, and what the relations between them,
for I had measured them with care, you would not believe
me. And this is not the moment to jeopardize my credit.
Sometimes you would think I was writing for the public.
And in spite of all the pains I had lavished on these prob-
lems, I was more than ever stupefied by the complexity of
this innumerable dance, involving doubtless other deter-
minants of which I had not the slightest idea. And I said,
with rapture, Here is something I can study all my life, and
never understand. And all during this long journey home,
when I racked my mind for a little joy in store, the thought
of my bees and their dance was the nearest thing to comfort. For I was still eager for my little joy, from time to
time! And I admitted with good grace the possibility that
this dance was after all no better than the dances of the
people of the West, frivolous and meaningless. But for me,
sitting near my sun-drenched hives, it would always be a
noble thing to contemplate, too noble ever to be sullied by
the cogitations of a man like me, exiled in his manhood.
And I would never do my bees the wrong I had done my
God, to whom I had been taught to ascribe my angers, fears,
desires, and even my body.

I have spoken of a voice giving me orders, or rather ad-

vice. It was on the way home I heard it for the first time.
I paid no attention to it.

Physically speaking it seemed to me I was now becoming
rapidly unrecognizable. And when I passed my hands over
my face, in a characteristic and now more than ever pardon-
able gesture, the face my hands felt was not my face any
more, and the hands my face felt were my hands no longer.
And yet the gist of the sensation was the same as in the
far-off days when I was well-shaven and perfumed and proud
of my intellectual's soft white hands. And this belly I did
not know remained my belly, my old belly, thanks to I
know not what intuition. And to tell the truth I not only
knew who I was, but I had a sharper and clearer sense of
my identity than ever before, in spite of its deep lesions and
the wounds with which it was covered. And from this point
of view I was less fortunate than my other acquaintances. I
am sorry if this last phrase is not so happy as it might be.
It deserved, who knows, to be without ambiguity.

Then there are the clothes that cleave so close to the
body and are so to speak inseparable from it, in time of
peace. Yes, I have always been very sensitive to clothing,
though not in the least a dandy. I had not to complain of
mine, tough and of good cut. I was of course inadequately
covered, but whose fault was that? And I had to part with
my straw, not made to resist the rigours of winter, and with
my stockings (two pairs) which the cold and damp, the
trudging and the lack of laundering facilities had literally
annihilated. But I let out my braces to their fullest extent and
my knickerbockers, very baggy as the fashion is, came
down to my calves. And at the sight of the blue flesh, between
the knickerbockers and the tops of my boots, I sometimes
thought of my son and the blow I had fetched him, so avid
is the mind of the flimsiest analogy. My boots became rigid,
from lack of proper care. So skin defends itself, when dead
and tanned. The air coursed through them freely, preserving perhaps my feet from freezing. And I had likewise sadly
to part with my drawers (two pairs). They had rotted, from
constant contact with my incontinences. Then the seat of
my breeches, before it too decomposed, sawed my crack
from Dan to Beersheba. What else did I have to discard?
My shirt? Never! But I often wore it inside out and back to

front. Let me see. I had four ways of wearing my shirt. Front to front right side out, front to front inside out, back to front right side out, back to front inside out. And the fifth day I began again. It was in the hope of making it last. Did this make it last? I do not know. It lasted. To major things the surest road is on the minor pains bestowed, if you don't happen to be in a hurry. But what else did I have to discard? My hard collars, yes, I discarded them all, and even before they were quite worn and torn. But I kept my tie, I even wore it, knotted round my bare neck, out of sheer bravado I suppose. It was a spotted tie, but I forget the colour.

When it rained, when it snowed, when it hailed, then I found myself faced with the following dilemma. Was I to go on leaning on my umbrella and get drenched or was I to stop and take shelter under my open umbrella? It was a false dilemma, as so many dilemmas are. For on the one hand all that remained of the canopy of my umbrella was a few flitters of silk fluttering from the stays and on the other I could have gone on, very slowly, using the umbrella no longer as a support, but as a shelter. But I was so accustomed on the one hand to the perfect watertightness of my expensive umbrella, and on the other hand to being unable to walk without its support, that the dilemma remained entire, for me. I could of course have made myself a stick, out of a branch, and gone on, in spite of the rain, the snow, the hail, leaning on the stick and the umbrella open above me. But I did not, I do not know why. But when the rain descended and the other things that descend upon us from above, sometimes I pushed on, leaning on the umbrella, getting drenched, but most often I stopped dead, opened the umbrella above me and waited for it to be over. Then I got equally drenched. But this was not the point. And if it had suddenly begun to rain manna I would have waited, stock still, under my umbrella, for it to be over, before taking advantage of it. And when my arm was weary of holding up the umbrella, then I gave it to the other hand. And with my free hand I slapped and rubbed every part of my body within its reach, in order to keep the blood trickling freely, or I drew it over my face, in a gesture that was characteristic, of me. And the long spike of my umbrella was like a

finger. My best thoughts came to me during these halts.
But when it was clear that the rain, etc., would not stop all
day, or all night, then I did the sensible thing and built
myself a proper shelter. But I did not like proper shelters,
made of boughs, any more. For soon there were no more
leaves, but only the needles of certain conifers. But this
was not the real reason why I did not like proper shelters
any more, no. But when I was inside them I could think
of nothing but my son's raincoat, I literally saw it, I saw
nothing else, it filled all space. It was in reality what our
English friends call a trench-coat, and I could smell the
rubber, though trench-coats are not rubberized as a rule.
So I avoided as far as possible having recourse to proper
shelters, made of boughs, preferring the shelter of my faithful umbrella, or of a tree, or of a hedge, or of a bush, or of
a ruin.

The thought of taking to the road, to try and get a lift,
never crossed my mind.

The thought of turning for help to the villages, to the
peasants, would have displeased me, if it had occurred to me.

I reached home with my fifteen shillings intact. No, I
spent two. This is how.

I had to suffer other molestations than this, other offences,
but I shall not record them. Let us be content with para-
digms. I may have to suffer others in the future. This is not
certain. But they will never be known. This is certain.

It was evening. I was waiting quietly, under my umbrella,
for the weather to clear, when I was brutally accosted from
behind. I had heard nothing. I had been in a place where I
was all alone. A hand turned me about. It was a big ruddy
farmer. He was wearing an oilskin, a bowler hat and welling-
tons. His chubby cheeks were streaming, the water was
dripping from his bushy moustache. But why describe him?
We glared at each other with hatred. Perhaps he was the
same who had so politely offered to drive us home in his
car. I think not. And yet his face was familiar. Not only
his face. He held a lantern in his hand. It was not lit. But
he might light it at any moment. In the other he held a
spade. To bury me with if necessary. He seized me by the
jacket, by the lapel. He had not yet begun to shake me
exactly, he would shake me in his own good time, not before.

He merely cursed me. I wondered what I could have done,
to put him in such a state. I must have raised my eyebrows.
But I always raise my eyebrows, they are almost in my hair,
my brow is nothing but wales and furrows. I understood
finally that I did not own the land. It was his land. What
was I doing on his land? If there is one question I dread,
to which I have never been able to invent a satisfactory
reply, it is the question what am I doing. And on someone
else's land to make things worse! And at night! And in
weather not fit for a dog! But I did not lose my presence of
mind. It is a vow, I said. I have a fairly distinguished voice,
when I choose. I must have impressed him. He unhanded me.
A pilgrimage, I said, following up my advantage. He asked
me where to. He was lost. To the Turdy Madonna, I said.
The Turdy Madonna? he said, as if he knew Turdy like the
back of his hand and there were no Madonna in the length
and breadth of it. But where is the place in which there is
no Madonna? Herself, I said. The black one? he said, to
try me. She is not black that I know of, I said. Another
would have lost countenance. Not I. I knew my yokels and
their weak points. You'll never get there, he said. It's thanks
to her I lost my infant boy, I said, and kept his mamma.
Such sentiments could not fail to please a cattle breeder.
Had he but known! I told him more fully what alas had
never happened. Not that I miss Ninette. But she, at least,
who knows, in any case, yes, a pity, no matter. She is the
Madonna of pregnant women, I said, of pregnant married
women, and I have vowed to drag myself miserably to her
niche, and thank her. This incident gives a feeble idea of
my ability, even at this late period. But I had gone a little
too far, for the vicious look came back into his eye. May I
ask you a favour, I said, God will reward you. I added,
God sent you to me, this evening. Humbly to ask a favour of
people who are on the point of knocking your brains out
sometimes produces good results. A little hot tea, I implored, without sugar or milk, to revive me. To grant such
a small favour to a pilgrim on the rocks was frankly a
temptation difficult to resist. Oh all right, he said, come
back to the house, you can dry yourself, before the fire.
But I cannot, I cannot, I cried, I have sworn to make a
bee-line to her! And to efface the bad impression created

by these words I took a florin from my pocket and gave
it to him. For your poor-box, I said. And I added, because
of the dark, A florin for your poor-box. It's a long way,
he said. God will go with you, I said. He thought it over.
Well he might. Above all nothing to eat, I said, no really,
I must not eat. Ah Moran, wily as a serpent, there was
never the like of old Moran. Of course, I would have preferred violence, but I dared not take the risk. Finally he
took himself off telling me to stay where I was. I do not
know what was in his mind. When I judged him at a safe
remove I closed the umbrella and set off in the opposite
direction, at right angles to the way I was going, in the
driving rain. That was how I spent a florin.

Now I may make an end.

I skirted the graveyard. It was night. Midnight perhaps.
The lane is steep, I laboured. A little wind was chasing the
clouds over the faint sky. It is a great thing to own a plot
in perpetuity, a very great thing indeed. If only that were the
only perpetuity. I came to the wicket. It was locked. Very
properly. But I could not open it. The key went into the hole,
but would not turn. Long disuse? A new lock? I burst it open.
I drew back to the other side of the lane and hurled myself at it. I had come home, as Youdi had commanded me.
In the end I got to my feet. What smelt so sweet? The lilacs?
The primroses perhaps. I went towards my hives. They
were there, as I feared. I lifted the top off one and laid it
on the ground. It was a little roof, with a sharp ridge, and
steep overhanging slopes. I put my hand in the hive, moved
it among the empty trays, felt along the bottom. It encountered, in a corner, a dry light ball. It crumbled under my
fingers. They had clustered together for a little warmth, to
try and sleep. I took out a handful. It was too dark to see,
I put it in my pocket. It weighed nothing. They had been
left out all winter, their honey taken away, without sugar.
Yes, now I may make an end. I did not go to the hen-
house. My hens were dead too, I knew they were dead. They
had not been killed in the same way, except the grey one
perhaps, that was the only difference. My bees, my hens,
I had deserted them. I went towards the house. It was in
darkness. The door was locked. I burst it open. Perhaps I
could have opened it, with one of my keys. I turned the

switch. No light. I went to the kitchen, to Martha's room.
No one. There is nothing more to tell. The house was empty.
The company had cut off the light. They have offered to
let me have it back. But I told them they could keep it.
That is the kind of man I have become. I went back to
the garden. The next day I looked at my handful of bees.
A little dust of annulets and wings. I found some letters,
at the foot of the stairs, in the box. A letter from Savory.
My son was well. He would be. Let us hear no more about
him. He has come back. He is sleeping. A letter from Youdi,
in the third person, asking for a report. He will get his report. It is summer again. This time a year ago I was setting
out. I am clearing out. One day I received a visit from Gaber.
He wanted the report. That's funny, I thought I was done
with people and talk. Call back, I said. One day I received
a visit from Father Ambrose. Is it possible! he said when
he saw me. I think he really liked me, in his own way. I
told him not to count on me any more. He began to talk.
He was right. Who is not right? I left him. I am clearing
out. Perhaps I shall meet Molloy. My knee is no better.
It is no worse either. I have crutches now. I shall go faster,
all will go faster. They will be happy days. I shall learn.
All there was to sell I have sold. But I had heavy debts. I
have been a man long enough, I shall not put up with it any
more, I shall not try any more. I shall never light this lamp
again. I am going to blow it out and go into the garden. I
think of the long May days, June days, when I lived in the
garden. One day I talked to Hanna. She gave me news of
Zulu, of the Elsner sisters. She knew who I was, she was
not afraid of me. She never went out, she disliked going
out. She talked to me from her window. The news was bad,
but might have been worse. There was a bright side. They
were lovely days. The winter had been exceptionally rigorous,
everybody said so. We had therefore a right to this superb
summer. I do not know if we had a right to it. My birds had
not been killed. They were wild birds. And yet quite trust-
ing. I recognized them and they seemed to recognize me.
But one never knows. Some were missing and some were
new. It tried to understand their language better. Without
having recourse to mine. They were the longest, loveliest days
of all the year. I lived in the garden. I have spoken of a

voice telling me things. I was getting to know it better now, to understand what it wanted. It did not use the words that Moran had been taught when he was little and that he in his turn had taught to his little one. So that at first I did not know what it wanted. But in the end I understood this language. I understood it, I understood it, all wrong perhaps. That is not what matters. It told me to write the report. Does this mean I am freer now than I was? I do not know. I shall learn. Then I went back into the house and wrote, It is midnight. The rain is beating on the windows. It was not midnight. It was not raining.

MALONE DIES

Translated from the French by the author

I shall soon be quite dead at last in spite of all. Perhaps next month. Then it will be the month of April or of May. For the year is still young, a thousand little signs tell me so. Perhaps I am wrong, perhaps I shall survive Saint John the Baptist's Day and even the Fourteenth of July, festival of freedom. Indeed I would not put it past me to pant on to the Transfiguration, not to speak of the Assumption. But I do not think so, I do not think I am wrong in saying that these rejoicings will take place in my absence, this year. I have that feeling, I have had it now for some days, and I credit it. But in what does it differ from those that have abused me ever since I was born? No, that is the kind of bait I do not rise to any more, my need for prettiness is gone. I could die to-day, if I wished, merely by making a little effort, if I could wish, if I could make an effort. But it is just as well to let myself die, quietly, without rushing things. Something must have changed. I will not weigh upon the balance any more, one way or the other. I shall be neutral and inert. No difficulty there. Throes are the only trouble, I must be on my guard against throes. But I am less given to them now, since coming here. Of course I still have my little fits of impatience, from time to time, I must be on my guard against them, for the next fortnight or three weeks. Without exaggeration to be sure, quietly crying and laughing, without working myself up into a state. Yes, I shall be natural at last, I shall suffer more, then less, without drawing any conclusions, I shall pay less heed to myself, I shall be neither hot nor cold any more, I shall be tepid, I shall die tepid, without enthusiasm. I shall not watch myself die, that would spoil everything. Have I watched myself live? Have I ever complained? Then why rejoice now? I am content, necessarily,

179

but not to the point of clapping my hands. I was always content, knowing I would be repaid. There he is now, my old debtor. Shall I then fall on his neck? I shall not answer any more questions. I shall even try not to ask myself any more. While waiting I shall tell myself stories, if I can. They will not be the same kind of stories as hitherto, that is all. They will be neither beautiful nor ugly, they will be calm, there will be no ugliness or beauty or fever in them any more, they will be almost lifeless, like the teller. What was that I said? It does not matter. I look forward to their giving me great satisfaction, some satisfaction. I am satisfied, there, I have enough, I am repaid, I need nothing more. Let me say before I go any further that I forgive nobody. I wish them all an atrocious life and then the fires and ice of hell and in the execrable generations to come an honoured name. Enough for this evening.

This time I know where I am going, it is no longer the ancient night, the recent night. Now it is a game, I am going to play. I never knew how to play, till now. I longed to, but I knew it was impossible. And yet I often tried. I turned on all the lights, I took a good look all round, I began to play with what I saw. People and things ask nothing better than to play, certain animals too. All went well at first, they all came to me, pleased that someone should want to play with them. If I said, Now I need a hunchback, immediately one came running, proud as punch of his fine hunch that was going to perform. It did not occur to him that I might have to ask him to undress. But it was not long before I found myself alone, in the dark. That is why I gave up trying to play and took to myself for ever shapelessness and speechlessness, incurious wondering, darkness, long stumbling with outstretched arms, hiding. Such is the earnestness from which, for nearly a century now, I have never been able to depart. From now on it will be different. I shall never do anything any more from now on but play. No, I must not begin with an exaggeration. But I shall play a great part of the time, from now on, the greater part, if I can. But perhaps I shall not succeed any better than hitherto. Perhaps as hitherto I shall find myself abandoned, in the dark, without anything to play with. Then I shall play with myself. To have been able to conceive such a plan is encouraging.

I must have thought about my time-table during the night. I think I shall be able to tell myself four stories, each one on a different theme. One about a man, another about a woman, a third about a thing and finally one about an animal, a bird probably. I think that is everything. Perhaps I shall put the man and the woman in the same story, there is so little difference between a man and a woman, between mine I mean. Perhaps I shall not have time to finish. On the other hand perhaps I shall finish too soon. There I am back at my old aporetics. Is that the word? I don't know. It does not matter if I do not finish. But if I finish too soon? That does not matter either. For then I shall speak of the things that remain in my possession, that is a thing I have always wanted to do. It will be a kind of inventory. In any case that is a thing I must leave to the very last moment, so as to be sure of not having made a mistake. In any case that is a thing I shall certainly do, no matter what happens. It will not take me more than a quarter of an hour at the most. That is to say it could take me longer, if I wished. But should I be short of time, at the last moment, then a brief quarter of an hour would be all I should need to draw up my inventory. My desire is henceforward to be clear, without being finical. I have always wanted that too. It is obvious I may suddenly expire, at any moment. Would it not then be better for me to speak of my possessions without further delay? Would not that be wiser? And then if necessary at the last moment correct any inaccuracies. That is what reason counsels. But reason has not much hold on me, just now. All things run together to encourage me. But can I really resign myself to the possibility of my dying without leaving an inventory behind? There I am back at my old quibbles. Presumably I can, since I intend to take the risk. All my life long I have put off this reckoning, saying, Too soon, too soon. Well it is still too soon. All my life long I have dreamt of the moment when, edified at last, in so far as one can be before all is lost, I might draw the line and make the tot. This moment seems now at hand. I shall not lose my head on that account. So first of all my stories and then, last of all, if all goes well, my inventory. And I shall begin, that they may plague me no more, with the man and woman. That will be the first story, there is not matter there for two. There will therefore be only three stories after all, that one, then the one about the animal, then the one about the thing, a stone probably. That is all very clear. Then I shall deal with my possessions. If after all that I am still alive I shall take the necessary steps to ensure my not having made a mistake. So much for that. I used not to know where I was going, but I knew I would arrive, I knew there would be an end to the long blind road. What half-truths, my God. No matter. It is playtime now. I find it hard to get used to that idea. The old fog calls. Now the case is reversed, the way well charted and little hope of coming to its end. But I have high hopes. What am I doing now, I wonder, losing time or gaining it? I have also decided to remind myself briefly of my present state before embarking on my stories. I think this is a mistake. It is a weakness. But I shall indulge in it. I shall play with all the more ardour afterwards. And it will be a pendant to the inventory. Aesthetics are therefore on my side, at least a certain kind of aesthetics. For I shall have to become earnest again to be able to speak of my possessions. There it is then divided into five, the time that remains. Into five what? I don't know. Everything divides into itself, I suppose. If I start trying to think again I shall make a mess of my decease. I must say there is something very attractive about such a prospect. But I am on my guard. For the past few days I have been finding something attractive about everything. To return to the five. Present state, three stories, inventory, there. An occasional interlude is to be feared. A full programme. I shall not deviate from it any further than I must. So much for that. I feel I am making a great mistake. No matter.

Present state. This room seems to be mine. I can find no other explanation to my being left in it. All this time. Unless it be at the behest of one of the powers that be. That is hardly likely. Why should the powers have changed in their attitude towards me? It is better to adopt the simplest explanation, even if it is not simple, even if it does not explain very much. A bright light is not necessary, a taper is all one needs to live in strangeness, if it faithfully burns. Perhaps I came in for the room on the death of whoever was in it before me. I enquire no further in any case. It is not a room in a hospital, or in a madhouse, I can feel that. I have listened

at different hours of the day and night and never heard anything suspicious or unusual, but always the peaceful sounds
of men at large, getting up, lying down, preparing food, coming and going, weeping and laughing, or nothing at all, no
sounds at all. And when I look out of the window it is clear
to me, from certain signs, that I am not in a house of rest
in any sense of the word. No, this is just a plain private room
apparently, in what appears to be a plain ordinary house. I do
not remember how I got here. In an ambulance perhaps,
a vehicle of some kind certainly. One day I found myself here,
in the bed. Having probably lost consciousness somewhere, I
benefit by a hiatus in my recollections, not to be resumed until
I recovered my senses, in this bed. As to the events that led
up to my fainting and to which I can hardly have been oblivious, at the time, they have left no discernible trace, on my
mind. But who has not experienced such lapses? They are
common after drunkenness. I have often amused myself with
trying to invent them, those same lost events. But without
succeeding in amusing myself really. But what is the last
thing I remember, I could start from there, before I came to
my senses again here? That too is lost. I was walking certainly, all my life I have been walking, except the first few
months and since I have been here. But at the end of the
day I did not know where I had been or what my thoughts
had been. What then could I be expected to remember, and
with what? I remember a mood. My young days were more
varied, such as they come back to me, in fits and starts. I
did not know my way about so well then. I have lived in a
kind of coma. The loss of consciousness for me was never
any great loss. But perhaps I was stunned with a blow, on
the head, in a forest perhaps, yes, now that I speak of a forest
I vaguely remember a forest. All that belongs to the past.
Now it is the present I must establish, before I am avenged.
It is an ordinary room. I have little experience of rooms, but
this one seems quite ordinary to me. The truth is, if I did
not feel myself dying, I could well believe myself dead,
expiating my sins, or in one of heaven's mansions. But I feel
at last that the sands are running out, which would not be
the case if I were in heaven, or in hell. Beyond the grave,
the sensation of being beyond the grave was stronger with
me six months ago. Had it been foretold to me that one day

I should feel myself living as I do to-day, I should have smiled.
It would not have been noticed, but I would have known I
was smiling. I remember them well, these last few days, they
have left me more memories than the thirty thousand odd
that went before. The reverse would have been less surprising.
When I have completed my inventory, if my death is not
ready for me then, I shall write my memoirs. That's funny,
I have made a joke. No matter. There is a cupboard I have
never looked into. My possessions are in a corner, in a little
heap. With my long stick I can rummage in them, draw
them to me, send them back. My bed is by the window. I lie
turned towards it most of the time. I see roofs and sky, a
glimpse of street too, if I crane. I do not see any fields or
hills. And yet they are near. But are they near? I don't know.
I do not see the sea either, but I hear it when it is high. I
can see into a room of the house across the way. Queer things
go on there sometimes, people are queer. Perhaps these are
abnormal. They must see me too, my big shaggy head up
against the window-pane. I never had so much hair as now,
nor so long, I say it without fear of contradiction. But at
night they do not see me, for I never have a light. I have
studied the stars a little here. But I cannot find my way about
among them. Gazing at them one night I suddenly saw myself
in London. Is it possible I got as far as London? And what
have stars to do with that city? The moon on the other hand
has grown familiar, I am well familiar now with her changes
of aspect and orbit, I know more or less the hours of the
night when I may look for her in the sky and the nights when
she will not come. What else? The clouds. They are varied,
very varied. And all sorts of birds. They come and perch on
the window-sill, asking for food! It is touching. They rap
on the window-pane, with their beaks. I never give them
anything. But they still come. What are they waiting for? They
are not vultures. Not only am I left here, but I am looked
after! This is how it is done now. The door half opens, a
hand puts a dish on the little table left there for that purpose,
takes away the dish of the previous day, and the door closes
again. This is done for me every day, at the same time
probably. When I want to eat I hook the table with my stick
and draw it to me. It is on castors, it comes squeaking and
lurching towards me. When I need it no longer I send it back

to its place by the door. It is soup. They must know I am
toothless. I eat it one time out of two, out of three, on an
average. When my chamber-pot is full I put it on the table,
beside the dish. Then I go twenty-four hours without a pot.
No, I have two pots. They have thought of everything. I am
naked in the bed, in the blankets, whose number I increase
and diminish as the seasons come and go. I am never hot,
never cold. I don't wash, but I don't get dirty. If I get dirty
somewhere I rub the part with my finger wet with spittle.
What matters is to eat and excrete. Dish and pot, dish and
pot, these are the poles. In the beginning it was different.
The woman came right into the room, bustled about, enquired
about my needs, my wants. I succeeded in the end in getting
them into her head, my needs and my wants. It was not easy.
She did not understand. Until the day I found the terms, the
accents, that fitted her. All that must be half imagination.
It was she who got me this long stick. It has a hook at one
end. Thanks to it I can control the furthest recesses of my
abode. How great is my debt to sticks! So great that I almost
forget the blows they have transferred to me. She is an old
woman. I don't know why she is good to me. Yes, let us
call it goodness, without quibbling. For her it is certainly
goodness. I believe her to be even older than I. But rather
less well preserved, in spite of her mobility. Perhaps she goes
with the room, in a manner of speaking. In that case she
does not call for separate study. But it is conceivable that
she does what she does out of sheer charity, or moved
with regard to me by a less general feeling of compassion or
affection. Nothing is impossible, I cannot keep on denying
it much longer. But it is more convenient to suppose that
when I came in for the room I came in for her too. All I
see of her now is the gaunt hand and part of the sleeve. Not
even that, not even that. Perhaps she is dead, having pre-
deceased me, perhaps now it is another's hand that lays and
clears my little table. I don't know how long I have been
here, I must have said so. All I know is that I was very old
already before I found myself here. I call myself an octo-
genarian, but I cannot prove it. Perhaps I am only a quin-
quagenarian, or a quadragenarian. It is ages since I counted
them, my years I mean. I know the year of my birth, I have
not forgotten that, but I do not know what year I have got

to now. But I think I have been here for some very considerable time. For there is nothing the various seasons can
do to me, within the shelter of these walls, that I do not
know. That is not to be learnt in one year or two. In a
flicker of my lids whole days have flown. Does anything
remain to be said? A few words about myself perhaps. My
body is what is called, unadvisedly perhaps, impotent. There
is virtually nothing it can do. Sometimes I miss not being
able to crawl around any more. But I am not much given
to nostalgia. My arms, once they are in position, can exert
a certain force. But I find it hard to guide them. Perhaps the
red nucleus has faded. I tremble a little, but only a little.
The groaning of the bedstead is part of my life, I would not
like it to cease, I mean I would not like it to decrease. It is
on my back, that is to say prostrate, no, supine, that I feel
best, least bony. I lie on my back, but my cheek is on the
pillow. I have only to open my eyes to have them begin again,
the sky and smoke of mankind. My sight and hearing are very
bad, on the vast main no light but reflected gleams. All my
senses are trained full on me, me. Dark and silent and stale,
I am no prey for them. I am far from the sounds of blood
and breath, immured. I shall not speak of my sufferings.
Cowering deep down among them I feel nothing. It is there
I die, unbeknown to my stupid flesh. That which is seen, that
which cries and writhes, my witless remains. Somewhere
in this turmoil thought struggles on, it too wide of the mark.
It too seeks me, as it always has, where I am not to be
found. It too cannot be quiet. On others let it wreak its dying
rage, and leave me in peace. Such would seem to be my
present state.

The man's name is Saposcat. Like his father's. Christian
name? I don't know. He will not need one. His friends call
him Sapo. What friends? I don't know, A few words about
the boy. This cannot be avoided.

He was a precocious boy. He was not good at his lessons,
neither could he see the use of them. He attended his classes
with his mind elsewhere, or blank.

He attended his classes with his mind elsewhere. He liked
sums, but not the way they were taught. What he liked was

the manipulation of concrete numbers. All calculation seemed
to him idle in which the nature of the unit was not specified.
He made a practice, alone and in company, of mental arithmetic. And the figures then marshalling in his mind thronged
it with colours and with forms.

What tedium.

He was the eldest child of poor and sickly parents. He often
heard them talk of what they ought to do in order to have
better health and more money. He was struck each time by
the vagueness of these palavers and not surprised that they
never led to anything. His father was a salesman, in a shop.
He used to say to his wife, I really must find work for the
evenings and the Saturday afternoon. He added, faintly, And
the Sunday. His wife would answer, But if you do any more
work you'll fall ill. And Mr. Saposcat had to allow that he would
indeed be ill-advised to forego his Sunday rest. These people
at least are grown up. But his health was not so poor that he
could not work in the evenings of the week and on the Saturday afternoon. At what, said his wife, work at what? Perhaps
secretarial work of some kind, he said. And who will look
after the garden? said his wife. The life of the Saposcats was
full of axioms, of which one at least established the criminal
absurdity of a garden without roses and with its paths and
lawns uncared for. I might perhaps grow vegetables, he said.
They cost less to buy, said his wife. Sapo marvelled at these
conversations. Think of the price of manure, said his mother.
And in the silence which followed Mr. Saposcat applied his
mind, with the earnestness he brought to everything he did,
to the high price of manure which prevented him from sup-
porting his family in greater comfort, while his wife made
ready to accuse herself, in her turn, of not doing all she might.
But she was easily persuaded that she could not do more
without exposing herself to the risk of dying before her time.
Think of the doctor's fees we save, said Mr. Saposcat. And
the chemist's bills, said his wife. Nothing remained but to
envisage a smaller house. But we are cramped as it is, said
Mrs. Saposcat. And it was an understood thing that they
would be more and more so with every passing year until the
day came when, the departure of the first-born compensating

the arrival of the new-born, a kind of equilibrium would be
attained. Then little by little the house would empty. And at
last they would be all alone, with their memories. It would
be time enough then to move. He would be pensioned off,
she at her last gasp. They would take a cottage in the country
where, having no further need of manure, they could afford
to buy it in cartloads. And their children, grateful for the
sacrifices made on their behalf, would come to their assistance. It was in this atmosphere of unbridled dream that these
conferences usually ended. It was as though the Saposcats
drew the strength to live from the prospect of their impotence.
But sometimes, before reaching that stage, they paused to
consider the case of their first-born. What age is he now?
asked Mr. Saposcat. His wife provided the information, it
being understood that this was of her province. She was
always wrong. Mr. Saposcat took over the erroneous figure,
murmuring it over and over to himself as though it were
a question of the rise in price of some indispensable com-
modity, such as butcher's meat. And at the same time he
sought in the appearance of his son some alleviation of what
he had just heard. Was it at least a nice sirloin? Sapo looked
at his father's face, sad, astonished, loving, disappointed,
confident in spite of all. Was it on the cruel flight of the years
he brooded, or on the time it was taking his son to command
a salary? Sometimes he stated wearily his regret that his son
should not be more eager to make himself useful about the
place. It is better for him to prepare his examinations, said
his wife. Starting from a given theme their minds laboured
in unison. They had no conversation properly speaking. They
made use of the spoken word in much the same way as the
guard of a train makes use of his flags, or of his lantern. Or
else they said, This is where we get down. And their son
once signalled, they wondered sadly if it was not the mark of
superior minds to fail miserably at the written paper and cover
themselves with ridicule at the viva voce. They were not always content to gape in silence at the same landscape. At
least his health is good, said Mr. Saposcat. Not all that, said
his wife. But no definite disease, said Mr. Saposcat. A nice
thing that would be, at his age, said his wife. They did not
know why he was committed to a liberal profession. That was
yet another thing that went without saying. It was therefore

impossible he should be unfitted for it. They thought of him as a doctor for preference. He will look after us when we are old, said Mrs. Saposcat. And her husband replied, I see him rather as a surgeon, as though after a certain age people were inoperable.

What tedium. And I call that playing. I wonder if I am not talking yet again about myself. Shall I be incapable, to the end, of lying on any other subject? I feel the old dark gathering, the solitude preparing, by which I know myself, and the call of that ignorance which might be noble and is mere poltroonery. Already I forget what I have said. That is not how to play. Soon I shall not know where Sapo comes from, nor what he hopes. Perhaps I had better abandon this story and go on to the second, or even the third, the one about the stone. No, it would be the same thing. I must simply be on my guard, reflecting on what I have said before I go on and stopping, each time disaster threatens, to look at myself as I am. That is just what I wanted to avoid. But there seems to be no other solution. After that mud-bath I shall be better able to endure a world unsullied by my presence. What a way to reason. My eyes, I shall open my eyes, look at the little heap of my possessions, give my body the old orders I know it cannot obey, turn to my spirit gone to rack and ruin, spoil my agony the better to live it out, for already from the world that parts at last its labia and lets me go.

I have tried to reflect on the beginning of my story. There are things I do not understand. But nothing to signify. I can go on.

Sapo had no friends — no, that won't do.

Sapo was on good terms with his little friends, though they did not exactly love him. The dolt is seldom solitary. He boxed and wrestled well, was fleet of foot, sneered at his teachers and sometimes even gave them impertinent answers. Fleet of foot? Well well. Pestered with questions one day he cried, Haven't I told you I don't know! Much of his free time he spent confined in school doing impositions and often he did not get home before eight o'clock

at night. He submitted with philosophy to these vexations.
But he would not let himself be struck. The first time an
exasperated master threatened him with a cane, Sapo snatched
it from his hand and threw it out of the window, which was
closed, for it was winter. This was enough to justify his
expulsion. But Sapo was not expelled, either then or later.
I must try and discover, when I have time to think about
it quietly, why Sapo was not expelled when he so richly
deserved to be. For I want as little as possible of darkness
in his story. A little darkness, in itself, at the time, is nothing. You think no more about it and you go on. But I
know what darkness is, it accumulates, thickens, then suddenly bursts and drowns everything.

I have not been able to find out why Sapo was not expelled. I shall have to leave this question open. I try not
to be glad. I shall make haste to put a safe remove between
him and this incomprehensible indulgence, I shall make him
live as though he had been punished according to his deserts.
We shall turn our backs on this little cloud, but we shall
not let it out of our sight. It will not cover the sky without
our knowing, we shall not suddenly raise our eyes, far from
help, far from shelter, to a sky as black as ink. That is
what I have decided. I see no other solution. It is the best
I can do.

At the age of fourteen he was a plump rosy boy. His
wrists and ankles were thick, which made his mother say
that one day he would be even bigger than his father.
Curious deduction. But the most striking thing about him
was his big round head horrid with flaxen hair as stiff
and straight as the bristles of a brush. Even his teachers could
not help thinking he had a remarkable head and they were
all the more irked by their failure to get anything into it.
His father would say, when in good humour, One of these
days he will astonish us all. It was thanks to Sapo's skull
that he was enabled to hazard this opinion and, in defiance
of the facts and against his better judgment, to revert to it
from time to time. But he could not endure the look in
Sapo's eyes and went out of his way not to meet it. He
has your eyes, his wife would say. Then Mr. Saposcat chafed

to be alone, in order to inspect his eyes in the mirror. They were palest blue. Just a shade lighter, said Mrs. Saposcat.

Sapo loved nature, took an interest

This is awful.

Sapo loved nature, took an interest in animals and plants and willingly raised his eyes to the sky, day and night. But he did not know how to look at all these things, the looks he rained upon them taught him nothing about them. He confused the birds with one another, and the trees, and could not tell one crop from another crop. He did not associate the crocus with the spring nor the chrysanthemum with Michaelmas. The sun, the moon, the planets and the stars did not fill him with wonder. He was sometimes tempted by the knowledge of these strange things, sometimes beautiful, that he would have about him all his life. But from his ignorance of them he drew a kind of joy, as from all that went to swell the murmur, You are a simpleton. But he loved the flight of the hawk and could distinguish it from all others. He would stand rapt, gazing at the long pernings, the quivering poise, the wings lifted for the plummet drop, the wild reascent, fascinated by such extremes of need, of pride, of patience and solitude.

I shall not give up yet. I have finished my soup and sent back the little table to its place by the door. A light has just gone on in one of the two windows of the house across the way. By the two windows I mean those I can see always, without raising my head from the pillow. By this I do not mean the two windows in their entirely, but one in its entirety and part of the other. It is in this latter that the light has just gone on. For an instant I could see the woman coming and going. Then she drew the curtain. Until tomorrow I shall not see her again, her shadow perhaps from time to time. She does not always draw the curtain. The man has not yet come home. Home. I have demanded certain movements of my legs and even feet. I know them well and could feel the effort they made to obey. I have lived with them that little space of time, filled with drama, between the message received and the piteous response. To old dogs the hour comes when, whistled by their master setting forth

with his stick at dawn, they cannot spring after him. Then
they stay in their kennel, or in their basket, though they are
not chained, and listen to the steps dying away. The man
too is sad. But soon the pure air and the sun console him,
he thinks no more about his old companion, until evening.
The lights in his house bid him welcome home and a feeble
barking makes him say, It is time I had him destroyed.
There's a nice passage. Soon it will be even better, soon things
will be better. I am going to rummage a little in my possessions. Then I shall put my head under the blankets. Then
things will be better, for Sapo and for him who follows
him, who asks nothing but to follow in his footsteps, by
clear and endurable ways.

Sapo's phlegm, his silent ways, were not of a nature to
please. In the midst of tumult, at school and at home, he
remained motionless in his place, often standing, and gazed
straight before him with eyes as pale and unwavering as a
gull's. People wondered what he could brood on thus, hour
after hour. His father supposed him a prey to the first
flutterings of sex. At sixteen I was the same, he would say.
At sixteen you were earning your living,· said his wife. So
I was, said Mr. Saposcat. But in the view of his teachers
the signs were rather those of besottedness pure and simple.
Sapo dropped his jaw and breathed through his mouth.
It is not easy to see in virtue of what this expression is
incompatible with erotic thoughts. But indeed his dream
was less of girls than of himself, his own life, his life to be.
That is more than enough to stop up the nose of a lucid
and sensitive boy, and cause his jaw temporarily to sag.
But it is time I took a little rest, for safety's sake.

I don't like those gull's eyes. They remind me of an
old shipwreck, I forget which. I know it is a small thing.
But I am easily frightened now. I know those little phrases
that seem so innocuous and, once you let them in, pollute
the whole of speech. *Nothing is more real than nothing.*
They rise up out of the pit and know no rest until they drag
you down into its dark. But I am on my guard now.

Then he was sorry he had not learnt the art of thinking,

beginning by folding back the second and third fingers the better to put the index on the subject and the little finger on the verb, in the way his teacher had shown him, and sorry he could make no meaning of the babel raging in his head, the doubts, desires, imaginings and dreads. And a little less well endowed with strength and courage he too would have abandoned and despaired of ever knowing what manner of being he was, and how he was going to live, and lived vanquished, blindly, in a mad world, in the midst of strangers.

From these reveries he emerged tired and pale, which confirmed his father's impression that he was the victim of lascivious speculations. He ought to play more games, he would say. We are getting on, getting on. They told me he would be a good athlete, said Mr. Saposcat, and now he is not on any team. His studies take up all his time, said Mrs. Saposcat. And he is always last, said Mr. Saposcat. He is fond of walking, said Mrs. Saposcat, the long walks in the country do him good. Then Mr. Saposcat wried his face, at the thought of his son's long solitary walks and the good they did him. And sometimes he was carried away to the point of saying, It might have been better to have put him to a trade. Whereupon it was usual, though not compulsory, for Sapo to go away, while his mother exclaimed, Oh Adrian, you have hurt his feelings!

We are getting on. Nothing is less like me than this patient, reasonable child, struggling all alone for years to shed a little light upon himself, avid of the least gleam, a stranger to the joys of darkness. Here truly is the air I needed, a lively tenuous air, far from the nourishing murk that is killing me. I shall never go back into this carcass except to find out its time. I want to be there a little before the plunge, close for the last time the old hatch on top of me, say goodbye to the holds where I have lived, go down with my refuge. I was always sentimental. But between now and then I have time to frolic, ashore, in the brave company I have always longed for, always searched for, and which would never have me. Yes, now my mind is easy, I know the game is won, I lost them all till now, but it's the last that counts. A very fine achievement I must say, or rather would, if I did not fear to contradict myself. Fear to con-

tradict myself! If this continues it is myself I shall lose
and the thousand ways that lead there. And I shall resemble
the wretches famed in fable, crushed beneath the weight
of their wish come true. And I even feel a strange desire
come over me, the desire to know what I am doing, and
why. So I near the goal I set myself in my young days and
which prevented me from living. And on the threshold of
being no more I succeed in being another. Very pretty.

The summer holidays. In the morning he took private
lessons. You'll have us in the poorhouse, said Mrs. Saposcat. It's a good investment, said Mr. Saposcat. In the afternoon he left the house, with his books under his arm, on
the pretext that he worked better in the open air, no,
without a word. Once clear of the town he hid his books
under a stone and ranged the countryside. It was the season
when the labours of the peasants reach their paroxysm and the
long bright days are too short for all there is to do. And
often they took advantage of the moon to make a last
journey between the fields, perhaps far away, and the barn
or threshing floor, or to overhaul the machines and get them
ready for the impending dawn. The impending dawn.

I fell asleep. But I do not want to sleep. There is no
time for sleep in my time-table. I do not want — no, I
have no explanations to give. Coma is for the living. The
living. They were always more than I could bear, all, no,
I don't mean that, but groaning with tedium I watched them
come and go, then I killed them, or took their place, or
fled. I feel within me the glow of that old frenzy, but I
know it will set me on fire no more. I stop everything and
wait. Sapo stands on one leg, motionless, his strange eyes
closed. The turmoil of the day freezes in a thousand absurd
postures. The little cloud drifting before their glorious sun
will darken the earth as long as I please.

Live and invent. I have tried. I must have tried. Invent.
It is not the word. Neither is live. No matter. I have tried.
While within me the wild beast of earnestness padded up
and down, roaring, ravening, rending. I have done that. And
all alone, well hidden, played the clown, all alone, hour after
hour, motionless, often standing, spellbound, groaning. That's

right, groan. I couldn't play. I turned till I was dizzy,
clapped my hands, ran, shouted, saw myself winning, saw
myself losing, rejoicing, lamenting. Then suddenly I threw
myself on the playthings, if there were any, or on a child,
to change his joy to howling, or I fled, to hiding. The grown-
ups pursued me, the just, caught me, beat me, hounded
me back into the round, the game, the jollity. For I was
already in the toils of earnestness. That has been my disease.
I was born grave as others syphilitic. And gravely I struggled
to be grave no more, to live, to invent, I know what I
mean. But at each fresh attempt I lost my head, fled to my
shadows as to sanctuary, to his lap who can neither live nor
suffer the sight of others living. I say living without knowing
what it is. I tried to live without knowing what I was trying.
Perhaps I have lived after all, without knowing. I wonder
why I speak of all this. Ah yes, to relieve the tedium. Live
and cause to live. There is no use indicting words, they are
no shoddier than what they peddle. After the fiasco, the
solace, the repose, I began again, to try and live, cause to
live, be another, in myself, in another. How false all this
is. No time now to explain. I began again. But little by little
with a different aim, no longer in order to succeed, but in
order to fail. Nuance. What I sought, when I struggled out
of my hole, then aloft through the stinging air towards an
inaccessible boon, was the rapture of vertigo, the letting go,
the fall, the gulf, the relapse to darkness, to nothingness, to
earnestness, to home, to him waiting for me always, who
needed me and whom I needed, who took me in his arms
and told me to stay with him always, who gave me his place
and watched over me, who suffered every time I left him,
whom I have often made suffer and seldom contented, whom
I have never seen. There I am forgetting myself again.
My concern is not with me, but with another, far beneath me
and whom I try to envy, of whose crass adventures I can
now tell at last, I don't know how. Of myself I could never
tell, any more than live or tell of others. How could I
have, who never tried? To show myself now, on the point
of vanishing, at the same time as the stranger, and by the
same grace, that would be no ordinary last straw. Then live,
long enough to feel, behind my closed eyes, other eyes close.
What an end.

The market. The inadequacy of the exchanges between rural and urban areas had not escaped the excellent youth. He had mustered, on this subject, the following considerations, some perhaps close to, others no doubt far from, the truth.

In his country the problem — no, I can't do it.

The peasants. His visits to. I can't. Assembled in the farmyard they watched him depart, on stumbling, wavering feet, as though they scarcely felt the ground. Often he stopped, stood tottering a moment, then suddenly was off again, in a new direction. So he went, limp, drifting, as though tossed by the earth. And when, after a halt, he started off again, it was like a big thistledown plucked by the wind from the place where it had settled. There is a choice of images.

I have rummaged a little in my things, sorting them out and drawing them over to me, to look at them. I was not far wrong in thinking that I knew them off, by heart, and could speak of them at any moment, without looking at them. But I wanted to make sure. It was well I did. For now I know that the image of these objects, with which I have lulled myself till now, though accurate in the main, was not completely so. And I should be sorry to let slip this unique occasion which seems to offer me the possibility of something suspiciously like a true statement at last. I might feel I had failed in my duty! I want this matter to be free from all trace of approximativeness. I want, when the great day comes, to be in a position to enounce clearly, without addition or omission, all that its interminable prelude had brought me and left me in the way of chattels personal. I presume it is an obsession.

I see then I had attributed to myself certain objects no longer in my possession, as far as I can see. But might they not have rolled behind a piece of furniture? That would surprise me. A boot, for example, can a boot roll behind a piece of furniture? And yet I see only one boot. And behind what pieces of furniture? In this room, to the best of my knowledge, there is only one piece of furniture capable of intervening between me and my possessions, I refer to the cupboard. But it so cleaves to the wall, to the two walls, for it stands in the corner, that it seems part of

them. It may be objected that my button-boot, for it was
a kind of button-boot, is in the cupboard. I thought of that.
But I have gone through it, my stick has gone through the
cupboard, opening the doors, the drawers, for the first
time perhaps, and rooting everywhere. And the cupboard,
far from containing my boot, is empty. No, I am now
without this boot, just as I am now without certain other
objects of less value, which I thought I had preserved, among
them a zinc ring that shone like silver. I note on the other
hand, in the heap, the presence of two or three objects I
had quite forgotten and one of which at least, the bowl of
a pipe, strikes no chord in my memory. I do not remember
ever having smoked a tobacco-pipe. I remember the soap-pipe
with which, as a child, I used to blow bubbles, an odd bubble.
Never mind, this bowl is now mine, wherever it comes from.
A number of my treasures are derived from the same source.
I also discovered a little packet tied up in age-yellowed
newspaper. It reminds me of something, but of what? I
drew it over beside the bed and felt it with the knob of my
stick. And my hand understood, it understood softness and
lightness, better I think than if it had touched the thing
directly, fingering it and weighing it in its palm. I resolved,
I don't know why, not to undo it. I sent it back into the
corner, with the rest. I shall speak of it again perhaps, when
the time comes. I shall say, I can hear myself already, Item,
a little packet, soft, and light as a feather, tied up in newspaper. It will be my little mystery, all my own. Perhaps it is
a lakh of rupees. Or a lock of hair.

I told myself too that I must make better speed. True
lives do not tolerate this excess of circumstance. It is
there the demon lurks, like the gonococcus in the folds
of the prostrate. My time is limited. It is thence that one
fine day, when all nature smiles and shines, the rack lets
loose its black unforgettable cohorts and sweeps away the
blue for ever. My situation is truly delicate. What fine
things, what momentous things, I am going to miss through
fear, fear of falling back into the old error, fear of not
finishing in time, fear of revelling, for the last time, in a
last outpouring of misery, impotence and hate. The forms
are many in which the unchanging seeks relief from its
formlessness. Ah yes, I was always subject to the deep

thought, especially in the spring of the year. That one had
been nagging at me for the past five minutes. I venture to
hope there will be no more, of that depth. After all it is
not important not to finish, there are worse things than
velleities. But is that the point? Quite likely. All I ask is that
the last of mine, as long as it lasts, should have living for
its theme, that is all, I know what I mean. If it begins to
run short of life I shall feel it. All I ask is to know, before
I abandon him whose life has so well begun, that my death
and mine alone prevents him from living on, from winning,
losing, joying, suffering, rotting and dying, and that even
had I lived he would have waited, before he died, for his
body to be dead. That is what you might call taking a reef
in your sails.

My body does not yet make up its mind. But I fancy
it weighs heavier on the bed, flattens and spreads. My
breath, when it comes back, fills the room with its din,
though my chest moves no more than a sleeping child's.
I open my eyes and gaze unblinkingly and long at the
night sky. So a tiny tot I gaped, first at the novelties, then
at the antiquities. Between it and me the pane, misted and
smeared with the filth of years. I should like to breathe on
it, but it is too far away. It is such a night as Kasper David
Friedrich loved, tempestuous and bright. That name that
comes back to me, those names. The clouds scud, tattered
by the wind, across a limpid ground. If I had the patience
to wait I would see the moon. But I have not. Now that I
have looked I hear the wind. I close my eyes and it mingles
with my breath. Words and images run riot in my head,
pursuing, flying, clashing, merging, endlessly. But beyond
this tumult there is a great calm, and a great indifference,
never really to be troubled by anything again. I turn a
little on my side, press my mouth against the pillow, and
my nose, crush against the pillow my old hairs now no
doubt as white as snow, pull the blanket over my head. I
feel, deep down in my trunk, I cannot be more explicit,
pains that seem new to me. I think they are chiefly in my
back. They have a kind of rhythm, they even have a kind
of little tune. They are bluish. How bearable all that is,
my God. My head is almost facing the wrong way, like a

bird's. I part my lips, now I have the pillow in my mouth.
I have, I have. I suck. The search for myself is ended. I
am buried in the world, I knew I would find my place there
one day, the old world cloisters me, victorious. I am happy,
I knew I would be happy one day. But I am not wise.
For the wise thing now would be to let go, at this instant
of happiness. And what do I do? I go back again to the
light, to the fields I so longed to love, to the sky all astir
with little white clouds as white and light as snowflakes,
to the life I could never manage, through my own fault
perhaps, through pride, or pettiness, but I don't think so.
The beasts are at pasture, the sun warms the rocks and makes
them glitter. Yes, I leave my happiness and go back to the
race of men too, they come and go, often with burdens.
Perhaps I have judged them ill, but I don't think so, I have
not judged them at all. All I want now is to make a last
effort to understand, to begin to understand, how such
creatures are possible. No, it is not a question of understanding. Of what then? I don't know. Here I go none the
less, mistakenly. Night, storm and sorrow, and the catalepsies
of the soul, this time I shall see that they are good. The
last word is not yet said between me and — yes the last
word is said. Perhaps I simply want to hear it said again.
Just once again. No, I want nothing.

The Lamberts. The Lamberts found it difficult to live, I
mean to make ends meet. There was the man, the woman
and two children, a boy and a girl. There at least is something that admits of no controversy. The father was known
as Big Lambert, and big he was indeed. He had married
his young cousin and was still with her. This was his third
or fourth marriage. He had other children here and there,
grown men and women imbedded deep in life, hoping for
nothing more, from themselves or from others. They helped
him, each one according to his means, or the humour of
the moment, out of gratitude towards him but for whom
they had never seen the light of day, or saying, with indulgence, If it had not been he it would have been someone else. Big Lambert had not a tooth in his head and smoked
his cigarettes in a cigarette holder, while regretting his pipe.
He was highly thought of as a bleeder and disjointer of

pigs and greatly sought after, I exaggerate, in that capacity.
For his fee was lower than the butcher's, and he had even
been known to demand no more, in return for his services,
than a lump of gammon or a pig's cheek. How plausible
all that is. He often spoke of his father with respect and
tenderness. His like will not be seen again, he used to say,
once I am gone. He must have said this in other words. His
great days then fell in December and January, and from
February onwards he waited impatiently for the return of
that season, the principal event of which is unquestionably
the Saviour's birth, in a stable, while wondering if he would
be spared till then. Then he would set forth, hugging under
his arm, in their case, the great knives so lovingly whetted
before the fire the night before, and in his pocket, wrapped
in paper, the apron destined to protect his Sunday suit
while he worked. And at the thought that he, Big Lambert,
was on his way towards that distant homestead where all
was in readiness for his coming, and that in spite of his
great age he was still needed, and his methods preferred to
those of younger men, then his old heart exulted. From these
expeditions he reached home late in the night, drunk and
exhausted by the long road and the emotions of the day.
And for days afterwards he could speak of nothing but
the pig he had just dispatched, I would say into the other
world if I was not aware that pigs have none but this,
to the great affliction of his family. But they did not dare
protest, for they feared him. Yes, at an age when most
people cringe and cower, as if to apologize for still being
present, Lambert was feared and in a position to do as he
pleased. And even his young wife had abandoned all hope
of bringing him to heel, by means of her cunt, that trump
card of young wives. For she knew what he would do to her
if she did not open it to him. And he even insisted on her
making things easy for him, in ways that often appeared
to her exorbitant. And at the least show of rebellion on her
part he would run to the wash-house and come back with
the beetle and beat her until she came round to a better
way of thinking. All this by the way. And to return to our
pigs, Lambert continued to expatiate, to his near and dear
ones, of an evening, while the lamp burned low, on the
specimen he had just slaughtered, until the day he was sum-

moned to slaughter another. Then all his conversation was of this new pig, so unlike the other in every respect, so quite unlike, and yet at bottom the same. For all pigs are alike, when you get to know their little ways, struggle, squeal, bleed, squeal, struggle, bleed, squeal and faint away, in more or less the same way exactly, a way that is all their own and could never be imitated by a lamb, for example, or a kid. But once March was out Big Lambert recovered his calm and became his silent self again.

The son, or heir, was a great strapping lad with terrible teeth.

The farm. The farm was in a hollow, flooded in winter and in summer burnt to a cinder. The way to it lay through a fine meadow. But this fine meadow did not belong to the Lamberts, but to other peasants living at a distance. There jonquils and narcissi bloomed in extraordinary profusion, at the appropriate season. And there at nightfall, stealthily, Big Lambert turned loose his goats.

Strange to say this gift that Lambert possessed when it came to sticking pigs seemed of no help to him when it came to rearing them, and it was seldom his own exceeded nine stone. Clapped into a tiny sty on the day of its arrival, in the month of April, it remained there until the day of its death, on Christmas Eve. For Lambert persisted in dreading for his pigs, though every passing year proved him wrong, the thinning effects of exercise. Daylight and fresh air he dreaded for them too. And it was finally a weak pig, blind and lean, that he laid on its back in the box, having tied its legs, and killed, indignantly but without haste, upbraiding it the while for its ingratitude, at the top of his voice. For he could not or would not understand that the pig was not to blame, but he himself, who had coddled it unduly. And he persisted in his error.

Dead world, airless, waterless. That's it, reminisce. Here and there, in the bed of a crater, the shadow of a withered lichen. And nights of three hundred hours. Dearest of lights, wan, pitted, least fatuous of lights. That's it, babble. How long can it have lasted? Five minutes? Ten minutes? Yes, no more, not much more. But my sliver of sky is silvery with it yet. In the old days I used to count, up to three hundred, four hundred, and with other things too, the showers, the bells,

the chatter of the sparrows at dawn, or with nothing, for
no reason, for the sake of counting, and then I divided, by
sixty. That passed the time, I was time, I devoured the world.
Not now, any more. A man changes. As he gets on.

In the filthy kitchen, with its earth floor, Sapo had his place,
by the window. Big Lambert and his son left their work,
came and shook his hand, then went away, leaving him with
the mother and the daughter. But they too had their work, they
too went away and left him, alone. There was so much work,
so little time, so few hands. The woman, pausing an instant
between two tasks, or in the midst of one, flung up her arms
and, in the same breath, unable to sustain their great weight,
let them fall again. Then she began to toss them about in a
way difficult to describe, and not easy to understand. The
movements resembled those, at once frantic and slack, of an
arm shaking a duster, or a rag, to rid it of its dust. And so
rapid was the trepidation of the limp, empty hands that there
seemed to be four or five at the end of each arm, instead of
the usual one. At the same time angry unanswerable questions,
such as, What's the use? fell from her lips. Her hair came
loose and fell about her face. It was thick, grey and dirty,
for she had no time to tend it, and her face was pale and
thin and as though gouged with worry and its attendant rancours. The bosom — no, what matters is the head and then
the hands it calls to its help before all else, that clasp, wring,
then sadly resume their labour, lifting the old inert objects
and changing their position, bringing them closer together
and moving them further apart. But this pantomime and these
ejaculations were not intended for any living person. For
every day and several times a day she gave way to them,
within doors and without. Then she little cared whether she
was observed or not, whether what she was doing was urgent
or could wait, no, but she dropped everything and began to
cry out and gesticulate, the last of all the living as likely as not
and dead to what was going on about her. Then she fell silent
and stood stockstill a moment, before resuming whatever it
was she had abandoned or setting about some new task. Sapo
remained alone, by the window, the bowl of goat's milk on
the table before him, forgotten. It was summer. The room
was dark in spite of the door and window open on the great

outer light. Through these narrow openings, far apart, the
light poured, lit up a little space, then died, undiffused. It had
no steadfastness, no assurance of lasting as long as day lasted.
But it entered at every moment, renewed from without,
entered and died at every moment, devoured by the dark.
And at the least abatement of the inflow the room grew
darker and darker until nothing in it was visible any more.
For the dark had triumphed. And Sapo, his face turned
towards an earth so resplendent that it hurt his eyes, felt at
his back and all about him the unconquerable dark, and it
licked the light on his face. Sometimes abruptly he turned
to face it, letting it envelop and pervade him, with a kind
of relief. Then he heard more clearly the sounds of those at
work, the daughter calling to her goats, the father cursing
his mule. But silence was in the heart of the dark, the silence
of dust and the things that would never stir, if left alone.
And the ticking of the invisible alarm-clock was as the voice
of that silence which, like the dark, would one day triumph
too. And then all would be still and dark and all things at
rest for ever at last. Finally he took from his pocket the few
poor gifts he had brought, laid them on the table and went.
But it sometimes happened, before he decided to go, before
he went rather, for there was no decision, that a hen, taking
advantage of the open door, would venture into the room. No
sooner had she crossed the threshold than she paused, one leg
hooked up under her breech, her head on one side, blinking,
anxious. Then, reassured, she advanced a little further, jerkily,
with concertina neck. It was a grey hen, perhaps the grey
hen. Sapo got to know her well and, it seemed to him, to
be well known by her. If he rose to go she did not fly into
a flutter. But perhaps there were several hens, all grey and
so alike in other respects that Sapo's eye, avid of resem-
blances, could not tell between them. Sometimes she was
followed by a second, a third and even a fourth, bearing
no likeness to her, and but little to one another, in the matter
of plumage and entasis. These showed more confidence than
the grey, who had led the way and come to no harm. They
shone an instant in the light, grew dimmer and dimmer as
they advanced, and finally vanished. Silent at first, fearing
to betray their presence, they began gradually to scratch
and cluck, for contentment, and to relax their soughing

feathers. But often the grey hen came alone, or one of the
grey hens if you prefer, for that is a thing that will never be
known, though it might well have been, without much trouble.
For all that was necessary, in order that it might be known
whether there was only one grey hen or more than one, was
for someone to be present when all the hens came running
towards Mrs. Lambert as she cried, Tweet! Tweet!, and
banged on an old tin with an old spoon. But after all what
use would that have been? For it was quite possible there
were several grey hens, and yet only one in the habit of coming to the kitchen. And yet the experiment was worth making.
For it was quite possible there was only one grey hen, even
at feeding-time. Which would have clinched the matter. And
yet that is a thing that will never be known. For among those
who must have known, some are dead and the others have
forgotten. And the day when it was urgent for Sapo to have
this point cleared up, and his mind set at rest, it was too
late. Then he was sorry he had not understood, in time to
profit by it, the importance that those hours were one day to
assume, for him, those long hours in that old kitchen where,
neither quite indoors nor quite out of doors, he waited to be
on his feet again, and in motion, and while waiting noted
many things, among them this big, anxious, ashen bird,
poised irresolute on the bright threshold, then clucking and
clawing behind the range and fidgeting her atrophied wings,
soon to be sent flying with a broom and angry cries and soon
to return, cautiously, with little hesitant steps, stopping often
to listen, opening and shutting her little bright black eyes.
And so he went, all unsuspecting, with the fond impression of
having been present at everyday scenes of no import. He
stooped to cross the threshold and saw before him the well,
with its winch, chain and bucket, and often too a long line
of tattered washing, swaying and drying in the sun. He went
by the little path he had come by, along the edge of the
meadow in the shadow of the great trees that bordered the
stream, its bed a chaos of gnarled roots, boulders, and baked
mud. And so he went, often unnoticed, in spite of his strange
walk, his halts and sudden starts. Or the Lamberts saw him,
from far off or from near by, or some of them from far off
and the others from near by, suddenly emerge from behind
the washing and set off down the path. Then they did not

try to detain him or even call goodbye, unresentful at his
leaving them in a way that seemed so lacking in friendliness,
for they knew he meant no harm. Or if at the time they could
not help feeling a little hurt, this feeling was quite dispelled
a little later, when they found on the kitchen-table the
crumpled paper-bag containing a few little articles of haber-
dashery. And these humble presents, but oh how useful, and
this oh so delicate way of giving, disarmed them too at the
sight of the bowl of goat's milk only half emptied, or left
untouched, and prevented them from regarding this as an
affront, in the way tradition required. But it would appear
on reflection that Sapo's departure can seldom have escaped
them. For at the least movement within sight of their land,
were it only that of a little bird alighting or taking to wing,
they raised their heads and stared with wide eyes. And even
on the road, of which segments were visible more than a mile
away, nothing could happen without their knowledge, and
they were able not only to identify all those who passed along
it and whose remoteness reduced them to the size of a pin's
head, but also to divine whence they were coming, where they
were going, and for what purpose. Then they cried the news
to one another, for they often worked at a great distance
apart, or they exchanged signals, all erect and turned towards
the event, for it was one, before bowing themselves down to
the earth again. And at the first spell of rest taken in common,
about the table or elsewhere, each one gave his version of
what had passed and listened to those of the others. And
if at first they were not in agreement about what they had
seen, they talked it over doggedly until they were, in agreement I mean, or until they resigned themselves to never being
so. It was therefore difficult for Sapo to glide away unseen,
even in the deep shadow of the trees that bordered the stream,
even supposing him to have been capable of gliding, for his
movements were rather those of one floundering in a quag.
And all raised their heads and watched him as he went, then
looked at one another, before stooping to the earth again.
And on each face bent to the earth there played perhaps a
little smile, a little rictus rather, but without malice, each
wondering perhaps if the others felt the same thing and making the resolve to ask them, at their next meeting. But the
face of Sapo as he stumbled away, now in the shadow of

the venerable trees he could not name, now in the brightness of the waving meadow, so erratic was his course, the face of Sapo was always grave, or rather expressionless. And when he halted it was not the better to think, or the closer to pore upon his dream, but simply because the voice had ceased that told him to go on. Then with his pale eyes he stared down at the earth, blind to its beauty, and to its utility, and to the little wild many-coloured flowers happy among the crops and weeds. But these stations were short-lived, for he was still young. And of a sudden he is off again, on his wanderings, passing from light to shadow, from shadow to light, unheedingly.

When I stop, as just now, the noises begin again, strangely loud, those whose turn it is. So that I seem to have again the hearing of my boyhood. Then in my bed, in the dark, on stormy nights, I could tell from one another, in the outcry without, the leaves, the boughs, the groaning trunks, even the grasses and the house that sheltered me. Each tree had its own cry, just as no two whispered alike, when the air was still. I heard afar the iron gates clashing and dragging at their posts and the wind rushing between their bars. There was nothing, not even the sand on the paths, that did not utter its cry. The still nights too, still as the grave as the saying is, were nights of storm for me, clamorous with countless pantings. These I amused myself with identifying, as I lay there. Yes, I got great amusement, when young, from their so-called silence. The sound I liked best had nothing noble about it. It was the barking of the dogs, at night, in the clusters of hovels up in the hills, where the stone-cutters lived, like generations of stone-cutters before them. It came down to me where I lay, in the house in the plain, wild and soft, at the limit of earshot, soon weary. The dogs of the valley replied with their gross bay all fangs and jaws and foam. From the hills another joy came down, I mean the brief scattered lights that sprang up on their slopes at night-fall, merging in blurs scarcely brighter than the sky, less bright than the stars, and which the palest moon extinguished. They were things that scarcely were, on the confines of silence and dark, and soon ceased. So I reason now, at my ease. Standing before my high window I gave myself to them, waiting for them to end, for my joy to end, straining towards the joy of ended joy. But our business at the moment is less with these futilities than with my ears from which there spring two impetuous tufts of no doubt yellow hair, yellowed by wax and lack of care, and so long that the lobes are hidden. I note then, without emotion, that of late their hearing seems to have improved. Oh not that I was ever even incompletely deaf. But for a long time now I have been hearing things confusedly. There I go again. What I mean is possibly this, that the noises of the world, so various in themselves and which I used to be so clever at distinguishing from one another, had been dinning at me for so long, always the same old noises, as gradually to have merged into a single noise, so that all I heard was one vast continuous buzzing. The volume of sound perceived remained no doubt the same, I had simply lost the faculty of decomposing it. The noises of nature, of mankind and even my own, were all jumbled together in one and the same unbridled gibberish. Enough. I would willingly attribute part of my shall I say my misfortunes to this disordered sense were I not unfortunately rather inclined to look upon it as a blessing. Misfortunes, blessings, I have no time to pick my words, I am in a hurry to be done. And yet no, I am in no hurry. Decidedly this evening I shall say nothing that is not false, I mean nothing that is not calculated to leave me in doubt as to my real intentions. For it is evening, even night, one of the darkest I can remember, I have a short memory. My little finger glides before my pencil across the page and gives warning, falling over the edge, that the end of the line is near. But in the other direction, I mean of course vertically, I have nothing to guide me. I did not want to write, but I had to resign myself to it in the end. It is in order to know where I have got to, where he has got to. At first I did not write, I just said the thing. Then I forgot what I had said. A minimum of memory is indispensible, if one is to live really. Take his family, for example, I really know practically nothing about his family any more. But that does not worry me, there is a record of it somewhere. It is the one way to keep an eye on him. But as far as I myself am concerned the same necessity does not arise, or does it? And yet I write about myself with the same pencil and in the same exercise-book as about him. It is because it is no longer

I, I must have said so long ago, but another whose life is
just beginning. It is right that he too should have his little
chronicle, his memories, his reason, and be able to recognize
the good in the bad, the bad in the worst, and so grow gently
old all down the unchanging days and die one day like any
other day, only shorter. That is my excuse. But there must
be others, no less excellent. Yes. it is quite dark. I can see
nothing. I can scarcely even see the window-pane, or the wall
forming with it so sharp a contrast that it often looks like the
edge of an abyss. I hear the noise of my little finger as it
glides over the paper and then that so different of the pencil
following after. That is what surprises me and makes me say
that something must have changed. Whence that child I
might have been, why not? And I hear also, there we are at
last, I hear a choir, far enough away from me not to hear it
when it goes soft. It is a song I know, I don't know how, and
when it fades, and when it dies quite away, it goes on inside
me, but too slow, or too fast, for when it comes on the air
to me again it is not together with mine, but behind, or ahead.
It is a mixed choir, or I am greatly deceived. With children
too perhaps. I have the absurd feeling it is conducted by a
woman. It has been singing the same song for a long time
now. They must be rehearsing. It belongs already to the long
past, it has uttered for the last time the triumphal cry on
which it ends. Can it be Easter Week? Thus with the year
Seasons return. If it can, could not this song I have just heard,
and which quite frankly is not yet quite stilled within me,
could not this song have simply been to the honour and glory
of him who was the first to rise from the dead, to him who
saved me, twenty centuries in advance? Did I say the first?
The final bawl lends colour to this view.

I fear I must have fallen asleep again. In vain I grope, I
cannot find my exercise-book. But I still have the pencil in
my hand. I shall have to wait for day to break. God knows
what I am going to do till then.

I have just written, I fear I must have fallen, etc. I hope
this is not too great a distortion of the truth. I now add these
few lines, before departing from myself again. I do not depart
from myself now with the same avidity as a week ago for
example. For this must be going on now for over a week,

it must be over a week since I said, I shall soon be quite
dead at last, etc. Wrong again. That is not what I said, I
could swear to it, that is what I wrote. This last phrase seems
familiar, suddenly I seem to have written it somewhere before,
or spoken it, word for word. Yes, I shall soon be, etc., that
is what I wrote when I realized I did not know what I had
said, at the beginning of my say, and subsequently, and that
consequently the plan I had formed, to live, and cause to live,
at last, to play at last and die alive, was going the way of all
my other plans. I think the dawn was not so slow in coming
as I had feared, I really do. But I feared nothing, I fear nothing
any more. High summer is truly at hand. Turned towards the
window I saw the pane shiver at last, before the ghastly sunrise. It is no ordinary pane, it brings me sunset and it brings
me sunrise. The exercise-book had fallen to the ground. I
took a long time to find it. It was under the bed. How are
such things possible? I took a long time to recover it. I had
to harpoon it. It is not pierced through and through, but it is
in a bad way. It is a thick exercise-book. I hope it will see
me out. From now on I shall write on both sides of the page.
Where does it come from? I don't know. I found it, just like
that, the day I needed it. Knowing perfectly well I had no
exercise-book I rummaged in my possessions in the hope of
finding one. I was not disappointed, not surprised. If to-
morrow I needed an old love-letter I would adopt the same
method. It is ruled in squares. The first pages are covered
with ciphers and other symbols and diagrams, with here and
there a brief phrase. Calculations, I reckon. They seem to
stop suddenly, prematurely at all events. As though discouraged. Perhaps it is astronomy, or astrology. I did not
look closely. I drew a line, no, I did not even draw a line,
and I wrote, Soon I shall be quite dead at last, and so on,
without even going on to the next page, which was blank.
Good. Now I need not dilate on this exercise-book when it
comes to the inventory, but merely say, Item, an exercise-
book, giving perhaps the colour of the cover. But I may
well lose it between now and then, for good and all. The
pencil on the contrary is an old acquaintance, I must have
had it about me when I was brought here. It has five faces.
It is very short. It is pointed at both ends. A Venus. I hope
it will see me out. I was saying I did not depart from myself now

with quite the same alacrity. That must be in the natural
order of things, all that pertains to me must be written there,
including my inability to grasp what order is meant. For I
have never seen any sign of any, inside me or outside me.
I have pinned my faith to appearances, believing them to be
vain. I shall not go into the details. Choke, go down, come up,
choke, suppose, deny, affirm, drown. I depart from myself
less gladly. Amen. I waited for the dawn. Doing what? I don't
know. What I had to do. I watched for the window. I gave
rein to my pains, my impotence. And in the end it seemed
to me, for a second, that I was going to have a visit!

The summer holidays were drawing to a close. The decisive
moment was at hand when the hopes reposed in Sapo were
to be fulfilled, or dashed to the ground. He is trained to a hair,
said Mr. Saposcat. And Mrs. Saposcat, whose piety grew
warm in times of crisis, prayed for his success. Kneeling at
her bedside, in her night-dress, she ejaculated, silently, for
her husband would not have approved, Oh God grant he
pass, grant he pass, grant he scrape through!
When this first ordeal was surmounted there would be
others, every year, several times a year. But it seemed to
the Saposcats that these would be less terrible than the first
which was to give them, or deny them, the right to say, He
is doing his medicine, or, He is reading for the bar. For they
felt that a more or less normal if unintelligent youth, once
admitted to the study of these professions, was almost sure
to be certified, sooner or later, apt to exercise them. For they
had experience of doctors, and of lawyers, like most people.
One day Mr. Saposcat sold himself a fountain-pen, at a
discount. A Bird. I shall give it to him on the morning of
the examination, he said. He took off the long cardboard
lid and showed the pen to his wife. Leave it in its box! he
cried, as she made to take it in her hand. It lay almost hidden
in the scrolled leaflet containing the instructions for use. Mr.
Saposcat parted the edges of the paper and held up the box
for his wife to look inside. But she, instead of looking at the
pen, looked at him. He named the price. Might it not be
better, she said, to let him have it the day before, to give him
time to get used to the nib? You are right, he said, I had not
thought of that. Or even two days before, she said, to give

him time to change the nib if it does not suit him. A bird, its
yellow beak agape to show it was singing, adorned the lid,
which Mr. Saposcat now put on again. He wrapped with
expert hands the box in tissue-paper and slipped over it a
narrow rubber band. He was not pleased. It is a medium nib,
he said, and it will certainly suit him.

This conversation was renewed the next day. Mr. Saposcat
said, Might it not be better if we just lent him the pen and
told him he could keep it for his own, if he passed? Then we
must do so at once, said Mr. Saposcat, otherwise there is no
point in it. To which Mr. Saposcat made, after a silence, a
first objection, and then, after a second silence, a second
objection. He first objected that his son, if he received the
pen forthwith, would have time to break it, or lose it, before
the paper. He secondly objected that his son, if he received
the pen immediately, and assuming he neither broke nor lost
it, would have time to get so used to it and, by comparing it
with the pens of his less impoverished friends, so familiar with
its defects, that its possession would no longer tempt him. I
did not know it was an inferior article, said Mrs. Saposcat.
Mr. Saposcat placed his hand on the table-cloth and sat gazing
at it for some time. Then he laid down his napkin and left
the room. Adrian, cried Mrs. Saposcat, come back and finish
your sweet! Alone before the table she listened to the steps
on the garden-path, clearer, fainter, clearer, fainter.

The Lamberts. One day Sapo arrived at the farm earlier
than usual. But do we know what time he usually arrived?
Lengthening, fading shadows. He was surprised to see, at a
distance, in the midst of the young stubble, the father's
big red and white head. His body was in the hole or pit he
had dug for his mule, which had died during the night.
Edmund came out of the house, wiping his mouth, and
joined him. Lambert then climbed out of the hole and the
son went down into it. Drawing closer Sapo saw the mule's
black corpse. Then all became clear to him. The mule was
lying on its side, as was to be expected. The forelegs were
stretched out straight and rigid, the hind drawn up under
the belly. The yawning jaws, the wreathed lips, the enormous
teeth, the bulging eyes, composed a striking death's-head.
Edmund handed up to his father the pick, the shovel and

the spade and climbed out of the hole. Together they dragged
the mule by the legs to the edge of the hole and heaved it
in, on its back. The forelegs, pointing towards heaven, projected above the level of the ground. Old Lambert banged
them down with his spade. He handed the spade to his son
and went toward the house. Edmund began to fill up the
hole. Sapo stood watching him. A great calm stole over
him. Great calm is an exaggeration. He felt better. The end
of a life is always vivifying, Edmund paused to rest, leaned
panting on the spade and smiled. There were great pink
gaps in his front teeth. Big Lambert sat by the window,
smoking, drinking, watching his son. Sapo sat down before
him, laid his hand on the table and his head on his hand,
thinking he was alone. Between his head and his hand he
slipped the other hand and sat there marble still. Louis
began to talk. He seemed in good spirits. The mule, in his
opinion, had died of old age. He had bought it, two years
before, on its way to the slaughter-house. So he could not
complain. After the transaction the owner of the mule pre-
dicted that it would drop down dead at the first ploughing. But
Lambert was a connoisseur of mules. In the case of mules
it is the eye that counts, the rest is unimportant. So he
looked the mule full in the eye, at the gates of the slaughter-
house, and saw it could still be made to serve. And the
mule returned his gaze, in the yard of the slaughter-house.
As Lambert unfolded his story the slaughter-house loomed
larger and larger. Thus the site of the transaction shifted
gradually from the road that led to the slaughter-house to
the gates of the slaughter-house and thence to the yard
itself. Yet a little while and he would have contended
for the mule with the knacker. The look in his eye, he said,
was like a prayer to me to take him. It was covered with
sores, but in the case of mules one should never let oneself be deterred by senile sores. Someone said, He's done
ten miles already, you'll never get him home, he'll drop down
dead on the road. I thought I might screw six months out
of him, said Lambert, and I screwed two years. All the
time he told this story he kept his eyes fixed on his son.
There they sat, the table between them, in the gloom, one
speaking, the other listening, and far removed, the one from
what he said, the other from what he heard, and far from

each other. The heap of earth was dwindling, the earth shone strangely in the raking evening light, glowing in patches as though with its own fires, in the fading light. Edmund stopped often to rest, leaning on the spade and looking about him. The slaughter-house, said Lambert. that's where I buy my beasts, will you look at that loafer. He went out and set to work, beside his son. They worked together for a time, heedless of each other. Then the son dropped his shovel, turned aside and moved slowly away, passing from toil to rest in a single unbroken movement that did not seem of his doing. The mule was no longer visible. The face of the earth, on which it had plodded its life away, would see it no more, toiling before the plough or the dray. And Big Lambert would soon be able to plough and harrow the place where it lay, with another mule, or an old horse, or an old ox, bought at the knacker's yard, knowing that the share would not turn up the putrid flesh or be blunted by the big bones. For he knew how the dead and buried tend, contrary to what one might expect, to rise to the surface, in which they resembled the drowned. And he had made allowance for this when digging the hole. Edmund and his mother passed each other by in silence. She had been to see a neighbour, to borrow a pound of lentils for their supper. She was thinking of the handsome steelyard that served to weight them and wondering if it was true. Before her husband too she rapidly passed, without a glance, and in his attitude there was nothing to suggest that he had seen her either. She lit the lamp where it stood at its usual place on the chimney-piece, beside the alarm-clock, flanked in its turn by a crucifix hanging from a nail. The clock, being the lowest of the three, had to remain in the middle, and the lamp and crucifix could not change places because of the nail from which the latter was hung. She stood with her forehead and her hands pressed against the wall, until she might turn up the wick. She turned it up and put on the yellow globe which a large hole defaced. Seeing Sapo she first thought he was her daughter. Then her thoughts flew to the absent one. She set down the lamp on the table and the outer world went out. She sat down, emptied out the lentils on the table and began to sort them. So that soon there were two heaps on the table, one big heap getting

smaller and one small heap getting bigger. But suddenly
with a furious gesture she swept the two together, annihilat-
ing thus in less than a second the work of two or three
minutes. Then she went away and came back with a saucepan. It won't kill them, she said, and with the heel of her
hand she brought the lentils to the edge of the table and over
the edge into the saucepan, as if all that mattered was not
to be killed, but so clumsily and with such nervous haste
that a great number fell wide of the pan to the ground. Then
she took up the lamp and went out, to fetch wood perhaps,
or a lump of fat bacon. Now that it was dark again in the
kitchen the dark outside gradually lightened and Sapo, his
eye against the window-pane, was able to discern certain
shapes, including that of Big Lambert stamping the ground.
To stop in the middle of a tedious and perhaps futile task
was something that Sapo could readily understand. For a
great number of tasks are of this kind, without a doubt, and
the only way to end them is to abandom them. She could
have gone on sorting her lentils all night and never achieved
her purpose, which was to free them from all admixture.
But in the end she would have stopped, saying, I have done
all I can do. But she would not have done all she could have
done. But the moment comes when one desists, because it
is the wisest thing to do, discouraged, but not to the extent
of undoing all that has been done. But what if her purpose,
in sorting the lentils, were not to rid them of all that was
not lentil, but only of the greater part, what then? I don't
know. Whereas there are other tasks, other days, of which
one may fairly safely say that they are finished, though I
do not see which. She came back, holding the lamp high and
a little to one side, so as not to be dazzled. In the other
hand she held a white rabbit, by the hindlegs. For whereas
the mule had been black, the rabbit had been white. It was
dead already, it had ceased to be. There are rabbits that
die before they are killed, from sheer fright. They have
time to do so while being taken out of the hutch, often by
the ears, and disposed in the most convenient position to
receive the blow, whether on the back of the neck or on
some other part. And often you strike a corpse, without
knowing it. For you have just seen the rabbit alive and
well behind the wire meshing, nibbling at its leaves. And

you congratulate yourself on having succeeded with the first
blow, and not caused unnecessary suffering, whereas in
reality you have taken all that trouble for nothing. This
occurs most frequently at night, fright being greater in the
night. Hens on the other hand are more stubborn livers and
some have been observed, with the head already off, to
cut a few last capers before collapsing. Pigeons too are less
impressionable and sometimes even struggle before choking
to death. Mrs. Lambert was breathing hard. Little devil!
she cried. But Sapo was already far away, trailing his hand
in the high waving meadow grasses. Soon afterwards Lambert, then his son, attracted by the savoury smell, entered
the kitchen. Sitting at the table, face to face, their eyes
averted from each other's eyes, they waited. But the woman,
the mother, went to the door and called. Lizzy! she cried,
again and again. Then she went back to her range. She
had seen the moon. After a silence Lambert declared, I'll
kill Whitey to-morrow. Those of course were not the words
he used, but that was the meaning. But neither his wife nor
his son could approve him, the former because she would have
preferred him to kill Blackey, the latter because he held that to
kill the kids at such an early stage of their development, either
of them, it was all the same to him, would be premature.
But Big Lambert told them to hold their tongues and went
to the corner to fetch the case containing the knives, three
in number. All he had to do was to wipe off the grease and
whet them a little on one another. Mrs. Lambert went back
to the door, listened, called. In the far distance the flock
replied. She's coming, she said. But a long time passed
before she came. When the meal was over Edmund went
up to bed, so as to masturbate in peace and comfort before
his sister joined him, for they shared the same room. Not
that he was restrained by modesty, when his sister was there.
Nor was she, when her brother was there. Their quarters
were cramped, certain refinements were not possible.
Edmund then went up to bed, for no particular reason. He
would have gladly slept with his sister, the father too. I
mean the father would have gladly slept with his daughter,
the time was long past and gone when he would have gladly
slept with his sister. But something held them back. And
she did not seem eager. But she was still young. Incest then

was in the air. Mrs. Lambert, the only member of the house-
hold who had no desire to sleep with anybody, saw it
coming with indifference. She went out. Alone with his
daughter Lambert sat watching her. She was crouched
before the range, in an attitude of dejection. He told her
to eat and she began to eat the remains of the rabbit, out
of the pot, with a spoon. But it is hard to look steadily for
any length of time at a fellow-creature, even when you are
resolved to, and suddenly Lambert saw his daughter at
another place and otherwise engaged than in bringing the
spoon up from the pot into her mouth and down from her
mouth into the pot again. And yet he could have sworn
that he had not taken his eyes off her. He said, To-morrow
we'll kill Whitey, you can hold her if you like. But seeing
her still so bad, and her cheeks wet with tears, he went
towards her.

What tedium. If I went on to the stone? No, it would be
the same thing. The Lamberts, the Lamberts, does it matter
about the Lamberts? No, not particularly. But while I am
with them the other is lost. How are my plans getting on,
my plans, I had plans not so long ago. Perhaps I have
another ten years ahead of me. The Lamberts! I shall try
and go on all the same, a little longer, my thoughts elsewhere,
I can't stay here. I shall hear myself talking, afar off, from
my far mind, talking of the Lamberts, talking of myself, my
mind wandering, far from here, among its ruins.

Then Mrs. Lambert was alone in the kitchen. She sat
down by the window and turned down the wick of the lamp,
as she always did before blowing it out, for she did not like
to blow out a lamp that was still hot. When she thought the
chimney and shade had cooled sufficiently she got got up
and blew down the chimney. She stood a moment irresolute,
bowed forward with her hands on the table, before she sat
down again. Her day of toil over, day dawned on other toils
within her, on the crass tenacity of life and its diligent pains.
Sitting, moving about, she bore them better than in bed.
From the well of this unending weariness her sigh went up
unendingly, for day when it was night, for night when it was
day, and day and night, fearfully, for the light she had been

told about, and told she could never understand, because it
was not like those she knew, not like the summer dawn she
knew would come again, to her waiting in the kitchen, sitting up straight on the chair, or bowed down over the table,
with little sleep, little rest, but more than in her bed. Often
she stood up and moved about the room, or out and round
the ruinous old house. Five years now it had been going on,
five or six, not more. She told herself she had a woman's
disease, but half-heartedly. Night seemed less night in the
kitchen pervaded with the everyday tribulations, day less
dead. It helped her, when things were bad, to cling with her
fingers to the worn table at which her family would soon be
united, waiting for her to serve them, and to feel about her,
ready for use, the lifelong pots and pans. She opened the
door and looked out. The moon had gone, but the stars
were shinning. She stood gazing up at them. It was a scene
that had sometimes solaced her. She went to the well and
grasped the chain. The bucket was at the bottom, the wind-
lass locked. So it was. Her fingers strayed along the sinuous
links. Her mind was a press of formless questions, mingling
and crumbling limply away. Some seemed to have to do
with her daughter, that minor worry, now lying sleepless
in her bed, listening. Hearing her mother moving about, she
was on the point of getting up and going down to her. But
it was only the next day, or the day after, that she decided
to tell her what Sapo had told her, namely that he was going
away and would not come back. Then, as people do when
someone even insignificant dies, they summoned up such
memories as he had left them, helping one another and
trying to agree. But we all know that little flame and its
flickerings in the wild shadows. And agreement only comes
a little later, with the forgetting.

Mortal tedium. One day I took counsel of an Israelite on
the subject of conation. That must have been when I was
still looking for someone to be faithful to me, and for me
to be faithful to. Then I opened wide my eyes so that the
candidates might admire their bottomless depths and the
way they phosphoresced at all we left unspoken. Our faces
were so close that I felt on mine the wafts of hot air and
sprays of saliva, and he too, no doubt, on his. I can see him

still, the fit of laughter past, wiping his eyes and mouth, and
myself, with downcast eyes, pained by my wetted trousers
and the little pool of urine at my feet. Now that I have
no further use for him I may as well give his name, Jackson.
I was sorry he had not a cat, or a young dog, or better still
an old dog. But all he had to offer in the way of dumb companions was a pink and grey parrot. He used to try and
teach it to say, Nihil in intellectu, etc. These first three
words the bird managed well enough, but the celebrated
restriction was too much for it, all you heard was a series of
squawks. This annoyed Jackson, who kept nagging at it to
begin all over again. Then Polly flew into a rage and retreated
to a corner of its cage. It was a very fine cage, with every
convenience, perches, swings, trays, troughs, stairs and
cuttle-bones. It was even overcrowded, personally I would
have felt cramped. Jackson called me the merino, I don't
know why, perhaps because of the French expression. I
could not help thinking that the notion of a wandering
herd was better adapted to him than to me. But I have
never thought anything but wind, the same that was never
measured to me. My relations with Jackson were of short
duration. I could have put up with him as a friend, but
unfortunately he found me disgusting, as did Johnson, Wil-
son, Nicholson and Watson, all whore-sons. I then tried,
for a space, to lay hold of a kindred spirit among the inferior
races, red, yellow, chocolate, and so on. And if the plague-
stricken had been less difficult of access I would have
intruded on them too, ogling, sidling, leering, ineffing and
conating, my heart palpitating. With the insane too I failed,
by a hair's-breadth. That must have been the way with me
then. But the point is rather what is the way with me now.
When young the old filled me with wonder and awe. Bawling
babies are what dumbfound me now. The house is full of
them finally. Suave mari magno, especially for the old
salt. What tedium. And I thought I had it all thought out.
If I had the use of my body I would throw it out of the
window. But perhaps it is the knowledge of impotence that
emboldens me to that thought. All hangs together, I am in
chains. Unfortunately I do not know quite what floor I
am on, perhaps I am only on the mezzanine. The doors
banging, the steps on the stairs, the noises in the street, have

not enlightened me, on this subject. All I know is that the
living are there, above me and beneath me. It follows at
least that I am not in the basement. And do I not sometimes see the sky and sometimes, through my window, other
windows facing it apparently? But that proves nothing, I
do not wish to prove anything. Or so I say. Perhaps after
all I am in a kind of vault and this space which I take to be
the street in reality no more than a wide trench or ditch with
other vaults opening upon it. But the noises that rise up
from below, the steps that come climbing towards me?
Perhaps there are other vaults even deeper than mine, why
not? In which case the question arises again as to which
floor I am on there is nothing to be gained by my saying I
am in a basement if there are tiers of basements one on top
of another. But the noises that I say rise up from below, the
steps that I say come climbing towards me, do they really
do so? I have no proof that they do. To conclude from this that
I am a prey to hallucinations pure and simple is however a
step I hesitate to take. And I honestly believe that in this
house there are people coming and going and even convers-
ing, and multitudes of fine babies, particularly of late, which
the parents keep moving about from one place to another,
to prevent their forming the habit of motionlessness, in
anticipation of the day when they will have to move about
unaided. But all things considered I would be hard set to
say for certain where exactly they are, in relation to where
exactly I am. And when all is said and done there is nothing
more like a step that climbs than a step that descends or even
that paces to and fro forever on the same level, I mean for
one not only in ignorance of his position and consequently
of what he is to expect, in the way of sounds, but at the
same time more than half-deaf more than half the time.
There is naturally another possibility that does not escape
me, though it would be a great disappointment to have it
confirmed, and that is that I am dead already and that all
continues more or less as when I was not. Perhaps I expired
in the forest, or even earlier. In which case all the trouble
I have been taking for some time past, for what purpose I
do not clearly recall except that it was in some way connected
with the feeling that my troubles were nearly over, has
been to no purpose whatsoever. But my horse-sense tells me

I have not yet quite ceased to gasp. And it summons in support of this view various considerations having to do for example with the little heap of my possessions, my system of nutrition and elimination, the couple across the way, the changing sky, and so on. Whereas in reality all that is perhaps nothing but my worms. Take for example the light that reigns in this den and of which the least that can be said, really the least, is that it is bizarre. I enjoy a kind of night and day, admittedly, often it is even pitch dark, but in rather a different way from the way to which I fancy I was accustomed, before I found myself here. Example, there is nothing like examples, I was once in utter darkness and waiting with some impatience for dawn to break, having need of its light to see to certain little things which it is difficult to see to in the dark. And sure enough little by little the dark lightened and I was able to hook with my stick the objects I required. But the light, instead of being the dawn, turned out in a very short time to be the dusk. And the sun, instead of rising higher and higher in the sky as I confidently expected, calmy set, and night, the passing of which I had just celebrated after my fashion, calmly fell again. Now the reverse, as you might say, I mean day closing in the twilight of dawn, I must confess to never having experienced, and that goes to my heart, I mean that I cannot bring myself to declare that I experienced that too. And yet how often I have implored night to fall, all the livelong day, with all my feeble strength, and how often day to break, all the livelong night. But before leaving this subject and entering upon another, I feel it is my duty to say that it is never light in this place, never really light. The light is there, outside, the air sparkles, the granite wall across the way glitters with all its mica, the light is against my window, but it does not come through. So that here all bathes, I will not say in shadow, nor even half shadow, but in a kind of leaden light that makes no shadow, so that it is hard to say from what direction it comes, for it seems to come from all directions at once, and with equal force. I am convinced for example that at the present moment it is as bright under my bed as it is under the ceiling, which admittedly is not saying much, but I need say no more. And does not that amount to simply this, that there is really no colour in this place, except in so far as this kind of grey incandescence may be called a colour? Yes, no doubt one may speak of grey, personally I have no objection, in which case the issue here would lie between this grey and the black that it overlays more or less, I was going to say according to the time of day, but no, it does not always seem to depend on the time of day. I myself am very grey, I even sometimes have the feeling that I emit grey, in the same way as my sheets for example. And my night is not the sky's. Naturally black is black the whole world over. But how is it my little space is not visited by the luminaries I sometimes see shining afar and how is it the moon where Cain toils bowed beneath his burden never sheds its light on my face? In a word there seems to be the light of the outer world, of those who know the sun and moon emerge at such an hour and at such another plunge again below the surface, and who rely on this, and who know that clouds are always to be expected but sooner or later always pass away, and mine. But mine too has its alternations, I will not deny it, its dusks and dawns, but that is what I say, for I too must have lived, once, out there, and there is no recovering from that. And when I examine the ceiling and walls I see there is no possibility of my making light, artificial light, like the couple across the way for example. But someone would have to give me a lamp, or a torch, you know, and I don't know if the air here is of the kind that lends itself to the comedy of combustion. Mem, look for a match in my possessions, and see if it burns. The noises too, cries, steps, doors, murmurs, cease for whole days, their days. Then that silence of which, knowing what I know, I shall merely say that there is nothing, how shall I merely say, nothing negative about it. And softly my little space begins to throb again. You may say it is all in my head, and indeed sometimes it seems to me I am in a head and that these eight, no, six, these six planes that enclose me are of solid bone. But thence to conclude the head is mine, no, never. A kind of air circulates, I must have said so, and when all goes still I hear it beating against the walls and being beaten back by them. And then somewhere in midspace other waves, other onslaughts, gather and break, whence I suppose the faint sound of aerial surf that is my silence. Or else it is the sudden storm, analogous to those outside, rising and drowning the cries of the children, the dying, the lovers, so that in my innocence I say they cease, whereas in reality they never cease. It is difficult to decide. And in the skull is it a vacuum? I ask, And if I close my eyes, close them really, as others cannot, but as I can, for there are limits to my impotence, then sometimes my bed is caught up into the air and tossed like a straw by the swirling eddies, and I in it. Fortunately it is not so much an affair of eyelids, but as it were the soul that must be veiled, that soul denied in vain, vigilant, anxious, turning in its cage as in a lantern, in the night without haven or craft or matter or understanding. Ah yes, I have my little pastimes and they

What a misfortune, the pencil must have slipped from my fingers, for I have only just succeeded in recovering it after forty-eight hours (see above) of intermittent efforts. What my stick lacks is a little prehensile proboscis like the nocturnal tapir's. I should really lose my pencil more often, it might do me good, I might be more cheerful, it might be more cheerful. I have spent two unforgettable days of which nothing will ever be known, it is too late now, or still too soon, I forget which, except that they brought me the solution and conclusion of the whole sorry business, I mean the business of Malone (since that is what I am called now) and of the other, for the rest is no business of mine. And it was, though more unutterable, like the crumbling away of two little heaps of finest sand, or dust, or ashes, of unequal size, but diminishing together as it were in ratio, if that means anything, and leaving behind them, each in its own stead, the blessedness of absence. While this was going on I was struggling to retrieve my pencil, by fits and starts. My pencil. It is a little Venus, still green no doubt, with five or six facets, pointed at both ends and so short there is just room, between them, for my thumb and the two adjacent fingers, gathered together in a little vice. I use the two points turn and turn about, sucking them frequently, I love to suck. And when they go quite blunt I strip them with my nails which are long, yellow, sharp and brittle for want of chalk or is it phosphate. So little by little my little pencil

dwindles, inevitably, and the day is fast approaching when
nothing will remain but a fragment too tiny to hold. So I
write as lightly as I can. But the lead is hard and would
leave no trace if I wrote too lightly. But I say to myself,
Between a hard lead with which one dare not write too
lightly, if a trace is to be left, and a soft fat lead which blackens
the page almost without touching it, what possible difference
can there be, from the point of view of durability. Ah yes,
I have my little pastimes. The strange thing is I have another
pencil, made in France, a long cylinder hardly broached, in
the bed with me somewhere I think. So I have nothing to
worry about, on this score. And yet I do worry. Now while
I was hunting for my pencil I made a curious discovery. The
floor is whitening. I struck it several blows with my stick and
the sound it gave forth was at once sharp and dull, wrong
in fact. So it was not without some trepidation that I inspected the other great planes, above and all about me. And
all this time the sand kept trickling away and I saying to
myself, It is gone for ever, meaning of course the pencil.
And I saw that all these superficies, or should I say infra-
ficies, the horizontal as well as the perpendicular, though
they do not look particularly perpendicular from here, had
visibly blanched since my last examination of them, dating
from I know not when. And this is all the more singular as
the tendency of things in general is I believe rather to
darken, as time wears on, with of course the exception of
our mortal remains and certain parts of the body which
lose their natural color and from which the blood recedes
in the long run. Does this mean there is more light here
now, now that I know what is going on? No, I fear not, it
is the same grey as heretofore, literally sparkling at times,
then growing murky and dim, thickening is perhaps the
word, until all things are blotted out except the window
which seems in a manner of speaking to be my umbilicus,
so that I say to myself, When it too goes out I shall know
more or less where I am. No, all I mean is this, that when I
open staring wide my eyes I see at the confines of this restless
gloom a gleaming and shimmering as of bones, which was
not hitherto the case, to the best of my knowledge. And I
can even distinctly remember the paper-hangings or wall-
paper still clinging in places to the walls and covered with

a writhing mass of roses, violets and other flowers in such
profusion that it seemed to me I had never seen so many
in the whole course of my life, nor of such beauty. But
now they seem to be all gone, quite gone, and if there were
no flowers on the ceiling there was no doubt something
else, cupids perhaps, gone too, without leaving a trace. And
while I was busy pursuing my pencil a moment came when
my exercise-book, almost a child's, fell also to the ground.
But it I very soon recovered, slipping the hook of my stick
into one of the rents in the cover and hoisting it gently
towards me. And during all this time, so fertile in incidents
and mishaps, in my head I suppose all was streaming and
emptying away as though a sluice, to my great joy, until
finally nothing remained, either of Malone or of the other.
And what is more I was able to follow without difficulty the
various phases of this deliverance and felt no surprise at its
irregular course, now rapid, now slow, so crystal clear was
my understanding of the reasons why this could not be
otherwise. And I rejoiced furthermore, quite apart from the
spectacle, at the thought that I now knew what I had to do,
I whose every move has always been a groping, and whose
motionlessness too was a kind of groping, yes, I have greatly
groped stockstill. And here again naturally I was utterly deceived, I mean in imagining I had grasped at last the true
nature of absurd tribulations, but not so utterly as to feel
the need to reproach myself with it now. For even as I
said, How easy and beautiful it all is!, in the same breath I
said, All will grow dark again. And it is without excessive
sorrow that I see us again as we are, namely to be removed
grain by grain until the hand, wearied, begins to play,
scooping us up and letting us trickle back into the same
place, dreamily as the saying is. For I knew it would be so,
even as I said, At last! And I must say that to me at least
and for as long as I can remember the sensation is familiar
of a blind and tired hand delving feebly in my particles and
letting them trickle between its fingers. And sometimes, when
all is quiet, I feel it plunged in me up to the elbow, but
gentle, and as though sleeping. But soon it stirs, wakes,
fondles, clutches, ransacks, ravages, avenging its failure to
scatter me with one sweep. I can understand. But I have
felt so many strange things, so many baseless things as-

suredly, that they are perhaps better left unsaid. To speak
for example of the times when I go liquid and become like
mud, what good would that do? Or of the others when I
would be lost in the eye of a needle, I am so hard and con-
tracted? No, those are well-meaning squirms that get me
nowhere. I was speaking then was I not of my little pastimes
and I think about to say that I ought to content myself with
them, instead of launching forth on all this ballsaching
poppycock about life and death, if that is what it is all
about, and I suppose it is, for nothing was ever about anything else to the best of my recollection. But what it is all
about exactly I could no more say, at the present moment,
than take up my bed and walk. It's vague, life and death. I
must have had my little private idea on the subject when
I began, otherwise I would not have begun, I would have
held my peace, I would have gone on peacefully being bored
to howls, having my little fun and games with the cones and
cylinders, the millet grains beloved of birds and other panics,
until someone was kind enough to come and coffin me. But
it is gone clean out of my head, my little private idea. No
matter, I have just had another. Perhaps it is the same one
back again, ideas are so alike, when you get to know them.
Be born, that's the brainwave now, that is to say live long
enough to get acquainted with free carbonic gas, then say
thanks for the nice time and go. That has always been my
dream at bottom, all the things that have always been my
dream at bottom, so many strings and never a shaft. Yes,
an old foetus, that's what I am now, hoar and impotent,
mother is done for, I've rotted her, she'll drop me with the
help of gangrene, perhaps papa is at the party too, I'll land
headforemost mewling in the charnel-house, not that I'll
mewl, not worth it. All the stories I've told myself, clinging
to the putrid mucus, and swelling, swelling, saying, Got
it at last, my legend. But why this sudden heat, has anything happened, anything changed? No, the answer is no,
I shall never get born and therefore never get dead, and
a good job too. And if I tell of me and of that other who
is my little one, it is as always for want of love, well I'll
be buggered, I wasn't expecting that, want of a homuncule,
I can't stop. And yet it sometimes seems to me I did get
born and had a long life and met Jackson and wandered in

the towns, the woods and wildernesses and tarried by the
seas in tears before the islands and peninsulas where night
lit the little brief yellow lights of man and all night the
great white and colored beams shining in the caves where
I was happy, crouched on the sand in the lee of the rocks
with the smell of the seaweed and the wet rock and the
howling of the wind the waves whipping me with foam
or sighing on the beach softly clawing the shingle, no, not
happy, I was never that, but wishing night would never end
and morning never come when men wake and say, Come
on, we'll soon be dead, let's make the most of it. But what
matter whether I was born or not, have lived or not, am
dead or merely dying, I shall go on doing as I have always
done, not knowing what it is I do, nor who I am, nor where
I am, nor if I am. Yes, a little creature, I shall try and make
a little creature, to hold in my arms, a little creature in my
image, no matter what I say. And seeing what a poor thing
I have made, or how like myself, I shall eat it. Then be
alone a long time, unhappy, not knowing what my prayer
should be nor to whom.

I have taken a long time to find him again, but I have
found him. How did I know it was he, I don't know. And
what can have changed him so? Life perhaps, the struggle
to love, to eat, to escape the redressers of wrongs. I slip
into him, I suppose in the hope of learning something. But
it is a stratum, strata, without debris or vestiges. But before
I am done I shall find traces of what was. I ran him down
in the heart of the town, sitting on a bench. How did I
know it was he? The eyes perhaps. No, I don't know
how I knew, I'll take back nothing. Perhaps it is not he.
No matter, he is mine now, living flesh and needless to say
male, living with that evening life which is like a convales-
cence, if my memories are mine, and which you savour
doddering about in the wake of the fitful sun, or deeper
than the dead, in the corridors of the underground railway
and the stench of their harassed mobs scurrying from cradle
to grave to get to the right place at the right time. What
more do I want? Yes, those were the days, quick to night
and well beguiled with the search for warmth and reasonably
edible scraps. And you imagine it will be so till the end.
But suddenly all begins to rage and roar again, you are

lost in forests of high threshing ferns or whirled far out
on the face of wind-swept wastes, till you being to wonder
if you have not died without knowing and gone to hell or
been born again into an even worse place than before. Then
it is hard to believe in those brief years when the bakers
were often indulgent, at close of day, and baking-apples,
I was always a great man for apples, to be had almost for
the whining if you knew your way about, and a little sunshine and shelter for those who direly needed them. And
there he is as good as gold on the bench, his back to the
river, and dressed as follows, though clothes don't matter,
I know, I know, but he'll never have any others, if I know
anything about it. He has had them a long time already, to
judge by their decay, but no matter, they are the last. But
most remarkable of all is his greatcoat, in the sense that
it covers him completely and screens him from view. For
it is so well buttoned, from top to bottom, by means of
fifteen buttons at the very least, set at intervals of three or
four inches at the very most, that nothing is to be seen of
what goes on inside. And even the two feet, flat on the
ground demurely side by side, even they are partly hidden
by this coat, in spite of the double flexion of the body,
first at the base of the trunk, where the thighs form a right
angle with the pelvis, and then again at the knees, where
the shins resume the perpendicular. For the posture is completely lacking in abandon, and but for the absence of
bonds you might think he was bound to the bench, the posture is so stiff and set in the sharpness of its planes and
angles, like that of the Colossus of Memnon, dearly loved
son of Dawn. In other words, when he walks, or simply
stands stockstill, the tails of this coat literally sweep the
ground and rustle like a train, when he walks. And indeed
this coat terminates in a fringe, like certain curtains, and
the thread of the sleeves too is bare and frayed into long
waving strands that flutter in the wind. And the hands too
are hidden. For the sleeves of this vast rag are of a piece
with its other parts. But the collar has remained intact,
being of velvet or perhaps shag. Now as to the colour of
this coat, for colour too is an important consideration, there
is no good denying it, all that can be said is that green
predominates. And it might safely be wagered that this

coat, when new, was of a fine plain green colour, what
you might call cab green, for there used to be cabs and
carriages rattling through the town with panels of a handsome bottle green, I must have seen them myself, and even
driven in them, I would not put it past me. But perhaps I
am wrong to call this coat a greatcoat and perhaps I should
rather call it an overcoat or even cover-me-down, for that
is indeed the impression it gives, that it covers the whole
body all over, with the exception obviously of the head which
emerges, lofty and impassive, clear of its embrace. Yes,
passion has marked the face, action too possibly, but it
seems to have ceased from suffering, for the time being.
But one never knows, does one? Now with regard to the
buttons of this coat, they are not so much genuine buttons
as little wooden cylinders two or three inches long, with
a hole in the middle for the thread, for one hole is ample,
though two and even four are more usual, and this because
of the inordinate distension of the buttonholes consequent
on wear and tear. And cylinders is perhaps an exaggeration,
for if some of these little sticks or pegs are in fact cylindrical,
still more have no definable form. But all are roughly two
and a half inches long and thus prevent the lappets from
flying apart, all have this feature in common. Now with
regard to the material of this coat, all that can be said is
that it looks like felt. And the various dints and bulges
inflicted upon it by the spasms and contortions of the
body subsist long after the fit is past. So much for this
coat. I'll tell myself stories about the boots another time,
if I can. The hat, as hard as iron, superbly domed above
its narrow guttered rim, is marred by a wide crack or rent
extending in front from the crown down and intended probably to facilitate the introduction of the skull. For coat and
hat have this much in common, that whereas the coat is
too big, the hat is too small. And though the edges of the
split brim close on the brow like the jaws of a trap, nevertheless the hat is attached, by a string, for safety, to the
topmost button of the coat, because, never mind. And were
there nothing more to be said about the structure of this
hat, the important thing would still remain unsaid, meaning
of course its colour, of which all that can be said is this,
that a strong sun full upon it brings out shimmers of buff and

pearl grey and that otherwise it verges on black, without however ever really approaching it. And it would not surprise me to learn that this hat once belonged to a sporting gentleman, a turf-man or breeder of rams. And if we now turn to consider this coat and this hat, no longer separately, but in relation to each other, we are very soon agreeably surprised to see how well they are assorted. And it would not surprise me to learn that they had been bought, one at the hatter's, the other at the tailor's, perhaps the same day and by the same toff, for such men exist, I mean fine handsome men six foot tall and over and all in keeping but the head, small from over-breeding. And it is a pleasure to find oneself again in the presence of one of those immutable relations between harmoniously perishing terms and the effect of which is this, that when weary to death one is almost resigned to — I was going to say to the immortality of the soul, but I don't see the connexion. But to pass on now to the garments that really matter, subjacent and even intimate, all that can be said is that this for the moment is delicate ground. For Sapo — no, I can't call him that any more, and I even wonder how I was able to stomach such a name till now. So then for, let me see, for Macmann, that's not much better but there is no time to lose, for Macmann might be stark staring naked under this surtout for all anyone would be any the wiser. The trouble is he does not stir. Since morning he has been here and now it is evening. The tugs, their black funnels striped with red, tow to their moorings the last barges, freighted with empty barrels. The water cradles already the distant fires of the sunset, orange, rose and green, quenches them in its ruffles and then in trembling pools spreads them bright again. His back is turned to the river, but perhaps it appears to him in the dreadful cries of the gulls that evening assembles, in paroxysms of hunger, round the outflow of the sewers, opposite the Bellevue Hotel. Yes, they too, in a last frenzy before night and its high crags, swoop ravening about the offal. But his face is towards the people that throng the streets at this hour, their long day ended and the whole long evening before them. The doors open and spew them out, each door its contingent. For an instant they cluster in a daze, huddled on the sidewalk or in the gutter, then set off singly

on their appointed ways. And even those who know themselves condemned, at the outset, to the same direction, for
the choice of directions at the outset is not great, take leave
of one another and part, but politely, with some polite excuse,
or without a word, for they all know one another's little
ways. And God help him who longs, for once, in his recovered freedom, to walk a little way with a fellow-creature,
no matter which, unless of course by a merciful chance he
stumble on one in the same plight. Then they take a few
paces happily side by side, then part, each one muttering
perhaps, Now there will be no holding him. At this hour
then erotic craving accounts for the majority of couples.
But these are few compared to the solitaries pressing forward
through the throng, obstructing the access to places of
amusement, bowed over the parapets, propped against
vacant walls. But soon they come to the appointed place,
at home or at some other home, or abroad, as the saying
is, in a public place, or in a doorway in view of possible
rain. And the first to arrive have seldom long to wait, for
all hasten towards one another, knowing how short the time
in which to say all the things that lie heavy on the heart
and conscience and to do all the things they have to do
together, things one cannot do alone. So there they are for
a few hours in safety. Then the drowsiness, the little memor-
andum book with its little special pencil, the yawned goodbyes. Some even take a cab to get more quickly to the
rendezvous or, when the fun is over, home or to the hotel,
where their comfortable bed is waiting for them. Then you
see the last stage of the horse, between its recent career as
a pet horse, or a race-horse, or a pack-horse, or a plough-
horse, and the shambles. It spends most of its time standing
still in an attitude of dejection, its head hanging as low
as the shafts and harness permit, that is to say almost to the
cobble-stones. But once in motion it is transformed, momentarily, perhaps because of the memories that motion
revives, for the mere fact of running and pulling cannot give
it much satisfaction, under such conditions. But when the
shafts tilt up, announcing that a fare has been taken on
board, or when on the contrary the backband begins to
gall its spine, according as the passenger is seated facing
the way he is going or, what is perhaps even more restful,

with his back to it, then it rears its head, stiffens its houghs
and looks almost content. And you see the cabman too, all
alone on his box ten feet from the ground, his knees
covered at all seasons and in all weathers with a kind of rug
as a rule originally brown, the same precisely which he has
just snatched from the rump of his horse. Furious and livid
perhaps from want of passengers, the least fare seems to
excite him to a frenzy. Then with his huge exasperated hands
he tears at the reins or, half rising and leaning out over his
horse, brings them down with a crack all along its back.
And he launches his equipage blindly through the dark
thronging streets, his mouth full of curses. But the passenger,
having named the place he wants to go and knowing himself as helpless to act on the course of events as the dark
box that encloses him, abandons himself to the pleasant feeling of being freed from all responsibility, or he ponders on
what lies before him, or on what lies behind him, saying,
Twill not be ever thus, and then in the same breath, But
twas ever thus, for there are not five hundred different kinds
of passenger. And so they hasten, the horse, the driver and
the passenger, towards the appointed place, by the shortest
route or deviously, through the press of other misplaced
persons. And each one has his reasons, while wondering
from time to time what they are worth, and if they are the
true ones, for going where he is going rather than somewhere else, and the horse hardly less darkly than the men,
though as a rule it will not know where it is going until
it gets there, and not always even then. And if as suggested
it is dusk, then another phenomenon to be observed is the
number of windows and shop-windows that light up an
instant, almost after the fashion of the setting sun, though
that all depends on the season. But for Macmann, thank
God, he's still there, for Macmann it is a true spring evening,
an equinoctial gale howls along the quays bordered by high
red houses, many of which are warehouses. Or it is perhaps
an evening in autumn and these leaves whirling in the air,
whence it is impossible to say, for here there are no trees,
are perhaps no longer the first of the year, barely green,
but old leaves that have known the long joys of summer
and now are good for nothing but to lie rotting in a heap,
now that men and beasts have no more need of shade, on

the contrary, nor birds of nests to lay and hatch out in,
and trees must blacken even where no heart beats, though
it appears that some stay green forever, for some obscure
reason. And it is no doubt all the same to Macmann whether
it is spring or whether it is autumn, unless he prefers summer to winter or inversely, which is improbable. But it
must not be thought he will never move again, out of this
place and attitude, for he has still the whole of his old
age before him, and then that kind of epilogue when it is
not very clear what is happening and which does not seem
to add very much to what has already been acquired or
to shed any great light on its confusion, but which no
doubt has its usefulness, as hay is left out to dry before
being garnered. He will therefore rise, whether he likes it
or not, and proceed by other places to another place, and
then by others still to yet another, unless he comes back
here where he seems to be snug enough, but one never knows,
does one? And so on, on, for long years. Because in order
not to die you must come and go, come and go, unless
you happen to have someone who brings you food wherever
you happen to be, like myself. And you can remain for two,
three and even four days without stirring hand or foot, but
what are four days when you have all old age before you,
and then the languors of evaporation, a drop in the ocean.
It is true you know nothing of this, you flatter yourself
you are hanging by a thread like all mankind, but that
is not the point. For there is no point, no point in not
knowing this or that, either you know all or you know
nothing, and Macmann knows nothing. But he is concerned
only with his ignorance of certain things, of those that appall
him among others, which is only human. But it is bad policy,
for on the fifth day rise you must, and rise in fact you do,
but with how much greater pains than if you had made up
your mind to it the day before, or better still two days
before, and why add to your pains, it's bad policy, assuming
you do add to them, and nothing is less certain. For on the
fifth day, when the problem is how to rise, the fourth and
third do not matter any more, all that matters is how to
rise, for you are half out of your mind. And sometimes you
cannot, get to your feet I mean, and have to drag yourself
to the nearest plot of vegetables, using the tufts of grass

and asperities of the earth to drag yourself forward, or to
the nearest clump of brambles, where there are sometimes
good things to eat, if acid, and which are superior to the
plots in this, that you can crawl into them and hide, as you
cannot in a plot of ripe potatoes for example, and in this
also, that often you frighten the little wild things away, both
furred and feathered. For it is not as if he possessed the
means of accumulating, in a single day, enough food to keep
him alive for three weeks or a month, and what is a month
compared to the whole of second childishness, a drop in
a bucket. But he does not, possess them I mean, and could
not employ them even if he did, he feels so far from the
morrow. And perhaps there is none, no morrow any more,
for one who has waited so long for it in vain. And perhaps
he has come to that stage of his instant when to live is to
wander the last of the living in the depths of an instant without bounds, where the light never changes and the wrecks
look all alike. Bluer scarcely than white of egg the eyes
stare into the space before them, namely the fulness of the
great deep and its unchanging calm. But at long intervals
they close, with the gentle suddenness of flesh that tightens,
often without anger, and closes on itself. Then you see the
old lids all red and worn that seem hard set to meet, for
there are four, two for each lachrymal. And perhaps it is
then he sees the heaven of the old dream, the heaven of
the sea and of the earth too, and the spasms of the waves
from shore to shore all stirring to their tiniest stir, and
the so different motion of men for example, who are not
tied together, but free to come and go as they please. And
they make full use of it and come and go, their great balls
and sockets rattling and clacking like knackers, each on his
way. And when one dies the others go on, as if nothing had
happened.

I feel

I feel it's coming. How goes it, thanks, it's coming. I
wanted to be quite sure before I noted it. Scrupulous to the
last, finical to a fault, that's Malone, all over. I mean sure of
feeling that my hour is at hand. For I never doubted it would
come, sooner or later, except the days I felt it was past. For

my stories are all in vain, deep down I never doubted, even
the days abounding in proof to the contrary, that I was still
alive and breathing in and out the air of earth. At hand, that
is in two or three days, in the language of the days when they
taught me the names of the days and I marvelled at their
being so few and flourished my little fists, crying out for more,
and how to tell the time, and what are two or three days, more
or less, in the long run, a joke. But not a word and on with
the losing game, it's good for the health. And all I have to do
is go on though doomed to see the midsummer moon. For I
believe I have now reached what is called the month of May,
I don't know why, I mean why I believe that, for May comes
from Maia, hell, I remember that too, goddess of increase and
plenty, yes, I believe I have entered on the season of increase
and plenty, of increase at last, for plenty comes later, with the
harvest. So quiet, quiet. I'll be still here at All Saints, in the
middle of the chrysanthemums, no, this year I shall not hear
them howling over their charnels. But this sensation of dila-
tion is hard to resist. All strains towards the nearest deeps, and
notably my feet, which even in the ordinary way are so much
further from me than all the rest, from my head I mean, for
that is where I am fled, my feet are leagues away. And to call
them in, to be cleaned for example, would I think take me
over a month, exclusive of the time required to locate them.
Strange, I don't feel my feet any more, my feet feel nothing
any more, and a mercy it is. And yet I feel they are beyond
the range of the most powerful telescope. Is that what is
known as having a foot in the grave? And similarly for the
rest. For a mere local phenomenon is something I would not
have noticed, having been nothing but a series or rather a
succession of local phenomena all my life, without any result.
But my fingers too write in other latitudes and the air that
breathes through my pages and turns them without my knowing, when I doze off, so that the subject falls far from the
verb and the object lands somewhere in the void, is not the
air of this second-last abode, and a mercy it is. And perhaps
on my hands it is the shimmer of the shadows of leaves and
flowers and the brightness of a forgotten sun. Now my sex,
I mean the tube itself, and in particular the nozzle, from which
when I was yet a virgin clouts and gouts of sperm came streaming and splashing up into my face, a continuous flow, while

it lasted, and which must still drip a little piss from time to
time, otherwise I would be dead of uraemia, I do not expect
to see my sex again, with my naked eye, not that I wish to,
we've stared at each other long enough, in the eye, but it
gives you some idea. But that is not all and my extremities are
not only the parts to recede, in their respective directions, far
from it. For my arse for example, which can hardly be accused of being the end of anything, if my arse suddenly
started to shit at the present moment, which God forbid, I
firmly believe the lumps would fall out in Australia. And if
I were to stand up again, from which God preserve me, I
fancy I would fill a considerable part of the universe, oh not
more than lying down, but more noticeably. For it is a thing
I have often noticed, the best way to pass unnoticed is to lie
down flat and not move. And so there I am, who always
thought I would shrivel and shrivel, more and more, until in
the end I could be almost buried in a casket, swelling. No
matter, what matters is that in spite of my stories I continue
to fit in this room, let us call it a room, that's all that matters,
and I need not worry, I'll fit in it as long as needs be. And
if I succeed in breathing my last it will not be in the street,
or in a hospital, but here, in the midst of my possessions, beside this window that sometimes looks as if it were painted
on the wall, like Tiepolo's ceiling at Würzburg, what a tourist
I must have been, I even remember the diaeresis, if it is one.
If only I could be sure, of my deathbed I mean. And yet
how often I have seen this old head swing out through the
door, low, for my big old bones weigh heavy, and the door
is low, lower and lower in my opinion. And each time it bangs
against the jamb, my head does, for I am tall, and the landing
is small, and the man carrying my feet cannot wait, before
he starts down the stairs, for the whole of me to be out, on
the landing I mean, but he has to start turning before that,
so as not to bang into the wall, of the landing I mean. So
my head bangs against the jamb, it's inevitable. And it doesn't
matter to my head, in the state it is in, but the man carrying
it says, Eh Bob easy!, out of respect perhaps, for he doesn't
know me, he didn't know me, or for fear of hurting his
fingers. Bang! Easy! Right! The door!, and the room is vacant
at last and ready to receive, after disinfection, for you can't be
too careful, a large family or a pair of turtle doves. Yes, the

event is past, but it's too soon to use it, hence the delay,
that's what I tell myself. But I tell myself so many things,
what truth is there in all this babble? I don't know. I simply
believe I can say nothing that is not true, I mean that has
not happened, it's not the same thing but no matter. Yes,
that's what I like about me, at least one of the things, that
I can say, Up the Republic!, for example, or, Sweetheart!, for
example, without having to wonder if I should not rather
have cut my tongue out, or said something else. Yes, no
reflection is needed, before or after, I have only to open my
mouth for it to testify to the old story, my old story, and to
the long silence that has silenced me, so that all is silent. And
if I ever stop talking it will be because there is nothing more
to be said, even though all has not been said, even though
nothing has been said. But let us leave these morbid matters
and get on with that of my demise, in two or three days if
I remember rightly. Then it will be all over with the Murphys,
Merciers, Molloys, Morans and Malones, unless it goes on
beyond the grave. But sufficient unto the day, let us first
defunge, then we'll see. How many have I killed, hitting them
on the head or setting fire to them? Off-hand I can only think
of four, all unknowns, I never knew anyone. A sudden wish,
I have a sudden wish to see, as sometimes in the old days,
something, anything, no matter what, something I could not
have imagined. There was the old butler too, in London I
think, there's London again, I cut his throat with his razor,
that makes five. It seems to me he had a name. Yes, what I
need now is a touch of the unimaginable, coloured for preference, that would do me good. For this may well be my last
journey, down the long familiar galleries, with my little suns
and moons that I hang aloft and my pockets full of pebbles to
stand for men and their seasons, my last, if I'm lucky. Then
back here, to me, whatever that means, and no more leaving
me, no more asking me for what I haven't got. Or perhaps
we'll all come back, reunited, done with parting, done with
prying on one another, back to this foul little den all dirty
white and vaulted, as though hollowed out of ivory, an old
rotten tooth. Or alone, back alone, as alone as when I went,
but I doubt it, I can hear them from here, clamouring after
me down the corridors, stumbling through the rubble, beseeching me to take them with me. That settles that. I have

just time, if I have calculated right, and if I have calculated
wrong so much the better, I ask nothing better, besides I
haven't calculated anything, don't ask anything either, just
time to go and take a little turn, come back here and do
all I have to do, I forgot what, ah yes, put my possessions in
order, and then something else, I forget what, but it will
come back to me when the time comes. But before I go I
should like to find a hole in the wall behind which so much
goes on, such extraordinary things, and often coloured. One
last glimpse and I feel I could slip away as happy as if I were
embarking for — I nearly said for Cythera, decidedly it is
time for this to stop. After all this window is whatever I
want it to be, up to a point, that's right, don't compromise
yourself. What strikes me to begin with is how much rounder
it is than it was, so that it looks like a bull's-eye, or a port-
hole. No matter, provided there is something on the other
side. First I see the night, which surprises me, to my surprise,
I suppose because I want to be surprised, just once more. For in
the room it is not night, I know, here it is never really night, I
don't care what I said, but often darker than now, whereas out
there up in the sky it is black night, with few stars, just
enough to show that the black night I see is truly of mankind and not merely painted on the window-pane, for they
tremble, like true stars, as they would not do if they were
painted. And as if that were not enough to satisfy me it is
the outer world, the other world, suddenly the window across
the way lights up, or suddenly I realize it is lit up, for I am
not one of those people who can take in everything at a
single glance, but I have to look long and fixedly and give
things time to travel the long road that lies between me and
them. And that indeed is a happy chance and augurs well,
unless it be devised on purpose to make mock of me, for I
might have found nothing better to speed me from this place
than the nocturnal sky where nothing happens, though it is
full of tumult and violence, nothing unless you have the whole
night before you to follow the slow fall and rise of other
worlds, when there are any, or watch out for the meteors,
and I have not the whole night before me. And it does not
matter to me whether they have risen before dawn, or not
yet gone to bed, or risen in the middle of the night intending
perhaps to go back to bed when they have finished, and it

is enough for me to see them standing up against each other behind the curtain, which is dark, so that it is a dark light, if one may say so, and dim the shadow they cast. For they cleave so fast together that they seem a single body, and consequently a single shadow. But when they totter it is clear they are twain, and in vain they clasp with the energy of despair, it is clear we have here two distinct and separate bodies, each enclosed within its own frontiers, and having no need of each other to come and go and sustain the flame of life, for each is well able to do so, independently of the other. Perhaps they are cold, that they rub against each other so, for friction maintains heat and brings it back when it is gone. It is all very pretty and strange, this big complicated shape made up of more than one, for perhaps there are three of them, and how it sways and totters, but rather poor in colour. But the night must be warm, for of a sudden the curtain lifts on a flare of tender colour, pale blush and white of flesh, then pink that must come from a garment and gold too that I haven't time to understand. So it is not cold they are, standing so lightly clad by the open window. Ah how stupid I am, I see what it is, they must be loving each other, that must be how it is done. Good, that has done me good. I'll see now if the sky is still there, then go. They are right up against the curtain now, motionless. Is it possible they have finished already? They have loved each other standing, like dogs. Soon they will be able to part. Or perhaps they are just having a breather, before they tackle the titbit. Back and forth, back and forth, that must be wonderful. They seem to be in pain. Enough, enough, goodbye.

Caught by the rain far from shelter Macmann stopped and lay down, saying, The surface thus pressed against the ground will remain dry, whereas standing I would get uniformly wet all over, as if rain were a mere matter of drops per hour, like electricity. So he lay down, prostrate, after a moment's hesitation, for he could just as easily have lain down supine or, meeting himself half-way, on one of his two sides. But he fancied that the nape of the neck and the back right down to the loins were more vulnerable than the chest and belly, not realizing, any more than if he had been a crate of tomatoes, that all these parts are intimately and even indissolubly bound up together, at least until death do them part,

and to many another too of which he had no conception,
and that a drop of water out of season on the coccyx for example may lead to spasms of the risorius lasting for years as
when, having waded through a bog, you merely die of pneu-
monia and your legs none the worse for the wetting, but if
anything better, thanks perhaps to the action of the bog-
water. It was a heavy, cold and perpendicular rain, which
led Macmann to suppose it would be brief, as if there were
a relation between violence and duration, and that he would
spring to his feet in ten minutes or a quarter of an hour, his
front, no, his back, white with, no, front was right, his front
white with dust. This is the kind of story he has been telling
himself all his life, saying, This cannot possibly last much
longer. It was sometime in the afternoon, impossible to say
more, for hours and hours past it had been the same leaden
light, so it was very probably the afternoon, very. The still
air, though not cold as in winter, seemed without promise
or memory of warmth. Incommoded by the rain pouring into
his hat through the crack, Macmann took it off and laid
it on his temple, that is to say turned his head and pressed his
cheek to the ground. His hands at the ends of the long outstretched arms clutched the grass, each hand a tuft, with as
much energy as if he had been spread-eagled against the
face of a cliff. Let us by all means continue this description.
The rain pelted down on his back with the sound first of a
drum, but in a short time of washing, as when washing is
soused gurgling and squelching in a tub, and he distinguished
clearly and with interest the difference in noise of the rain
falling on him and falling on the earth. For this ear, which
is on the same plane as the cheek or nearly, was glued to the
earth in a way it seldom is in wet weather, and he could hear
the kind of distant roar of the earth drinking and the sighing
of the soaked bowed grasses. The idea of punishment came
to his mind, addicted it is true to that chimera and probably
impressed by the posture of the body and the fingers clenched
as though in torment. And without knowing exactly what
his sin was he felt full well that living was not a sufficient
atonement for it or that this atonement was in itself a sin,
calling for more atonement, and so on, as if there could be
anything but life, for the living. And no doubt he would
have wondered if it was really necessary to be guilty in order

to be punished but for the memory, more and more galling, of his having consented to live in his mother, then to leave her. And this again he could not see as his true sin, but as yet another atonement which had miscarried and, far from cleansing him of his sin, plunged him in it deeper than before. And truth to tell the ideas of guilt and punishment were confused together in his mind, as those of cause and effect so often are in the minds of those who continue to think. And it was often in fear and trembling that he suffered, saying, This will cost me dear. But not knowing how to go about it, in order to think and feel correctly, he would suddenly begin to smile for no reason, as now, as then, for already it is long since that afternoon, in March perhaps, or in November perhaps, in October rather, when the rain caught him far from shelter, to smile and give thanks for the teeming rain and the promise it contained of stars a little later, to light his way and enable him to get his bearings, should he wish to do so. For he did not know quite where he was, except that he was in a plain, and the mountains not far, nor the sea, nor the town, and that all he needed was a dust of light and a few fixed stars to enable him to make definite headway towards the one, or the other, or the third, or to hold fast where was, in the plain, as he might be pleased to decide. For in order to hold fast in the place where you happen to be you need light too, unless you go round in circles, which is practically impossible in the dark, or halt and wait, motionless, for day to dawn again, and then you die of cold, unless it does not happen to be cold. But Macmann would have been more than human, after forty or forty-five minutes of sanguine expectation, seeing the rain persist as heavy as ever and day recede at last, if he had not begun to reproach himself with what he had done, namely with having lain down on the ground instead of continuing on his course, in as straight a line as possible, in the hope of chancing sooner or later on a tree, or a ruin. And instead of being astonished at such long and violent rain, he was astonished at not having understood, from the moment the first timid drops began to fall, that it was going to rain violently and long and that he must not stop and lie down, but on the contrary press forward, as fast as his legs could carry him, for he was no more than human, than the son and grandson and greatgrandson of humans. But between him and those grave and sober men, first bearded, then moustached, there was this difference, that his semen had never done any harm to anyone. So his link with his species was through his ascendants only, who were all dead, in the fond hope they had perpetuated themselves. But the better late than never thanks to which true men, true links, can acknowledge the error of their ways and hasten on the next, was beyond the power of Macmann, to whom it sometimes seemed that he could grovel and wallow in his mortality until the end of time and not have done. And without going so far as that, he who has waited long enough will wait for ever. And there comes the hour when nothing more can happen and nobody can come and all is ended but the waiting that knows itself in vain. Perhaps he had come to that. And when (for example) you die, it is too late, you have been waiting too long, you are no longer sufficiently alive to be able to stop. Perhaps he had come to that. But apparently not, though acts don't matter, I know, I know, nor thoughts. For having reproached himself with what he had done, and with his monstrous error of appreciation, instead of springing up and hurrying on he turned over on his back, thus offering all his front to the deluge. And it was then his hair appeared clearly for the first time since his walks bareheaded in the smiling haunts of his youth, his hat having remained in the place which his head had just left. For when, lying on your stomach in a wild and practically illimitable part of the country, you turn over on your back, then there is a sideways movement of the whole body, including the head, unless you make a point of avoiding it, and the head comes to rest at x inches approximately from where it was before, x being the width of the shoulders in inches, for the head is right in the middle of the shoulders. But when you are in a narrow bed, I mean one just wide enough to contain you, a pallet shall we say, then it is in vain you turn over on your back, then back over on your stomach, the head remains always in the same place, unless you make a point of inclining it to the right or to the left, and some there doubtless are who go to this trouble, in the hope of finding a little freshness. He tried to look at the dark streaming mass which was all that remained of sky and air, but the

rain hurt his eyes and shut them. He opened his mouth and
lay for a long time thus, his mouth open and his hands also
and as far apart as possible from each other. For it is a
curious thing, one tends less to clutch the ground when on
one's back than when on one's stomach, there is a curious
remark which might be worth following up. And just as an
hour before he had pulled up his sleeves the better to clutch
the grass, so now he pulled them up again the better to feel
the rain pelting down on his palms, also called the hollows
of the hands, or the flats, it all depends. And in the midst —
but I was nearly forgetting the hair, which from the point of
view of colour was to white very much as the hour's gloom
to black and from the point of view of length very long
what is more, very long behind and very long on either side.
And on a dry and windy day it would have gone romping in
the grass almost like grass itself. But the rain glued it to
the ground and churned it up with the earth and grass into
a kind of muddy pulp, not a muddy pulp, a kind of muddy
pulp. And in the midst of his suffering, for one does not remain
so long in such a position without being incommoded, he began
to wish that the rain would never cease nor consequently his
sufferings or pain, for the cause of his pain was almost
certainly the rain, recumbency in itself not being particularly
unpleasant, as if there existed a relation between that which
suffers and that which causes to suffer. For the rain could
cease without his ceasing to suffer, just as he could cease
to suffer without the rain's ceasing on that account. And
on him already this important quarter-truth was perhaps
beginning to dawn. For while deploring he could not spend
the rest of his life (which would thereby have been agreeably
abridged) under this heavy, cold (without being icy) and
perpendicular rain, now supine, now prone, he was quarter-
inclined to wonder if he was not mistaken in holding it
responsible for his sufferings and if in reality his discomfort
was not the effect of quite a different cause or set of causes.
For people are never content to suffer, but they must have
heat and cold, rain and its contrary which is fine weather, and
with that love, friendship, black skin and sexual and peptic
deficiency for example, in short the furies and frenzies
happily too numerous to be numbered of the body including
the skull and its annexes, whatever that means, such as the

clubfoot, in order that they may know very precisely what exactly it is that dares prevent their happiness from being unalloyed. And sticklers have been met with who had no peace until they knew for certain whether their carcinoma was of the pylorus or whether on the contrary it was not rather of the duodenum. But these are flights for which Macmann was not yet fledged, and indeed he was rather of the earth earthy and ill-fitted for pure reason, especially in the circumstances in which we have been fortunate enough to circumscribe him. And to tell the truth he was by temperament more reptile than bird and could suffer extensive mutilation and survive, happier sitting than standing and lying down than sitting, so that he sat and lay down at the least pretext and only rose again when the élan vital or struggle for life began to prod him in the arse again. And a good half of his existence must have been spent in a motionlessness akin to that of stone, not to say the three quarters, or even the four fifths, a motionlessness at first skin-deep, but which little by little invaded, I will not say the vital parts, but at least the sensibility and understanding. And it must be presumed that he received from his numerous forbears, through the agency of his papa and his mama, a cast-iron vegetative system, to have reached the age he has just reached and which is nothing or very little compared to the age he will reach, as I know to my cost, without any serious mishap, I mean one of a nature to carry him off on the spot. For no one ever came to his help, to help him avoid the thorns and snares that attend the steps of innocence, and he could never count on any other craft than his own, any other strength, to go from morning to evening and then from evening to morning without mortal hurt. And notably he never received any gifts of cash, or very seldom, and very paltry, which would not have mattered if he had been able to earn, in the sweat of his brow or by making use of his intelligence. But when given the job of weeding a plot of young carrots for example, at the rate of threepence or even sixpence an hour, it often happened that he tore them all up, through absent-mindedness, or carried away by I know not what irresistible urge that came over him at the sight of vegetables, and even of flowers, and literally blinded him to his true interests, the urge to make a clean sweep and have nothing before his eyes but a patch

244

SAMUEL BECKETT

of brown earth rid of its parasites, it was often more than
he could resist. Or without going so far as that, suddenly all
swam before his eyes, he could no longer distinguish the
plants destined for the embellishment of the home or the
nutrition of man and beast from the weeds which are said
to serve no useful purpose, but which must have their usefulness too, for the earth to favour them so, such as squitch
beloved of dogs and from which man too in his turn has
succeeded in extracting a brew, and the hoe fell from his
hands. And even with such humble occupations as street-
cleaning to which with hopefulness he had sometimes turned,
on the off chance of his being a born scavenger, he did not
succeed any better. And even he himself was compelled to
admit that the place swept by him looked dirtier at his departure than on his arrival, as if a demon had driven him
to collect, with the broom, shovel and barrow placed gratis
at his disposal by the corporation, all the dirt and filth which
chance had withdrawn from the sight of the tax-payer and
add them thus recovered to those already visible and which
he was employed to move. With the result that at the end
of the day, throughout the sector consigned to him, one
could see the peels of oranges and bananas, cigarette-butts,
unspeakable scraps of paper, dogs' and horses' excrement
and other muck, carefully concentrated all along the sidewalk or distributed on the crown of the street, as though in
order to inspire the greatest possible disgust in the passers-by
or provoke the greatest possible number of accidents, some
fatal, by means of the slip. And yet he had done his honest best
to give satisfaction, taking as his model his more experienced
colleagues, and doing as they did. But it was truly as if he
were not master of his movements and did not know what
he was doing, while he was doing it, nor what he had done,
once he had done it. For someone had to say to him, Look
at what you have done, sticking his nose in it so to speak,
otherwise he did not realize, but thought he had done as
any man of good will would have done in his place and with
very much the same results, in spite of his lack of experience.
And yet when it came to doing some little thing for himself,
as for example when he had to repair or replace one of his
buttons or pegs, which were not long-lived being mostly of
green wood and exposed to all the rigours of the temperate

zone, then he really exhibited a certain dexterity, without the
help of any other apparatus than his bare hands. And indeed
he had devoted to these little tasks a great part of his existence, that it is to say of the half or quarter of his existence
associated with more or less coordinated movements of the
body. For he had to, he had to, if he wished to go on coming
and going on the earth, which to tell the truth he did not,
particularly, but he had to, for obscure reasons known who
knows to God alone, though to tell the truth God does not
seem to need reasons for doing what he does, and for omit-
ting to do what he omits to do, to the same degree as his
creatures, does he? Such then seemed to be Macmann, seen
from a certain angle, incapable of weeding a bed of pansies
or marigolds and leaving one standing and at the same time
well able to consolidate his boots with willow bark and
thongs of wicker, so that he might come and go on the earth
from time to time and not wound himself too sorely on the
stones, thorns and broken glass provided by the carelessness
or wickedness of man, with hardly a complaint, for he had
to. For he was incapable of picking his steps and choosing
where to put down his feet (which would have permitted
him to go barefoot). And even had he been so he would
have been so to no great purpose, so little was he master of
his movements. And what is the good of aiming at the smooth
and mossy places when the foot, missing its mark, comes
down on the flints and shards or sinks up to the knee in
the cowpads? But to pass on now to considerations of another
order, it is perhaps not inappropriate to wish Macmann,
since wishing costs nothing, sooner or later a general paralysis
sparing at a pinch the arms if that is conceivable, in a place
impermeable as far as possible to wind, rain, sound, cold,
great heat (as in the seventh century) and daylight, with one
or two eiderdowns just in case and a charitable soul say once
a week bearing eating-apples and sardines in oil for the purpose of postponing as long as possible the fatal hour, it
would be wonderful. But in the meantime in the end, the rain
still falling with unabated violence in spite of his having
turned over on his back, Macmann grew restless, flinging
himself from side to side as though in a fit of the fever,
buttoning himself and unbuttoning and finally rolling over and
over in the same direction, it little matters which, with a

brief pause after each roll to begin with, then without break. And in theory his hat should have followed him, seeing it was tied to his coat, and the string twisted itself about his neck, but not at all, for theory is one thing and reality another, and the hat remained where it was, I mean in its place, like a thing forsaken. But perhaps one day a high wind would come and send it, dry and light again, bowling and bounding over the plain until it came to the town, or the ocean, but not necessarily. Now it was not the first time that Macmann rolled upon the ground, but he had always done so without ulterior locomotive motive. Whereas then, as he moved further and further from the place where the rain had caught him far from shelter and which thanks to the hat continued to contrast with the surrounding space, he realized he was advancing with regularity, and even a certain rapidity, along the arc of a gigantic circle probably, for he assumed that one of his extremities was heavier than the other, without knowing quite which, but not by much. And as he rolled he conceived and polished the plan of continuing to roll on all night if necessary, or at least until his strength should fail him, and thus approach the confines of this plain which to tell the truth he was in no hurry to leave, but nevertheless was leaving, he knew it. And without reducing his speed he began to dream of a flat land where he would never have to rise again and hold himself erect in equilibrium, first on the right foot for example, then on the left, and where he might come and go and so survive after the fashion of a great cylinder endowed with the faculties of cognition and volition. And without exactly building castles in Spain, for that

Quick quick my possessions. Quiet, quiet, twice, I have time, lots of time, as usual. My pencil, my two pencils, the one of which nothing remains between my huge fingers but the lead fallen from the wood and the other, long and round, in the bed somewhere, I was holding it in reserve, I won't look for it, I know it's there somewhere, if I have time when I've finished I'll look for it, if I don't find it I won't have it, I'll make the correction, with the other, if anything remains of it. Quiet, quiet. My exercise-book, I don't see it, but I

feel it in my left hand, I don't know where it comes from,
I didn't have it when I came here, but I feel it is mine. That's
the style, as if I were sweet and seventy. In that case the bed
would be mine too, and the little table, the dish, the pots,
the cupboard, the blankets. No, nothing of all that is mine.
But the exercise-book is mine, I can't explain. The two
pencils then, the exercise-book and then the stick, which I
did not have either when I came here, but which I consider
mine, I must have described it long ago. I am quiet, I have
time, but I shall describe as little as possible. It is with me
in the bed, under the blankets, there was a time I used to
rub myself against it saying, It's a little woman. But it is so
long that it sticks out under the pillow and finishes far
behind me. I continue from memory. It is black dark. I can
hardly see the window. It must be letting in the night again.
Even if I had time to rummage in my possessions, to bring
them over to the bed one by one or tangled together as is
often the way with forsaken things, I would not see anything.
And perhaps indeed I have the time, let us assume I have
the time, and proceed as if I had not. But it cannot be so
long since I checked and went through all my things, in the
light, in anticipation of this hour. But since then I must have
forgotten it all. A needle stuck into two corks to prevent it
from sticking into me, for if the point pricks less than the
eye, no, that's wrong, for if the point pricks more than the
eye, the eye pricks too, that's wrong too. Round the shank,
between the two corks, a wisp of black thread clings. It is a
pretty little object, like a — no, it is like nothing. The bowl
of my pipe, though I never used a tobacco-pipe. I must have
found it somewhere, on the ground, when out walking. There
it was, in the grass, thrown away because it could no longer
serve, the stem having broken off (I suddenly remember
that) just short of the bowl. This pipe could have been re-
paired, but he must have said, Bah, I'll buy myself another.
But all I found was the bowl. But all that is mere supposition.
Perhaps I thought it pretty, or felt for it that foul feeling of
pity I have so often felt in the presence of things, especially
little portable things in wood and stone, and which made me
wish to have them about me and keep them always, so that
I stooped and picked them up and put them in my pocket,
often with tears, for I wept up to a great age, never having

really evolved in the fields of affection and passion, in spite
of my experiences. And but for the company of these little
objects which I picked up here and there, when out walking, and which sometimes gave me the impression that
they too needed me, I might have been reduced to the
society of nice people or to the consolations of some religion
or other, but I think not. And I loved, I remember, as I
walked along, with my hands deep in my pockets, for I am
trying to speak of the time when I could still walk without a
stick and a fortiori without crutches, I loved to finger and ca-
ress the hard shapely objects that were there in my deep pockets, it was my way of talking to them and reassuring them.
And I loved to fall asleep holding in my hand a stone, a horse
chestnut or a cone, and I would be still holding it when I
woke, my fingers closed over it, in spite of sleep which makes
a rag of the body, so that it may rest. And those of which
I wearied, or which were ousted by new loves, I threw away,
that is to say I cast round for a place to lay them where they
would be at peace forever, and no one ever find them short
of an extraordinary hazard, and such places are few and far
between, and I laid them there. Or I buried them, or threw
them into the sea with all my strength as far as possible from
the land, those I knew for certain would not float, even
briefly. But many a wooden friend too I have sent to the
bottom, weighted with a stone. Until I realized it was wrong
of me. For when the string is rotted they would rise to the
surface, if they have not already done so, and return to the
land, sooner or later. In this way I disposed of things I loved
but could no longer keep, because of new loves. And often
I missed them. But I had hidden them so well that even I
could never find them again. That's the style, as if I still had
time to kill. And so I have, deep down I know it well. Then
why play at being in a hurry? I don't know. Perhaps I am
in a hurry after all, it was the impression I had a short
time ago. But my impressions. And what after all if I were
not so anxious as I make out to recall to mind all that is
left to me of all I ever had, a good dozen objects at least to
put it mildly? No no, I must. Then it's something else. Where
were we? My bowl. So I never got rid of it. I used it as a
receptable, I kept things in it, I wonder what I could have
kept in it, so small a space, and I made a little cap for it,

out of tin. Next. Poor Macmann. Decidedly it will never
have been given to me to finish anything, except perhaps
breathing. One must not be greedy. But is this how one
chokes? Presumably. And the rattle, what about the rattle?
Perhaps it is not de rigueur after all. To have vagitated and
not be bloody well able to rattle. How life dulls the power
to protest to be sure. I wonder what my last words will be,
written, the others do not endure, but vanish, into thin air.
I shall never know. I shall not finish this inventory either, a
little bird tells me so, the paraclete perhaps, psittaceously
named. Be it so. A club in my case, I can't help it, I must
state the facts, without trying to understand, to the end.
There are moments when I feel I have been here always,
perhaps even was born here. Then it passes. That would explain
many things. Or that I have come back after a long absence.
But I have done with feelings and hypotheses. This club is
mine and that is all about it. It is stained with blood, but
insufficiently, insufficiently. I have defended myself, ill, but
I have defended myself. That is what I tell myself sometimes.
One boot, originally yellow, I forget for which foot. The
other, its fellow, has gone. They took it away, at the beginning, before they realized I should never walk again. And
they left the other, in the hope I would be saddened, seeing
it there, without its fellow. Men are like that. Or perhaps it
is on top of the cupboard. I have looked for it everywhere,
with my stick, but I never thought of the top of the cupboard.
Till now. And as I shall never look for it any more, or anything else, either on top of the cupboard or anywhere else,
it is no longer mine. For only those things are mine the
whereabouts of which I know well enough to be able to lay
hold of them, if necessary, that is the definition I have
adopted, to define my possessions. For otherwise there would
be no end to it. But in any case there will be no end to it.
It did not greatly resemble — but it is wrong of me to dwell
upon it — the one I have preserved, the yellow one, remarkable for the number of its eyeholes, I never saw a boot with
so many eyeholes, useless for the most part, having ceased
to be holes, and become slits. All these things are together in
the corner in a heap. I could lay hold of them, even now,
in the dark, I need only to wish to do so. I would identify
them by touch, the message would flow all along the stick,

I would hook the desired object and bring it over to the bed, I would hear it coming towards me over the floor, gliding, jogging, less and less dear, I would hoist it up on the bed in such a way as not to break the window or damage the ceiling, and at last I would have it in my hands. If it was my hat I might put it on, that would remind me of the good old days, though I remember them sufficiently well. It has lost its brim, it looks like a bell-glass to put over a melon. In order to put it on and take it off you have to grasp it like a great ball, between your palms. It is perhaps the only object in my possession the history of which I have not forgotten, I mean counting from the day it became mine. I know in what circumstances it lost its brim, I was there at the time, it was so that I might keep it on while I slept. I should rather like it to be buried with me, a harmless whim, but what steps should I take? Mem, put it on on the off chance, well wedged down, before it is too late. But all in due time. Should I go on I wonder. I feel I am perhaps attributing to myself things I no longer possess and reporting as missing others that are not missing. And I feel there are others, over there in the corner, belonging to a third category, that of those of which I know nothing and with regard to which therefore there is little danger of my being wrong, or of my being right. And I remind myself also that since I last went through my possessions much water has passed beneath Butt Bridge, in both directions. For I have sufficiently perished in this room to know that some things go out, and other things come in, through I know not what agency. And among those that go out there are some that come back, after a more or less prolonged absence, and others that never come back. With the result that, among those that come in, some are familiar to me, others not. I don't understand. And, stranger still, there exists a whole family of objects, having apparently very little in common, which have never left me, since I have been here, but remained quietly in their place, in the corner, as in any ordinary uninhabited room. Or else they were very quick. How false all that rings. But there is no guarantee things will be ever thus. I cannot account in any other way for the changing aspect of my possessions. So that, strictly speaking, it is impossible for me to know, from one moment to the next, what is mine and what is not, according to my

definition. So I wonder if I should go on, I mean go on
drawing up an inventory corresponding perhaps but faintly
to the facts, and if I should not rather cut it short and devote
myself to some other form of distraction, of less consequence,
or simply wait, doing nothing, or counting perhaps, one, two,
three and so on, until all danger to myself from myself is past
at last. That is what comes of being scrupulous. If I had a
penny I would let it make up my mind. Decidedly the night
is long and poor in counsel. Perhaps I should persist until
dawn. All things considered. Good idea, excellent. If at dawn
I am still there I shall take a decision. I am half asleep. But
I dare not sleep. Rectifications in extremis, in extremissimis,
are always possible after all. But have I not perhaps just
passed away? Malone, Malone, no more of that. Perhaps I
should call in all my possessions such as they are and take
them into bed with me. Would that be of any use? I suppose
not. But I may. I have always that resource. When it is light
enough to see. Then I shall have them all around me, on
top of me, under me, in the corner there will be nothing left,
all will be in the bed, with me. I shall hold my photograph
my scrap of newspaper perhaps, or my buttons, and I shall
put on my hat. Perhaps I shall have something in my mouth,
my scrap of newspaper perhaps, or my buttons, and I shall
be lying on other treasures still. My photograph. It is not a
photograph of me, but I am perhaps at hand. It is an ass, taken
from in front and close up, at the edge of the ocean, it is
not the ocean, but for me it is the ocean. They naturally tried
to make it raise its head, so that its beautiful eyes might be
impressed on the celluloid, but it holds it lowered. You can tell
by its ears that it is not pleased. They put a boater on its
head. The thin hard parallel legs, the little hooves light and
dainty on the sand. The outline is blurred, that's the operator's
giggle shaking the camera. The ocean looks so unnatural that
you'd think you were in a studio, but is it not rather the
reverse I should say? No trace left of any clothes for example,
apart from the boot, the hat and three socks, I counted them.
Where have my clothes disappeared, my greatcoat, my
trousers and the flannel that Mr. Quin gave me, with the
remark that he did not need it any more? Perhaps they were
burnt. But our business is not with what I have no longer,
such things do not count at such a moment, whatever people

may say. In any case I think I'll stop. I was keeping the best
for the end, but I don't feel very well, perhaps I'm going,
that would surprise me. It is a passing weakness, everyone has
experienced that. One weakens, then it passes, one's strength
comes back and one resumes. That is probably what is happening to me. I yawn, would I yawn if it was serious? Why
not? I would gladly eat a little soup, if there was any left.
No, even if there was some left I would not eat it. So there.
It is some days now since my soup was renewed, did I mention that? I suppose so. It is in vain I dispatch my table to
the door, bring it back beside me, move it to and fro in the
hope that the noise will be heard and correctly interpreted
in the right quarters, the dish remains empty. One of the pots
on the other hand remains full, and the other is filling slowly.
If I ever succeed in filling it I shall empty them both out on
the floor, but it is unlikely. Now that I have stopped eating
I produce less waste and so eliminate less. The pots do not
seem to be mine, I simply have the use of them. They answer
to the definition of what is mine, but they are not mine.
Perhaps it is the definition that is at fault. They have each
two handles or ears, projecting above the rim and facing
each other, into which I insert my stick. In this way I move
my pots about, lift them up and set them down. Nothing
has been left to chance. Or is it a happy chance? I can therefore easily turn them upside down, if I am driven to it, and
wait for them to empty, as long as necessary. After this
passing reference to my pots I feel a little more lively. They
are not mine, but I say my pots, as I say my bed, my window,
as I say me. Nevertheless I shall stop. It is my possessions
have weakened me, if I start talking about them again I shall
weaken again, for the same causes give rise to the same
effects. I should have liked to speak of the cap of my bicycle-
bell, of my half-crutch, the top half, you'd think it was a
baby's crutch. But I can still do so, what is there to prevent
me? I don't know. I can't. To think I shall perhaps die of
hunger, after all, of starvation rather, after having struggled
successfully all my life against that menace. I can't believe
it. There is a providence for impotent old men, to the end.
And when they cannot swallow any more someone rams a
tube down their gullet, or up their rectum, and fills them full
of vitaminized pap, so as not to be accused of murder. I shall

therefore die of old age pure and simple, glutted with days
as in the days before the flood, on a full stomach. Perhaps
they think I am dead. Or perhaps they are dead themselves.
I say they, though perhaps I should not. In the beginning,
but it was in the beginning, I used to see an old woman,
then for a time an old yellow arm, then for a time an old
yellow hand. But these were probably no more than the agents
of a consortium. And indeed the silence at times is such
that the earth seems uninhabited. That is what comes of the
taste for generalisation. You have only to hear nothing for
a few days, in your hole, nothing but the sounds of things,
and you begin to fancy yourself the last of human kind. What
if I started to scream? Not that I wish to draw attention to
myself, simply to try and find out if there is someone about.
But I don't like screaming. I have spoken softly, gone my
ways softly, all my days, as behoves one who has nothing
to say, nowhere to go, and so nothing to gain by being seen
or heard. Not to mention the possibility of there being not
a living soul within a radius of one hundred yards and then
such multitudes· of people that they are walking on top of
one another. They do not dare come near me. In that case I
could scream my head off to no purpose. I shall try all the
same. I have tried. I heard nothing out of the ordinary. No,
I exaggerate, I heard a kind of burning croak deep down in
the windpipe, as when one has heartburn. With practice I
might produce a groan, before I die. I am not sleepy any
more. In any case I must not sleep any more. What tedium.
I have missed the ebb. Did I say I only say a small proportion of the things that come into my head? I must have. I
choose those that seem somehow akin. It is not always easy.
I hope they are the most important. I wonder If I shall ever
be able to stop. Perhaps I should throw away my lead. I
could never retrieve it now. I might be sorry. My little lead. It
is a risk I do not feel inclined to take, just now. What then?
I wonder if I could not contrive, wielding my stick like a
punt-pole, to move my bed. It may well be on castors, many
beds are. Incredible I should never have thought of this, all
the time I have been here.. I might even succeed in steering it,
it is so narrow, through the door, and even down the stairs,
if there is a stairs that goes down. To be off and away. The
dark is against me, in a sense. But I can always try and see if

the bed will move. I have only to set the stick against the
wall and push. And I can see myself already, if successful,
taking a little turn in the room, until it is light enough for me
to set forth. At least while thus employed I shall stop telling
myself lies. And then, who knows, the physical effort may
polish me off, by means of heart failure.

I have lost my stick, That is the outstanding event of the
day, for it is day again. The bed has not stirred. I must have
missed my point of purchase, in the dark. Sine qua non,
Archimedes was right. The stick, having slipped, would have
plucked me from the bed if I had not let it go. It would of
course have been better for me to relinquish my bed than
to lose my stick. But I had not time to think. The fear of
falling is the source of many a folly. It is a disaster. I suppose
the wisest thing now is to live it over again, meditate upon it
and be edified. It is thus that man distinguishes himself from
the ape and rises, from discovery to discovery, ever higher,
towards the light. Now that I have lost my stick I realize what
it is I have lost and all it meant to me. And thence ascend,
painfully, to an understanding of the Stick, shorn of all its
accidents, such as I had never dreamt of. What a broadening
of the mind. So that I half discern, in the veritable catastrophe
that has befallen me, a blessing in disguise. How comforting
that is. Catastrophe too in the ancient sense no doubt. To
be buried in lava and not turn a hair, it is then a man shows
what stuff he is made of. To know you can do better next
time, unrecognizably better, and that there is no next time,
and that it is a blessing there is not, there is a thought to
be going on with. I thought I was turning my stick to the
best possible account, like a monkey scratching its fleas with
the key that opens its cage. For it is obvious to me now that
by making a more intelligent use of my stick I might have
extracted myself from my bed and perhaps even got myself
back into it, when tired of rolling and dragging myself about
the floor or on the stairs. That would have introduced a little
variety into my decomposition. How is it that never occurred
to me? It is true I had no wish to leave my bed. But can the
sage have no wish for something the very possibility of which
he does not conceive? I don't understand. The sage perhaps.

But I? It is day again, at least what passes for such here. I must have fallen asleep after a brief bout of discouragement, such as I have not experienced for a long time. For why be discouraged, one of the thieves was saved, that is a generous percentage. I see the stick on the floor, not far from the bed. That is to say I see part of it, as of all one sees. It might just as well be at the equator, or one of the poles. No, not quite, for perhaps I shall devise a way of retrieving it, I am so ingenious. All is not then yet quite irrevocably lost. In the meantime nothing is mine any more, according to my definition, if I remember rightly, except my exercise-book, my lead and the French pencil, assuming it really exists. I did well to stop my inventory, it was a happy thought. I feel less weak, perhaps they fed me while I slept. I see the pot, the one that is not full, it is lost to me too. I shall doubtless be obliged to forget myself in the bed, as when I was a baby. At least I shall not be skelped. But enough about me. You would thing I was relieved to be without my stick. I think I know how I might retrieve it. But something occurs to me. Are they depriving me of soup on purpose to help me die? One judges people too hastily. But in that case why feed me during my sleep? But there is no proof they have. But if they wished to help me would it not be more intelligent to give me poisoned soup, large quantities of poisoned soup? Perhaps they fear an autopsy. It is obvious they see a long way ahead. That reminds me that among my possessions I once had a little phial, unlabelled, containing pills. Laxatives? Sedatives? I forget. To turn to them for calm and merely obtain a diarrhoea, my, that would be annoying. In any case the question does not arise I am calm, insufficiently, I still lack a little calm. But enough about me. I'll see if there is anything in my little idea, I mean how to retrieve my stick. The fact is I must be very weak. If there is, anything in it I mean, I shall try and get myself out of the bed, for a start. If not I do not know what I shall do. Go and see how Macmann is getting on perhaps. I have always that resource. Why this need of activity? I am growing nervous.

One day, much later, to judge by his appearance, Macmann came to again, once again, in a kind of asylum. At first he did not know it was one, being plunged within it, but he was

told so as soon as he was in a condition to receive news. They
said in substance, You are now in the House of Saint John
of God, with the number one hundred and sixty-six. Fear
nothing, you are among friends. Friends! Well well. Take no
thought for anything, it is we shall think and act for you,
from now forward. We like it. Do not thank us therefore.
In addition to the nourishment carefully calculated to keep
you alive, and even well, you will receive, every Saturday,
in honour of our patron, an imperial half-pint of porter and
a plug of tobacco. Then followed instructions regarding his
duties and prerogatives, for he was credited with a certain
number of prerogatives, notwithstanding the bounties show-
ered upon him. Stunned by this torrent of civility, for he had
eluded charity all his days, Macmann did not immediately
grasp that he was being spoken to. The room, or cell, in
which he lay, was thronged with men and women dressed
in white. They swarmed about his bed, those in the rear
rising on tiptoe and craning their necks to get a better view
of him. The speaker was a man, naturally, in the flower and
the prime of life, his features stamped with mildness and
severity in equal proportions, and he wore a scraggy beard
no doubt intended to heighten his resemblance to the Messiah.
To tell the truth, yet again, he did not so much read as
improvise, or recite, to judge by the paper he held in his hand
and on which from time to time he cast an anxious eye. He
finally handed this paper to Macmann, together with the
stump of an indelible pencil, the point of which he first wetted
with his lips, and requested him to sign, adding that it was
a mere formality. And when Macmann had obeyed, either because he was afraid of being punished if he refused or
because he did not realize the seriousness of what he was
doing, the other took back the paper, examined it and said,
Mac what? It was then a woman's voice, extraordinarily shrill
and unpleasant, was heard to say, Mann, his name is Macmann. This woman was standing behind him, so that he could
not see her, and in each hand she clutched a bar of the bed.
Who are you? said the speaker. Someone replied, But it is
Moll, can't you see, her name is Moll. The speaker turned
towards this informant, glared at him for a moment, then
dropped his eyes. To be sure, he said, to be sure, I am out of
sorts. He added, after a pause, Nice name, without its being

quite clear whether this little tribute was aimed at the nice name of Moll or at the nice name of Macmann. Don't push, for Jesus' sake! he said, irritably. Then, suddenly turning, he cried, What in God's name are you all pushing for for Christ's sake? And indeed the room was filling more and more. under the influx of fresh spectators. Personally I'm going, said the speaker. Then all retreated, in great jostle and dis-order, each one striving to be first out through the door, with the sole exception of Moll, who did not stir. But when all were gone she went to the door and shut it, then came back and sat down on a chair by the bed. She was a little old woman, immoderately ill-favoured of both face and body. She seems called on to play a certain part in the remarkable events, which I hope, will enable me to make an end. The thin yellow arms contorted by some kind of bone deformation, the lips so broad and thick that they seemed to devour half the face, were at first sight her most revolting features. She wore by way of ear-rings two long ivory crucifixes which swayed wildly at the least movement of her head.

I pause to record that I feel in extraordinary form. De-lirium perhaps.

It seemed probable to Macmann that he was committed to the care and charge of this person. Correct. For it had been decreed, by those in authority, that one hundred and sixty-six was Moll's, she having applied for him, formally. She brought him food (one large dish daily, to eat first hot, then cold), emptied his chamber-pot every morning first thing and showed him how to wash himself, his face and hands every day, and the other parts of the body successively in the course of the week, Monday the feet, Tuesday the legs up to the knees, Wednesday the thighs, and so on, culminating on Sunday with the neck and ears, no, Sunday he rested from washing. She swept the floor, shook up the bed from time to time and seemed to take an extreme pleasure in polishing until they shone the frosted lights of the unique window, which was never opened. She informed Macmann, when he did some-thing, if that thing was permitted or not, and similarly, when he remained inert, whether or not he was entitled to. Does this mean that she stayed with him all the time? Why no, and no doubt she had other attentions to bestow elsewhere,

and other instructions to give. But in the early stages, before
he had grown used to this new tide in his fortune, she
assuredly left him alone as little as possible and even watched
over him part of the night. How understanding she was, and
how good-natured, appears from the following anecdote. One
day, not long after his admission, Macmann realized he was
wearing instead of his usual accoutrement, a long loose smock
of course linen, or possibly drugget. He at once began to
clamour loudly for his clothes, including probably the contents of his pockets, for he cried, My things! My things!, over
and over again, tossing about in the bed and beating the blanket
with his palms. Then Moll sat down on the edge of the bed
and distributed her hands as follows, one on top of one of
Macmann's, the other on his brow. She was so small that
her feet did not reach the floor. When he was a little calmer
she told him that his clothes had certainly ceased to exist and
could not therefore be returned to him. With regard to the
objects found in the pockets, they had been assessed as quite
worthless and fit only to be thrown away with the exception
of a little silver knife-rest which he could have back at any
time. But these declarations so distressed him that she hastened
to add, with a laugh, that she was only joking and that in
reality his clothes, cleaned, pressed, mended, strewn with
mothballs and folded away in a cardboard box bearing his
name and number, were as safe as if they had been received in
deposit by the Bank of England. But as Macmann continued
vehemently to demand his things, as if he did not understand
a word of what she had just told him, she was obliged to
invoke the regulations which tolerated on no account that
an inmate should resume contact with the trappings of his
derelict days until such time as he might be discharged. But
as Macmann continued passionately to clamour for his things,
and notably for his hat, she left him, saying he was not reasonable. And she came back a little later, holding with the tips
of her fingers the hat in question, retrieved perhaps from the
rubbish-heap at the end of the vegetable-garden, for to know
everything takes too long, for it was fringed with manure
and seemed to be rotting away. And what is more she suffered
him to put it on, and even helped him to do so, helping him
to sit up in the bed and arranging his pillows in such a way
that he might remain propped up without fatigue. And she

contemplated with tenderness the old bewildered face relaxing, and in its tod of hair the mouth trying to smile, and the little red eyes turning timidly towards her as if in gratitude or rolling towards the recovered hat, and the hands raised to set it on more firmly and returning to rest trembling on the blanket. And at last a long look passed between them and Moll's lips puffed and parted in a dreadful smile, which made Macmann's eyes waver like those of an animal glared on by its master and compelled then finally to look away. End of anecdote. This must be the selfsame hat that was abandoned in the middle of the plain, its resemblance to it is so great, allowance being made for the additional wear and tear. Can it be then that it is not the same Macmann at all, after all, in spite of the great resemblance (for those who know the power of the passing years), both physical and otherwise. It is true the Macmanns are legion in the island and pride themselves, what is more, with few exceptions, on having one and all, in the last analysis, sprung from the same illustrious ball. It is therefore inevitable they should resemble one another, now and then, to the point of being confused even in the minds of those who wish them well and would like nothing better than to tell between them. No matter, any old remains of flesh and spirit do, there is no sense in stalking people. So long as it is what is called a living being you can't go wrong, you have the guilty one. For a long time he did not stir from his bed, not knowing if he could walk, or even stand, and fearing to run foul of the authorities, if he could. Let us then first consider this first phase of Macmann's stay in the House of Saint John of God. We shall then pass on to the second, and even to the third, if necessary.

A thousand little things to report, very strange, in view of my situation, if I interpret them correctly. But my notes have a curious tendency, as I realize at last, to annihilate all they purport to record. So I hasten to turn aside from this extraordinary heat, to mention only it, which has seized on certain parts of my economy, I will not specify which. And to think I was expecting rather to grow cold, if anything!

This first phase, that of the bed, was characterized by the evolution of the relationship between Macmann and his keeper. There sprang up gradually between them a kind of intimacy which, at a given moment, led them to lie together and copulate as best they could. For given their age and scant experience of carnal love, it was only natural they should not succeed, at the first shot, in giving each other the impression they were made for each other. The spectacle was then offered of Macmann trying to bundle his sex into his partner's like a pillow into a pillow-slip, folding it in two, and stuffing it in with his fingers. But far from losing heart they warmed to their work. And though both were completely impotent they finally succeeded, summoning to their aid all the resources of the skin, the mucus and the imagination, in striking from their dry and feeble clips a kind of sombre gratification. So that Moll exclaimed, being (at that stage) the more expansive of the two, Oh would we had but met sixty years ago! But on the long road to this what flutterings, alarms and bashful fumblings, of which only this, that they gave Macmann some insight into the meaning of the expression, Two is company. He then made unquestionable progress in the use of the spoken word and learnt in a short time to let fall, at the right time, the yesses, noes, mores, and enoughs that keep love alive. It was also the occasion of his penetrating into the enchanted world of reading, thanks to the inflammatory letters which Moll brought and put into his hands. And the memories of school are so tenacious, for those who have been there, that he was soon able to dispense with the explanations of his correspondent and understand all unaided, holding the sheet of paper as far from his eyes as his arms permitted. While he read Moll held a little aloof, with downcast eyes, saying to herself, Now he's at the part where, and a little later, Now he's at the part where, and so remained until the rustle of the sheet going back into the envelope announced that he had finished. Then she turned eagerly towards him, in time to see him raise the letter to his lips or press it against his heart, another reminiscence of the fourth form. Then he gave it back to her and she put it under his pillow with the others there already, arranged in chronological order and tied together by a favour. These letters did not much vary in form and tenor, which greatly facilitated matters for Macmann. Example. Sweetheart, Not one day goes by that I do not give thanks to God, on my bended knees, for having found

you, before I die. For we shall soon die, you and I, that is
obvious. That it may be at the same moment exactly is all
I ask. In any case I have the key of the medicine cupboard.
But let us profit first by this superb sundown, after the long
day of storm. Are you not of this opinion? Sweetheart! Ah
would we had met but seventy years ago! No, all is for the
best, we shall not have time to grow to loathe each other,
to see our youth slip by, to recall with nausea the ancient
rapture, to seek in the company of third parties, you on the
one hand, I on the other, that which together we can no
longer compass, in a word to get to know each other. One
must look things in the face, must one not, sweet pet? When
you hold me in your arms, and I you in mine, it naturally
does not amount to much, compared to the transports of
youth, and even middle age. But all is relative, let us bear
that in mind, stags and hinds have their needs and we have
ours. It is even astonishing that you manage so well, I can
hardly get over it, what a chaste and sober life you must
have led. I too, you must have noticed it. Consider moreover that the flesh is not the end-all and the be-all, especially
at our age, and name me the lovers who can do with their
eyes what we can do with ours, which will soon have seen
all there is for them to see and have often great difficulty
in remaining open, and with their tenderness, without the
help of passion, what by this means alone we realize daily,
when separated by our respective obligations. Consider furthermore, since there is nothing more for us to hide, that I
was never beautiful or well-proportioned, but ugly and even
misshapen, to judge by the testimonies I have received. Papa
notably used to say that people would run a mile from me,
I have not forgotten the expression. And you, sweet, even
when you were of an age to quicken the pulse of beauty, did
you exhibit the other requisites? I doubt it. But with the passing of the years we have become scarcely less hideous than
even our best favored contemporaries and you, in particular,
have kept your hair. And thanks to our having never served,
never understood, we are not without freshness and innocence,
it seems to me. Moral, for us at last it is the season of love,
let us make the most of it, there are pears that only ripen in
December. Do not fret about our methods, leave all that to me,
and I warrant you we'll surprise each other yet. With regard

to tetty-beshy I must beg to differ, it is well worth persevering with, in my opinion. Follow my instructions, you'll come back for more. For shame, you dirty old man! It's all these bones that makes it awkward, that I grant you. Well, we must just accept ourselves as we are. And above all *not fret*, these are trifles. Let us think of the hours when, spent, we lie twined together in the dark, our hearts labouring as one, and listen to the wind saying what it is to be abroad, at night, in winter, and what it is to have been what we have been, and sink together, in an unhappiness that has no name. That is how we must look at things. So courage, my sweet old hairy Mac, and oyster kisses just where you think from your own Sucky Moll. P.S. I enquire about the oysters, I have hopes. Such was the rather rambling style of the declarations which Moll, despairing no doubt of giving vent to her feelings by the normal channels, addressed three or four times a week to Macmann, who never answered, I mean in writing, but manifested by every other means in his power how pleased he was to receive them. But towards the close of this idyll, that is to say when it was too late, he began to compose brief rimes of curious structure, to offer to his mistress, for he felt she was drifting away from him. Example.

> *Hairy Mac and Sucky Molly*
> *In the ending days and nights*
> *Of unending melancholy*
> *Love it is at last unites.*

Other example.

> *To the lifelong promised land*
> *Of the nearest cemetery*
> *With his Sucky hand in hand*
> *Love it is at last leads Hairy.*

He had time to compose ten or twelve more or less in this vein, all remarkable for their exaltation of love regarded as a kind of lethal glue, a conception frequently to be met with in mystic texts. And it is extraordinary that Macmann should have succeeded, in so short a time and after such inauspicious beginnings, in elevating himself to a view of this altitude.

And one can only speculate on what he might have achieved if he had become acquainted with true sexuality at a less advanced age.

I am lost. Not a word.

Inauspicious beginnings indeed, during which his feeling for Moll was frankly one of repugnance. Her lips in particular repelled him, those selfsame lips, or so little changed as to make no matter, that some months later he was to suck with grunts of pleasure, so that at the very sight of them he not only closed his eyes, but covered them with his hands for greater safety. She it was therefore who at this period exerted herself in tireless ardours, which may serve to explain why she seemed to weaken in the end and stand in her turn in need of stimulation. Unless it was simply a question of health. Which does not exclude a third hypothesis, namely that Moll, having finally decided that she had been mistaken in Macmann and that he was not the man she had taken him for, sought a means of putting an end to their intercourse, but gently, in order not to give him a shock. Unfortunately our concern here is not with Moll, who after all is only a female, but with Macmann, and not with the close of their relations, but rather with the beginning. Of the brief period of plenitude between these two extremes, when between warming up of the one party and the cooling down of the other there was established a fleeting equality of temperature, no further mention will be made. For if it is indispensable to have in order not to have had and in order to have no longer, there is no obligation to expatiate upon it. But let us rather let events speak for themselves, that is more or less the right tone. Example. One day, just as Macmann was getting used to being loved, though without as yet responding as he was subsequently to do, he thrust Moll's face away from his on the pretext of examining her ear-rings. But as she made to return to the charge he checked her again with the first words that came into his head, namely, Why two Christs?, implying that in his opinion one was more than sufficient. To which she made the absurd reply, Why two ears? But obtained his forgiveness a moment later, saying, with a smile (she smiled at the least thing), Besides they are the thieves, Christ is in my mouth. Then parting her jaws and pulling down her blobber-lip she discovered, breaking with its solitary fang the monotony of the gums, a long yellow canine bared to the roots and carved, with the drill probably, to represent the celebrated sacrifice. With the forefinger of her free hand she fingered it. It's loose, she said, one of these fine mornings I'll wake up and find I've swallowed it, perhaps I should have it out. She let go her lip, which sprang back into place with a smack. This incident made a strong impression on Macmann and Moll rose with a bound in his affections. And in the pleasure he was later to enjoy, when he put his tongue in her mouth and let it wander over her gums, this rotten crucifix had assuredly its part. But from these harmless aids what love is free? Sometimes it is an object, a garter I believe or a sweat-absorber for the armpit. And sometimes it is the simple image of a third party. A few words in conclusion on the decline of this liaison. No, I can't.

Weary with my weariness, white last moon, sole regret, not even. To be dead, before her, on her, with her, and turn, dead on dead, about poor mankind, and never have to die any more, from among the living. Not even, not even that. My moon was here below, far below, the little I was able to desire. And one day, soon, soon, one earthlit night, be- neath the earth, a dying being will say, like me, in the earth- light, Not even, not even that, and die, without having been able to find a regret.

Moll. I'm going to kill her. She continued to look after Macmann, but she was no longer the same. When she had finished cleaning up she sat down on a chair, in the middle of the room, and remained without stirring. If he called her she went and perched on the edge of the bed and even sub- mitted to be titillated. But it was obvious her thoughts were elsewhere and her only wish to return to her chair and resume the now familiar gesture of massaging her stomach, slowly, weighing on it with her two hands. She was also beginning to smell. She had never smelt sweet, but between not smelling sweet and giving off the smell she was giving off now there is a gulf. She was also subject to fits of vomit- ing. Turning away, so that her lover should only see her convulsive back, she vomited at length on the floor. And these dejections remained sometimes for hours where they fell, until such time as she had the strength to go and fetch what was needed to clean up the mess. Half a century younger she might have been taken for pregnant. At the same time her hair began to fall out in abundance and she confessed to Macmann that she did not dare comb it any more, for fear of making it fall out even faster. He said to himself with satisfaction, She tells me everything. But these were small things compared to the change in her complexion, now rapidly turning from yellow to saffron. The sight of her so diminished did not damp Macmann's desire to take her, all stinking, yellow, bald and vomiting, in his arms. And he would certainly have done so had she not been opposed to it. One can understand him (her too). For when one has within reach the one and only love requited of a life so monstrously prolonged, it is natural one should wish to profit by it, before it is too late, and refuse to be deterred by feelings of squeamishness excusable in the faint-hearted, but which true love disdains. And though all pointed to Moll's being out of sorts, Macmann could not help interpreting her attitude as a falling off of her affection for him. And perhaps indeed there was something of that too. At all events the more she declined the more Macmann longed to crush her to his breast, which is at least sufficiently curious and unusual to deserve of mention. And when she turned and looked at him (and from time to time she did so still), with eyes in which he fancied he could read boundless regret and love, then a kind of frenzy seized upon him and he began to belabour with his fists his chest, his head and even the mattress, writhing and crying out, in the hope perhaps she would take pity on him and come and comfort him and dry his tears, as on the day when he had demanded his hat. No, it was not that, it was without malice he cried, writhed and beat his breast, for she made no attempt to stop him and even left the room if it went on too long for her liking. Then, all alone and unobserved, he continued to behave as if beside himself, which is proof positive, is it not, that he was disinterested, unless of course he suspected her of having stopped outside the door to listen. And when he grew calm again at last he mourned the long immunity he had lost, from shelter, charity

and human tenderness. And he even carried his inconsequence
to the length of wondering what right anyone had to take
care of him. In a word most evil days, for Macmann. For
Moll too probably, naturally, admittedly. It was at this time
she lost her tooth. It fell unaided from the socket, happily
in the day time, so that she was able to recover it and put
it away in a safe place. Macmann said to himself, when she
told him, There was a time she would have made me a
present of it, or at least shown it to me. But a little later
he said, firstly, To have told me, when she need not have, is
a mark of confidence and affection, and secondly, But I would
have known in any case, when she opened her mouth to
speak or smile, and finally, But she does not speak or smile
any more. One morning early a man whom he had never
seen came and told him that Moll was dead. There's one out
of the way at least. My name is Lemuel, he said, though my
parents were probably Aryan, and it is in my charge you are
from now on. Here is your porridge. Eat while it is boiling.

A last effort. Lemuel gave the impression of being slightly
more stupid than malevolent, and yet his malevolence was
considerable. When Macmann, more and more disturbed by
his situation apparently and what is more now capable of
isolating and expressing well enough to be understood a little
of the little that passed through his mind, when Macmann I
say asked a question it was seldom he got an immediate
answer. When asked for example to state whether Saint John
of Gods was a private institution or run by the State, a hospice
for the aged and infirm or a madhouse, if once in one might
entertain the hope of one day getting out and, in the affirma-
tive, by means of what steps, Lemuel remained for a long time
plunged in thought, sometimes for as long as ten minutes or a
quarter of an hour, motionless or if you prefer scratching his
head or his armpit, as if such questions had never crossed his
mind, or possibly thinking about something quite different.
And if Macmann, growing impatient or perhaps feeling he
had not made himself clear, ventured to try again, an imper-
ious gesture bid him be silent. Such was this Lemuel, viewed
from a certain angle. Or he cried, stamping the ground with
indescribable nervousness, Let me think, you shite! It usually

ended by his saying he did not know. But he was subject to
almost hypomaniacal fits of good-humor. Then he would add,
But I'll enquire. And taking out a note-book as fat as a ship's
log he made note, murmuring, Private or state, mad or like
me, how out, etc. Macmann could then be sure he would
never hear any more about it. May I get up? he said one day.
Already in Moll's lifetime he had expressed the wish to get up
and go out into the fresh air, but timidly, as when one asks
for the moon. And he had then been told that if he was good
he might indeed be let up one day, and out into the pure
plateau air, and that on that day, in the great hall where the
staff assembled at dawn before entering on their duties, there
would be seen pinned on the board a note thus conceived, Let
one hundred and sixty-six get up and go out. For when it
came to the regulations Moll was inflexible and their voice
was stronger than the voice of love, in her heart, whenever
they made themselves heard there simultaneously. The oysters
for example, which the Board had refused in a note calling
her attention to the article whereby they were prohibited, but
which she could easily have smuggled in, Macmann never saw
sight or sign of the oysters. But Lemuel was made of sterner
stuff, in this connexion, and far from being a stickler for the
statutes seemed to have little or no acquaintance with them.
Indeed the question might have arisen, in the mind of one
looking down upon the scene, as to whether he had all his
wits about him. For when not rooted to the spot in a daze
he was to be seen, with heavy, furious reeling tread, stamping
up and down for hours on end, gesticulating and ejaculating
unintelligible words. Flayed alive by memory, his mind crawling with cobras, not daring to dream or think and powerless
not to, his cries were of two kinds, those having no other
cause than moral anguish and those, similar in every respect,
by means of which he hoped to forestall same. Physical pain,
on the contrary, seemed to help him greatly. And one day
rolling up the leg of his trousers, he showed Macmann his
shin covered with bruises, scars and abrasions. Then produc-
ing smartly a hammer from an inner pocket he dealt himself,
right in the middle of his ancient wounds, so violent a blow
that he fell down backwards, or perhaps I should say forwards.
But the part he struck most readily, with his hammer, was
the head, and that is understandable, for it too is a bony part,

and sensitive, and difficut to miss, and the seat of all the shit
and misery, so you rain blows upon it, with more pleasure
than on the leg for example, which never did you any harm,
it's only human. Up! cried Macmann. Let me up! Lemuel
came to a standstill. What? he roared. Up! cried Macmann.
Let me up! Let me up!

I have had a visit. Things were going too well. I had
forgotten myself, lost myself. I exaggerate. Things were not
going too badly. I was elsewhere. Another was suffering. Then
I had the visit. To bring me back to dying. If that amuses
them. The fact is they don't know, neither do I, but they
think they know. An aeroplane passes, flying low, with a
noise like thunder. It is a noise quite unlike thunder, one says
thunder but one does not think it, it is just a loud, fleeting
noise, nothing more, unlike any other. It is certainly the first
time I have heard it here, to my knowledge. But I have heard
aeroplanes elsewhere and have even seen them in flight, I
saw the very first in flight and then in the end the latest
models, oh not the very latest, the very second-latest, the
very antepenultimate. I was present at one of the first loop-
ings of the loop, so help me God. I was not afraid. It was
above a racecourse, my mother held me by the hand, She kept
saying, It's a miracle, a miracle. Then I changed my mind. We
were not often of the same mind. One day we were walking
along the road, up a hill of extraordinary steepness, near
home I imagine, my memory is full of steep hills, I get
them confused. I said, The sky is further away than you think,
is it not, mama? It was without malice, I was simply thinking
of all the leagues that separated me from it. She replied, to me
her son, It is precisely as far away as it appears to be. She was
right. But at the time I was aghast. I can still see the spot,
opposite Tyler's gate. A market-gardener, he had only one
eye and wore sidewhiskers. That's the idea, rattle on. You
could see the sea, the islands, the headlands, the isthmuses,
the coast stretching away to north and south and the crooked
moles of the harbor. We were on our way home from the
butcher's. My mother? Perhaps it is just another story, told
me by some one who found it funny. The stories I was told,
at one time! And all funny, not one not funny. In any case

here I am back in the shit. The aeroplane, on the other hand,
has just passed over at two hundred miles an hour perhaps. It's
a good speed, for the present day. I am with it in spirit,
naturally. All the things I was always with in spirit. In body
no. Not such a fool. Here is the programme anyhow, the end
of the programme. They think they can confuse me and
make me lose sight of my programmes. Proper cunts whoever
they are. Here it is. Visit, various remarks, Macmann continued, agony recalled. Macmann continued, then mixture of
Macmann and agony as long as possible. It does not depend
on me, my lead is not inexhaustible, nor my exercise-book,
nor Macmann, nor myself in spite of appearances. That all
may be wiped out at the same instant is all I ask, for the
moment. The visit. I felt a violent blow on the head. He had
perhaps been there for some time. One does not care to be
kept waiting for ever, one draws attention to oneself as best
one can, it's human. I don't doubt he gave me due warning,
before he hit me. I don't know what he wanted. He's gone
now. What an idea, all the same, to hit me on the head. The
light has been queer ever since, oh I insinuate nothing, dim
and at the same time radiant, perhaps I have concussion. His
mouth opened, his lips worked, but I heard nothing. He
might as well have said nothing. And yet I am not deaf, witness the aeroplane, if I hear nothing it is because there is
nothing to hear. But perhaps life has dulled my irritability to
specifically human sounds. I myself for example make no
sound, well well, can't go back on it now, no, not the tiniest.
And yet I pant, cough, moan and gulp right up against my ear,
I could swear to it. In other words I do not know to what I
owe the honor. He seemed vexed. Must I describe him? Why
not? He may be important. I had a clear view of him. Black
suit of antiquated cut, or perhaps come back into the fashion,
black tie, snow-white shirt, heavily starched clown's cuffs almost entirely covering the hands, oily black hair, a long,
dismal, glabrous, floury face, sombre lacklustre eyes, medium
height and build, block-hat pressed delicately to stomach with
fingertips, then without warning a gesture of extraordinary
suddenness and precision slapped on skull. A folding-rule,
together with a fin of white hankerchief, emerged from the
breast pocket. I took him at first for the undertaker's man,
annoyed at having called prematurely. He remained some

time, seven hours at least. Perhaps he hoped to have the
satisfaction of seeing me expire before he left, that would
probably have saved him time and trouble. For a moment
I thought he was going to finish me off. What a hope, it
would have been a crime. He must have left at six o'clock,
his working day ended. The light is queer ever since. That is
to say he went a first time, came back some hours later, then
left for good. He must have been here from nine to twelve,
then from two to six, now I have it. He kept looking at his
watch, a turnip. Perhaps he will come back to-morrow. It
was in the morning he hit me, about ten o'clock probably. In
the afternoon he did not touch me, though I did not see him
immediately, he was already in position when I saw him,
standing beside the bed. I speak of morning and afternoon and
of such and such an hour, if you simply must speak of people
you simply must put yourself in their place, it is not difficult.
The only thing you must never speak of is your happiness, I
can think of nothing else for the moment. Better even not to
think of it. Standing by the bed he watched me. Seeing my
lips move, for I tried to speak he stooped down to me. I had
things to ask him, to give me my stick for example. He would
have refused. Then with clasped hands and tears in my eyes
I would have begged it of him as a favour. This humiliation
has been denied to me thanks to my aphony. My voice has
gone dead, the rest will follow. I could have written, on a
page of my exercise-book, and shown to him, Please give me
back my stick, or, Be so kind as to hand me up my stick. But
I had hidden the exercise-book under the blanket, so that he
might not take it from me. I did so without thinking that
he had been there for some time (otherwise he would not
have struck me) watching me writing, for I must have been
writing when he came, and that consequently he could easily
have taken my exercise-book if he had wished, and without
thinking either that he was watching me when I slipped it out of
sight, and that consequently the only effect of my precaution
was to draw his attention to the very object I wished to hide
from him. There's reasoning for you. For of all I ever had in
this world all has been taken from me, except the exercise-
book, so I cherish it, it's human. The lead too, I was forgetting
the lead, but what is lead, without paper? He must have said
to himself, over his lunch, This afternoon I'll take his exercise-

book from him, he seems to cherish it. But when he came
back from his lunch the exercise-book was no longer in the
place where he had seen me put it, he had not thought of
that. His umbrella, have I mentioned his umbrella, the tightest
rolled I ever saw? Shifting it every few minutes from one
hand to the other he leaned his weight upon it, standing beside
the bed. Then it bent. He made use of it to raise my blankets.
It was with this umbrella that I thought he was going to kill
me, with its long sharp point, he had only to plunge it in
my heart. Wilful murder, people would have said. Perhaps
he will come back to-morrow, better equipped, or with an
assistant, now that he is familiar with the premises. But if he
watched me I too watched him, I think we gazed at each
other literally for hours, without winking. He probably imagined he could stare me down, because I am old and helpless.
The poor bastard. It was so long since I had seen a biped of
this description that I had my eyes out on stalks, as the saying
is, for fear of not being able to credit them. I said to myself,
One of these days they'll start grazing the trees. And the face
they have! I had forgotten. At a certain moment, incommoded
by the smell probably, he squeezed himself in between the
bed and the wall, to try and open the window. He couldn't.
In the morning I didn't take my eyes off him. But in the
afternoon I slept a little. I don't know what he did while I
was asleep, rummaged in my possessions probably, with his
umbrella, they are scattered all over the floor now. I thought
for a moment he had been sent by the funeral people. Those
who have enabled me to live till now will no doubt see to it
that I am buried with a minimum of ceremony. Here lies
Malone at last, with the dates to give a faint idea of the time
he took to be excused and then to distinguish him from his
namesakes, numerous in the island and beyond the grave.
Funny I never ran into one, to my knowledge, not one. There
is still time. Here lies a ne'er-do-well, six feet under hell. But
for a moment only, I mean half-an-hour at most. Then I
tried him with other functions, all equally disappointing.
Strange need to know who people are and what they do for
a living and what they want with you. In spite of the ease
with which he wore his black and manipulated his umbrella
and his consummate mastery of the block-hat, I had for a
time the impression he was disguised, but from what if I may

say so, and as what? At a given moment, yet another, he took
fright, for his breath came faster and he moved away from the
bed. It was then I saw he was wearing brown boots, which
gave me such a shock as no words can convey. They were
copiously caked with fresh mud and I said to myself, Through
what sloughs has he had to toil to reach me? I wonder if
he was looking for something in particular, it would be so nice
to know. I shall tear a page out of my exercise-book and re-
produce upon it, from memory, what follows, and show it
to him to-morrow, or to-day, or some other day, if he ever
comes back. 1. Who are you? 2. What do you do, for a living? 3. Are you looking for something in particular? What
else? 4. Why are you so cross? 5. Have I offended you? 6. Do
you know anything about me? 7. It was wrong of you to
strike me. 8. Give me my stick. 9. Are you your own employer? 10. If not who sends you? 11. Put back my things where
you found them. 12. Why has my soup been stopped? 13. For
what reason are my pots no longer emptied? 14. Do you
think I shall last much longer? 15. May I ask you a favour?
16. Your conditions are mine. 17. Why brown boots and
whence the mud? 18. You couldn't by any chance let me have
the butt of a pencil? 19. Number your answers. 20. Don't go,
I haven't finished. Will one page suffice? There cannot be
many left. I might as well ask for a rubber while I am about
it. 21. Could you lend me an India rubber? When he had gone
I said to myself, But surely I have seen him somewhere before. And the people I have seen have seen me too, I can guarantee that. But of whom may it not be said, I know that man?
Drivel, drivel. And then at evening morning is so far away.
I had stopped looking at him. I had got used to him. I was
thinking of him, trying to understand, you can't do that and
look at the same time. I did not even see him go. Oh he did
not vanish, after the fashion of a ghost, no, I heard him, the
clank when he took out his watch, the satisfied thump of the
umbrella on the floor, the rightabout, the rapid steps towards
the door, its soft closing and finally, I am sorry to say, a gay
and lively whistle dying away. What have I omitted? Little
things, nothings. They will come back to me later, make me
see more clearly what has happened and say, Ah if I had only
known then, now it is too late. Yes, little by little I shall see
him as he just has been, or as he should have been for me to

be able to say, yet again, Too late, too late. There's feeling for you. Or he is perhaps just the first of a series of visitors, all different. They are going to relay one another, and they are numerous. To-morrow perhaps he will be wearing leggings, riding-breeches and a check cap, with a whip in his hand to make up for the umbrella and a horse-shoe in his button-hole. All the people I have caught a glimpse of, at close quarters or at a distance, may file past from now on, that is obvious. There even may be women with children, I have caught a glimpse of a few, they will all be armed with something to lean on and rummage in my things with, they will all give me a clout on the head to begin with and then spend the rest of the day glaring at me in anger and disgust. I shall have to revise my questionnaire so as to adapt it to all and sundry. Perhaps one, one day, unmindful of his instructions, will give me my stick. Or I might be able to catch one, a little girl for example, and half strangle her, three quarters, until she promises to give me my stick, give me soup, empty my pots, kiss me, fondle me, smile to me, give me my hat, stay with me, follow the hearse weeping into her handkerchief, that would be nice. I am such a good man, at bottom, such a good man, how is it nobody ever noticed it? A little girl would be into my barrow, she would undress before me, sleep beside me, have nobody but me, I would jam the bed against the door to prevent her running away, but then she would throw herself out of the window, when they got to know she was with me they would bring soup for two, I would teach her love and loathing, she would never forget me, I would die delighted, she would close my eyes and put a plug in my arsehole, as per instructions. Easy, Malone, take it easy, you old whore. That reminds me, how long can one fast with impunity? The Lord Mayor of Cork lasted for ages, but he was young, and then he had political convictions, human ones too probably, just plain human convictions. And he allowed himself a sip of water from time to time, sweetened probably. Water, for pity's sake! How is it I am not thirsty. There must be drinking going on inside me, my secretions. Yes, let us talk a little about me, that will be a rest from all these blackguards. What light! Foretaste of paradise? My head. On fire, full of boiling oil. What shall I die of, in the end? A transport of blood to the brain? That would be the last straw.

The pain is almost unbearable, upon my soul it is. Incandescent migraine. Death must take me for someone else. It's the heart's fault, as in the bosom of the match king, Schneider, Schroeder, I forget. It too is burning, with shame, of itself, of me, of them, shame of everything, except of beating apparently. It's nothing, mere nervousness. And who knows, perhaps the first to fail will be my breath, after all. After each avowal, before and during, what swirling murmurs. The window says break of day, rack of tattered rainclouds stampeding. Have a nice time. Far from this molten gloom. Yes, my last gasps are not what they might be, the bellows won't go down, the air is choking me, perhaps it is a little lacking in oxygen. Macmann pygmy beneath the great black gesticulating pines gazes at the distant raging sea. The others are there too, or at their windows, like me, but on their feet, they must be able to move, or to be moved, no, not like me, they can't do anything for anybody, clinging to the shivering poplars, or at their windows, listening. But perhaps I should finish with myself first, in so far naturally as such a thing is possible. The speed I am turning at now make things difficult admittedly, but it probably can only increase, that is the thing to be considered. Mem, add to the questionnaire, If you happen to have a match try and light it. How is it I heard nothing when he spoke to me and yet I heard him leave, whistling? Perhaps he only feigned to speak to me, to try and make me think I had gone deaf. Do I hear anything at the present instant? Let me see. No, the answer is no. Neither the wind, nor the sea, nor the paper, nor the air I exhale with such labour. But this innumerable babble, like a multitude whispering? I don't understand. With my distant hand I count the pages that remain. They will do. This exercise-book is my life, this child's exercise-book, it has taken me a long time to resign myself to that. And yet I shall not throw it away. For I want to put down in it, for the last time, those I have called to my help, but ill, so that they did not understand, so that they may cease with me. Now rest.

Wearing over his long shirt a great striped cloak reaching down to his ankles Macmann took the air in all weathers, from morning to night. And more than once they had been obliged to go out looking for him with lanterns, to bring him

back to his cell, for he had remained deaf to the call of the
bell and to the shouts and threats first of Lemuel, then of
the other keepers. Then the keepers, in their white clothes,
armed with sticks and lanterns, spread out from the buildings
and beat the thickets, the copses and the fern-brakes, calling
the fugitive by name and threatening him with the direst
reprisals if he did not surrender immediately. But they
finally remarked that he hid, when he did, always in the same
place and such a deployment of force was unnecessary. From
then on it was Lemuel who went out alone, in silence, as
always when he knew what he had to do, straight to the bush
in which Macmann had made his lair, whenever this was
necessary. My God. And often the two of them remained
there for some time, in the bush, before going in, huddled together, for the lair was small, saying nothing, perhaps listening to the noises of the night, the owls, the wind in the leaves,
the sea when it was high enough to make its voice heard, and
then the other night sounds that you cannot tell the meaning
of. And it sometimes happened that Macmann, weary of not
being alone went away alone and back into his cell and
remained there until Lemuel rejoined him, much later. It was
a genuine English park, though far from England, extravagantly unformal, luxuriant to the point of wildness, the trees
at war with one another, and the bushes, and the wild flowers
and weeds, all ravening for earth and light. One evening
Macmann went back to his cell with a branch torn from a
dead bramble, for use as a stick to support him as he walked.
Then Lemuel took it from him and struck him with it over and
over again, no, that won't work, then Lemuel called a keeper by
the name of Pat, a thorough brute though puny in appearance,
and said to him, Pat, will you look at that. Then Pat snatched
the stick from Macmann who, seeing the turn things were taking was holding it clutched tight in his two hands, and struck
him with it until Lemuel told him to stop, and even for some
little time afterwards. All this without a word of explanation.
So that a little later Macmann, having brought back from his
walk a hyacinth he had torn up bulb and roots in the hope of
being able to keep it a little longer thus than if he had simply
plucked it, was fiercely reprimanded by Lemuel who wrenched
the pretty flower from his hands and threatened to hand him
over to Jack again, no, to Pat again, Jack is a different one.

And yet the fact of having half demolished the bush, a kind of laurel, in order to hide in it, had never brought upon his head the least reproof. This is not necessarily surprising, there was no proof against him. Had he been questioned about it he would naturally have told the truth, for he did not suspect he had done anything wrong. But they must have assumed he would do nothing but lie and stoutly deny and that it was therefore useless to press him with questions. Besides no questions were ever asked in the House of Saint John of God, but stern measures were simply taken, or not taken, according to the dictates of a peculiar logic. For, when you come to think of it, in virtue of what possible principle of justice can a flower in the hand fasten on the bearer the crime of having gathered it? Or was the mere fact of holding it for all to see in itself a felony, analogous to that of the receiver or fence? And if so would it not have been preferable to make this known, quite plainly and frankly, to all concerned, so that the sense of guilt, instead of merely following on the guilty act, might precede and accompany it as well? Problem. But nicely posed, I think, very nicely indeed. Thanks to the white cloak with its blue butcher stripes no confusion was possible between the Macmanns on the one hand and the Lemuels, Pats and Jacks on the other. The birds. Numerous and varied in the dense foliage they lived without fear all the year round, or in fear only of their congeners, and those which in summer or in winter flew off to other climes came back the following winter or the following summer, roughly speaking. The air was filled with their voices, especially at dawn and dusk, and those which set off in flocks in the morning, such as the crows and starlings, for distant pastures, came back the same evening all joyous to the sanctuary, where their sentinels awaited them. The gulls were many in stormy weather which paused here on their flight inland. They wheeled long in the cruel air, screeching with anger, then settled in the grass or on the house-tops, mistrustful of the trees. But that is all beside the point, like so many things. All is pretext, Sapo and the birds, Moll, the peasants, those who in the towns seek one another out and fly from one another, my doubts which do not interest me, my situation, my possessions, pretext for not coming to the point, the abandoning, the raising of the arms and going down, without further splash, even though it may annoy the bathers. Yes, there is no good

pretending, it is hard to leave everything. The horror-worn
eyes linger abject on all they have beseeched so long, in a last
prayer, the true prayer at last, the one that asks for nothing.
And it is then a little breath of fulfillment revives the dead
longings and a murmer is born in the silent world, reproach-
ing you affectionately with having despaired too late. The
last word in the way of viaticum. Let us try it another way.
The pure plateau

   Try and go on. The pure plateau air. Yes, it was a plateau,
Moll had not lied, or rather a great mound with gentle slopes.
The entire top was occupied by the domain of Saint John and
there the wind blew almost without ceasing, causing the stout-
est trees to bend and groan, breaking the boughs, tossing the
bushes, lashing the ferns to fury, flattening the grass and whirling leaves and flowers far away. I hope I have not forgotten
anything. Good. A high wall encompassed it about, without
however shutting off the view, unless you happened to be in
its lee. How was this possible? Why thanks to the rising
ground to be sure, culminating in a summit called the Rock,
because of the rock that was on it. From here a fine view was
to be obtained of the plain, the sea, the mountains, the smoke
of the town and the buildings of the institution, bulking large
in spite of their remoteness and all astir with little dots or
flecks forever appearing and disappearing, in reality the keepers coming and going, perhaps mingled with I was going to
say with the prisoners! For seen from this distance the striped
cloak had no stripes, nor indeed any great resemblance to a
cloak at all. So that one could only say, when the first shock
of surprise was past, Those are men and women, you know,
people, without being able to specify further. A stream at
long intervals bestrid — but to hell with all this fucking
scenery. Where could it have risen anyway, tell me that.
Underground perhaps. In a word a little Paradise for those
who like their nature sloven. Macmann sometimes wondered
what was lacking to his happiness. The right to be abroad in
all weathers morning, noon and night, trees and bushes with
outstretched branches to wrap him round and hide him, food
and lodging such as they were free of all charge, superb views
on every hand out over the lifelong enemy, a minimum of
persecution and corporal punishmen, the song of the birds,

no human contact except with Lemuel, who went out of his way
to avoid him, the faculties of memory and reflection stunned by
the incessant walking and high wind, Moll dead, what more
could he wish? I must be happy, he said, it is less pleasant than
I should have thought. And he clung closer and closer to the
wall, but not too close, for it was guarded, seeking a way
out into the desolation of having nobody and nothing, the
wilds of the hunted, the scant bread and the scant shelter and
the black joy of the solitary way, in helplessness and will-less-
ness, through all the beauty, the knowing and the loving.
Which he stated by saying, for he was artless, I have had
enough, without pausing a moment to reflect on what it was
he had enough of or to compare it with what it had been he
had had enough of, until he lost it, and would have enough of
again, when he got it back again, and without suspecting that
the thing so often felt to be excessive, and honored by such a
variety of names, was perhaps in reality always one and the
same. But there was one reflecting in his place and setting
down coldly the sign of equality where it was needed, as if
that could make any difference. So he had only to go on gasping, in his artless way, Enough! Enough!, as he crept along by
the wall under the cover of the bushes, searching for a
breach through which he might slip out, under cover of
night, or a place with footholds where he might climb over.
But the wall was unbroken and smooth and topped uninter-
ruptedly with broken glass of a bottle green. But let us
cast a glance at the main entrance, wide enough to admit
two large vehicles abreast and flanked by two charming
lodges covered with Virginia creeper and occupied by large
deserving families, to judge by the swarms of little brats
playing nearby, pursuing one another with cries of joy, rage
and grief. But space hemmed him in on every side and
held him in its toils, with the multitude of other faintly
stirring, faintly struggling things, such as the children, the
lodges and the gates, and like a sweat of things the moments
streamed away in a great chaotic conflux of oozings and
torrents, and the trapped huddled things changed and died
each one according to its solitude. Beyond the gate, on the
road, shapes passed that Macmann could not understand,
because of the bars, because of all the trembling and raging
behind him and beside him, because of the cries, the sky,

the earth enjoining him to fall and his long blind life. A keeper came out of one of the lodges, in obedience to a telephone-call probably, all in white, a long black object in his hand, a key, and the children lined up along the drive. Suddenly there were women. All fell silent. The heavy gates swung open, driving the keeper before them. He backed away, then suddenly turned and fled to his doorstep. The road appeared, white with dust, bordered with dark masses, stretched a little way and ran up dead, against a narrow grey sky. Macmann let go the tree that hid him and turned back up the hill, not running, for he could hardly walk, but as fast as he could, bowed and stumbling, helping himself forward with the boles and boughs that offered. Little by little the haze formed again, and the sense of absence, and the captive things began to murmur again, each one to itself, and it was as if nothing had ever happened or would ever happen again.

Others besides Macmann strayed from morning to night, stooped under the heavy cloak, in the rare glades, among the trees that hid the sky and in the high ferns where they looked like swimmers. They seldom came near to one another, because they were few and the park was vast. But when chance brought one or more together, near enough for them to realize it had done so, then they hastened to turn back or, without going to such extremes, simply aside, as if ashamed to be seen by their fellows. But sometimes they brushed against one another without seeming to notice it, their heads buried in the ample hood.

Macmann carried with him and contemplated from time to time the photograph that Moll had given him, it was perhaps rather a daguerreotype. She was standing beside a chair and squeezing in her hands her long plaits. Traces were visible, behind her of a kind of trellis with clambering flowers, roses probably, they sometimes like to clamber. When giving this keep-sake to Macmann she had said, I was fourteen, I well remember the day, a summer day, it was my birthday, afterwards they took me to see Punch and Judy. Macmann remembered those words. What he liked best in this picture was the chair, the seat of which seemed to be made of straw. Diligently Moll pressed her lips together, in order to hide her great buck-teeth. The roses must have been pretty, they must have scented the air. In the end Macmann tore up this photograph and threw the bits in the air, one windy day. Then they scattered, though all subjected to the same conditions, as though with alacrity.

When it rained, when it snowed

On. One morning Lemuel, putting in the prescribed appearance in the great hall before setting out on his rounds, found pinned on the board a notice concerning him. Group Lemuel, excursion to the islands, weather permitting, with Lady Pedal, leaving one p.m. His colleagues observed him, sniggering and poking one another in the ribs. But they did not dare say anything. One woman however did pass a witty remark, to good effect. Lemuel was not liked, that was clear. But would he have wished to be, that is less clear. He initialed the notice and went away. The sun was dragging itself up, dispatching on its way what perhaps would be, thanks to it, a glorious May or April day, April more likely, it is doubtless the Easter week-end, spent by Jesus in hell. And it may well have been in honor of this latter that Lady Pedal had organized, for the benefit of Lemuel's group, this outing to the islands which was going to cost her dear, but she was well off and lived for doing good and bringing a little happiness into the lives of those less fortunate than herself, who was all right in her head and to whom life had always smiled or, as she had it herself, returned her smile, enlarged as in a convex mirror, or a concave, I forget. Taking advantage of the terrestrial atmosphere that dimmed its brightness Lemuel glared with loathing at the sun. He had reached his room, on the fourth or fifth floor, whence on countless occasions he could have thrown himself in perfect safety out of the window if he had been less weak-minded. The long silver carpet was in position, ending in a point, trembling across the calm repoussé sea. The room was small and absolutely empty, for Lemuel slept on the bare boards and even off them ate his lesser meals, now at one place, now at another. But what matter about Lemuel and his room? On. Lady Pedal was not the only one to take an interest

in the inmates of Saint John of God's, known pleasantly
locally as the Johnny Goddams, or the Goddam Johnnies,
not the only one to treat them on an average once every
two years to excursions by land and sea through scenery
renowned for its beauty or grandeur and even to entertain-
ments on the premises such as whole evenings of prestidigi-
tation and ventriloquism in the moonlight on the terrace, no,
but she was seconded by other ladies sharing her way of
thinking and similarly blessed in means and leisure. But
what matter about Lady Pedal? On. Carrying in one hand
two buckets wedged the one within the other Lemuel proceeded to the vast kitchen, full of stir and bustle at that hour.
Six excursion soups, he growled. What? said the cook. Six
excursion soups! roared Lemuel, dashing his buckets against
the oven, without however relinquishing the handles, for he
retained enough presence of mind to dread the thought of
having to stoop and pick them up again. The difference between an excursion soup and a common or house soup was
simply this, that the latter was uniformly liquid whereas the
former contained a piece of fat bacon intended to keep
up the strength of the excursionist until his return. When
his bucket had been filled Lemuel withdrew to a secluded
place, rolled up his sleeve to the elbow, fished up from the
bottom of the bucket one after another the six pieces of
bacon, his own and the five others, ate all the fat off them,
sucked the rinds and threw them back in the soup. Strange
when you come to think of it, but after all not so strange
really, that they should have issued six extra or excursion
soups at his mere demand, without requiring a written order.
The cells of the five were far apart and so astutely disposed
that Lemuel had never been able to determine how best,
that is to say with the minimum of fatigue and annoyance,
to visit them in turn. In the first a young man, dead young,
seated in an old rocking-chair, his shirt rolled up and his
hands on his thighs, would have seemed asleep had not his
eyes been wide open. He never went out, unless commanded
to do so, and then someone had to accompany him, in order
to make him move forward. His chamber-pot was empty,
whereas in his bowl the soup of the previous day had con-
gealed. The reverse would have been less surprising. But
Lemuel was used to this, so used that he had long since

ceased to wonder on what this creature fed. He emptied
the bowl into his empty bucket and from his full bucket
filled it with fresh soup. Then he went, a bucket in each
hand, whereas up to now a single hand had been enough
to carry the two buckets. Because of the excursion he
locked the door behind him, an unnecessary precaution. The
second cell, four or five hundred paces distant from the
first, contained one whose only really striking features were
his stature, his stiffness and his air of perpetually looking
for something while at the same time wondering what that
something could possibly be. Nothing in his person gave
any indication of his age, whether he was marvellously well-
preserved or on the contrary prematurely decayed. He was
called the Saxon, though he was far from being any such
thing. Without troubling to take off his shirt he had swathed
himself in his two blankets as in swaddlings and over and
above this rough and ready cocoon he wore his cloak. He
gathered it shiveringly about him, with one hand, for he
needed the other to help him in his investigation of all that
aroused his suspicions. Good-morning, good-morning, good-
morning, he said, with a strong foreign accent and darting
fearful glances all about him, fucking awful business this,
no, yes? Sudden starts instantly repressed dislodged him
imperceptibly from his coign of maximum vantage in the
centre of the room. What! he exclaimed. His soup, examined
drop by drop, had been transferred in its entirety to his pot.
Anxiously he watched Lemuel performing his office, filling
and emptying. Dreamt all night of that bloody man Quin
again, he said. It was his habit to go out from time to time,
into the air. But after a few steps he would halt, totter, turn
and hasten back into his cell, aghast at such depths of opacity.

In the third a small thin man was pacing up and down,
his cloak folded over his arm, an umbrella in his hand. Fine
head of white flossy hair. He was asking himself questions
in a low voice, reflecting, replying. The door had hardly
opened when he made a dart to get out, for he spent his
days ranging about the park in all directions. Without putting
down his buckets Lemuel sent him flying with a toss of his
shoulder. He lay where he had fallen, clutching his cloak
and umbrella. Then, having recovered from his surprise, he

began to cry. In the fourth a misshapen giant, bearded, occupied to the exclusion of all else in scratching himself,
intermittently. Sprawling on his pillow on the floor under
the window, his head sunk, his mouth open, his legs wide
apart, his knees raised, leaning with one hand on the ground
while the other came and went under his shirt, he awaited
his soup. When his bowl had been filled he stopped scratching and stretched out his hand towards Lemuel, in the daily
disappointed hope of being spared the trouble of getting up.
He still loved the gloom and secrecy of the ferns, but never
sought them out. The youth then, the Saxon, the thin one and
the giant. I don't know if they have changed, I don't remember. May the others forgive me. In the fifth Macmann,
half asleep.

A few lines to remind me that I too subsist. He has not
come back. How long ago is it now? I don't know. Long.
And I? Indubitably going, that's all that matters. Whence
this assurance? Try and think. I can't. Grandiose suffering.
I am swelling. What if I should burst? The ceiling rises
and falls, rises and falls, rhythmically, as when I was a
foetus. Also to be mentioned a noise of rushing water,
phenomenon mutatis mutandis perhaps analogous to that
of the mirage, in the desert. The window. I shall not see it
again. Why? Because, to my grief, I cannot turn my head.
Leaden light again, thick, eddying, riddled with little tunnels
through to brightness, perhaps I should say air, sucking air.
All is ready. Except me. I am being given, if I may venture
the expression, birth to into death, such is my impression.
The feet are clear already, of the great cunt of existence.
Favourable presentation I trust. My head will be the last to
die. Haul in your hands. I can't. The render rent. My story
ended I'll be living yet. Promising lag. That is the end of
me. I shall say I no more.

Surrounded by his little flock which after nearly two hours
of efforts he had succeeded in assembling, single-handed,
Pat having refused to help him, Lemuel stood on the terrace
waiting for Lady Pedal to arrive. Cords tethered by the
ankles the thin one to the youth, the Saxon to the giant, and
Lemuel held Macmann by the arm. Of the five it was Mac-

mann, furious at having been shut up in his cell all morning
and at a loss to understand what was wanted of him, whose
resistance had been the most lively. He had notably refused
to stir a step without his hat, with such fierce determination
that Lemuel had finally consented to his keeping it on, provided it was hidden by the hood. In spite of this Macmann
continued peevish and agitated, trying to free his arm and
saying over and over again, Let me go! Let me go! The
youth, tormented by the sun, was grabbing feebly at the
thin one's umbrella, saying Pasol! Pasol! The thin one re-
taliated with petulant taps on his hands and arms. Naughty!
he cried. Help! The giant had thrown his arms round the
Saxon's neck and hung there, his legs limp. The Saxon,
tottering, too proud to collapse, demanded to be enlightened
in tones without anger. Who is this shite anyhow, he said,
any of you poor buggers happen to know? The director, or
his delegate, also present, said dreamily from time to time,
Now, now, please. They were alone on the great terrace.
Can it be she fears a change of weather? said the director.
He added, turning towards Lemuel, I am asking you a question. The sky was cloudless, the air still. Where is the beautiful young man with the Messiah beard? But in that case
would she not have telephoned? said the director.

The waggonette. Up on the box, beside the coachman,
Lady Pedal. On one of the seats, set parallel to the wheels,
Lemuel, Macmann, the Saxon and the giant. On the other,
facing them, the youth, the thin one and two colossi dressed
in sailor-suits. As they passed through the gates the children
cheered. A sudden descent, long and steep, sent them plunging towards the sea. Under the drag of the brakes the wheels
slid more than they rolled and the stumbling horses reared
against the thrust. Lady Pedal clung to the box, her bust
flung back. She was a huge, big, tall, fat woman. Artificial
daisies with brilliant yellow disks gushed from her broad-
brimmed straw hat. At the same time behind the heavily
spotted fall-veil her plump red face appeared to pullulate.
The passengers, yielding with unanimous inertia to the
tilt of the seats, sprawled pell-mell beneath the box. Sit
back! cried Lady Pedal. Nobody stirred. What good would
that do? said one of the sailors. None, said the other. Should

they not all get down, said Lady Pedal to the coachman,
and walk? When they were safely at the bottom of the hill
at last Lady Pedal turned affably to her guests. Courage
my hearties! she said, to show she was not superior. The
waggonette jolted on with gathering speed. The giant lay
on the boards, between the seats. Are you the one in charge?
said Lady Pedal. One of the sailors leaned towards Lemuel
and said, She wants to know if you're the one in charge.
Fuck off, said Lemuel. The Saxon uttered a roar which Lady
Pedal, on the qui vive for the least sign of animation, was
pleased to interpret as a manifestation of joy. That's the
spirit! she cried. Sing! Make the most of this glorious day!
Banish your cares, for an hour or so! And she burst forth:

> *Oh the jolly spring*
> *Blue and sun and nests and flowers*
> *Alleluiah Christ is King*
> *Oh the happy happy hours*
> *Oh the jolly jolly —*

She broke off, discouraged. What is the matter with them?
she said. The youth, less youthful now, doubled in two, his
head swathed in the skirts of his cloak, seemed to be vomiting. His legs, monstrously bony and knock-kneed, were
knocking together at the knees. The thin one, shivering,
though in theory and Saxon is the shiverer, had resumed his
dialogue. Motionless and concentrated between the voices
he reinforced these with passionate gestures amplified by
the umbrella. And you? . . . Thanks . . . And you? . . .
THANKS! . . . True . . . Left . . . Try . . . Back . . .
Where? . . . On . . . No! . . . Right . . . Try . . . Do
you smell the sea, said Lady Pedal, I do. Macmann made
a bid for freedom. In vain. Lemuel produced a hatchet from
under his cloak and dealt himself a few smart blows on the
skull, with the heel, for safety. Nice jaunt we're having
said one of the sailors. Swell, said the other. Sun azure.
Ernest, hand out the buns, said Lady Pedal.

The boat. Room, as in the waggonette, for twice as many,
three times, four times, at a pinch. A land receding, another
approaching, big and little islands. No sound save the oars,

the rowlocks, the blue sea against the keel. In the stern-
sheets Lady Pedal, sad. What beauty! she murmured. Alone,
not understood, good, too good. Taking off her glove she
trailed in the transparent water her sapphire-laden hand. Four
oars, no rudder, the oars steer. My creatures, what of them?
Nothing. They are there, each as best he can, as best he can
be somewhere. Lemuel watches the mountains rising behind
the steeples beyond the harbour, no they are no more

No, they are no more than hills, they raise themselves
gently, faintly blue, out of the confused plain. It was there
somewhere he was born, in a fine house, of loving parents.
Their slopes are covered with ling and furze, its hot yellow
bells, better known as gorse. The hammers of the stone-
cutters ring all day like bells.

The island. A last effort. The islet. The shore facing the
open sea is jagged with creeks. One could live there, perhaps happy, if life were a possible thing, but nobody lives
there. The deep water comes washing into its heart, between high walls of rock. One day nothing will remain of
it but two islands, separated by a gulf, narrow at first, then
wider and wider as the centuries slip by, two islands, two
reefs. It is difficult to speak of man, under such conditions.
Come, Ernest, said Lady Pedal, let us find a place to picnic.
And you, Maurice, she added, stay by the dinghy. She called
that a dinghy. The thin one chafed to run about, but the
youth had thrown himself down in the shade of a rock, like
Sordello, but less noble, for Sordello resembled a lion at
rest, and clung to it with both hands. The poor creatures,
said Lady Pedal, let them loose. Maurice made to obey.
Keep off, said Lemuel. The giant had refused to leave the
boat, so that the Saxon could not leave it either. Macmann
was not free either, Lemuel held him by the waist, perhaps
lovingly. Well, said Lady Pedal, you are the one in charge.
She moved away with Ernest. Suddenly she turned and said,
You know, on the island, there are Druid

remains. She looked at them in turn. When we have had
our tea, she said, we shall hunt for them, what do you say?

Finally she moved away again, followed by Ernest carrying the hamper in his arms. When she had disappeared Lemuel released Macmann, went up behind Maurice who was sitting on a stone filling his pipe and killed him with the hatchet. We're getting on, getting on. The youth and the giant took no notice. The thin one broke his umbrella against the rock, a curious gesture. The Saxon cried, bending forward and slapping his thighs, Nice work, sir, nice work! A little later Ernest came back to fetch them. Going to meet him Lemuel killed him in his turn, in the same way as the other. It merely took a little longer. Two decent, quiet, harmless men, brothers-in-law into the bargain, there are billions of such brutes. Macmann's huge head. He has put his hat on again. The voice of Lady Pedal, calling. She appeared, joyous. Come along, she cried, all of you, before the tea gets cold. But at the sight of the late sailors she fainted, which caused her to fall. Smash her! screamed the Saxon. She had raised her veil and was holding in her hand a tiny sandwich. She must have broken something in her fall, her hip perhaps, old ladies often break their hips, for no sooner had she recovered her senses than she began to moan and groan, as if she were the only being on the face of the earth deserving of pity. When the sun had vanished, behind the hills, and the lights of the land began to glitter, Lemuel made Macmann and the two others get into the boat and got into it himself. Then they set out, all six, from the shore.

Gurgles of outflow.

This tangle of grey bodies is they. Silent, dim, perhaps clinging to one another, their heads buried in their cloaks, they lie together in a heap, in the night. They are far out in the bay. Lemuel has shipped his oars, the oars trail in the water. The night is strewn with absurd

absurd lights, the stars, the beacons, the buoys, the lights of earth and in the hills the faint fires of the blazing gorse. Macmann, my last, my possessions, I remember, he is there too, perhaps he sleeps. Lemuel

Lemuel is in charge, he raises his hatchet on which the
blood will never dry, but not to hit anyone, he will not hit
anyone, he will not hit anyone any more, he will not touch
anyone any more, either with it or with it or with it or with or

or with it or with his hammer or with his stick or with his
fist or in thought in dream I mean never he will never

or with his pencil or with his stick or

or light light I mean

never there he will never

never anything

there

any more

THE UNNAMABLE

Translated from the French by the author

Where now? Who now? When now? Unquestioning. I, say I. Unbelieving. Questions, hypotheses, call them that. Keep going, going on, call that going, call that on. Can it be that one day, off it goes on, that one day I simply stayed in, in where, instead of going out, in the old way, out to spend day and night as far away as possible, it wasn't far. Perhaps that is how it began. You think you are simply resting, the better to act when the time comes, or for no reason, and you soon find yourself powerless ever to do anything again. No matter how it happened. It, say it, not knowing what. Perhaps I simply assented at last to an old thing. But I did nothing. I seem to speak, it is not I, about me, it is not about me. These few general remarks to begin with. What am I to do, what shall I do, what should I do, in my situation, how proceed? By aporia pure and simple? Or by affirmations and negations invalidated as uttered, or sooner or later? Generally speaking. There must be other shifts. Otherwise it would be quite hopeless. But it is quite hopeless. I should mention before going any further, any further on, that I say aporia without knowing what it means. Can one be ephectic otherwise than unawares? I don't know. With the yesses and noes it is different, they will come back to me as I go along and how, like a bird, to shit on them all without exception. The fact would seem to be, if in my situation one may speak of facts, not only that I shall have to speak of things of which I cannot speak, but also, which is even more interesting, but also that I, which is if possible even more interesting, that I shall have to, I forget, no matter. And at the same time I am obliged to speak. I shall never be silent. Never.

I shall not be alone, in the beginning. I am of course alone. Alone. That is soon said. Things have to be soon said. And how can one be sure, in such darkness? I shall have company. In the beginning. A few puppets. Then I'll scatter them, to the winds, if I can. And things, what is the correct attitude to adopt towards things? And, to begin with, are they necessary? What a question. But I have few illusions, things are to be expected. The best is not to decide anything, in this connexion, in advance. If a thing turns up, for some reason or another, take it into consideration. Where there are people, it is said, there are things. Does this mean that when you admit the former you must also admit the latter? Time will tell. The thing to avoid, I don't know why, is the spirit of system. People with things, people without things, things without people, what does it matter, I flatter myself it will not take me long to scatter them, whenever I choose, to the winds. I don't see how. The best would be not to begin. But I have to begin. That is to say I have to go on. Perhaps in the end I shall smother in a throng. Incessant comings and goings, the crush and bustle of a bargain sale. No, no danger. Of that.

Malone is there. Of his mortal liveliness little trace remains. He passes before me at doubtless regular intervals, unless it is I who pass before him. No, once and for all, I do not move. He passes, motionless. But there will not be much on the subject of Malone, from whom there is nothing further to be hoped. Personally I do not intend to be bored. It was while watching him pass that I wondered if we cast a shadow. Impossible to say. He passes close by me, a few feet away, slowly, always in the same direction. I am almost sure it is he. The brimless hat seems to me conclusive. With his two hands he props up his jaw. He passes without a word. Perhaps he does not see me. One of these days I'll challenge him. I'll say, I don't know, I'll say something, I'll think of something when the time comes. There are no days here, but I use the expression. I see him from the waist up, he stops at the waist, as far as I am concerned. The trunk is erect. But I do not know whether he is on his feet or on his knees. He might also be seated. I see him in profile. Sometimes I wonder if it is not Molloy.

Perhaps it is Molloy, wearing Malone's hat. But it is more reasonable to suppose it is Malone, wearing his own hat. Oh look, there is the first thing, Malone's hat. I see no other clothes. Perhaps Molloy is not here at all. Could he be, without my knowledge? The place is no doubt vast. Dim intermittent lights suggest a kind of distance. To tell the truth I believe they are all here, at least from Murphy on, I believe we are all here, but so far I have only seen Malone. Another hypothesis, they were here, but are here no longer. I shall examine it after my fashion. Are there other pits, deeper down? To which one accedes by mine? Stupid obsession with depth. Are there other places set aside for us and this one where I am, with Malone, merely their narthex? I thought I had done with preliminaries. No no, we have all been here forever, we shall all be here forever, I know it.

No more questions. Is not this rather the place where one finishes vanishing? Will the day come when Malone will pass before me no more? Will the day come when Malone will pass before the spot where I was? Will the day come when another will pass before me, before the spot where I was? I have no opinion, on these matters.

Were I not devoid of feeling his beard would fill me with pity. It hangs down, on either side of his chin, in two twists of unequal length. Was there a time when I too revolved thus? No, I have always been sitting here, at this selfsame spot, my hands on my knees, gazing before me like a great horn-owl in an aviary. The tears stream down my cheeks from my unblinking eyes. What makes me weep so? From time to time. There is nothing saddening here. Perhaps it is liquefied brain. Past happiness in any case has clean gone from my memory, assuming it was ever there. If I accomplish other natural functions it is unawares. Nothing ever troubles me. And yet I am troubled. Nothing has ever changed since I have been here. But I dare not infer from this that nothing ever will change. Let us try and see where these considerations lead. I have been here, ever since I began to be, my appearances elsewhere having been put in by other parties. All has proceeded, all this time, in the utmost calm, the most perfect order, apart from one or two manifestations

the meaning of which escapes me. No, it is not that their
meaning escapes me, my own escapes me just as much. Here
all things, no, I shall not say it, being unable to. I owe my
existence to no one, these faint fires are not of those that
illuminate or burn. Going nowhere, coming from nowhere,
Malone passes. These notions of forbears, of houses where
lamps are lit at night, and other such, where do they come
to me from? And all these questions I ask myself. It is not
in a spirit of curiosity. I cannot be silent. About myself
I need know nothing. Here all is clear. No, all is not clear.
But the discourse must go on. So one invents obscurities.
Rhetoric. These lights for instance, which I do not require
to mean anything, what is there so strange about them, so
wrong? Is it their irregularity, their instability, their shining
strong one minute and weak the next, but never beyond the
power of one or two candles? Malone appears and disappears with the punctuality of clockwork, always at the
same remove, the same velocity, in the same direction, the
same attitude. But the play of the lights is truly unpredictable.
It is only fair to say that to eyes less knowing than mine
they would probably pass unseen. But even to mine do they
not sometimes do so? They are perhaps unwavering and
fixed and my fitful perceiving the cause of their inconstancy.
I hope I may have occasion to revert to this question. But
I shall remark without further delay, in order to be sure
of doing so, that I am relying on these lights, as indeed on
all other similar sources of credible perplexity, to help me
continue and perhaps even conclude. I resume, having no
alternative. Where was I? Ah yes, from the unexceptionable
order which has prevailed here up to date may I infer that
such will always be the case? I may of course. But the
mere fact of asking myself such a question gives me to
reflect. It is in vain I tell myself that its only purpose is to
stimulate the lagging discourse, this excellent explanation
does not satisfy me. Can it be I am the prey of a genuine
preoccupation, of a need to know as one might say? I don't
know. I'll try it another way. If one day a change were
to take place, resulting from a principle of disorder already
present, or on its way, what then? That would seem to
depend on the nature of the change. No, here all change
would be fatal and land me back, there and then, in all the

fun of the fair. I'll try it another way. Has nothing really changed since I have been here? No, frankly, hand on heart, wait a second, no, nothing, to my knowledge. But, as I have said, the place may well be vast, as it may well measure twelve feet in diameter. It comes to the same thing, as far as discerning its limits is concerned. I like to think I occupy the centre, but nothing is less certain. In a sense I would be better off at the circumference, since my eyes are always fixed in the same direction. But I am certainly not at the circumference. For if I were it would follow that Malone, wheeling about me as he does, would issue from the enceinte at every revolution, which is manifestly impossible. But does he in fact wheel, does he not perhaps simply pass before me in a straight line? No, he wheels, I feel it, and about me, like a planet about its sun. And if he made a noise, as he goes, I would hear him all the time, on my right hand, behind my back, on my left hand, before seeing him again. But he makes none, for I am not deaf, of that I am convinced, that is to say half-convinced. From centre to circumference in any case it is a far cry and I may well be situated somewhere between the two. It is equally possible, I do not deny it, that I too am in perpetual motion, accompanied by Malone, as the earth by its moon. In which case there would be no further grounds for my complaining about the disorder of the lights, this being due simply to my insistence on regarding them as always the same lights and viewed always from the same point. All is possible, or almost. But the best is to think of myself as fixed and at the centre of this place, whatever its shape and extent may be. This is also probably the most pleasing to me. In a word, no change apparently since I have been here, disorder of the lights perhaps an illusion, all change to be feared, incomprehensible uneasiness.

That I am not stone deaf is shown by the sounds that reach me. For though the silence here is almost unbroken, it is not completely so. I remember the first sound heard in this place, I have often heard it since. For I am obliged to assign a beginning to my residence here, if only for the sake of clarity. Hell itself, although eternal, dates from the revolt of Lucifer. It is therefore permissible, in the

light of this distant analogy, to think of myself as being
here forever, but not as having been here forever. This will
greatly help me in my relation. Memory notably, which I
did not think myself entitled to draw upon, will have its
word to say, if necessary. This represents at least a thousand
words I was not counting on. I may well be glad of them.
So after a long period of immaculate silence a feeble cry
was heard, by me. I do not know if Malone heard it too. I
was surprised, the word is not too strong. After so long
a silence a little cry, stifled outright. What kind of creature
uttered it and, if it is the same, still does, from time to time?
Impossible to say. Not a human one in any case, there are
no human creatures here, or if there are they have done with
crying. Is Malone the culprit? Am I? Is it not perhaps a simple
little fart, they can be rending? Deplorable mania, when
something happens, to inquire what. If only I were not
obliged to manifest. And why speak of a cry? Perhaps it
is something breaking, some two things colliding. There are
sounds here, from time to time, let that suffice. This cry to
begin with, since it was the first. And others, rather different.
I am getting to know them. I do not know them all. A man
may die at the age of seventy without ever having had the
possibility of seeing Halley's comet.

It would help me, since to me I must attribute a beginning,
if I could relate it to that of my abode. Did I wait somewhere for this place to be ready to receive me? Or did it
wait for me to come and people it? By far the better of
these hypotheses, from the point of view of usefulness, is
the former, and I shall often have occasion to fall back
on it. But both are distasteful. I shall say therefore that
our beginnings coincide, that this place was made for me,
and I for it, at the same instant. And the sounds I do not
yet know have not yet made themselves heard. But they will
change nothing. The cry changed nothing, even the first
time. And my surprise? I must have been expecting it.

It is no doubt time I gave a companion to Malone. But
first I shall tell of an incident that has only occurred once,
so far. I await its recurrence without impatience. Two shapes
then, oblong like man, entered into collision before me.

They fell and I saw them no more. I naturally thought of the pseudocouple Mercier-Camier. The next time they enter the field, moving slowly towards each other, I shall know they are going to collide, fall and disappear, and this will perhaps enable me to observe them better. Wrong. I continue to see Malone as darkly as the first time. My eyes being fixed always in the same direction I can only see, I shall not say clearly, but as clearly as the visibility permits, that which takes place immediately in front of me, that is to say, in the case before us, the collision, followed by the fall and disappearance. Of their approach I shall never obtain other than a confused glimpse, out of the corner of the eye, and what an eye. For their path too must be a curve, two curves, and meeting I need not say close beside me. For the visibility, unless it be the state of my eyesight, only permits me to see what is close beside me. I may add that my seat would appear to be somewhat elevated, in relation to the surrounding ground, if ground is what it is. Perhaps it is water or some other liquid. With the result that, in order to obtain the optimum view of what takes place in front of me, I should have to lower my eyes a little. But I lower my eyes no more. In a word, I only see what appears immediately in front of me, I only see what appears close beside me, what I best see I see ill.

Why did I have myself represented in the midst of men, the light of day? It seems to me it was none of my doing. We won't go into that now. I can see them still, my delegates. The things they have told me! About men, the light of day. I refused to believe them. But some of it has stuck. But when, through what channels, did I communicate with these gentlemen? Did they intrude on me here? No, no one has ever intruded on me here. Elsewhere then. But I have never been elsewhere. But it can only have been from them I learnt what I know about men and the ways they have of putting up with it. It does not amount to much. I could have dispensed with it. I don't say it was all to no purpose. I'll make use of it, if I'm driven to it. It won't be the first time. What puzzles me is the thought of being indebted for this information to persons with whom I can never have been in contact. Can it be innate knowledge? Like that of good and evil. This seems improbable to me. Innate knowl-

edge of my mother, for example, is that conceivable? Not for
me. She was one of their favourite subjects, of conversation.
They also gave me the low-down on God. They told me
I depended on him, in the last analysis. They had it on
the reliable authority of his agents at Bally I forget what,
this being the place, according to them, where the inestimable
gift of life had been rammed down my gullet. But what
they were most determined for me to swallow was my fellow-
creatures. In this they were without mercy. I remember
little or nothing of these lectures. I cannot have understood
a great deal. But I seem to have retained certain descriptions,
in spite of myself. They gave me courses on love, on intelligence, most precious, most precious. They also taught me
to count, and even to reason. Some of this rubbish has
come in handy on occasions, I don't deny it, on occasions
which would never have arisen if they had left me in peace.
I use it still, to scratch my arse with. Low types they must
have been, their pockets full of poison and antidote. Perhaps all this instruction was by correspondence. And yet I
seem to know their faces. From photographs perhaps. When
did all this nonsense stop? And has it stopped? A few last
questions. Is it merely a lull? There were four or five of
them at me, they called that presenting their report. One
in particular, Basil I think he was called, filled me with
hatred. Without opening his mouth, fastening on me his eyes
like cinders with all their seeing, he changed me a little more
each time into what he wanted me to be. Is he still glaring
at me, from the shadows? Is he still usurping my name, the
one they foisted on me, up there in their world, patiently,
from season to season? No no, here I am in safety, amusing
myself wondering who can have dealt me these insignificant
wounds.

The other advances full upon me. He emerges as from
heavy hangings, advances a few steps, looks at me, then
backs away. He is stooping and seems to be dragging invisible burdens. What I see best is his hat. The crown is all
worn through, like the sole of an old boot, giving vent to
a straggle of grey hairs. He raises his eyes and I feel the
long imploring gaze, as if I could do something for him.
Another impression, no doubt equally false, he brings me
presents and dare not give them. He takes them away again,

or he lets them fall, and they vanish. He does not come often, I cannot be more precise, but regularly assuredly. His visit has never coincided, up to now, with the transit of Malone. But perhaps some day it will. That would not necessarily be a violation of the order prevailing here. For if I can work out to within a few inches the orbit of Malone, assuming perhaps erroneously that he passes before me at a distance of say three feet, with regard to the other's career I must remain in the dark. For I am incapable not only of measuring time, which in itself is sufficient to vitiate all calculation in this connexion, but also of comparing their respective velocities. So I cannot tell if I shall ever have the good fortune to see the two of them at once. But I am inclined to think I shall. For if I were never to see the two of them at once, then it would follow, or should follow, that between their respective appearances the interval never varies. No, wrong. For the interval may vary considerably, and indeed it seems to me it does, without ever being abolished. Nevertheless I am inclined to think, because of this erratic interval, that my two visitors may some day meet before my eyes, collide and perhaps even knock each other down. I have said that all things here recur sooner or later, no, I was going to say it, then thought better of it. But is it not possible that this does not apply to encounters? The only encounter I ever witnessed, a long time ago now, has never yet been re-enacted. It was perhaps the end of something. And I shall perhaps be delivered of Malone and the other, not that they disturb me, the day I see the two of them at one and the same time, that is to say in collision. Unfortunately they are not the only disturbers of my peace. Others come towards me, pass before me, wheel about me. And no doubt others still, invisible so far. I repeat they do not disturb me. But in the long run it might become wearisome. I don't see how. But the possibility must be taken into account. One starts things moving without a thought of how to stop them. In order to speak. One starts speaking as if it were possible to stop at will. It is better so. The search for the means to put an end to things, an end to speech, is what enables the discourse to continue. No, I must not try to think, simply utter. Method or no method I shall have to banish them in the end, the beings, things, shapes, sounds and

lights with which my haste to speak has encumbered this
place. In the frenzy of utterance the concern with truth.
Hence the interest of a possible deliverance by means of
encounter. But not so fast. First dirty, then make clean.

Perhaps it is time I paid a little attention to myself, for
a change. I shall be reduced to it sooner or later. At first
sight it seems impossible. Me, utter me, in the same foul
breath as my creatures? Say of me that I see this, feel that,
fear, hope, know and do not know? Yes, I will say it, and
of me alone. Impassive, still and mute, Malone revolves, a
stranger forever to my infirmities, one who is not as I can
never not be. I am motionless in vain, he is the god. And
the other? I have assigned him eyes that implore me, offer-
ings for me, need of succour. He does not look at me, does
not know of me, wants for nothing. I alone am man and
all the rest divine.

Air, the air, is there anything to be squeezed from that
old chestnut? Close to me it is grey, dimly transparent,
and beyond that charmed circle deepens and spreads its
fine impenetrable veils. Is it I who cast the faint light that
enables me to see what goes on under my nose? There
is nothing to be gained, for the moment, by supposing so.
There is no night so deep, so I have heard tell, that it may
not be pierced in the end, with the help of no other light
than that of the blackened sky, or of the earth itself. Nothing
nocturnal here. This grey, first murky, then frankly opaque,
is luminous none the less. But may not this screen which
my eyes probe in vain, and see as denser air, in reality be
the enclosure wall, as compact as lead? To elucidate this
point I would need a stick or pole, and the means of plying
it, the former being of little avail without the latter, and
vice versa. I could also do, incidentally with future and
conditional participles. Then I would dart it, like a javelin,
straight before me and know, by the sound made, whether
that which hems me round, and blots out my world, is the
old void, or a plenum. Or else, without letting it go, I would
wield it like a sword and thrust it through empty air, or
against the barrier. But the days of sticks are over, here I
can count on my body alone, my body incapable of the

smallest movement and whose very eyes can no longer close
as they once could, according to Basil and his crew, to rest
me from seeing, to rest me from waking, to darken me to
sleep, and no longer look away, or down, or up open to
heaven, but must remain forever fixed and staring on the
narrow space before them where there is nothing to be
seen, 99% of the time. They must be as red as live coals.
I sometimes wonder if the two retinae are not facing each
other. And come to think of it this grey is shot with rose,
like the plumage of certain birds, among which I seem to
remember the cockatoo.

Whether all grow black, or all grow bright, or all remain
grey, it is grey we need, to begin with, because of what it
is, and of what it can do, made of bright and black, able
to shed the former, or the latter, and be the latter or the
former alone. But perhaps I am the prey, on the subject of
grey, in the grey, to delusions.

How, in such conditions, can I write, to consider only
the manual aspect of that bitter folly? I don't know. I could
know. But I shall not know. Not this time. It is I who
write, who cannot raise my hand from my knee. It is I who
think, just enough to write, whose head is far. I am Matthew
and I am the angel, I who came before the cross, before
the sinning, came into the world, came here.

I add this, to be on the safe side. These things I say,
and shall say, if I can, are no longer, or are not yet, or
never were, or never will be, or if they were, if they are,
if they will be, were not here, are not here, will not be
here, but elsewhere. But I am here. So I am obliged to
add this. I who am here, who cannot speak, cannot think,
and who must speak, and therefore perhaps think a little,
cannot in relation only to me who am here, to here where
I am, but can a little, sufficiently, I don't know how, unimportant, in relation to me who was elsewhere, who shall be
elsewhere, and to those places where I was, where I shall
be. But I have never been elsewhere, however uncertain
the future. And the simplest therefore is to say that what I
say, what I shall say, if I can, relates to the place where
I am, to me who am there, in spite of my inability to think

of these, or to speak of them, because of the compulsion
I am under to speak of them, and therefore perhaps think
of them a little. Another thing. What I say, what I may say,
on this subject, the subject of me and my abode, has already
been said since, having always been here, I am here still.
At last a piece of reasoning that pleases me, and worthy
of my situation. So I have no cause for anxiety. And yet I
am anxious. So I am not heading for disaster, I am not
heading anywhere, my adventures are over, my say said, I
call that my adventures. And yet I feel not. And indeed I
greatly fear, since my speech can only be of me and here, that
I am once more engaged in putting an end to both. Which
would not matter, far from it, but for the obligation, once
rid of them, to begin again, to start again from nowhere,
from no one and from nothing and win to me again, to me
here again, by fresh ways to be sure, or by the ancient ways,
unrecognizable at each fresh faring. Whence a certain confusion in the exordia, long enough to situate the condemned
and prepare him for execution. And yet I do not despair
of one day sparing me, without going silent. And that day,
I don't know why, I shall be able to go silent, and make an
end, I know it. Yes, the hope is there, once again, of not
making me, not losing me, of staying here, where I said I
have always been, but I had to say something quick, of ending here, it would be wonderful. But is it to be wished? Yes,
it is to be wished, to end would be wonderful, no matter who
I am, no matter where I am.

I hope this preamble will soon come to an end and the
statement begin that will dispose of me. Unfortunately I am
afraid, as always, of going on. For to go on means going
from here, means finding me, losing me, vanishing and beginning again, a stranger first, then little by little the same
as always, in another place, where I shall say I have always
been, of which I shall know nothing, being incapable of
seeing, moving, thinking, speaking, but of which little by
little, in spite of these handicaps, I shall begin to know
something, just enough for it to turn out to be the same
place as always, the same which seems made for me and
does not want me, which I seem to want and do not want,
take your choice, which spews me out or swallows me up,

I'll never know, which is perhaps merely the inside of my distant skull where once I wandered, now am fixed, lost for tininess, or straining against the walls, with my head, my hands, my feet, my back, and ever murmuring my old stories, my old story, as if it were the first time. So there is nothing to be afraid of. And yet I am afraid, afraid of what my words will do to me, to my refuge, yet again. Is there really nothing new to try? I mentioned my hope, but it is not serious. If I could speak and yet say nothing, really nothing? Then I might escape being gnawed to death as by an old satiated rat, and my little tester-bed along with me, a cradle, or be gnawed to death not so fast, in my old cradle, and the torn flesh have time to knit, as in the Caucasus, before being torn again. But it seems impossible to speak and yet say nothing, you think you have succeeded, but you always overlook something, a little yes, a little no, enough to exterminate a regiment of dragoons. And yet I do not despair, this time, while saying who I am, where I am, of not losing me, of not going from here, of ending here. What prevents the miracle is the spirit of method to which I have perhaps been a little too addicted. The fact that Prometheus was delivered twenty-nine thousand nine hundred and seventy years after having purged his offence leaves me naturally as cold as camphor. For between me and that miscreant who mocked the gods, invented fire, denatured clay and domesticated the horse, in a word obliged humanity, I trust there is nothing in common. But the thing is worth mentioning. In a word, shall I be able to speak of me and of this place without putting an end to us, shall I ever be able to go silent, is there any connexion between these two questions? Nothing like issues. There are a few to be going on with, perhaps one only.

All these Murphys, Molloys and Malones do not fool me. They have made me waste my time, suffer for nothing, speak of them when, in order to stop speaking, I should have spoken of me and of me alone. But I just said I have spoken of me, am speaking of me. I don't care a curse what I just said. It is now I shall speak of me, for the first time. I thought I was right in enlisting these sufferers of my pains. I was wrong. They never suffered my pains, their pains are nothing, compared to mine, a mere tittle of mine, the tittle I thought I could put from me, in order to witness it. Let them be gone now, them and all the others, those I have used and those I have not used, give me back the pains I lent them and vanish, from my life, my memory, my terrors and shames. There, now there is no one here but me, no one wheels about me, no one comes towards me, no one has ever met anyone before my eyes, these creatures have never been, only I and this black void have ever been. And the sounds? No, all is silent. And the lights, on which I had set such store, must they too go out? Yes, out with them, there is no light here. No grey either, black is what I should have said. Nothing then but me, of which I know nothing, except that I have never uttered, and this black, of which I know nothing either, except that it is black, and empty. That then is what, since I have to speak, I shall speak of, until I need speak no more. And Basil and his gang? Inexistent, invented to explain I forget what. Ah yes, all lies, God and man, nature and the light of day, the heart's outpourings and the means of understanding, all invented, basely, by me alone, with the help of no one, since there is no one, to put off the hour when I must speak of me. There will be no more about them.

I, of whom I know nothing, I know my eyes are open, because of the tears that pour from them unceasingly. I know I am seated, my hands on my knees, because of the pressure against my rump, against the soles of my feet, against the palms of my hands, against my knees. Against my palms the pressure is of my knees, against my knees of my palms, but what is it that presses against my rump, against the soles of my feet? I don't know. My spine is not supported. I mention these details to make sure I am not lying on my back, my legs raised and bent, my eyes closed. It is well to establish the position of the body from the outset, before passing on to more important matters. But what makes me say I gaze straight before me, as I have said? I feel my back straight, my neck stiff and free of twist and up on top of it the head, like the ball of the cup-and-ball in its cup at the end of the stick. These comparisons are uncalled-for. Then there is the way of flowing of my tears which flow all over my face, and even down

along the neck, in a way it seems to me they could not do if
the face were bowed, or lifted up. But I must not confuse the
unbowed head with the level gaze, nor the vertical with the
horizontal plane. This question in any case is secondary, since
I see nothing. Am I clothed? I have often asked myself this
question, then suddenly started talking about Malone's hat, or
Molloy's greatcoat, or Murphy's suit. If I am, I am but lightly. For I feel my tears coursing over my chest, my sides, and
all down my back. Ah yes, I am truly bathed in tears. They
gather in my beard and from there, when it can hold no
more — no, no beard, no hair either, it is a great smooth ball I
carry on my shoulders, featureless, but for the eyes, of which
only the sockets remain. And were it not for the distant
testimony of my palms, my soles, which I have not yet been
able to quash, I would gladly give myself the shape, if not the
consistency, of an egg, with two holes no mattter where to prevent it from bursting, for the consistency is more like that of
mucilage. But softly, softly, otherwise I'll never arrive. In the
matter of clothes then I can think of nothing for the moment
but possibly puttees, with perhaps a few rags clinging to me
here and there. No more obscenities either. Why should I
have a sex, who have no longer a nose? All those things have
fallen, all the things that stick out, with my eyes my hair, without leaving a trace, fallen so far so deep that I heard nothing,
perhaps are falling still, my hair slowly like soot still, of the
fall of my ears heard nothing. Mean words, and needless,
from the mean old spirit, I invented love, music, the smell of
flowering currant, to escape from me. Organs, a without, it's
easy to imagine, a god, it's unavoidable, you imagine them, it's
easy, the worst is dulled, you doze away, an instant. Yes, God,
fomenter of calm, I never believed, not a second. No more
pauses either. Can I keep nothing then, nothing of what has
borne my poor thoughts, bent beneath my words, while I hid?
I'll dry these streaming sockets too, bung them up, there, it's
done, no more tears, I'm a big talking ball, talking about
things that do not exist, or that exist perhaps, impossible to
know, beside the point. Ah yes, quick let me change my tune.
And after all why a ball, rather than something else, and why
big? Why not a cylinder, a small cylinder? An egg, a medium
egg? No no, that's the old nonsense, I always knew I was
round, solid and round, without daring to say so, no asperi-

ties, no apertures, invisible perhaps, or as vast as Sirius in the
Great Dog, these expressions mean nothing. All that matters
is that I am round and hard, there must be reasons for that,
for my being round and hard rather than of some irregular
shape and subject to the dents and bulges incident to shock,
but I have done with reasons. All the rest I renounce, including this ridiculous black which I thought for a moment wor-
thier than grey to enfold me. What rubbish all this stuff about
light and dark. And how I have luxuriated in it. But do I roll,
in the manner of a true ball? Or am I in equilibrium somewhere,
on one of my numberless poles? I feel strongly tempted to
inquire. What reams of discourse I could elicit from this
seemingly so legitimate preoccupation. But which would not
be credited to me. No, between me and the right to silence,
the living rest, stretches the same old lesson, the one I once
knew by heart and would not say, I don't know why, perhaps
for fear of silence, or thinking any old thing would do, and
so for preference lies, in order to remain hidden, no importance. But now I shall say my old lesson, if I can remember it.
Under the skies, on the roads, in the towns, in the woods, in
the hills, in the plains, on the shores, on the seas, behind my
mannikins, I was not always sad, I wasted my time, abjured
my rights, suffered for nothing, forgot my lesson. Then a little
hell after my own heart, not too cruel, with a few nice damned
to foist my groans on, something sighing off and on and the
distant gleams of pity's fires biding their hour to promote us
to ashes. I speak, speak, because I must, but I do not listen,
I seek my lesson, my life I used to know and would not confess, hence possibly an occasional slight lack of limpidity.
And perhaps now again I shall do no more than seek my
lesson, to the self-accompaniment of a tongue that is not mine.
But instead of saying what I should not have said, and what
I shall say no more, if I can, and what I shall say perhaps, if
I can, should I not rather say some other thing, even though
it be not yet the thing? I'll try, I'll try in another present,
even though it be not yet mine, without pauses, without tears,
without eyes, without reasons. Let it be assumed then that I
am at rest, though this is unimportant, at rest or forever moving, through the air or in contact with other surfaces, or that
I sometimes move, sometimes rest, since I feel nothing, neither
quietude nor change, nothing that can serve as a point of

departure towards an opinion on this subject, which would not
greatly matter if I possessed some general notions, and then
the use of reason, but there it is, I feel nothing, know nothing,
and as far as thinking is concerned I do just enough to
preserve me from going silent, you can't call that thinking.
Let us then assume nothing, neither that I move, nor that I
don't, it's safer, since the thing is unimportant, and pass on
to those that are. Namely? This voice that speaks, knowing
that it lies, indifferent to what it says, too old perhaps and too
abased ever to succeed in saying the words that would be its
last, knowing itself useless and its uselessness in vain, not
listening to itself but to the silence that it breaks and whence
perhaps one day will come stealing the long clear sigh of
advent and farewell, is it one? I'll ask no more questions,
there are no more questions, I know none any more. It issues
from me, it fills me, it clamours against my walls, it is not
mine, I can't stop it, I can't prevent it, from tearing me,
racking me, assailing me. It is not mine, I have none, I have
no voice and must speak, that is all I know, its round that I
must revolve, of that I must speak, with this voice that is not
mine, but can only be mine, since there is no one but me, or
if there are others, to whom it might belong, they have never
come near me, I won't delay just now to make this clear.
Perhaps they are watching me from afar, I have no objection,
as long as I don't see them, watching me like a face in the
embers which they know is doomed to crumble, but it takes
too long, it's getting late, eyes are heavy and tomorrow they
must rise betimes. So it is I who speak, all alone, since I
can't do otherwise. No, I am speechless. Talking of speaking,
what if I went silent? What would happen to me then? Worse
than what is happening? But fie these are questions again.
That is typical. I know no more questions and they keep on
pouring out of my mouth. I think I know what it is, it's to
prevent the discourse from coming to an end, this futile
discourse which is not credited to me and brings me not a
syllable nearer silence. But now I am on my guard, I shall
not answer them anymore, I shall not pretend any more to
answer them. Perhaps I shall be obliged, in order not to peter
out, to invent another fairy-tale, yet another, with heads,
trunks, arms, legs and all that follows, let loose in the change-
less round of imperfect shadow and dubious light. But I hope

and trust not. But I always can if necessary. For while
unfolding my facetiae, the last time that happened to me, or
to the other who passes for me, I was not inattentive. And
it seemed to me then that I heard a murmur telling of another
and less unpleasant method of ending my troubles and that I
even succeeded in catching, without ceasing for an instant to
emit my he said, and he said to himself, and he asked, and he
answered, a certain number of highly promising formulae and
which indeed I promised myself to turn to good account at
the first opportunity, that is to say as soon as I had finished
with my troop of lunatics. But all has gone clean from my
head. For it is difficult to speak, even any old rubbish, and at
the same time focus one's attention on another point, where
one's true interest lies, as fitfully defined by a feeble murmur
seeming to apologize for not being dead. And what it seemed
to me I heard then, concerning what I should do, and say, in
order to have nothing further to do, nothing further to say,
it seemed to me I only barely heard it, because of the noise I
was engaged in making elsewhere, in obedience to the unintelligible terms of an incomprehensible damnation. And yet
I was sufficiently impressed by certain expressions to make a
vow, while continuing my yelps, never to forget them and,
what is more, to ensure they should engender others and finally,
in an irresistible torrent, banish from my vile mouth all other
utterance, from my mouth spent in vain with vain inventons
all other utterance but theirs, the true at last, the last at last.
But all is forgotten and I have done nothing, unless what I
am doing now is something, and nothing could give me greater
satisfaction. For if I could hear such a music at such a time,
I mean while floundering through a ponderous chronicle of
moribunds in their courses, moving, clashing, writhing or
fallen in short-lived swoons, with how much more reason
should I not hear it now, when supposedly I am burdened with
myself alone. But this is thinking again. And I see myself
slipping, though not yet at the last extremity, towards the
resorts of fable. Would it not be better if I were simply to keep
on saying babababa, for example, while waiting to ascertain the
true function of this venerable organ? Enough questions,
enough reasoning, I resume, years later, meaning I suppose
that I went silent, that I can go silent. And now this noise
again. That is all rather obscure. I say years, though here

there are no years. What matter how long? Years is one of
Basil's ideas. A short time, a long time, it's all the same. I
kept silence, that's all that counts, if that counts, I have forgotten if that is supposed to count. And now it is taken from
me again. Silence, yes, but what silence! For it is all very fine
to keep silence, but one has also to consider the kind of
silence one keeps. I listened. One might as well speak and be
done with it. What liberty! I strained my ear towards what
must have been my voice still, so weak, so far, that it was
like the sea, a far calm sea dying — no, none of that,
no beach, no shore, the sea is enough, I've had enough of
shingle, enough of sand, enough of earth, enough of sea too.
Decidedly Basil is becoming important, I'll call him Mahood
instead, I prefer that, I'm queer. It was he told me stories
about me, lived in my stead, issued forth from me, came back
to me, entered back into me, heaped stories on my head. I
don't know how it was done. I always liked not knowing, but
Mahood said it wasn't right. He didn't know either, but it
worried him. It is his voice which has often, always, mingled
with mine, and sometimes drowned it completely. Until he
left me for good, or refused to leave me any more, I don't
know. Yes, I don't know if he's here now or far away, but
I don't think I am far wrong in saying that he has ceased
to plague me. When he was away I tried to find myself again,
to forget what he had said, about me, about my misfortunes,
fatuous misfortunes, idiotic pains, in the light of my true situation, revolting word. But his voice continued to testify for me,
as though woven into mine, preventing me from saying who I
was, what I was, so as to have done with saying, done with
listening. And still today, as he would say, though he plagues
me no more his voice is there, in mine, but less, less. And
being no longer renewed it will disappear one day, I hope,
from mine, completely. But in order for that to happen I
must speak, speak. And at the same time, I do not deceive
myself, he may come back again, or go away again and then
come back again. Then my voice, the voice, would say,
That's an idea, now I'll tell one of Mahood's stories, I need
a rest. Yes, that's how it would happen. And it would say,
Then refreshed, set about the truth again, with redoubled
vigour. To make me think I was a free agent. But it would
not be my voice, not even in part. That is how it would be

done. Or quietly, stealthily, the story would begin, as if nothing had happened and I still the teller and the told. But I would be fast asleep, my mouth agape, as usual, I would look the same as usual. And from my sleeping mouth the lies would pour, about me. No, not sleeping, listening, in tears. But now, is it I now, I on me? Sometimes I think it is. And then I realize it is not. I am doing my best, and failing again, yet again. I don't mind failing, it's a pleasure, but I want to go silent. Not as just now, the better to listen, but peacefully, victorious, without ulterior object. Then it would be a life worth having, a life at last. My speech-parched voice at rest would fill with spittle, I'd let it flow over and over, happy at last, dribbling with life, my pensum ended, in the silence. I spoke, I must have spoken, of a lesson, it was pensum I should have said, I confused pensum with lesson. Yes, I have a pensum to discharge, before I can be free, free to dribble, free to speak no more, listen no more, and I've forgotten what it is. There at last is a fair picture of my situation. I was given a pensum, at birth perhaps, as a punishment for having been born perhaps, or for no particular reason, because they dislike me, and I've forgotten what it is. But was I ever told? Squeeze, squeeze, not too hard, but squeeze a little longer, this is perhaps about you, and your goal at hand. After ten thousand words? Well let us say one goal, after it there will be others. Speak, yes, but to me, I have never spoken enough to me, never listened enough to me, never replied enough to me, never had pity enough on me, I have spoken for my master, listened for the words of my master never spoken, Well done, my child, well done, my son, you may stop, you may go, you are free, you are acquitted, you are pardoned, never spoken. My master. There is a vein I must not lose sight of. But for the moment my concern— but before I forget, there may be more than one, a whole college of tyrants, differing in their views as to what should be done with me, in conclave since time began or a little later, listening to me from time to time, then breaking up for a meal or a game of cards—my concern is with the pensum of which I think I may safely say, without loss of face, that it is in some way related to that lesson too hastily proclaimed, too hastily denied. For all I need say is this, that if I have a pensum to perform it is because I could not say my lesson,

and that when I have finished my pensum I shall still have
my lesson to say, before I have the right to stay quiet in my
corner, alive and dribbling, my mouth shut, my tongue at
rest, far from all disturbance, all sound, my mind at peace,
that is to say empty. But this does not get me very far. For
even should I hit upon the right pensum, somewhere in this
churn of words at last, I would still have to reconstitute the
right lesson, unless of course the two are one and the same,
which obviously is not impossible either. Strange notion in
any case, and eminently open to suspicion, that of a task to
be performed, before one can be at rest. Strange task, which
consists in speaking of oneself. Strange hope, turned towards
silence and peace. Possessed of nothing but my voice, the
voice, it may seem natural, once the idea of obligation has
been swallowed, that I should interpret it as an obligation
to say something. But is it possible? Bereft of hands, perhaps
it is my duty to clap or, striking the palms together, to call
the waiter, and of feet, to dance the Carmagnole. But let us
first suppose, in order to get on a little, then we'll suppose
something else, in order to get on a little further, that it is in
fact required of me that I say something, something that is
not to be found in all I have said up to now. That seems a
reasonable assumption. But thence to infer that the something required is something about me suddenly strikes me as
unwarranted. Might it not rather be the praise of my master,
intoned, in order to obtain his forgiveness? Or the admission
that I am Mahood after all and these stories of a being whose
identity he usurps, and whose voice he prevents from being
heard, all lies from beginning to end? And what if Mahood were
my master? I'll leave it at that, for the time being. So many
prospects in so short a time, it's too much. Decidedly it
seems impossible, at this stage, that I should dispense with
questions, as I promised myself I would. No, I merely swore
I'd stop asking them. And perhaps before long, who knows, I
shall light on the happy combination which will prevent them
from ever arising again in my — let us not be over-nice —
mind. For what I am doing is not being done without a minimum of mind. Not mine perhaps, granted, with pleasure, but I
draw on it, at least I try and look as if I did. Rich matter there,
to be exploited, fatten you up, suck it to the core, keep you
going for years, tasty into the bargain, I quiver at the thought,

give you my word, spoken in jest, quiver and hurry on, all
life before me, on and forget, what I was saying, just now,
something important, it's gone, it'll come back, no regrets,
as good as new, unrecognizable, let's hope so, some day when
I feel more on for high-class nuts to crack. On. The master.
I never paid him enough attention. No more perhapses either,
that old trick is worn to a thread. I'll forbid myself everything,
then go on as if I hadn't. The master. A few allusions here
and there, as to a satrap, with a view to enlisting sympathy.
They clothed me and gave me money, that kind of thing, the
light touch. Then no more. Or Moran's boss, I forget his
name. Ah yes, certain things, things I invented, hoping for
the best, full of doubts, croaking with fatigue, I remember certain things, not always the same. But to investigate this
matter seriously, I mean with as much futile ardour as that
of the underling, which I hoped was mine, close to mine, the
road to mine, no, that never occurred to me. And if it occurs
to me now it is because I have despaired of mine. A moment
of discouragement, to strike while hot. My master then,
assuming he is solitary, in my image, wishes me well, poor
devil, wishes my good, and if he does not seem to do very
much in order not to be disappointed it is because there is
not very much to be done or, better still, because there is
nothing to be done, otherwise he would have done it, my
great and good master, that must be it, long ago, poor devil.
Another supposition, he has taken the necessary steps, his
will is done as far as I am concerned (for he may have other
protégés) and all is well with me without my knowing it.
Cases one and two. I'll consider the former first, if I can.
Then I'll admire the latter, if my eyes are still open. This
sounds like one of Malone's anecdotes. But quick, consider,
before you forget. There he is then, the unfortunate brute,
quite miserable because of me, for whom there is nothing
to be done, and he so anxious to help, so used to giving
orders and to being obeyed. There he is, ever since I came
into the world, possibly at his instigation, I wouldn't put it
past him, commanding me to be well, you know, in every
way, no complaints at all, with as much success as if he were
shouting at a lump of inanimate matter. If he is not pleased
with this panegyric I hope I may be—I nearly said hanged,
but that I hope in any case, without restriction, I nearly said

con, that would cut my cackle. Ah for a neck! I want all to
be well with you, do you hear me, that's what he keeps on
dinning at me. To which I reply, in a respectful attitude, I
too, your Lordship. I say that to cheer him up, he sounds so
unhappy. I am good-hearted, on the surface. No, we have
no conversation, never a mum of his mouth to me. He's out
of luck, that's certain, perhaps he didn't choose me. What he
means by good, my good, is another problem. He is capable
of wanting me to be happy, such a thing has been known, it
appears. Or to serve a purpose. Or the two at once! A little
more explicitness on his part, since the initiative belongs to
him, might be a help, as well from his point of view as from
the one he attributes to me. Let the man explain himself and
have done with it. It's none of my business to ask him questions, even if I knew how to reach him. Let him inform me
once and for all what exactly it is he wants from me, for me.
What he wants is my good, I know that, at least I say it, in
the hope of bringing him round to a more reasonable frame
of mind, assuming he exists and, existing, hears me. But what
good, there must be more than one. The supreme perhaps. In
a word let him enlighten me, that's all I ask, so that I may at
least have the satisfaction of knowing in what sense I leave
to be desired. If he wants me to say something, for my good
naturally, he has only to tell me what it is and I'll let it out
with a roar straight away. It's true he may have already told
me a hundred times. Well, let him make it a hundred and one,
this time I'll try and pay attention. But perhaps I malign him
unjustly, my good master, perhaps he is not solitary like me,
not free like me, but associated with others, equally good,
equally concerned with my welfare, but differing as to its
nature. Every day, up above, I mean up above me, from one
set hour to another set hour, everything there being set and
settled except what is to be done with me, they assemble to
discuss me. Or perhaps it's a meeting of deputies, with
instructions to elaborate a tentative agreement. The fact of
my continuing, while they are thus engaged, to be what I
have always been is naturally preferable to a lame resolution,
voted perhaps by a majority of one, or drawn from an old
hat. They too are unhappy, all this time, each one to the best
of his capacity, because all is not well with me. And now
enough of that. If that doesn't mollify them so much the

worse for me, I can still conceive of such a thing. But one more suggestion before I forget and go on to serious matters. Why don't they wash their hands of me and set me free? That might do me good. I don't know. Perhaps then I could go silent, for good and all. Idle talk, idle talk, I am free, abandoned. All for nothing again. Even Mahood has left me, I'm alone. All this business of a labour to accomplish, before I can end, of words to say, a truth to recover, in order to say it, before I can end, of an imposed task, once known, long neglected, finally forgotten, to perform, before I can be done with speaking, done with listening, I invented it all, in the hope it would console me, help me to go on, allow me to think of myself as somewhere on a road, moving, between a beginning and an end, gaining ground, losing ground, getting lost, but somehow in the long run making headway. All lies. I have nothing to do, that is to say nothing in particular. I have to speak, whatever that means. Having nothing to say, no words but the words of others, I have to speak. No one compels me to, there is no one, it's an accident, a fact. Nothing can ever exempt me from it, there is nothing, nothing to discover, nothing to recover, nothing that can lessen what remains to say, I have the ocean to drink, so there is an ocean then. Not to have been a dupe, that will have been my best possession, my best deed, to have been a dupe, wishing I wasn't, thinking I wasn't, knowing I was, not being a dupe of not being a dupe. For any old thing, no, that doesn't work, that should work, but it doesn't. Labyrinthine torment that can't be grasped, or limited, or felt, or suffered, no, not even suffered, I suffer all wrong too, even that I do all wrong too, like an old turkey-hen dying on her feet, her back covered with chickens and the rats spying on her. Next instalment, quick. No cries, above all no cries, be urbane, a credit to the art and code of dying, while the others cackle, I can hear them from here, like the crackling of thorns, no I forgot, it's impossible, it's myself I hear, howling behind my dissertation. So not any old thing. Even Mahood's stories are not any old thing, though no less foreign, to what, to that unfamiliar native land of mine, as unfamiliar as that other where men come and go, and feel at home, on tracks they have made themselves, in order to visit one another with the maximum of convenience and dispatch, in the light of a choice of luminaries pissing on the darkness turn about, so that it is never dark, never deserted, that must be terrible. So be it. Not any old thing, but as near as no matter. Mahood. Before him there were others, taking themselves for me, it must be a sinecure handed down from generation to generation, to judge by their family air. Mahood is no worse than his predecessors. But before executing his portrait, full length on his surviving leg, let me note that my next vice-exister will be a billy in the bowl, that's final, with his bowl on his head and his arse in the dust, plump down on thousand-breasted Tellus, it'll be softer for him. Faith that's an idea, yet another, mutilate, mutilate, and perhaps some day, fifteen generations hence, you'll succeed in beginning to look like yourself, among the passers-by. In the meantime it's Mahood, this caricature is he. What if we were one and the same after all, as he affirms, and I deny? And I been in the places where he says I have been, instead of having stayed on here, trying to take advantage of his absence to unravel my tangle? Here, in my domain, what is Mahood doing in my domain, and how does he get here? There I am launched again on the same old hopeless business, there we are face to face, Mahood and I, if we are twain, as I say we are. I never saw him, I don't see him, he has told me what he is like, what I am like, they have all told me that, it must be one of their principal functions. It isn't enough that I should know what I'm doing, I must also know what I'm looking like. This time I am short of a leg. And yet it appears I have rejuvenated. That's part of the programme. Having brought me to death's door, senile gangrene, they whip off a leg and yip off I go again, like a young one, scouring the earth for a hole to hide in. A single leg and other distinctive stigmata to go with it, human to be sure, but not exaggeratedly, lest I take fright and refuse to nibble. He'll resign himself in the end, he'll own up in the end, that's the watchword. Let's try him this time with a hairless wedgehead, he might fancy that, that kind of talk. With the solitary leg in the middle, that might appeal to him. The poor bastards. They could clap an artificial anus in the hollow of my hand and still I wouldn't be there, alive with their life, not far short of a man, just barely a man, sufficiently a man to have hopes one day of being one, my avatars behind me. And yet sometimes it seems to me I am there, among the incriminated scenes, tottering under the attributes peculiar

to the lords of creation, dumb with howling to be put out of
my misery, and all round me the spinach blue rustling with
satisfaction. Yes, more than once I almost took myself for
the other, all but suffered after his fashion, the space of an
instant. Then they uncorked the champagne. One of us at
last! Green with anguish! A real little terrestrial! Choking
in the chlorophyll! Hugging the slaughter-house walls! Paltry
priests of the irrepressible ephemeral, how they must hate me.
Come, my lambkin, join in our gambols, it's soon over, you'll
see, just time to frolic with a lambkinette, that's jam. Love,
there's a carrot never fails, I always had to thread some old
bodkin. And that's the kind of jakes in which I sometimes
dreamt I dwelt, and even let down my trousers. Mahood
himself nearly codded me more than once. I've been he an
instant, hobbling through a nature which, it is only fair to say,
was on the barren side and, what is more, it is only just to
add, tolerably deserted to begin with. After each thrust
of my crutches I stopped, to devour a narcotic and measure
the distance gone, the distance yet to go. My head is there too,
broad at the base, its slopes denuded, culminating in a ridge
or crowning glory strewn with long waving hairs like those
that grow on naevi. No denying it, I'm confoundedly well
informed. You must allow it was tempting. I say an instant,
perhaps it was years. Then I withdrew my adhesion, it was
getting too much of a good thing. I had already advanced a
good ten paces, if one may call them paces, not in a straight
line I need hardly say, but in a sharp curve which, if I continued to follow it, seemed likely to restore me to my point
of departure, or to one adjacent. I must have got embroiled
in a kind of inverted spiral, I mean one the coils of which,
instead of widening more and more, grew narrower and
narrower and finally, given the kind of space in which I
was supposed to evolve, would come to an end for lack of
room. Faced then with the material impossibility of going
any further I should no doubt have had to stop, unless of
course I elected to set off again at once in the opposite
direction, to unscrew myself as it were, after having screwed
myself to a standstill, which would have been an experience
rich in interest and fertile in surprises if I am to believe what
I once was told, in spite of my protests, namely that there is
no road so dull, on the way out, but it has quite a different

aspect, quite a different dullness, on the way back, and vice
versa. No good wriggling, I'm a mine of useless knowledge.
But a difficulty arises here. For if by dint of winding myself
up, if I may venture that ellipse, it doesn't often happen to
me now, if by dint of winding myself up, I don't seem to
have gained much time, if by dint of winding myself up I
must inevitably find myself stuck in the end, once launched in
the opposite direction should I not normally unfold ad
infinitum, with no possibility of ever stopping, the space in
which I was marooned being globular, or is it the earth, no
matter, I know what I mean. But where is the difficulty?
There was one a moment ago, I could swear to it. Not to
mention that I could quite easily at any moment, literally
any, run foul of a wall, a tree or similar obstacle, which of
course it would be prohibited to circumvent, and thereby
have an end put to my gyrations as effectively as by the kind
of cramp just mentioned. But obstacles, it appears, can be
removed in the fullness of time, but not by me, me they would
stop dead forever, if I lived among them. But even without
such aids it seems to me that once beyond the equator you
would start turning inwards again, out of sheer necessity,
I somehow have that feeling. At the particular moment I
am referring to, I mean when I took myself for Mahood, I
must have been coming to the end of a world tour, perhaps
not more than two or three centuries to go. My state of
decay lends colour to this view, perhaps I had left my leg
behind in the Pacific, yes, no perhaps about it, I had, somewhere off the coast of Java and its jungles red with rafflesia
stinking of carrion, no, that's the Indian Ocean, what a
gazeteer I am, no matter, somewhere round there. In a
word I was returning to the fold, admittedly reduced, and
doubtless fated to be even more so, before I could be restored
to my wife and parents, you know, my loved ones, and clasp
in my arms, both of which I had succeeded in preserving,
my little ones born in my absence. I found myself in a kind
of vast yard or campus, surrounded by high walls, its surface
an amalgam of dirt and ashes, and this seemed sweet to me
after the vast and heaving wastes I had traversed, if my
information was correct. I almost felt out of danger! At the
centre of this enclosure stood a small rotunda, windowless,
but well furnished with loopholes. Without being quite sure I

had seen it before, I had been so long from home, I kept
saying to myself, Yonder is the nest you should never have
left, there your dear absent ones are awaiting your return,
patiently, and you too must be patient. It was swarming with
them, grandpa, grandma, little mother and the eight or nine
brats. With their eyes glued to the slits and their hearts
going out to me they surveyed my efforts. This yard so long
deserted was now enlivened, for them, by me. So we turned,
in our respective orbits, I without, they within. At night,
keeping watch by turns, they observed me with the help of
a searchlight. So the seasons came and went. The children
increased in stature, the periods of Ptomaine grew pale, the
ancients glowered at each other, muttering, to themselves,
I'll bury you yet, or, You'll bury me yet. Since my arrival
they had a subject of conversation, and even of discussion,
the same as of old, at the moment of my setting forth,
perhaps even an interest in life, the same as of old. Time
hung less heavy on their hands. What about throwing him
a few scraps? No no, it might upset him. They did not want
to check the impetus that was sweeping me towards them.
You wouldn't know him! True, papa, and yet you can't
mistake him. They who in the ordinary way never answered
when spoken to, my elders, my wife, she who had chosen me,
rather than one of her suitors. A few more summers and
he'll be in our midst. Where am I going to put him? In the
basement? Perhaps after all I am simply in the basement.
What possesses him to be stopping all the time? Oh he was
always like that, ever since he was a mite, always stopping,
wasn't he, Granny? Yes indeed, never easy, always stopping.
According to Mahood I never reached them, that is to say they
all died first, the whole ten or eleven of them, carried off by
sausage-poisoning, in great agony. Incommoded first by their
shrieks, then by the stench of decomposition, I turned sadly
away. But not so fast, otherwise we'll never arrive. It's no longer
I in any case. He'll never reach us if he doesn't get a move on.
He looks as if he had slowed down, since last year. Oh the
last laps won't take him long. My missing leg didn't seem to
affect them, perhaps it was already missing when I left. What
about throwing him a sponge? No no, it might confuse him.
In the evening, after supper, while my wife kept her eye on
me, gaffer and gammer related my life history, to the sleepy

children. Bedtime story atmosphere. That's one of Mahood's
favourite tricks, to produce ostensibly independent testimony
in support of my historical existence. The instalment over,
all joined in a hymn, Safe in the arms of Jesus, for example,
or, Jesus lover of my soul, let me to thy bosom fly, for
example. Then they went to bed, with the exception of the
one on watch duty. My parents differed in their views on
me, but they were agreed I had been a fine baby, at the very
beginning, the first fortnight or three weeks. And yet he was
a fine baby, with these words they invariably closed their
relations. Often they fell silent, engulfed in their memories.
Then it was usual for one of the children to launch, by way
of envoy, the consecrated phrase, And yet he was a fine baby.
A burst of clear and innocent laughter, from the mouths of
those whom sleep had not yet overcome, greeted this premature conclusion. And the narrators themselves, torn from
their melancholy thoughts, could scarce forbear to smile.
Then they all rose, with the exception of my mother whose
knees couldn't support her, and sang, Gentle Jesus, meek
and mild, for example, or, Jesus, my one, my all, hear me
when I call, for example. He too must have been a fine
baby. Finally my wife announced the latest news, for them to
take to bed with them. He's backing away again, or, He's
stopped to scratch himself, or, You should have seen him
hopping sidelong, or, Oh look children, quick he's down on
his hands and knee, admittedly that must have been worth
seeing. It was then customary that someone should ask her
if I was approaching none the less, if in spite of everything
I was making headway, they couldn't bear the thought of
going to bed, those who were still awake, without the assurance that I wasn't losing ground. Ptoto set their minds at
rest. I had moved, no further proof was needed. I had been
drawing near for so long now that provided I remained in
motion there could be no cause for anxiety. I was launched,
there was no reason why I should suddenly begin to retreat,
I just wasn't made that way. Then having kissed all round
and wished one another happy dreams they retired, with the
exception of the watch. What about hailing him? Poor Papa,
he burned to encourage me vocally. Stick it, lad, it's your
last winter. But in view of the trouble I was having, the
trouble I was taking, they held him back, pointing out that

the moment was ill-chosen to give me a shock. But what
were my own feelings at this period? What was I thinking
of? With what? Was I having difficulty with my morale? The
answer to all that is this, I quote Malone, that I was entirely
absorbed in the business on hand and not at all concerned to
know precisely, or even approximately, what it consisted in.
The only problem for me was how to continue, since I could
not do otherwise, to the best of my declining powers, in the
motion which had been imparted to me. This obligation, and
the quasi-impossibility of fulfilling it, engrossed me in a
purely mechanical way, excluding notably the free play of
the intelligence and sensibility, so that my situation rather
resembled that of an old broken-down cart or bat-horse
unable to receive the least information either from its instinct
or from its observation as to whether it is moving towards the
stable or away from it, and not greatly caring either way. The
question, among others, of how such things are possible had
long since ceased to preoccupy me. This touching picture
of my situation I found by no means unattractive and as I
recall it I find myself wondering again if I was not in fact
the creature revolving in that yard, as Mahood assured me.
Well supplied with pain-killers I drew upon them freely,
without however permitting myself the lethal dose that would
have cut short my functions, whatever they may have been.
Having somehow or other remarked the habitation and even
admitted to myself that I had perhaps seen it before, I gave
it no further thought, nor to the near and dear ones that filled
it to overflowing, in a mounting fever of impatience. Though
now close at hand, as the crow flies, to my goal, I did not
quicken my step. I could have no doubt, but I had to husband
my strength, if I was ever to arrive. I had no wish to arrive,
but I had to do my utmost, in order to arrive. A desirable
goal, no, I never had time to dwell on that. To go on, I still
call that on, to go on and get on has been my only care, if
not always in a straight line, at least in obedience to the figure
assigned to me, there was never any room in my life for anything else. Still Mahood speaking. Never once have I stopped.
My halts do not count. Their purpose was to enable me to
go on. I did not use them to brood on my lot, but to rub myself as best I might with Elliman's Embrocation, for example,
or to give myself an injection of laudanum, no easy matters

for a man with only one leg. Often the cry went up, He's
down! But in reality I had sunk to the ground of my own
free will, in order to be rid of my crutches and have both
hands available to minister to myself in peace and comfort.
Admittedly it is difficult, for a man with but one leg, to sink
to earth in the full force of the expression, particularly when
he is weak in the head and the sole surviving leg flaccid for
want of exercise, or from excess of it. The simplest thing
then is to fling away the crutches and collapse. That is what
I did. They were therefore right in saying I had fallen, they
were not far wrong. Oh I have also been known to fall
involuntarily, but not often, an old warrior like me, you can
imagine. But have it any way you like. Up or down, taking
my anodynes, waiting for the pain to abate, panting to be on
my way again, I stopped, if you insist, but not in the sense
they meant when they said, He's down again, he'll never
reach us. When I penetrate into that house, if I ever do, it
will be to go on turning, faster and faster, more and more
convulsive, like a constipated dog, or one suffering from worms,
overturning the furniture, in the midst of my family all trying
to embrace me at once, until by virtue of a supreme spasm
I am catapulted in the opposite direction and gradually leave
backwards, without having said good-evening. I must really
lend myself to this story a little longer, there may possibly be
a grain of truth in it. Mahood must have remarked that I
remained sceptical, for he casually let fall that I was lacking
not only a leg, but an arm also. With regard to the homolo-
gous crutch, I seemed to have retained sufficient armpit to
hold and manoeuvre it, with the help of my unique foot to kick
the end of it forward as occasion required. But what shocked
me profoundly, to such a degree that my mind (Mahood
dixit) was assailed by insuperable doubts, was the suggestion
that the misfortune experienced by my family and brought to
my notice first by the noise of their agony, then by the smell
of their corpses, had caused me to turn back. From that
moment on I ceased to go along with him. I'll explain why,
that will permit me to think of something else and in the first
place of how to get back to me, back to where I am waiting
for me, I'd just as soon not, but it's my only chance, at least
I think so, the only chance I have of going silent, of saying
something at last that is not false, if that is what they want,

so as to have nothing more to say. My reasons. I'll give three
or four, that ought to be enough for me. First this family of
mine, the mere fact of having a family should have put me
on my guard. But my good will at certain moments is such,
and my longing to have floundered however briefly, however
feebly, in the great life torrent streaming from the earliest
protozoa to the very latest humans, that I, no, parenthesis
unfinished. I'll begin again. My family. To begin with it had
no part or share in what I was doing. Having set forth from
that place, it was only natural I should return to it, given the
accuracy of my navigation. And my family could have moved
to other quarters during my absence, and settled down a
hundred leagues away, without my deviating by as much as
a hair's-breadth from my course. As for the screams of pain
and wafts of decomposition, assuming I was capable of
noticing them, they would have seemed to me quite in the
natural order of things, such as I had come to know it. If
before such manifestations I had been compelled each time
to turn aside, I should not have got very far. Washed on the
surface only by the rains, my head cracking with unutterable
imprecations, it was from myself I should have had to turn
aside, before all else. After all perhaps I was doing so, that
would account for my vaguely circular motion. Lies, lies,
mine was not to know, nor to judge, nor to rail, but to go.
That the bacillus botulinus should have exterminated my entire
kith and kin, I shall never weary of repeating this, was something I could readily admit, but only on condition that my
personal behaviour had not to suffer by it. Let us rather
consider what really took place, if Mahood was telling the
truth. And why should he have lied to me, he so anxious to
obtain my adhesion, to what now that I come to think of it,
to his conception of me? Why? For fear of paining me
perhaps. But I am there to be pained, that is what my tempters
have never grasped. What they all wanted, each according to
his particular notion of what is endurable, was that I should
exist and at the same time be only moderately, or perhaps I
should say finitely pained. They have even killed me off, with
the friendly remark that having reached the end of my endurance I had no choice but to disappear. The end of my
endurance! It was one second they should have schooled me
to endure, after that I would have held out for all eternity,

whistling a merry tune. The hard knocks they invented for
me! But the bouquet was this story of Mahood's in which
I appear as upset at having been delivered so economically
of a pack of blood relations, not to mention the two cunts
into the bargain, the one for ever accursed that ejected me into
this world and the other, infundibuliform, in which, pumping
my likes, I tried to take my revenge. To tell the truth, let us
be honest at least, it is some considerable time now since I
last knew what I was talking about. It is because my thoughts
are elsewhere. I am therefore forgiven. So long as one's
thoughts are somewhere everything is permitted. On then,
without misgiving, as if nothing had happened. And let us
consider what really took place, if Mahood was telling the
truth when he represented me as rid at one glorious sweep of
parents, wife and heirs. I've plenty of time to blow it all sky-
high, this circus where it is enough to breathe to qualify for
asphyxiation, I'll find a way out of it, it won't be like the
other times. But I should not like to defame my defamer. For
when he made me turn and set off in the other direction,
before I had exhausted the possibilities of the one I was
pursuing, he had not in mind a shrinking of the spirit, not for
a moment, but a purely physiological commotion, followed by
a simple desire to vomit, corresponding respectively to the
howls of my family as they grudgingly succumbed and the
subsequent stench, this latter compelling me to beat in retreat
under penalty of losing consciousness entirely. This version
of the facts having been restored, it only remains to say it is no
better than the other and no less incompatible with the kind
of creature I might just conceivably have been if they had
known how to take me. So let us consider now what really
occurred. Finally I found myself, without surprise, within the
building, circular in form as already stated, its ground-floor
consisting of a single room flush with the arena, and there
completed my rounds, stamping under foot the unrecognizable
remains of my family, here a face, there a stomach, as the
case might be, and sinking into them with the ends of my
crutches, both coming and going. To say I did so with satisfaction would be stretching the truth. For my feeling was
rather one of annoyance at having to flounder in such muck
just at the moment when my closing contortions called for a
firm and level surface. I like to fancy, even if it is not true,

that it was in mother's entrails I spent the last days of my
long voyage, and set out on the next. No, I have no preference, Isolde's breast would have done just as well, or papa's
private parts, or the heart of one of the little bastards. But
is it certain? Would I have not been more likely, in a sudden
access of independence, to devour what remained of the
fatal corned-beef? How often did I fall during these final
stages, while the storms raged without? But enough of this
nonsense. I was never anywhere but here, no one ever got
me out of here. Enough of acting the infant who has been
told so often how he was found under a cabbage that in the
end he remembers the exact spot in the garden and the kind
of life he led there before joining the family circle. There
will be no more from me about bodies and trajectories, sky
and earth, I don't know what it all is. They have told me,
explained to me, described to me, what it all is, what it looks
like, what it's all for, one after the other, thousands of times,
in thousands of connexions, until I must have begun to look
as if I understood. Who would ever think, to hear me, that
I've never seen anything, never heard anything but their
voices? And man, the lectures they gave me on men, before
they even began trying to assimilate me to him! What I
speak of, what I speak with, all comes from them. It's all the
same to me, but it's no good, there's no end to it. It's of me
now I must speak, even if I have to do it with their language,
it will be a start, a step towards silence and the end of madness, the madness of having to speak and not being able to,
except of things that don't concern me, that don't count, that
I don't believe, that they have crammed me full of to prevent
me from saying who I am, where I am, and from doing what
I have to do in the only way that can put an end to it, from
doing what I have to do. How they must hate me! Ah a nice
state they have me in, but still I'm not their creature, not quite,
not yet. To testify to them, until I die, as if there was any
dying with that tomfoolery, that's what they've sworn they'll
bring me to. Not to be able to open my mouth without
proclaiming them, and our fellowship, that's what they
imagine they'll have me reduced to. It's a poor trick that consists in ramming a set of words down your gullet on the
principle that you can't bring them up without being branded
as belonging to their breed. But I'll fix their gibberish for

them. I never understood a word of it in any case, not a word of the stories it spews, like gobbets in a vomit. My inability to absorb, my genius for forgetting, are more than they reckoned with. Dear incomprehension, it's thanks to you I'll be myself, in the end. Nothing will remain of all the lies they have glutted me with. And I'll be myself at last, as a starveling belches his odourless wind, before the bliss of coma. But who, they? Is it really worth while inquiring? With my cogged means? No, but that's no reason not to. On their own ground, with their own arms, I'll scatter them, and their miscreated puppets. Perhaps I'll find traces of myself by the same occasion. That's decided then. What is strange is that they haven't been pestering me for some time past, yes, they've inflicted the notion of time on me too. What conclusion, using their methods, am I to draw from this? Mahood is silent, that is to say his voice continues, but is no longer renewed. Do they consider me so plastered with their rubbish that I can never extricate myself, never make a gesture but their cast must come to life? But within, motionless, I can live, and utter me, for no ears but my own. They loaded me down with their trappings and stoned me through the carnival. I'll sham dead now, whom they couldn't bring to life, and my monster's carapace will rot off me. But it's entirely a matter of voices, no other metaphor is appropriate. They've blown me up with their voices, like a balloon, and even as I collapse it's them I hear. Who, them? And why nothing more from them lately? Can it be they have abandoned me, saying, Very well, there's nothing to be done with him, let's leave it at that, he's not dangerous. Ah but the little murmur of unconsenting man, to murmur what it is their humanity stifles, the little gasp of the condemned to life, rotting in his dungeon garrotted and racked, to gasp what it is to have to celebrate banishment, beware. No, they have nothing to fear, I am walled round with their vociferations, none will ever know what I am, none will ever hear me say it, I won't say it, I can't say it, I have no language but theirs, no, perhaps I'll say it, even with their language, for me alone, so as not to have not lived in vain, and so as to go silent, if that is what confers the right to silence, and it's unlikely, it's they who have silence in their gift, they who decide, the same old gang, among themselves, no matter, to hell with silence, I'll say what

I am, so as not to have not been born for nothing, I'll fix their
jargon for them, then any old thing, no matter what, whatever
they want, with a will, till time is done, at least with a good
grace. First I'll say what I'm not, that's how they taught me
to proceed, then what I am, it's already under way, I have
only to resume at the point where I let myself be cowed. I
am neither, I needn't say, Murphy, nor Watt, nor Mercier,
nor—no, I can't even bring myself to name them, nor any
of the others whose very names I forget, who told me I was
they, who I must have tried to be, under duress, or through
fear, or to avoid acknowledging me, not the slightest connexion. I never desired, never sought, never suffered, never
partook in any of that, never knew what it was to have,
things, adversaries, mind, senses. But enough of this. There
is no use denying, no use harping on the same old thing I
know so well, and so easy to say, and which simply amounts
in the end to speaking yet again in the way they intend me
to speak, that is to say about them, even with execration and
disbelief. Perhaps they exist in the way they have decreed
will be mine, it's possible, I don't know and I'm not interested.
If they had taught me how to wish I'd wish they did. There's
no getting rid of them without naming them and their con-
traptions, that's the thing to keep in mind. I might as well
tell another of Mahood's stories and no more about it, to be
understood in the way I was given to understand it, namely
as being about me. That's an idea. To heighten my disgust.
I'll recite it. This will leave me free to consider how I may
best proceed with my own affair, beginning again at the point
where I had to interrupt it, under duress, or through fear, or
through ignorance. It will be the last story. I'll try and look
as if I was telling it willingly, to keep them quiet in case they
should feel like refreshing my memory, on the subject of my
behaviour above in the island, among my compatriots, contemporaries, coreligionists and companions in distress. This
will leave me free to consider how to set about showing myself
forth. No one will be any the wiser. But who are these
maniacs let loose on me from on high for what they call my
good, let us first try and throw a little light on that. To tell the
truth—no, first the story. The island, I'm on the island, I've
never left the island, God help me. I was under the impression I spent my life in spirals round the earth. Wrong, it's

on the island I wind my endless ways. The island, that's all the earth I know. I don't know it either, never having had the stomach to look at it. When I come to the coast I turn back inland. And my course is not helicoidal, I got that wrong too, but a succession of irregular loops, now sharp and short as in the waltz, now of a parabolic sweep that embraces entire boglands, now between the two, somewhere or other, and invariably unpredictable in direction, that is to say determined by the panic of the moment. But at the period I refer to now this active life is at an end, I do not move and never shall again, unless it be under the impulsion of a third party. For of the great traveller I had been, on my hands and knees in the later stages, then crawling on my belly or rolling on the ground, only the trunk remains (in sorry trim), surmounted by the head with which we are already familiar, this is the part of myself the description of which I have best assimilated and retained. Stuck like a sheaf of flowers in a deep jar, its neck flush with my mouth, on the side of a quiet street near the shambles, I am at rest at last. If I turn, I shall not say my head, but my eyes, free to roll as they list, I can see the statue of the apostle of horse's meat, a bust. His pupilless eyes of stone are fixed upon me. That makes four, with those of my creator, omnipresent, do not imagine I flatter myself I am privileged. Though not exactly in order I am tolerated by the police. They know I am speechless and consequently incapable of taking unfair advantage of my situation to stir up the population against its governors, by means of burning oratory during the rush hour or subversive slogans whispered, after nightfall, to belated pedestrians the worse for drink. And since I have lost all my members, with the exception of the onetime virile, they know also that I shall not be guilty of any gestures liable to be construed as inciting to alms, a prisonable offence. The fact is I trouble no one, except possibly that category of hypersensitive persons for whom the least thing is an occasion for scandal and indignation. But even here the risk is negligible, such people avoiding the neighborhood for fear of being overcome at the sight of the cattle, fat and fresh from their pastures, trooping towards the humane killer. From this point of view the spot is well chosen, from my point of view. And even those sufficiently unhinged to be affected by the spectacle I offer, I mean upset

and temporarily diminished in their capacity for work and
aptitude for happiness, need only look at me a second time,
those who can bring themselves to do it, to have immediately
their minds made easy. For my face reflects nothing but the
satisfaction of one savouring a well-earned rest. It is true my
mouth was hidden, most of the time, and my eyes closed. Ah
yes, sometimes it's in the past, sometimes in the present. And
alone perhaps the state of my skull, covered with pustules
and bluebottles, these latter naturally abounding in such a
neighborhood, preserved me from being an object of envy
for many, and a source of discontent. I hope this gives a fair
picture of my situation. Once a week I was taken out of my
receptacle, so that it might be emptied. This duty fell to the
proprietress of the chop-house across the street and she performed it punctually and without complaint, beyond an occasional good-natured reflection to the effect that I was a nasty
old pig, for she had a kitchen-garden. Without perhaps having
exactly won her heart it was clear I did not leave her
indifferent. And before putting me back she took advantage of the circumstance that my mouth was accessible to stick
into it a chunk of lights or a marrow-bone. And when snow
fell she covered me with a tarpaulin still watertight in places.
It was under its shelter, snug and dry, that I became acquainted with the boon of tears, while wondering to what I was
indebted for it, not feeling moved. And this not merely once,
but every time she covered me, that is to say twice or three
times a year. Yes, it was fatal, no sooner had the tarpaulin
settled over me, and the precipitate steps of my benefactress
died away, than the tears began to flow. Is this, was this to
be interpreted as an effect of gratitude? But in that case
should not I have felt grateful? Besides I realized darkly that
if she took care of me thus, it was not solely out of goodness,
or else I had not rightly understood the meaning of goodness,
when it was explained to me. It must not be forgotten that I
represented for this woman an undeniable asset. For quite
apart from the services I rendered to her lettuce, I constituted
for her establishment a kind of landmark, not to say an adver-
tisement, far more effective than for example a chef in
cardboard, pot-bellied in profile and full face wafer thin. That
she was well aware of this is shown by the trouble she had
taken to festoon my jar with Chinese lanterns, of a very pretty

effect in the twilight, and a fortiori in the night. And the jar itself, so that the passer-by might consult with greater ease the menu attached to it, had been raised on a pedestal at her own expense. It is thus I learnt that her turnips in gravy are not so good as they used to be, but that on the other hand her carrots, equally in gravy, are even better than formerly. The gravy has not varied. This is the kind of language I can almost understand, these the kind of clear and simple notions on which it is possible for me to build, I ask for no other spiritual nourishment. A turnip, I know roughly what a turnip is like, a carrot too, particularly the Flakkee, or Colmar Red. I seem to grasp at certain moments the nuance that divides bad from worse. And if I do not always feel the full force of yesterday and today, this does not detract very much from the satisfaction I feel at having penetrated the gist of the matter. Of her salad, for example, I never heard anything but praise. Yes, I represent for her a tidy little capital and, if I should ever happen to die, I am convinced she would be genuinely annoyed. This should help me to live. I like to fancy that when the fatal hour of reckoning comes, if it ever does, and my debt to nature is paid off at last, she will do her best to prevent the removal, from where it now stands, of the old vase in which I shall have accomplished my vicissitudes. And perhaps in the place now occupied by my head she will set a melon, or a vegetable-marrow, or a big pineapple with its little tuft, or better still, I don't know why, a swede, in memory of me. Then I shall not vanish quite, as is so often the way with people when buried. But it is not to speak of her that I have started lying again. *De nobis ipsis silemus*, decidedly that should have been my motto. Yes, they gave me some lessons in pigsty latin too, it looks well, sprinkled through the perjury. It is perhaps worth noting that snow alone, provided of course it is heavy, entitles me to the tarpaulin. No other form of filthy weather lets loose in her the maternal instinct, in my favour. I have tried to make her understand, dashing my head angrily against the neck of the jar, that I should like to be shrouded more often. At the same time I let my spittle flow over, in an attempt to show my displeasure. In vain. I wonder what explanation she can have found to account for this behaviour. She must have talked it over with her husband and probably been told that I was merely stifling, that is just the

reverse of the truth. But credit where credit is due, we made
a balls of it between us, I with my signs and she with her
reading of them. This story is no good, I'm beginning almost
to believe it. But let us see how it is supposed to end, that will
sober me. The trouble is I forget how it goes on. But did I
ever know? Perhaps it stops there, perhaps they stopped it
there, saying, who knows, There you are now, you don't need
us any more. This in fact is one of their favourite devices, to
stop suddenly at the least sign of adhesion from me, leaving
me high and dry, with nothing for my renewal but the life
they have imputed to me. And it is only when they see me
stranded that they take up again the thread of my misfortunes,
judging me still insufficiently vitalized to bring them to a successful conclusion alone. But instead of making the junction, I
have often noticed this, I mean instead of resuming me at the
point where I was left off, they pick me up at a much later stage,
perhaps thereby hoping to induce in me the illusion that I
had got through the interval all on my own, lived without
help of any kind for quite some time, and with no recollection
of by what means or in what circumstances, or even died, all
on my own, and come back to earth again, by way of the
vagina like a real live baby, and reached a ripe age, and even
senility, without the least assistance from them and thanks
solely to the hints they had given me. To saddle me with a
lifetime is probably not enough for them, I have to be given
a taste of two or three generations. But it's not certain. Perhaps all they have told me has reference to a single existence,
the confusion of identities being merely apparent and due to
my inaptitude to assume any. If I ever succeed in dying under
my own steam, then they will be in a better position to decide
if I am worthy to adorn another age, or to try the same one
again, with the benefit of my experience. I may therefore
perhaps legitimately suppose that the one-armed one-legged
wayfarer of a moment ago and the wedge-headed trunk in
which I am now marooned are simply two phases of the same
carnal envelope, the soul being notoriously immune from de-
terioration and dismemberment. Having lost one leg, what
indeed more likely than that I should mislay the other? And
similarly for the arms. A natural transition in sum. But what
then of that other old age they bestowed upon me, if I remember right, and that other middle age, when neither legs nor

arms were lacking, but simply the power to profit by them?
And of that kind of youth in which they had to give me up
for dead? If I have a warm place, it is not in their hearts. Oh
I don't say they haven't done all they could to be agreeable to
me, to get me out of here, on no matter what pretext, in no
matter what disguise. All I reproach them with is their insistence. For beyond them is that other who will not give me
quittance until they have abandoned me as inutilizable and
restored me to myself. Then at last I can set about saying
what I was, and where, during all this long lost time. But who
is he, if my guess is right, who is waiting for that, from me?
And who these others whose designs are so different? And
into whose hands I play when I ask myself such questions?
But do I, do I? In the jar did I ask myself questions? And
in the arena? I have dwindled, I dwindle. Not so long ago,
with a kind of shrink of my head and shoulders, as when
one is scolded, I could disappear. Soon, at my present rate of
decrease, I may spare myself this effort. And spare myself the
trouble of closing my eyes, so as not to see the day, for they
are blinded by the jar a few inches away. And I have only
to let my head fall forward against the wall to be sure that
the light from above, which at night is that of the moon, will
not be reflected there either, in those little blue mirrors, I used
to look at myself in them, to try and brighten them. Wrong
again, wrong again, this effort and this trouble will not be
spared me. For the woman, displeased at seeing me sink lower
and lower, has raised me up by filling the bottom of my jar
with sawdust which she changes every week, when she makes
my toilet. It is softer than the stone, but less hygienic. And
I had got used to the stone. Now I'm getting used to the sawdust. It's an occupation. I could never bear to be idle, it saps
one's energy. And I open and close my eyes, open and close,
as in the past. And I move my head in and out, in and out,
as heretofore. And often at dawn, having left it out all night,
I bring it in, to mock the woman and lead her astray. For
in the morning, when she has rattled up her shutters, the first
look of her eyes still moist with fornication is for the jar. And
when she does not see my head she comes running to find out
what has happened. For either I have escaped during the
night or else I have shrunk again. But just before she reaches
me I up with it like a jack-in-the-box, the old eyes glaring up

at her. I mentioned I cannot turn my head, and this is true, my neck having stiffened prematurely. But this does not mean it is always facing in the same direction. For with a kind of tossing and writhing I succeed in imparting to my trunk the degree of rotation required, and not merely in one direction, but in the other also. My little game, which I should have thought inoffensive, has cost me dear, and yet I could have sworn I was insolvable. It is true one does not know one's riches until they are lost and I probably have others still that only await the thief to be brought to my notice. And today, if I can still open and close my eyes, as in the past, I can no longer, because of my roguish character, move my head in and out, as in the good old days. For a collar, fixed to the mouth of the jar, now encircles my neck, just below the chin. And my lips which used to be hidden, and which I sometimes pressed against the freshness of the stone, can now be seen by all and sundry. Did I say I catch flies? I snap them up, clack! Does this mean I still have my teeth? To have lost one's limbs and preserved one's dentition, what a mockery! But to revert now to the gloomy side of this affair, I may say that this collar, or ring, of cement, makes it very awkward for me to turn, in the way I have said. I take advantage of this to learn to stay quiet. To have forever before my eyes, when I open them, approximately the same set of hallucinations exactly, is a joy I might never have known, but for my cang. There is really only one thing that worries me, and that is the prospect of being throttled if I should ever happen to shorten further. Asphyxia! I who was always the respiratory type, witness this thorax still mine, together with the abdomen. I who murmured, each time I breathed in, Here comes more oxygen, and each time I breathed out, There go the impurities, the blood is bright red again. The blue face! The obscene protrusion of the tongue! The tumefaction of the penis! The penis, well now, that's a nice surprise, I'd forgotten I had one. What a pity I have no arms, there might still be something to be wrung from it. No, tis better thus. At my age, to start masturbating again, it would be indecent. And fruitless. And yet one can never tell. With a yo heave ho, concentrating with all my might on a horse's rump, at the moment when the tail rises, who knows, I might not go altogether empty-handed away. Heaven, I almost felt it flutter! Does this mean they did not geld me? I could have sworn they had gelt me. But perhaps I am getting mixed up with other scrota. Not another stir out of it in any case. I'll concentrate again. A Clydesdale. A Suffolk stallion. Come come, a little cooperation please, finish dying, it's the least you might do, after all the trouble they've taken to bring you to life. The worst is over. You've been sufficiently assassinated, sufficiently suicided, to be able now to stand on your own feet, like a big boy. That's what I keep telling myself. And I add, quite carried away, Slough off this mortal inertia, it is out of place, in this society. They can't do everything. They have put you on the right road, led you by the hand to the very brink of the precipice, now it's up to you, with an unassisted last step, to show them your gratitude. I like this colourful language, these bold metaphors and apostrophes. Through the splendours of nature they dragged a paralytic and now there's nothing more to admire it's my duty to jump, that it may be said, There goes another who has lived. It does not seem to occur to them that I was never there, that this glassy eye, this fallen chap and the foam at the mouth owe nothing to the Bay of Naples, or Auber- villiers. The last step! I who could never manage the first. But perhaps they would consider themselves sufficiently rewarded if I simply waited for the wind to blow me over. That by all means, it's in my repertory. The trouble is there is no wind equal to it. The cliff would have to cave in under me. If only I were alive inside one might look forward to heart-failure, or to a nice little infarctus somewhere or other. It's usually with sticks they put me out of their agony, the idea being to demonstrate, to the backers, and bystanders, that I had a beginning, and an end. Then planting the foot on my chest, where all is as usual, to the assembly, Ah if you had seen him fifty years ago, what push, what go! Knowing per- fectly well they have to begin me all over again. But perhaps I exaggerate my need of them. I accuse myself of inertia, and yet I move, at least I did, can I by any chance have missed the tide? Let us consider the head. There something seems to stir, from time to time, no reason therefore to despair of a fit of apoplexy. What else? The organs of digestion and evacua- tion, though sluggish, are not wholly inactive, as is shown by the attentions I receive. It's encouraging. While there's life there's hope. The flies, considered as traumatic agents, hardly call for mention. I suppose they might bring me typhus. No, that's rats. I have seen a few, but they are not yet reduced to me. A lowly tapeworm? Not interesting. It is clear in any case that I have lost heart too lightly, it is quite possible I have all that is required to give them satisfaction. But already I'm beginning to be there no more, in that calamitous street they made so clear to me. I could describe it, I could have, a moment ago, as if I had been there, in the form they chose for me, diminished certainly, not the man I was, not much longer for this world, but the eyes still open to impressions, and one ear, sufficiently, and the head sufficiently obedient, to provide me at least with a vague idea of the elements to be eliminated from the setting in order for all to be empty and silent. That was always the way. Just at the moment when the world is assembled at last, and it begins to dawn on me how I can leave it, all fades and disappears. I shall never see this place again, where my jar stands on its pedestal, with its garland of many-coloured lanterns, and me inside it, I could not cling to it. Perhaps they will have me struck by lightning, for a change, or poleaxed, one merry bank-holiday evening, then bundled in my shroud and whisked away, out of sight and mind. Or removed alive, for a change, shifted and deposited elsewhere, on the off chance. And at my next appearance, if I ever appear again, all will be new, new and strange. But little by little I'll get used to it, admonished by them, used to the scene, used to me, and little by little the old problem will raise its horrid head, how to live, with their kind of life, for a single second, young or old, without aid and assistance. And thus reminded of other attempts, in other circumstances, I shall start asking myself questions, prompted by them, like those I have been asking, concerning me, and them, and these sudden shifts of time and age, and how to succeed at last where I had always failed, so that they may be pleased with me, and perhaps leave me in peace at last, and free to do what I have to do, namely try and please the other, if that is what I have to do, so that he may be pleased with me, and leave me in peace at last, and give me quittance, and the right to rest, and silence, if that is in his gift. It's a lot to expect of one creature, it's a lot to ask, that he should first behave as if he were not, then as if he were, before being admitted to that peace where he neither is, nor is not, and

where the language dies that permits of such expressions. Two
falsehoods, two trappings, to be borne to the end, before I
can be let loose, alone, in the unthinkable unspeakable, where
I have not ceased to be, where they will not let me be. It
will perhaps be less restful than I appear to think, alone there
at last, and never importuned. No matter, rest is one of their
words, think is another. But here at last, is seems to me, is
food for delirium. What a shame if I should pitch on something and never notice it, another candle throw its little light
and I be none the wiser. Yes, I feel the moment has came
for me to look back, if I can, and take my bearings, if I am to
go on. If only I knew what I have been saying. Bah, no
need to worry, it can only have been one thing, the same as
ever. I have my faults, but changing my tune is not one of
them. I have only to go on, as if there was something to be
done, something begun, somewhere to go. It all boils down to
a question of words, I must not forget this, I have not forgotten it. But I must have said this before, since I say it now.
I have to speak in a certain way, with warmth perhaps, all is
possible, first of the creature I am not, as if I were he, and
then, as if I were he, of the creature I am. Before I can etc.
It's a question of voices, of voices to keep going, in the right
manner, when they stop, on purpose, to put me to the test,
as now the one whose burden is roughly to the effect that I
am alive. Warmth, ease, conviction, the right manner, as if it
were my own voice, pronouncing my own words, words
pronouncing me alive, since that's how they want me to be,
I don't know why, with their billions of quick, their trillions
of dead, that's not enough for them, I too must contribute my
little convulsion, mewl, howl, gasp and rattle, loving my neighbour and blessed with reason. But what is the right manner, I
don't know. It is they who dictate this torrent of balls, they
who stuffed me full of these groans that choke me. And out
it all pours unchanged, I have only to belch to be sure of
hearing them, the same old sour teachings I can't change a
tittle of. A parrot, that's what they're up against, a parrot.
If they had told me what I have to say, in order to meet with
their approval, I'd be bound to say it, sooner or later. But God
forbid, that would be too easy, my heart wouldn't be in it, I
have to puke my heart out too, spew it up whole along with
the rest of the vomit, it's then at last I'll look as if I mean

what I'm saying, it won't be just idle words. Well, don't lose
hope, keep your mouth open and your stomach turned,
perhaps you'll come out with it one of these days. But the
other voice, of him who does not share this passion for the
animal kingdom, who is waiting to hear from me, what is its
burden? Nice point, too nice for me. For on the subject of
me properly so called, I know what I mean, so far as I know
I have receved no information up to date. May one speak
of a voice, in these conditions? Probably not. And yet I do.
The fact is all this business about voices requires to be revised,
corrected and then abandoned. Hearing nothing I am none
the less a prey to communications. And I speak of voices!
After all, why not, so long as one knows it's untrue. But
there are limits, it appears. Let them come. So nothing about
me. That is to say no connected statement. Faint calls, at
long intervals. Hear me! Be yourself again! Someone has
therefore something to say to me. But never the least news
concerning me, beyond the insinuation that I am not in a
condition to receive any, since I am not there, which I knew
already. I have naturally remarked, in a moment of excep-
tional receptivity, that these exhortations are conveyed to me
by the same channel as that used by Malone and Co for their
transports. That's suspicious, or rather would be if I still
hoped to obtain, from these revelations to come, some truth
of more value than those I have been plastered with ever since
they took it into their heads I had better exist. But this fond
hope, which buoyed me up as recently as a moment ago, if
I remember right, has now passed from me. Two labours then,
to be distinguished perhaps, as the mine from the quarry,
on the plane of the effort required, but identically deficient
in charm and interest. I. Who might that be? The galley-man,
bound for the Pillars of Hercules, who drops his sweep under
cover of night and crawls between the thwarts, towards the
rising sun, unseen by the guard, praying for storm. Except
that I've stopped praying for anything. No no, I'm still a sup-
pliant. I'll get over it, between now and the last voyage, on
this leaden sea. It's like the other madness, the mad wish to
know, to remember, one's transgressions. I won't be caught
at that again, I'll leave it to this year's damned. And now let
us think no more about it, think no more about anything,
think no more. He alone or they a many, all solicit me in

the same tongue, the only one they taught me. They told me there were others, I don't regret not knowing them. The moment the silence is broken in this way it can only mean one thing. Orders, prayers, threats, praise, reproach, reasons. Praise, yes, they gave me to understand I was making progress. Well done, sonny, that will be all for today, run along now back to your dark and see you tomorrow. And there I am, with my white beard, sitting among the children, babbling, cringing from the rod. I'll die in the lower third, bowed down with years and impositions, four foot tall again, like when I had a future, bare-legged in my old black pinafore, wetting my drawers. Pupil Mahood, for the twenty-five thousandth time, what is a mammal? And I'll fall down dead, worn out by the rudiments. But I'll have made progress, they told me so, only not enough, not enough. Ah! Where was I, in my lessons? That is what has had a fatal effect on my development, my lack of memory, no doubt about it. Pupil Mahood, repeat after me, Man is a higher mammal. I couldn't. Always talking about mammals, in this menagerie. Frankly, between ourselves, what the hell could it matter to pupil Mahood, that man was this rather than that? Presumably nothing has been lost in any case, since here it all comes slobbering out again, let loose by the nightmare. I'll have my bellyful of mammals, I can see that from here, before I wake. Quick, give me a mother and let me suck her white, pinching my tits. But it's time I gave this solitary a name, nothing doing without proper names. I therefore baptise him Worm. It was high time. Worm. I don't like it, but I haven't much choice. It will be my name too, when the time comes, when I needn't be called Mahood any more, if that happy time ever comes. Before Mahood there were others like him, of the same breed and creed, armed with the same prong. But Worm is the first of his kind. That's soon said. I must not forget I don't know him. Perhaps he too will weary, renounce the task of forming me and make way for another, having laid the foundations. He has not yet been able to speak his mind, only murmur, I have not ceased to hear his murmur, all the while the others discoursed. He has survived them all, Mahood too, if Mahood is dead. I can hear him yet, faithful, begging me to still this dead tongue of the living. I imagine that is what he says, in his unchanging tone. If I could

be silent I would better understand what he wants of me,
wants me to be, wants me to say. Why doesn't he thunder it
at me and get it over? Too easy, it is I who must be silent,
hold my breath. But there is something wrong here. For if
Mahood were silent, Worm would be silent too. That the
impossible should be asked of me, good, what else could be
asked of me? But the absurd! Of me whom they have reduced to reason. It is true poor Worm is not to blame for this.
That's soon said. But let me complete my views, before I
shit on them. For if I am Mahood, I am Worm too, plop. Or
if I am not yet Worm, I shall be when I cease to be Mahood,
plop. On now to serious matters. No, not yet. Another of
Mahood's yarns perhaps, to perfect my besotment. No, not
worth the trouble, it will come at its appointed hour, the
record is in position from time immemorial. Yes, the big
words must out too, all be taken as it comes. The problem
of liberty too, as sure as fate, will come up for my consideration at the pre-established moment. But perhaps I have been
too hasty in opposing these two fomenters of fiasco. Is it
not the fault of one that I cannot be the other? Accomplices
therefore. That's the way to reason, warmly. Or is one to
postulate a tertius gaudens, meaning myself, responsible for
the double failure? Shall I come upon my true countenance
at last, bathing in a smile? I have the feeling I shall be spared
this spectacle. At no moment do I know what I'm talking
about, nor of whom, nor of where, nor how, nor why, but I
could employ fifty wretches for this sinister operation and
still be short of a fifty-first, to close the circuit, that I know,
without knowing what it means. The essential is never to
arrive anywhere, never to be anywhere, neither where Mahood is, nor where Worm is, nor where I am, it little matters
thanks to what dispensation. The essential is to go on squirming forever at the end of the line, as long as there are waters
and banks and ravening in heaven a sporting God to plague
his creature, per pro his chosen shits. I've swallowed three
hooks and am still hungry. Hence the howls. What a joy to
know where one is, and where one will stay, without being
there. Nothing to do but stretch out comfortably on the
rack, in the blissful knowledge you are nobody for all eternity.
A pity I should have to give tongue at the same time, it
prevents it from bleeding in peace, licking the lips. Well I

suppose one can't have everything, so late in the proceedings.
They'll surely bring me to the surface one day or another
and all then sink their differences and agree it was not worth
while going to so much trouble for such a paltry kill, for such
paltry killers. What silence then! And now let's see what
news there is of Worm, just to please the old bastard. I'll
soon know if the other is still after me. But even if he isn't
nothing will come of it, he won't catch me, I won't be
delivered from him, I mean Worm, I swear it, the other never
caught me, I was never delivered from him, it's past history,
up to the present. I am he who will never be caught, never
delivered, who crawls between the thwarts, towards the new
day that promises to be glorious, festooned with lifebelts,
praying for rack and ruin. The third line falls plumb from the
skies, it's for her majesty my soul, I'd have hooked her on
it long ago if I knew where to find her. That brings us up
to four, gathered together. I knew it, there might be a hundred of us and still we'd lack the hundred and first, we'll
always be short of me. Worm, I nearly said Watt, Worm,
what can I say of Worm, who hasn't the wit to make himself
plain, what to still this gnawing of termites in my Punch and
Judy box, what that might not just as well be said of the other?
Perhaps it's by trying to be Worm that I'll finally succeed in
being Mahood, I hadn't thought of that. Then all I'll have to do
is be Worm. Which no doubt I shall achieve by trying to be
Jones. Then all I'll have to do is be Jones. Stop, perhaps he'll
spare me that, have compassion and let me stop. The dawn
will not be always rosy. Worm, Worm, it's between the three
of us now, and the devil take the hindmost. It seems to me
besides that I must have already made, contrary to what it
seems to me I must have already said, some efforts in this
direction. I should have noted them, if only in my head.
But Worm cannot note. There at least is a first affirmation,
I mean negation, on which to build. Worm cannot note. Can
Mahood note? That's it, weave, weave. Yes, it is the characteristic, among others, of Mahood to note, even if he does
not always succeed in doing so, certain things, perhaps I
should say all things, so as to turn them to account, for his
governance. And indeed we have seen him do so, in the yard,
in his jar, in a sense. I knew I had only to try and talk of
Worm to begin talking of Mahood, with more felicity and

understanding than ever. How close to me he suddenly seems,
squinting up at the medals of the hippophagist Ducroix. It
is the hour of the apéritif, already people pause, to read the
menu. Charming hour of the day, particularly when, as sometimes happens, it is also that of the setting sun whose last
rays, raking the street from end to end, lend to my cenotaph
an interminable shadow, astraddle of the gutter and the sidewalk. There was a time I used to contemplate it, when I was
freer to turn my head than now, since being put in the collar.
Then over there, far from me, I knew my head was lying,
and people treading on it, and on my flies, which went on
gliding none the less, prettily on the dark ground. And I saw
the people coming towards me, all along my shadow, followed
by long faithful trembling shadows. For sometimes I confuse
myself with my shadow, and sometimes don't. And sometimes
I don't confuse myself with my jar, and sometimes do. It all
depends what mood we're in. And often I went on looking
without flinching until, ceasing to be, I ceased to see. Delicious
instant truly, coinciding from time to time, as already observed, with that of the apéritif. But this joy, which for my
part I should have thought harmless, and without danger for
the public, is something I have to go without now that the
collar holds my face turned towards the railings, just above
the menu, for it is important that the prospective customer
should be able to compose his meal without the risk of being
run over. The meat, in this quarter, has a high reputation, and
people come from a distance, from great distances, on purpose
to relish it. Which having done they hurry away. By ten
o'clock in the evening all is silent, as the grave, as they say.
Such is the fruit of my observations accumulated over a long
period of years and constantly subjected to a process of induction. Here all is killing and eating. This evening there is
tripe. It's a winter dish, or a late autumn one. Soon Marguerite
will come and light me up. She is late. Already more than one
passer-by has flashed his lighter under my nose the better to
decipher what I shall now describe, by way of elegant variation, as the bill of fare. Please God nothing has happened to
my protectress. I shall not hear her coming, I shall not hear
her steps, because of the snow. I spent all morning under my
cover. When the first frosts come she makes me a nest of
rags, well tucked in all round me, to preserve me from chills.

It's snug. I wonder will she powder my skull this evening, with her great puff. It's her latest invention. She's always thinking of something new, to relieve me. If only the earth would quake! The shambles swallow me up! Through the railings, at the end of a vista between two blocks of buildings, the sky appears to me. A bar moves over and shuts it off, whenever I please. If I could raise my head I'd see it streaming into the main of the firmament. What is there to add, to these particulars? The evening is still young, I know that, don't let us go just yet, not yet say goodbye once more forever, to this heap of rubbish. What about trying to cogitate, while waiting for something intelligible to take place? Just this once. Almost immediately a thought presents itself, I should really concentrate more often. Quick let me record it before it vanishes. How is it the people do not notice me? I seem to exist for none but Madeleine. That a passer-by pressed for time, in headlong flight or hot pursuit, should have no eyes for me, that I can conceive. But the idlers come to hear the cattle's bellows of pain and who, time obviously heavy on their hands, pace up and down waiting for the slaughter to begin? The hungry compelled by the position of the menu, and whether they like it or not, to post themselves literally face to face with me, in the full blast of my breath? The children on their way to and from their playgrounds beyond the gates, all out for a bit of fun? It seems to me that even a human head, recently washed and with a few hairs on top, should be quite a popular curiosity in the position occupied by mine. Can it be out of discretion, and a reluctance to hurt, that they affect to be unaware of my existence? But this is a refinement of feeling which can hardly be attributed to the dogs that come pissing against my abode, apparently never doubting that it contains some flesh and bones. It follows therefore that I have no smell either. And yet if anyone should have a smell, it is I. How, under these conditions, can Mahood expect me to behave normally? The flies vouch for me, if you like, but how far? Would they not settle with equal appetite on a lump of cowshit? No, as long as this point is not cleared up to my satisfaction, or as long as I am not distinguished by some sense organs other than Madeleine's, it will be impossible for me to believe, sufficiently to pursue my act, the things that are told about me. I should further remark, with regard to this testimony which I consider indispensable, that I shall soon be in no fit condition to receive it, so greatly have my faculties declined, in recent times. It is obvious we have here a principle of change pregnant with possibilities. But say I succeed in dying, to adopt the most comforting hypothesis, without having been able to believe I ever lived, I know to my cost it is not that they wish for me. For it has happened to me many times already, without their having granted me as much as a brief sick-leave among the worms, before resurrecting me. But who knows, this time, what the future holds in store. That qua sentient and thinking being I should be going downhill fast is in any case an excellent thing. Perhaps some day some gentleman, chancing to pass my way with his sweetheart on his arm, at the precise moment when my last is favouring me with a final smack of the flight of time, will exclaim, loud enough for me to hear, Oh I say, this man is ailing, we must call an ambulance! Thus with a single stone, when all hope seemed lost, the two rare birds. I shall be dead, but I shall have lived. Unless one is to suppose him victim of a hallucination. Yes, to dispel all doubt his betrothed would need to say, You are right, my love, he looks as if he were going to throw up. Then I'd know for certain and giving up the ghost be born at last, to the sound perhaps of one of those hiccups which mar alas too often the solemnity of the passing. When Mahood I once knew a doctor who held that scientifically speaking the latest breath could only issue from the fundament and this therefore, rather than the mouth, the orifice to which the family should present the mirror, before opening the will. However this may be, and without dwelling further on these macabre details, it is certain I was grievously mistaken in supposing that death in itself could be regarded as evidence, or even a strong presumption, in support of a preliminary life. And I for my part have no longer the least desire to leave this world, in which they keep trying to foist me, without some kind of assurance that I was really there, such as a kick in the arse, for example, or a kiss, the nature of the attention is of little importance, provided I cannot be suspected of being its author. But let two third parties remark me, there, before my eyes, and I'll take care of the rest. How all becomes clear and simple when one opens

an eye on the within, having of course previously exposed it
to the without, in order to benefit by the contrast. I should
be sorry, though exhausted personally, to abandon prematurely
this rich vein. For I shall not come back to it in a hurry,
ah no. But enough of this cursed first person, it is really
too red a herring, I'll get out of my depth if I'm not careful.
But what then is the subject? Mahood? No, not yet. Worm?
Even less. Bah, any old pronoun will do, provided one sees
through it. Matter of habit. To be adjusted later. Where
was I? Ah yes, the bliss of what is clear and simple. The
next thing is somehow to connect this with the unhappy
Madeleine and her great goodness. Attentions such as hers,
the pertinacity with which she continues to acknowledge
me, do not these sufficiently attest my real presence here,
in the Rue Brancion, never heard of in my island home?
Would she rid me of my paltry excrements every Sunday,
make me a nest at the approach of winter, protect me from
the snow, change my sawdust, rub salt into my scalp, I hope
I'm not forgetting anything, if I were not there? Would she
have put me in a cang, raised me on a pedestal, hung me
with lanterns, if she were not convinced of my substantiality?
How happy I should be to submit to this evidence and to the
execution upon me of the sentence it entails. Unfortunately
I regard it as highly subject to caution, not to say unallowable.
For what is one to think of the redoubled attentions she
has been lavishing on me for some time past? How different
from the serenity of our early relations, when I saw her only
once a week. No, there is no getting away from it, this woman
is losing faith in me. And she is trying to put off the moment
when she must finally confess her error by coming every
few minutes to see if I am still more or less imaginable in
situ. Similarly the belief in God, in all modesty be it said,
is sometimes lost following a period of intensified zeal and
observance, it appears. Here I pause to make a distinction
(I must be still thinking). That the jar is really standing
where they say, all right, I wouldn't dream of denying it,
after all it's none of my business, though its presence at such
a place, about the reality of which I do not propose to
quibble either, does not strike me as very credible. No, I
merely doubt that I am in it. It is easier to raise a shrine
than bring the deity down to haunt it. But what's all this

confusion now? That's what comes of distinctions. No matter.
She loves me, I've always felt it. She needs me. Her chop-
house, her husband, her children if she has any, are not
enough, there is in her a void that I alone can fill. It is not
surprising then she should have visions. There was a time I
thought she was perhaps a near relation, mother, sister,
daughter, or suchlike, perhaps even a wife, and that she was
sequestrating me. That is to say Mahood, seeing how little
impressed I was by his chief witness, whispered this suggestion
in my ear, adding, I didn't say anything. I must admit it is
not so preposterous as it looks at first sight, it even accounts
for certain bizarreries which had not yet struck me at the
time of its formulation, among others my inexistence in the
eyes of those who are not in the know, that is to say
all mankind. But assuming I was being stowed away in a public place, why go to such trouble to draw attention to my head,
artistically illuminated from dusk to midnight? You may of
course retort that results are all that count. Another thing
however. This woman has never spoken to me, to the best
of my knowledge. If I have said anything to the contrary
I was mistaken. If I say anything to the contrary again I
shall be mistaken again. Unless I am mistaken now. Into
the dossier with it in any case, in support of whatever thesis
you fancy. Never an affectionate word, never a reprimand.
For fear of bringing me to the public notice? Or lest the illusion should be dispelled? I shall now sum up. The moment
is at hand when my only believer must deny me. Nothing
has happened. The lanterns have not been lit. Is it the same
evening? Perhaps dinner is over. Perhaps Marguerite has
come and gone, come again and gone again, without my
having noticed her. Perhaps I have blazed with all my usual
brilliance, for hours on end, all unsuspecting. And yet something has changed. It is not a night like other nights. Not
because I see no stars, it is not often I see a star, away up
in the depths of the sliver of sky I command. Not because
I don't see anything, not even the railings, that has often
happened. Not because of the silence either, it is a silent
place, at night. And I am half-deaf. It is not the first time
I have strained my ears in vain for the stables' muffled
sounds. All of a sudden a horse will neigh. Then I'll know
that nothing has changed. Or I'll see the lantern of the

watchman, swinging knee-high in the yard. I must be patient.
It is cold, this morning it snowed. And yet I don't feel the
cold on my head. Perhaps I am still under the tarpaulin,
perhaps she flung it over me again, for fear of more snow
in the night, while I was meditating. But the sensation I so
love, of the tarpaulin weighing on my head, is lacking too.
Has my head lost all feeling? Or did I have a stroke, while
I was meditating? I don't know. I shall be patient, asking
no more questions, on the qui vive. Hours have passed, it
must be day again, nothing has happened, I hear nothing.
I placed them before their responsibilities, perhaps they have
let me go. For this feeling of being entirely enclosed, and yet
nothing touching me, is new. The sawdust no longer presses
against my stumps, I don't know where I end. I left it yesterday, Mahood's world, the street, the chop-house, the
slaughter, the statue and, through the railings, the sky like a
slate-pencil. I shall never hear again the lowing of the cattle,
nor the clinking of the forks and glasses, nor the angry voices
of the butchers, nor the litany of the dishes and the prices.
There will never be another woman wanting me in vain to
live, my shadow at evening will not darken the ground. The
stories of Mahood are ended. He has realized they could
not be about me, he has abandoned, it is I who win, who
tried so hard to lose, in order to please him, and be left in
peace. Having won, shall I be left in peace? It doesn't look
like it, I seem to be going on talking. In any case all these
suppositions are probably erroneous. I shall no doubt be
launched again, girt with better arms, against the fortress
of mortality. What is more important is that I should know
what is going on now, in order to announce it, as my function requires. It must not be forgotten, sometimes I forget,
that all is a question of voices. I say what I am told to say,
in the hope that some day they will weary of talking at me.
The trouble is I say it wrong, having no ear, no head, no
memory. Now I seem to hear them say it is Worm's voice
beginning, I pass on the news, for what it is worth. Do they
believe I believe it is I who am speaking? That's theirs too.
To make me believe I have an ego all my own, and can
speak of it, as they of theirs. Another trap to snap me up
among the living. It's how to fall into it they can't have explained to me sufficiently. They'll never get the better of my

stupidity. Why do they speak to me thus? Is it possible certain
things change on their passage through me, in a way they
can't prevent? Do they believe I believe it is I who am asking
these questions? That's theirs too, a little distorted perhaps.
I don't say it's not the right method. I don't say they won't
catch me in the end. I wish they would, to be thrown away.
It's this hunt that is tiring, this unending being at bay. Images,
they imagine that by piling on the images they'll entice me
in the end. Like the mother who whistles to prevent baby's
bladder from bursting, there's another. They, yes, now they're
all in the same galley. Worm to play, his lead, I wish him a
happy time. To think I thought he was against what they
were trying to do with me! To think I saw in him, if not me,
a step towards me! To get me to be he, the anti-Mahood,
and then to say, But what am I doing but living, in a kind
of way, the only possible way, that's the combination. Or
by the absurd prove to me that I am, the absurd of not being
able. Unfortunately it is no help my being forewarned, I
never remain so for long. In any case I wish him every success, in his courageous undertaking. And I am even prepared
to collaborate with him, as with Mahood and Co, to the best
of my ability, being unable to do otherwise, and knowing
my ability. Worm, to say he does not know what he is, where
he is, what is happening, is to underestimate him. What he
does not know is that there is anything to know. His senses
tell him nothing, nothing about himself, nothing about the
rest, and this distinction is beyond him. Feeling nothing,
knowing nothing, he exists nevertheless, but not for himself,
for others, others conceive him and say, Worm is, since we
conceive him, as if there could be no being but being conceived, if only by the beer. Others. One alone, then others.
One alone turned towards the all-impotent, all-nescient, that
haunts him, then others. Towards him whom he would nour-
ish, he the famished one, and who, having nothing human,
has nothing else, has nothing, is nothing. Come into the
world unborn, abiding there unliving, with no hope of death,
epicentre of joys, of griefs, of calm. Who seems the truest
possession, because the most unchanging. The one outside of
life we always were in the end, all our long vain life long.
Who is not spared by the mad need to speak, to think, to
know where one is, where one was, during the wild dream,

up above, under the skies, venturing forth at night. The one
ignorant of himself and silent, ignorant of his silence and
silent, who could not be and gave up trying. Who crouches
in their midst who see themselves in him and in their eyes
stares his unchanging stare. Thanks for these first notions.
And it's not all. He who seeks his true countenance, let him
be of good cheer, he'll find it, convulsed with anguish, the
eyes out on stalks. He who longs to have lived, while he was
alive, let him be reassured, life will tell him how. That's all
very comforting. Worm, be Worm, you'll see, it's impossible,
what a velvet glove, a little worn at the knuckles with all
the hard hitting. Bah, let's turn the black eye. And the starch-
ing begin at last, of this old clout so patiently pawed in vain,
as limp and drooping still as the first day. But it is solely a
question of voices, no other image is appropriate. Let it go
through me at last, the right one, the last one, his who has
none, by his own confession. Do they think they'll lull me,
with all this hemming and hawing? What can it matter to
me, that I succeed or fail? The undertaking is none of mine,
if they want me to succeed I'll fail, and vice versa, so as not
to be rid of my tormentors. Is there a single word of mine
in all I say? No, I have no voice, in this matter I have none.
That's one of the reasons why I confused myself with Worm.
But I have no reasons either, no reason, I'm like Worm,
without voice or reason, I'm Worm, no, if I were Worm I
wouldn't know it, I wouldn't say it, I wouldn't say anything,
I'd be Worm. But I don't say anything, I don't know anything, these voices are not mine, nor these thoughts, but the
voices and thoughts of the devils who beset me. Who make
me say that I can't be Worm, the inexpugnable. Who make
me say that I am he perhaps, as they are. Who make me
say that since I can't be he I must be he. That since I couldn't
be Mahood, as I might have been, I must be Worm, as I
cannot be. But is it still they who say that when I have failed
to be Worm I'll be Mahood, automatically, on the rebound?
As if, and a little silence, as if I were big enough now to
take a hint and understand, certain things, but they're wrong,
I need explanations, of everything, and even then, I don't
understand, that's how I'll sicken them in the end, by my
stupidity, so they say, to lull me, to make me think I'm
stupider than I am. And is it still they who say that when I

surprise them all and am Worm at last, then at last I'll be
Mahood, Worm proving to be Mahood the moment one is
he? Ah if they could only begin, and do what they want
with me, and succeed at last, in doing what they want with
me, I'm ready to be whatever they want, I'm tired of being
matter, matter, pawed and pummelled endlessly in vain. Or
give me up and leave me lying in a heap, in such a heap
that none would ever be found again to try and fashion it.
But they are not of the same mind, they are all of the same
kidney and yet they don't know what they want to do with
me, they don't know where I am, or what I'm like, I'm like
dust, they want to make a man out of dust. Listen to them,
losing heart! That's to lull me, till I imagine I hear myself
saying, myself at last, to myself at last, that it can't be they,
speaking thus, that it can only be I, speaking thus. Ah if
I could only find a voice of my own, in all this babble, it
would be the end of their troubles, and of mine. That's why
there are all these little silences, to try and make me break
them. They think can't bear silence, that some day, somehow,
my horror of silence will force me to break it. That's why they
are always leaving off, to try and drive me to extremities.
But they dare not be silent for long, the whole fabrication
might collapse. It's true I dread these gulfs they all bend over,
straining their ears for the murmur of a man. It isn't silence,
it's pitfalls, into which nothing would please me better than
to fall, with the little cry that might be taken for human,
like a wounded wistiti, the first and last, and vanish for
good and all, having squeaked. Well, if they ever succeed in
getting me to give a voice to Worm, in a moment of euphory,
perhaps I'll succeed in making it mine, in a moment of confusion. There we have the stake. But they won't. Did they
ever get Mahood to speak? It seems to me not. I think Murphy spoke now and then, the others too perhaps, I don't
remember, but it was clumsily done, you could see the
ventriloquist. And now I feel it's about to begin. They must
consider me sufficiently stupefied with all their balls about
being and existing. Yes, now that I've forgotten who Worm
is, where he is, what he's like, I'll begin to be he. Anything
rather than these college quips. Quick, a place. With no way
in, no way out, a safe place. Not like Eden. And Worm
inside. Feeling nothing, knowing nothing, capable of nothing,

wanting nothing. Until the instant he hears the sound that will never stop. Then it's the end, Worm no longer is. We know it, but we don't say it, we say it's the awakening, the beginning of Worm, for now we must speak, and speak of Worm. It's no longer he, but let us proceed as if it were still he, he at last, who hears, and trembles, and is delivered over, to affliction and the struggle to withstand it, the starting eye, the labouring mind. Yes, let us call that thing Worm, so as to exclaim, the sleight of hand accomplished, Oh look, life again, life everywhere and always, the life that's on every tongue, the only possible! Poor Worm, who thought he was different, there he is in the madhouse for life. Where am I? That's my first question, after an age of listening. From it, when it hasn't been answered, I'll rebound towards others, of a more personal nature, much later. Perhaps I'll even end up, before regaining my coma, by thinking of myself as living, technically speaking. But let us proceed with method. I shall do my best, as always, since I cannot do otherwise. I shall submit, more corpse-obliging than ever. I shall transmit the words as received, by the ear, or roared through a trumpet into the arsehole, in all their purity, and in the same order, as far as possible. This infinitesimal lag, between arrival and departure, this trifling delay in evacuation, is all I have to worry about. The truth about me will boil forth at last, scalding, provided of course they don't start stuttering again. I listen. Enough procrastination. I'm Worm, that is to say I am no longer he, since I hear. But I'll forget that in the heat of misery, I'll forget I am no longer Worm, but a kind of tenth-rate Toussaint L'Ouverture, that's what they're counting on. Worm then I catch this sound that will never stop, monotonous beyond words and yet not altogether devoid of a certain variety. At the end of I know not what eternity, they don't say, this has sufficiently exasperated my intelligence for it to grasp that the nuisance is a voice and that the realm of nature, in which I flatter myself I have a foot already, has other noises to offer which are even more unpleasant and may be relied on to make themselves heard before long. Don't tell me after that I had no predispositions for a man's estate. What a weary way since that first disaster, what nerves torn from the heart of insentience, with the appertaining terror and the cerebellum on fire. It took him a long time to adapt himself to this excoriation. To realize pooh it's nothing. A mere bagatelle. The common lot. A harmless joke. That will not last for ever. For me to gather while I may. They mentioned roses. I'll smell them before I'm finished. Then they'll put the accent on the thorns. What prodigious variety! The thorns they'll have to come and stick into me, as into their unfortunate Jesus. No, I need nobody, they'll start sprouting under my arse, unaided, some day I feel myself soaring above my condition. A billybowl of thorns and the air perfume-laden. But not so fast. I still leave much to be desired, I have no technique, none. For example, in case you don't believe me, I don't yet know how to move, either locally, in relation to myself, or bodily, in relation to the rest of the shit. I don't know how to want to, I want to in vain. What doesn't come to me from me has come to the wrong address. Similarly my understanding is not yet sufficiently well-oiled to function without the pressure of some critical circumstance, such as a violent pain felt for the first time. Some nice point in semantics, for example, of a nature to accelerate the march of the hours, could not retain my attention. For others the time-abolishing joys of impersonal and disinterested speculation. I only think, if that is the name for this vertiginous panic as of hornets smoked out of their nest, once a certain degree of terror has been exceeded. Does this mean I am less exposed to doing so, by the grace of inurement? To argue so would be to underestimate the extent of the repertory in which I am plunged and which, it appears, is nothing compared to what is in store for me at the conclusion of the novitiate. These lights gleaming low afar, then rearing up in a blaze and sweeping down upon me, blinding, to devour me, are merely one example. My familiarity with them avails me nothing, they invariably give me to reflect. Each time, at the last moment, just as I begin to scorch, they go out, smoking and hissing, and yet each time my phlegm is shattered. And in my head, which I am beginning to locate to my satisfaction, above and a little to the right, the sparks spirt and dash themselves out against the walls. And sometimes I say to myself I am in a head, it's terror makes me say it, and the longing to be in safety, surrounded on all sides by massive bone. And I add that I am foolish to let myself be frightened by another's thoughts, lacerating my sky with harmless fires and assail-

ing me with noises signifying nothing. But one thing at a time.
And often all sleeps, as when I was really Worm, except this
voice which has denatured me, which never stops, but often
grows confused and falters, as if it were going to abandon me.
But it is merely a passing weakness, unless it is done on
purpose, to teach me hope. Strange thing, ruined as I am and
still young in this abjection they have brought me to, I sometimes seem to remember what I was like when I was Worm,
and not yet delivered into their hands. That's to tempt me
into saying, I am indeed Worm after all, and into thinking that
after all he may have become the thing that I have become.
But it doesn't work. But they will devise another means, less
childish, of getting me to admit, or pretend to admit, that I
am he whose name they call me by, and no other. Or they'll
wait, counting on my weariness, as they press me ever harder,
to wipe him from my memory who cannot be brought to the
pass they have brought me to, not to mention yesterday, not
to mention tomorrow. And yet it seems to me I remember,
and shall never forget, what I was like when I was he, before
all became confused. But that is of course impossible, since
Worm could not know what he was like, or who he was, that's
how they want me to reason. And it seems to me too, which
is even more deplorable, that I could become Worm again,
if I were left in peace. This transmission is really excellent.
I wonder if it's going to get us somewhere. If only they would
stop talking for nothing, pending their stopping everything.
Nothing? That's soon said. It is not for me to judge. What
would I judge with? It's more provocation. They want me to
lose patience and rush, suddenly beside myself, to their rescue.
How transparent that all is! Sometimes I say to myself, they
say to me, Worm says to me, the subject matters little, that
my purveyors are more than one, four or five. But it's more
likely the same foul brute all the time, amusing himself
pretending to be a many, varying his register, his tone, his accent and his drivel. Unless it comes natural to him. A bare and
rusty hook I might accept. But all these titbits! But there are
long silences too, at long intervals, during which, hearing nothing, I say nothing. That is to say I hear murmuring, if I listen
hard enough, but it's not for me, it's for them alone, they are
putting their heads together again. I don't hear what they
say, all I know is they are still there, they haven't done, with

me. They have moved a little aside. Secrets. Or if there is only
one it is he alone, taking counsel with himself, muttering
and chewing his moustache, getting ready for a fresh flow of
inanity. To think of me eavesdropping, me, when silence falls!
Ah a nice state they have me in. But it's with the hope there is
no one left. But this is not the time to speak of that. Good.
Of what is it the time to speak? Of Worm, at last. Good. We
must first, to begin with, go back to his beginnings and then,
to go on with, follow him patiently through the various stages,
taking care to show their fatal concatenation, which have
made him what I am. The whole to be tossed off with bra-
vura. Then notes from day to day, until I collapse. And
finally, to wind up with, song and dance of thanksgiving by
victim, to celebrate his nativity. Please God nothing goes
wrong. Mahood I couldn't die. Worm will I ever get born?
It's the same problem. But perhaps not the same personage
after all. The scytheman will tell, it's all one to him. But let
us go back as planned, afterwards we'll fall forward as
projected. The reverse would be more like it. But not by
much. Upstream, downstream, what matter, I begin by the
ear, that's the way to talk. Before that it was the night of
time. Whereas ever since, what radiance! Now at least I know
where I am, as far as my origins go, I mean my origins considered as a subject of conversation, that's what counts. The
moment one can say, Someone is on his way, all is well.
Perhaps I have still a thousand years to go. No matter. He's
on his way. I begin to be familiar with the premises. I wonder
if I couldn't sneak out by the fundament, one morning, with
the French breakfast. No, I can't move, not yet. One minute
in a skull and the next in a belly, strange, and the next nowhere in particular. Perhaps it's Botal's Foramen, when all
about me palpitates and labours. Bait, bait. Can it be I have
a friend among them, shaking his head in sorrow and saying
nothing or only, from time to time, Enough, enough. One
can be before beginning, they have set their hearts on that.
They want me roots and all. This onward-rushing time is the
same which used to sleep. And this silence they yelp against
in vain and which one day will be restored, the same as in
the past. Perhaps a little the worse for wear. Agreed, agreed, I
who am on my way, words bellying out my sails, am also that
unthinkable ancestor of whom nothing can be said. But

perhaps I shall speak of him some day, and of the impenetrable age when I was he, some day when they fall silent,
convinced at last I shall never get born, having failed to be
conceived. Yes, perhaps I shall speak of him, for an instant,
like the echo that mocks, before being restored to him, the
one they could not part me from. And indeed they are weakening already, it's perceptible. But it's a feint, to have me rejoice without cause, after their fashion, and accept terms, for
the sake of peace at any price. But I can do nothing, that is
what they seem to forget at each instant. I can't rejoice and I
can't grieve, it's in vain they explained to me how it's done, I
never understood. And what terms? I don't know what it is
they want. I say what it is, but I don't know. I emit sounds,
better and better it seems to me. If that's not enough for
them I can't help it. If I speak of a head, referring to me,
it's because I hear it being spoken of. But why keep on saying the same thing? They hope things will change one day, it's
natural. That one day on my windpipe, or some other section
of the conduit, a nice little abscess will form, with an idea
inside, point of departure for a general infection. This would
enable me to jubilate like a normal person, knowing why.
And in no time I'd be a network of fistulae, bubbling with
the blessed pus of reason. Ah if I were flesh and blood, as
they are kind enough to posit, I wouldn't say no, there might
be something in their little idea. They say I suffer like true
thinking flesh, but I'm sorry, I feel nothing. Mahood I felt
a little, now and then, but what good did that do them? No,
they'd be better advised to try something else. I felt the cang,
the flies, the sawdust under my stumps, the tarpaulin on my
skull, when they were mentioned to me. But can that be called
a life which vanishes when the subject is changed? I don't
see why not. But they must have decreed it can't. They are
too hard to please, they ask too much. They want me to have
a pain in the neck, irrefragable proof of animation, while
listening to talk of the heavens. They want me to have a mind
where it is known once and for all that I have a pain in the
neck, that flies are devouring me and that the heavens can
do nothing to help. Let them scourge me without ceasing and
evermore, more and more lustily (in view of the habituation
factor), in the end I might begin to look as if I had grasped
the meaning of life. They might even take a breather from

time to time, without my ceasing to howl. For they would
have warned me, before they started, You must howl, do you
hear, otherwise it proves nothing. And worn out at last, or
feeble with old age, and my cries having ceased for want of
nourishment, they could pronounce me dead with every
appearance of veracity. And without ever having had to move
I would have gained my rest and heard them say, striking
softly together their dry old hands as if to shake off the dust,
He'll never move again. No, that would be too simple. We
must have the heavens and God knows what besides, lights,
luminaries, the three-monthly ray of hope and the gleam of
consolation. But let us close this parenthesis and, with a
light heart, open the next. The noise. How long did I remain
a pure ear? Up to the moment when it could go on no
longer, being too good to last, compared to what was coming.
These millions of different sounds, always the same, recurring
without pause, are all one requires to sprout a head, a bud
to begin with, finally huge, its function first to silence, then
to extinguish when the eye joins in, and worse than the evil,
its treasure-house. But no lingering on this thin ice. The
mechanism matters little, provided I succeed in saying, before
I go deaf, It's a voice, and it speaks to me. In inquiring,
boldly, if it is not mine. In deciding, it doesn't matter how,
that I have none. In blowing darkly hot and cold, with con-
comitant identical sensations. It's a starting-point, he's off,
they don't see me, but they hear me, panting, riveted, they
don't know I'm riveted. He knows they are words, he is not
sure they are not his, that's how it begins, with such a start
no one ever looked back, one day he'll make them his, when
he thinks he is alone, far from all men, out of range of every
voice, and come to the light of day they keep telling him of.
Yes, I know they are words, there was a time I didn't, as I
still don't know if they are mine. Their hopes are therefore
founded. In their shoes I'd be content with my knowing what
I know, I'd demand no more of me than to know that what
I hear is not the innocent and necessary sound of dumb things
constrained to endure, but the terror-stricken babble of the
condemned to silence. I would have pity, give me quittance,
not harry me into appearing my own destroyer. But they are
severe, greedy, no less, perhaps more, than when I was playing
Mahood. Instead of drawing in their horns! It's true I have

not spoken yet. In at one ear and incontinent out through the
mouth, or the other ear, that's possible too. No sense in multiplying the occasions of error. Two holes and me in the middle, slightly choked. Or a single one, entrance and exit, where
the words swarm and jostle like ants, hasty, indifferent,
bringing nothing, taking nothing away, too light to leave a
mark. I shall not say I again, ever again, it's too farcical. I
shall put in its place, whenever I hear it, the third person, if
I think of it. Anything to please them. It will make no difference. Where I am there is no one but me, who am not. So
much for that. Words, he says he knows they are words. But
how can he know, who has never heard anything else? True.
Not to mention other things, many others, to which the
abundance of matter has unfortunately up to now prohibited
the least allusion. For example, to begin with, his breathing.
There he is now with breath in his nostrils, it only remains
for him to suffocate. The thorax rises and falls, the wear and
tear are in full spring, the rot spreads downwards, soon he'll
have legs, the possibility of crawling. More lies, he doesn't
breathe yet, he'll never breathe. Then what is this faint noise,
as of air stealthily stirred, recalling the breath of life, to those
whom it corrodes? It's a bad example. But these lights that
go out hissing? Is it not more likely a great crackle of laughter,
at the sight of his terror and distress? To see him flooded with
light, then suddenly plunged back in darkness, must strike
them as irresistibly funny. But they have been there so long
now, on every side, they may have made a hole in the wall,
a little hole, to glue their eyes to, turn about. And these
lights are perhaps those they shine upon him, from time to
time, in order to observe the progress he is making. But this
question of lights deserves to be treated in a section apart,
it is so intriguing, and at length, composedly, and so it will
be, at the first opportunity, when time is not so short, and the
mind more composed. Resolution number twenty-three. And
in the meantime the conclusion to be drawn? That the only
noises Worm has had till now are those of mouths? Correct.
Not forgetting the groaning of the air beneath the burden.
He's coming, that's the main thing. When on earth later on
the storms rage, drowning momentarily the free expression
of opinion, he'll know what is afoot, that the end of the world
is not at hand. No, in the place where he is he cannot learn,

the head cannot work, he knows no more than on the first day, he merely hears, and suffers, uncomprehending, that must be possible. A head has grown out of his ear, the better to enrage him, that must be it. The head is there, glued to the ear, and in it nothing but rage, that's all that matters, for the time being. It's a transformer in which sound is turned, without the help of reason, to rage and terror, that's all that is required, for the moment. The circumvolutionisation will be seen too later, when they get him out. Why then the human voice, rather than a hyena's howls or the clanging of a hammer? Answer, so that the shock may not be too great, when the writhings of true lips meet his gaze. Between them they find a rejoinder to everything. And how they enjoy talking, they know there is no worse torment, for one not in the conversation. They are numerous, all round, holding hands perhaps, an endless chain, taking turns to talk. They wheel, in jerks, so that the voice always comes from the same quarter. But often they all speak at once, they all say simultaneously the same thing exactly, but so perfectly together that one would take it for a single voice, a single mouth, if one did not know that God alone can fill the rose of the winds, without moving from his place. One, but not Worm, who says nothing, knows nothing, yet. Similarly turn about they benefit by the peephole, those who care to. While one speaks another peeps, the one no doubt whose voice is next due and whose remarks may possibly have reference to what he may possibly have seen, this depending on whether what he has seen has aroused his interest to the extent of appearing worthy of remark, even indirectly. But what hope has sustained them, all the time they have been thus employed? For it is difficult not to suppose them sustained by some form of hope. And what is the nature of the change they are on the look out for, gluing one eye to the hole and closing the other. They have no pedagogic purpose in view, that's definite. There is no question of imparting to him any instruction whatsoever, for the moment. This catechist's tongue, honeyed and perfidious, is the only one they know. Let him move, try and move, that's all they ask, for the moment. No matter where he goes, being at the centre, he will go towards them. So he is at the centre, there is a clue of the highest interest, it matters little to what. They look, to see if he has stirred. He is nothing but a shapeless heap, without a face capable of reflecting the niceties of a torment, but the disposition of which, its greater or lesser degree of crouch and huddleness, is no doubt expressive, for specialists, and enables them to assess the chances of its suddenly making a bound, or dragging its coils faintly away, as if stricken to death. Somewhere in the heap an eye, a wild equine eye, always open, they must have an eye, they see him possessed of an eye. No matter where he goes he will go towards them, towards their song of triumph, when they know he has moved, or towards their sudden silence, when they know he has moved, to make him think he did well to move, or towards the voice growing softer, as if receding, to make him think he is drawing away from them, but not yet far enough, whereas he is drawing nearer, nearer and nearer. No, he can't think anything, can't judge of anything, but the kind of flesh he has is good enough, will try and go where peace seems to be, drop and lie when it suffers no more, or less, or can go no further. Then the voice will begin again, low at first, then louder, coming from the quarter they want him to retreat from, to make him think he is pursued and struggle on, towards them. In this way they'll bring him to the wall, and even to the precise point where they have made other holes through which to pass their arms and seize him. How physical this all is! And then, unable to go any further, because of the obstacle, and unable to go any further in any case, and not needing to go any further for the moment, because of the great silence which has fallen, he will drop, assuming he had risen, but even a reptile can drop, after a long flight, the expression may be used without impropriety. He will drop, it will be his first corner, his first experience of the vertical support, the vertical shelter, reinforcing those of the ground. That must be something, while waiting for oblivion, to feel a prop and buckler, not only for one of one's six planes, but for two, for the first time. But Worm will never know this joy but darkly, being less than a beast, before he is restored, more or less, to that state in which he was before the beginning of his prehistory. Then they will lay hold of him and gather him into their midst. For if they could make a small hole for the eye, then bigger ones for the arms, they can make one bigger still for the transit of Worm, from darkness to light. But what is the

good of talking about what they will do as soon as Worm
sets himself in motion, so as to gather him without fail into
their midst, since he cannot set himself in motion, though he
often desires to, if when speaking of him one may speak of
desire, and one may not, one should not, but there it is, that
is the way to speak of him, that is the way to speak to him,
as if he were alive, as if he could understand, as if he could
desire, even if it serves no purpose, and it serves none. And
it is a blessing for him he cannot stir, even though he suffers
because of it, for it would be to sign his life-warrant, to stir
from where he is, in search of a little calm and something of
the silence of old. But perhaps one day he will stir, the day
when the little effort of the early stages, infinitely weak, will
have become, by dint of repetition, a great effort, strong
enough to tear him from where he lies. Or perhaps one day
they will leave him in peace, letting go their hands, filling
up the holes and departing, towards more profitable occupations, in Indian file. For a decision must be reached, the scales
must tilt, to one side or the other. No, one can spend one's
life thus, unable to live, unable to bring to life, and die in
vain, having done nothing, been nothing. It is strange they
do not go and fetch him in his den, since they seem to have
access to it. They dare not, the air in the midst of which he
lies is not for them, and yet they want him to breathe theirs.
They could set a dog on him perhaps, with instructions to
drag him out. But no dog would survive there either, not for
one second. With a long pole perhaps, with a hook at the end.
But the place where he lies is vast, that's interesting, he is far,
too far for them to reach him even with the longest pole.
That tiny blur, in the depths of the pit, is he. There he is
now in a pit, no avenue will have been left unexplored. They
say they see him, the blur is what they see, they say the blur
is he, perhaps it is. They say he hears them, they don't know,
perhaps he does, yes, he hears, nothing else is certain. Worm
hears, though hear is not the word, but it will do, it will have
to do. They look down upon him then, according to the latest
news, he'll have to climb to reach them. Bah, the latest news,
the latest news is not the last. The slopes are gentle that meet
where he lies, they flatten out under him, it is not a meeting,
it is not a pit, that didn't take long, soon we'll have him
perched on an eminence. They don't know what to say, to be

able to believe in him, what to invent, to be reassured, they
see nothing, they see grey, like still smoke, unbroken, where
he might be, if he must be somewhere, where they have
decreed he is, into which they launch their voices, one after
another, in the hope of dislodging him, hearing him stir, seeing
him loom within reach of their gaffs, hooks, barbs, grapnels,
saved at last, home at last. And now that's enough about them,
their usefulness is over, no, not yet, let them stay, they may
still serve, stay where they are, turning in a ring, launching
their voices, through the hole, there must be a hole for the
voices too. But is it them he hears? Are they really necessary
that he may hear, they and kindred puppets? Enough con-
cessions, to the spirit of geometry. He hears, that's all about
it, he who is alone, and mute, lost in the smoke, it is not real
smoke, there is no fire, no matter, strange hell that has no
heating, no denizens, perhaps it's paradise, perhaps it's the
light of paradise, and the solitude, and this voice the voice of
the blest interceding invisible, for the living, for the dead, all
is possible. It isn't the earth, that's all that counts, it can't be
the earth, it can't be a hole in the earth, inhabited by Worm
alone, or by others if you like, huddled in a heap like him,
mute, immovable, and this voice the voice of those who mourn
them, envy them, call on them and forget them, that would
account for its incoherence, all is possible. Yes, so much the
worse, he knows it is a voice, how is not known, nothing is
known, he understands nothing it says, just a little, almost
nothing, it's inexplicable, but it's necessary, it's preferable,
that he should understand just a little, almost nothing, like a
dog that always gets the same filth flung to it, the same orders,
the same threats, the same cajoleries. That settles that, the
end is in sight. But the eye, let's leave him his eye too, it's to
see with, this great wild black and white eye, moist, it's to
weep with, it's to practise with, before he goes to Kil-
larney. What does he do with it, he does nothing with it, the
eye stays open, it's an eye without lids, no need for lids here,
where nothing happens, or so little, if he could blink he might
miss the odd sight, if he could close it, the kind he is, he'd
never open it again. Tears gush from it practically without
ceasing, why is not known, nothing is known, whether it's with
rage, or whether it's with grief, the fact is there, perhaps it's
the voice that makes it weep, with rage, or some other passion,

or at having to see, from time to time, some sight or other,
perhaps that's it, perhaps he weeps in order not to see, though
it seems difficult to credit him with an initiative of this complexity. The rascal, he's getting humanized, he's going to lose
if he doesn't watch out, if he doesn't take care, and with what
could he take care, with what could he form the faintest
conception of the condition they are decoying him into, with
their ears, their eyes, their tears and a brainpan where anything may happen. That's his strength, his only strength, that
he understands nothing, can't take thought, doesn't know what
they want, doesn't know they are there, feels nothing, ah but
just a moment, he feels, he suffers, the noise makes him suffer,
and he knows, he knows it's a voice, and he understands, a
few expressions here and there, a few intonations, ah it looks
bad, bad, no, perhaps not, for it's they describe him thus,
without knowing, thus because they need him thus, perhaps
he hears nothing, suffers nothing, and this eye, more mere
imagination. He hears, true, though it's they again who say
it, but this can't be denied, this is better not denied. Worm
hears, that's all can be said for certain, whereas there was a
time he didn't, the same Worm, according to them, he has
therefore changed, that's grave, gravid, who knows to what
lengths he may be carried, no, he can be relied on. The eye
too, of course, is there to put him to flight, make him take
fright, badly enough to break his bonds, they call that bonds,
they want to deliver him, ah mother of God, the things one
has to listen to, perhaps it's tears of mirth. Well, no matter,
let's drive on now to the end of the joke, we must be nearly
there, and see what they have to offer him, in the way of buga-
boos. Who, we? Don't all speak at once, there's no sense in
that either. All will come right, later on in the evening, everyone gone and silence restored. In the meantime no sense in
bickering about pronouns and other parts of blather. The
subject doesn't matter, there is none. Worm being in the
singular, as it turned out, they are in the plural, to avoid
confusion, confusion is better avoided, pending the great
confounding. Perhaps there is only one of them, one would
do the trick just as well, but he might get mixed up with his
victim, that would be abominable, downright masturbation.
We're getting on. Nothing much then in the way of sights
for sore eyes. But who can be sure who has not been there,

has not lived there, they call that living, for them the spark is
present, ready to burst into flame, all it needs is preaching
on, to become a living torch, screams included. Then they may
go silent, without having to fear an embarrassing silence, when
steps are heard on graves as the saying is, genuine hell, Decidedly this eye is hard of hearing. Noises travel, traverse walls,
but may the same be said of appearances? By no means,
generally speaking. But the present case is rather special. But
what appearances, it is always well to try and find out what
one is talking about, even at the risk of being deceived. This
grey to begin with, meant to be depressing no doubt. And
yet there is yellow in it, pink too apparently, it's a nice grey,
of the kind recommended as going with everything, urinous
and warm. In it the eye can see, otherwise why the eye, but
dimly, that's right, no superfluous particulars, later to be
controverted. A man would wonder where his kingdom ended,
his eye strive to penetrate the gloom, and he crave for a stick,
an arm, fingers apt to grasp and then release, at the right moment, a stone, stones, or for the power to utter a cry and wait,
counting the seconds, for it to come back to him, and suffer,
certainly, at having neither voice nor other missile, nor limbs
submissive to him, bending and unbending at the word of
command, and perhaps even regret being a man, under such
conditions, that is to say a head abandoned to its ancient
solitary resources. But Worm suffers only from the noise
which prevents him from being what he was before, admire
the nuance. If it's the same Worm, and they have set their
hearts on it. And if it is not it makes no difference, he suffers
as he has always suffered, from this noise that prevents nothing, that must be feasible. In any case this grey can hardly
be said to add to his misery, brightness would be better suited
for that purpose, since he cannot close his eye. He cannot
avert it either, nor lower it, nor lift it up, it remains trained
on the same tiny field, a stranger forever to the boons and
blessings of accommodation. But perhaps one day brightness
will come, little by little, or rapidly, or in a sudden flood, and
then it is hard to see how Worm could stay, and it is also
hard to see how he could go. But impossible situations cannot
be prolonged, unduly, the fact is well known, either they
disperse, or else they turn out to be possible after all, it's only
to be expected, not to mention other possibilities. Let there

then be light, it will not necessarily be disastrous. Or let there
be none, we'll manage without it. But these lights, in the
plural, which rear aloft, swell, sweep down and go out hissing,
reminding one of the naja, perhaps the moment has come
to throw them into the balance and have done with this tedious
equipoise, at last. No, the moment has not yet come, to do
that. Ha. None of your hoping here, that would spoil everything. Let others hope for him, outside, in the cool, in the
light, if they have a wish to, or if they are obliged to, or if
they are paid to, yes, they must be paid to hope, they hope
nothing, they hope things will continue as they are, it's a soft
job, their thoughts wander as they call on Jude, it's praying
they are, praying for Worm, praying to Worm, to have pity,
pity on them, pity on Worm, they call that pity, merciful God,
the things one has to put up with, fortunately it all means
nothing to him. Currish obscurity, to thy kennel, hell-hound!
Grey. What else? Calm, calm, there must be something else,
to go with this grey, which goes with everything. There must
be something of everything here, as in every world, a little of
everything. Mighty little, it seems. Beside the point in any
case. What balls is going on before the impotent crystalline,
that's all that needs to be imagined. A face, how encouraging that would be, if it could be a face, every now and then,
always the same, methodically varying its expressions, doggedly demonstrating all a true face can do, without ever ceasing to be recognizable as such, passing from unmixed joy to
the sullen fixity of marble, via the most characteristic shades
of disenchantment, how pleasant that would be. Worth ten of
Saint Anthony's pig's arse. Passing by at the right distance,
the right level, say once a month, that's not exorbitant, full
face and profile, like criminals. It might even pause, open its
mouth, raise its eyebrows, bless its soul, stutter, mutter, howl,
groan and finally shut up, the chaps clenched to cracking
point, or fallen, to let the dribble out. That would be nice. A
presence at last. A visitor, faithful, with his visiting-day, his
visiting-hour, never staying too long, it would be wearisome,
or too little, it would not be enough, but just the necessary
time for the hope to be born, grow, languish and die, say five
minutes. And even should the notion of time dawn on his
darkness, at this punctual image of the countenance everlasting, who could blame him? Involving very naturally that

of space, they have taken to going hand in hand, in certain
quarters, it's safer. And the game would be won, lost and won,
he'd be somehow suddenly among us, among the rendezvous,
and people saying, Look at old Worm, waiting for his sweetheart, and the flowers, look at the flowers, you'd think he was
asleep, you know old Worm, waiting for his love, and the
daisies, look at the daisies, you'd think he was dead. That
would be worth seeing. Fortunately it's all a dream. For here
there is no face, nor anything resembling one, nothing to
reflect the joy of living and succedanea, nothing for it but to
try something else. Some simple thing, a box, a piece of wood,
to come to rest before him for an instant, once a year, once
every two years, a ball, revolving one knows not how about
one knows not what, about him, every two years, every three
years, frequency unimportant in the early stages, without
stopping, it needn't stop, that would be better than nothing,
he'd hear it approaching, hear it receding, it would be an
event, he might learn to count, the minutes, the hours, to fret,
be brave, have patience, lose patience, turn his head, roll his
eye, a big stone, and faithful, that would be better than nothing, pending the hearts of flesh. And even should his start off,
his heart that is, on its waltz, in his ear, tralatralay
pom pom, again, tralatralay pom pom, re mi re do
bang bang bang, who could reprehend him? Unfortunately
we must stick to the facts, for what else is there, to stick
to, to cling to, when all founders, but the facts, when there
are any, still floating, within reach of the heart, happy
expression that, of the heart crying out, The facts are there,
the facts are there, and then more calmly, when the danger
is past, the continuation, namely, in the case before us, Here
there is no wood, nor any stone, or if there is, the facts are
there, it's as if there wasn't, the facts are there, no vegetables,
no minerals, only Worm, kingdom unknown, Worm is there,
as it were, as it were. But not too fast, it's too soon, to return,
to where I am, empty-handed, in triumph, to where I'm waiting, calm, passably calm, knowing, thinking I know, that
nothing has befallen me, nothing will befall me, nothing good,
nothing bad, nothing to be the death of me, nothing to be the
life of me, it would be premature. I see me, I see my place,
there is nothing to show it, nothing to distinguish it, from all
the other places, they are mine, all mine, if I wish, I wish

none but mine, there is nothing to mark it, I am there so little,
I see it, I feel it round me, it enfolds me, it covers me,
if only this voice would stop, for a second, it would
seem long to me, a second of silence. I'd listen, I'd know
if it was going to start again, or if it was stilled for ever,
what would I know it with, I'd know. And I'd keep
on listening, to try and advance in their good graces,
keep my place in their favour, and be ready, in case
they judged fit to take me in hand again, or I'd stop, stop
listening, is it possible that one day I shall stop listening, without having to fear the worst, namely, I don't know, what can
be worse than this, a woman's voice perhaps, I hadn't thought
of that, they might engage a soprano. But let us leave these
dreams and try again. If only I knew what they want, they
want me to be Worm, but I was, I was, what's wrong, I
was, but ill, it must be that, it can only be that, what else
can it be, but that, I didn't report in the light, the light
of day, in their midst, to hear them say, Didn't we tell you
you were alive and kicking? I have endured, that must
be it, I shouldn't have endured, but I feel nothing, yes
yes, this voice, I have endured it, I didn't fly from it, I
should have fled, Worm should have fled, but where,
how, he's riveted, Worm should have dragged himself away,
no matter where, towards them, towards the azure, but
how could he, he can't stir, it needn't be bonds, there are no
bonds here, it's as if he were rooted, that's bonds if you like,
the earth would have to quake, it isn't earth, one doesn't know
what it is, it's like sargasso, no, it's like molasses, no, no
matter, an eruption is what's needed, to spew him into the
light. But what calm, apart from the discourse, not a breath,
it's suspicious, the calm that precedes life, no no, not all this
time, it's like slime, paradise, it would be paradise, but for
this noise, it's life trying to get in, no, trying to get him out, or
little bubbles bursting all around, no, there's no air here, air is
to make you choke, light is to close your eyes, that's where he
must go, where it's never dark, but here it's never dark either,
yes, here it's dark, it's they who make this grey, with their
lamps. When they go, when they go silent, it will be dark, not
a sound, not a glimmer, but they'll never go, yes, they'll go,
they'll go silent perhaps and go, one day, one evening,
slowly, sadly, in Indian file, casting long shadows, towards

their master, who will punish them, or who will spare them, what else is there, up above, for those who lose, punishment, pardon, so they say. What have you done with your material? We have left it behind. But commanded to say whether yes or no they filled up the holes, have you filled up the holes yes or no, they will say yes and no, or some yes, others no, at the same time, not knowing what answer the master wants, to his question. But both are defendable, both yes and no, for they filled up the holes, if you like, and if you don't like they didn't, for they didn't know what to do, on departing, whether to fill up the holes or, on the contrary, leave them gaping wide. So they fixed their lamps in the holes, their long lamps, to prevent them from closing of themselves, it's like potter's clay, their powerful lamps, lit and trained on the within, to make him think they are still there, notwithstanding the silence, or to make him think the grey is natural, or to make him go on suffering, for he does not suffer from the noise alone, he suffers from the grey too, from the light, he must, it's preferable, or to make it possible for them to come back, if the master commands them to, without his knowing they have gone, as if he could know, or for no other reason than their ignorance of what to do, whether to fill up the holes or let them fill up of themselves, it's like shit, there we have it at last, there it is at last, the right word, one has only to seek, seek in vain, to be sure of finding in the end, it's a question of elimination. Enough now about holes. The grey means nothing, the grey silence is not necessarily a mere lull, to be got through somehow, it may be final, or it may not. But the lamps unattended will not burn on forever, on the contrary, they will go out, little by little, without attendants to charge them anew, and go silent, in the end. Then it will be black. But it is with the black as with the grey, the black proves nothing either, as to the nature of the silence which it inspissates (as it were). For they may come back, long after the lights are spent, having pleaded for years in vain before the master and failed to convince him there is nothing to be done, with Worm, for Worm. Then all will start over again, obviously. So it will never be known, Worm will never know, let the silence be black, or let it be grey, it can never be known, as long as it lasts, whether it is final, or whether it is a mere

lull, and what a lull, when he must listen, strain his ears for
the murmurs of olden silences, hold himself ready for the next
instalment, under pain of supplementary thunderbolts. But
Worm must not be confused with another. Though this has
no importance, as it happens. For he who has once had to
listen will listen always, whether he knows he will never hear
anything again, or whether he does not. In other words, they
like other words, no doubt about it, silence once broken will
never again be whole. Is there then no hope? Good gracious,
no, heavens, what an idea! Just a faint one perhaps, but which
will never serve. But one forgets. And if there is only one he
will depart all alone, towards his master, and his long shadow
will follow him, across the desert, it's a desert, that's news,
Worm will see the light in a desert, the light of day, the desert
day, the day they catch him, it's the same as everywhere else,
they say not, they say it's purer, clearer, fat lot of difference
that will make, oh it is not necessarily the Sahara, or Gobi,
there are others, it's the ozone that matters, in the beginning,
yes indeed, in the end too, it sterilizes. But this livid eye, what
use is it to him? To see the light, they call that seeing, no
objection, since it causes him suffering, they call that suffering,
they know how to cause suffering, the master explained to
them, Do this, do that, you'll see him squirm, you'll hear him
weep. He weeps, it's a fact, oh not a very firm one, to be
made the most of quick. As for the squirming, nothing doing.
But there is always this to be said, things are only beginning,
though long since begun, they will not lose heart, they'll
remember the motto of William the Silent and keep on talking,
that's what they're paid for, not for results. Enough about
them, they can speak of nothing else, all is theirs, but for
them there would be nothing, not even Worm, he's an idea
they have, a word they use, when speaking of them, enough
about them. But this grey, this light, if he could escape from
this light, which makes him suffer, is it not obvious it would
make him suffer more and more, in whatever direction he
went, since he is at the centre, and drive him back there,
after forty or fifty vain excursions? No, that is not obvious.
For it is obvious the light would lessen as he went towards
it, they would see to that, to make him think he was on the
right road and so bring him to the wall. Then the blaze, the
capture and the paean. As long as he suffers there's hope,

even though they need none, to make him suffer. But how can they know he suffers? Do they see him? They say they do. But it's impossible. Hear him? Certainly not. He makes no noise. A little with his whinging perhaps. In any case they are easy, rightly or wrongly, in their minds, he suffers, and thanks to them. Oh not yet sufficiently, but gently does it, an excess of severity at this stage might darken his understanding forever. Another thing. The problem is delicate. The dulling effect of habit, how do they deal with that? They can combat it of course, raising the voice, increasing the light. But suppose, instead of suffering less, as time flies, he continues to suffer as much, precisely, as the first day. That must be possible. And but suppose, instead of suffering less than the first day, or no less, he suffers more and more, as time flies, and the metamorphosis is accomplished, of unchanging future into unchangeable past. Eh? Another thing, but of a different order. The affair is thorny. Is not a uniform suffering preferable to one which, by its ups and downs, is liable at certain moments to encourage the view that perhaps after all it is not eternal? That must depend on the object pursued. Namely? A little fit of impatience, on the part of the patient. Thank you. That is the immediate object. Afterwards there will be others. Afterwards he'll be given lessons in keeping quiet. But for the moment let him toss and turn at least, roll on the ground, damn it all, since there's no other remedy, anything at all, to relieve the monotony, damn it all, look at the burnt alive, they don't have to be told, when not lashed to the stake, to rush about in every direction, without method, crackling, in search of a little cool, there are even those whose sang-froid is such that they throw themselves out of the window. No one asks him to go to those lengths. But simply to discover, without further assistance from without, the alleviations of flight from self, that's all, he won't go far, he needn't go far. Simply to find within himself a palliative for what he is, through no fault of his own. Simply to imitate the hussar who gets up on a chair the better to adjust the plume of his busby, it's the least he might do. No one asks him to think, simply to suffer, always in the same way, without hope of diminution, without hope of dissolution, it's no more complicated than that. No need to think in order to despair. Agreed then on monotony, it's more stimulating. But how can it be ensured? No matter, no matter how, they are doing the best they can, with the miserable means at their disposal, a voice, a little light, poor devils, that's what they're paid for, they say, No sign of hardening, no sign of softening, impossible to say, no matter, it's a good average, we have only to continue, one day he'll understand, one day he'll thrill, the little spasm will come, a change in the eye, and cast him up among us. To be on the watch and never sight, to listen for the moan that never comes, that's not a life worth living either. And yet it's theirs. He is there, says the master, somewhere, do as I tell you, bring him before me, he's lacking to my glory. But one last effort, one more, that's the spirit, that's the way, each time as if it were the last, the only way not to lose ground. A great gulp of stinking air and off we go, we'll be back in a second. Forward! That's soon said. But where is forward? And why? The dirty pack of fake maniacs, they know I don't know, they know I forget all they say as fast as they say it. These little pauses are a poor trick too. When they go silent, so do I. A second later, I'm a second behind them, I remember a second, for the space of a second, that is to say long enough to blurt it out, as received, while receiving the next, which is none of my business either. Not an instant I can call my own and they want me to know where next to turn. Ah I know what I'd know, and where I'd turn, if I had a head that worked. Let them tell me again what I'm doing, if they want me to look as if I were doing it. This tone, these words, to make me think they come from me. Always the same old dodges, ever since they took it into their heads that my existence is only a question of time. I think I must have blackouts, whole sentences lost, no, not whole. Perhaps I've missed the keyword to the whole business. I wouldn't have understood it, but I would have said it, that's all that's required, it would have spoken in my favour, next time they judge me, well well, so they judge me from time to time, they neglect nothing. Perhaps one day I'll know, say, what I'm guilty of. How many of us are there altogether, finally? And who is holding forth at the moment? And to whom? And about what? These are futile teasers. Let them put into my mouth at last the words that will save me, damn me, and no more talk about it, no more talk about anything. But this is my punishment, my crime is my punishment, that's what they

judge me for, I expiate vilely, like a pig, dumb, uncomprehending, possessed of no utterance but theirs. They'll clap me
in a dungeon, I'm in a dungeon, I've always been in a dungeon, I hear everything, every word they say, it's the only
sound, as if I were speaking, to myself, out loud, in the end
you don't know any more, a voice that never stops, where it's
coming from. Perhaps there are others here, with me, it's
dark, very properly, it is not necessarily an oubliette for one,
or one other, perhaps I havè a companion in misfortune,
given to talking, or condemned to talk, you know, any old
thing, out loud, without ceasing, but I think not, what do I
think not, that I have a companion in misfortune, that's it,
that would surprise me, they loathe me, but not to that extent,
they say that would surprise me. I must doze off from time to
time, with open eyes, and yet nothing changes, ever. Gaps,
there have always been gaps, it's the voice stopping, it's the
voice failing to carry to me, what can it matter, perhaps it's
important, the result is the same, one perhaps that doesn't
count, exceptionally. They shut me up here, now they're trying to get me out, to shut me up somewhere else, or to let me
go, they are capable of putting me out just to see what I'd do.
Standing with their backs to the door, their arms folded, their
legs crossed, they would observe me. Or all they did was to
find me here, on their arrival, or long afterwards. They are not
interested in me, only in the place, they want the place
for one of their own. What can one do but speculate,
speculate, until one hits on the happy speculation? When all
goes silent, and comes to an end, it will be because the words
have been said, those it behoved to say, no need to know
which, no means of knowing which, they'll be there somewhere, in the heap, in the torrent, not necessarily the last,
they have to be ratified by the proper authority, that takes
time, he's far from here, they bring him the verbatim report of
the proceedings, once in a way, he knows the words that
count, it's he who chose them, in the meantime the voice
continues, while the messenger goes towards the master, and
while the master examines the report, and while the messenger
comes back with the verdict, the words continue, the wrong
words, until the order arrives, to stop everything or to continue everything, no, superfluous, everything will continue
automatically, until the order arrives, to stop everything.

Perhaps they are somewhere there, the words that count, in what has just been said, the words it behoved to say, they need not be more than a few. They say they, speaking of them, to make me think it is I who am speaking. Or I say they, speaking of God knows what, to make me think it is not I who am speaking. Or rather there is silence, from the moment the messenger departs until he returns with his orders, namely, Continue. For there are long silences from time to time, truces, and then I hear them whispering, some perhaps whispering, It's over, this time we've hit the mark, and others, We'll have to go through it all again, in other words, or in the same words, arranged differently. Respite then, once in a way, if one can call that respite, when one waits to know one's fate, saying, Perhaps it's not that at all, and saying, Where do these words come from that pour out of my mouth, and what do they mean, no, saying nothing, for the words don't carry any more, if one can call that waiting, when there's no reason for it, and one listens, that stet, without reason, as one has always listened, because one day listening began, because it cannot stop, that's not a reason, if one can call that respite. But what's all this about not being able to die, live, be born, that must have some bearing, all this about staying where you are, dying, living, being born, unable to go forward or back, not knowing where you came from, or where you are, or where you're going, or that it's possible to be elsewhere, to be otherwise, supposing nothing, asking yourself nothing, you can't, you're there, you don't know who, you don't know where, the thing stays where it is, nothing changes, within it, outside it, apparently, apparently. And there is nothing for it but to wait for the end, nothing but for the end to come, and at the end all will be the same, at the end at last perhaps all the same as before, as all that livelong time when there was nothing for it but to get to the end, or fly from it, or wait for it, trembling or not, resigned or not, the nuisance of doing over, and of being, same thing, for one who could never do, never be. Ah if only this voice could stop, this meaningless voice which prevents you from being nothing, just barely prevents you from being nothing and nowhere, just enough to keep alight this little yellow flame feebly darting from side to side, panting, as if straining to tear itself from its wick, it should never have been lit, or it should never have been fed, or it should have been put out, put out, it should have been let go out. Regretting, that's what helps you on, that's what gets you on towards the end of the world, regretting what is, regretting what was, it's not the same thing, yes, it's the same, you don't know, what's happening, what's happened, perhaps it's the same, the same regrets, that's what transports you, towards the end of regretting. But a little animation now for pity's sake, it's now or never, a little spirit, it won't produce anything, not a budge, that doesn't matter, we are not tradesmen, and one never knows, does one, no. Perhaps Mahood will emerge from his urn and make his way towards Montmartre, on his belly, singing, I come, I come, my heart's delight. Or Worm, good old Worm, perhaps he won't be able to bear any more, of not being able, of not being able to bear any more, it would be a pity to miss that. If I were they I'd set the rats on him, water-rats, sewer-rats, they're the best, oh not too many, a dozen to a dozen and a half, that might help him make up his mind, to get going, and what an introduction, to his future attributes. No, it would be in vain, a rat wouldn't survive there, not one second. But let's have another squint at his eye, that's the place to look. A little raw perhaps, the white, with all the pissing, there's a gleam at last, one hesitates to say of intelligence. Apart from that the same as ever. A trifle more prominent perhaps, more paraphimotically globose. It seems to listen. It's weakening, that's unavoidable, glazing, it's high time to offer it something to bring it clean out of its socket, in ten years it will be too late. The mistake they make of course is to speak of him as if he really existed, in a specific place, whereas the whole thing is no more than a project for the moment. But let them blunder on to the end of their folly, then they can go into the question again, taking care not to compromise themselves by the use of terms, if not of notions, accessible to the understanding. In the same way the case of Mahood has been insufficiently studied. One may experience the need of such creatures, assuming they are twain, and even the presentiment of their possible reality, without all these blind and surly disquisitions. A little more reflection would have shown them that the hour to speak, far from having struck, might never strike. But they are compelled to speak, it is forbidden them to stop. Why then not speak of something else, something the existence of which seems in a certain measure already established, on the subject of which one may chatter away without blushing purple every thirty or forty thousand words at having to employ such locutions and which moreover, supreme guarantee, has caused the glibbest tongues to wag from time immemorial, it would be preferable. It's the old story, they want to be entertained, while doing their dirty work, no, not entertained, soothed, no, that's not it either, solaced, no, even less, no matter, with the result they achieve nothing, neither what they want, without knowing exactly what, nor the obscure infamy to which they are committed, the old story. You wouldn't think it was the same gang as a moment ago, or would you? What can you expect, they don't know who they are either, nor where they are, nor what they're doing, nor why everything is going so badly, so abominably badly, that must be it. So they build up hypotheses that collapse on top of one another, it's human, a lobster couldn't do it. Ah a nice mess we're in, the whole pack of us, is it possible we're all in the same boat, no, we're in a nice mess each one in his own peculiar way. I myself have been scandalously bungled, they must be beginning to realize it, I on whom all dangles, better still, about whom, much better, all turns, dizzily, yes yes, don't protest, all spins, it's a head, I'm in a head, what an illumination, sssst, pissed on out of hand. Ah this blind voice, and these moments of held breath when all listen wildly, and the voice that begins to fumble again, without knowing what it's looking for, and again the tiny silence, and the listening again, for what, no one knows, a sign of life perhaps, that must be it, a sign of life escaping someone, and bound to be denied if it came, that's it surely, if only all that could stop, there'd be peace, no, too good to be believed, the listening would go on, for the voice to begin again, for a sign of life, for some one to betray himself, or for something else, anything, what else can there be but signs of life, the fall of a pin, the stirring of a leaf, or the little cry that frogs give when the scythe slices them in half, or when they are spiked, in their pools, with a spear, one could multiply the examples, it would even be an excellent idea, but there it is, one can't. Perhaps it would be better

to be blind, the blind hear better, full of general knowledge
we are this evening, we have even piano-tuners up our
sleeve, they strike A and hear G, two minutes later, there's
nothing to be seen in any case, this eye is an oversight. But
this isn't Worm speaking. True, so far, who denies it, it
would be premature. Nor I, for that matter, and Mahood
is notoriously aphonic. But the question is not there, for
the moment, no one knows where it is, but it is not there,
for the time being. Ah yes, there's great fun to be had from
an eye, it weeps for the least little thing, a yes, a no, the
yesses make it weep, the noes too, the perhapses particularly,
with the result that the grounds for these staggering pro-
nouncements do not always receive the attention they deserve.
Mahood too, I mean Worm, no, Mahood, Mahood too is a
great weeper, in case it hasn't been mentioned, his beard
is soaking with the muck, it's quite ridiculous, especially as
it doesn't relieve him in the slightest, what could it possibly
relieve him of, the poor brute is as cold as a fish, incapable
even of cursing his creator, it's purely mechanical. But it's
time Mahood was forgotten, he should never have been
mentioned. No doubt. But is it possible to forget him? It is
true one forgets everything. And yet it is greatly to be feared
that Mahood will never let himself be completely resorbed.
Worm yes, Worm will vanish utterly, as if he had never
been, which indeed is probably the case, as if one could
ever vanish utterly without having been at some previous
stage. That's soon said. But Mahood too for that matter.
It's not clear, tut tut, it's not clear at all. No matter, Mahood
will stay where he was put, stuck up to his skull in his vase,
opposite the shambles, beseeching the passers-by, without a
word, or a gesture, or any play of his features, they don't
play, to perceive him ostensibly, concomitantly with the
day's dish, or independently, for reasons unknown, perhaps
in the hope of being proven in the swim, that is to say
guaranteed to sink, sooner or later, that must be it, such
notions may be entertained, without any process of thought.
I myself am exceptionally given to the tear, I should have
preferred this kept dark, in their position I should have
omitted this detail, the truth being I have no vent at my
disposal, neither the aforesaid nor those less noble, how
can one enjoy good health under such conditions, and what

is one to believe, that is not the point, to believe this or
that, the point is to guess right, nothing more, they say, If
it's not white it's very likely black, it must be admitted the
method lacks subtlety, in view of the intermediate shades
all equally worthy of a chance. The time they waste repeating
the same thing, when they must know pertinently it is not
the right one. Recriminations easily rebutted, if they chose
to take the trouble, and had the leisure, to reflect on their
inanity. But how can you think and speak at the same time,
how can you think about what you have said, may say, are
saying, and at the same time go on with the last-mentioned,
you think about any old thing, you say any old thing, more
or less, more or less, in a daze of baseless unanswerable
self-reproach, that's why they always repeat the same thing,
the same old litany, the one they know by heart, to try
and think of something different, of how to say something
different from the same old thing, always the same wrong
thing said always wrong, they can find nothing, nothing else
to say but the thing that prevents them from finding, they'd
do better to think of what they're saying, in order at least
to vary its presentation, that's what matters, but how can
you think and speak at the same time, without a special
gift, your thought's wander, your words too, far apart, no,
that's an exaggeration, apart, between them would be the
place to be, where you suffer, rejoice, at being bereft of
speech, bereft of thought, and feel nothing, hear nothing,
know nothing, say nothing, are nothing, that would be a
blessed place to be, where you are. It's a lucky thing they are
there, meaning anywhere, to bear the responsibility of this
state of affairs, with respect to which if one does not know
a great deal one knows at least this, that one would not
care to have it on one's conscience, to have it on one's
stomach is enough. Yes, I'm a lucky man to have them,
these voluble shades, I'll be sorry when they go, for I won't
have them always, not at this rate, they'll make me believe
I've piped up before they're done with me. The master in
any case, we don't intend, listen to them hedging, we don't
intend, unless absolutely driven to it, to make the mistake
of inquiring into him, he'd turn out to be a mere high official,
we'd end up by needing God, we have lost all sense of
decency admittedly, but there are still certain depths we prefer

not to sink to. Let us keep to the family circle, it's more intimate, we all know one another now, no surprises to be feared, the will has been opened, nothing for anybody. This eye, curious how this eye invites inspection, demands sympathy, solicits attention, implores assistance, to do what, it's not clear, to stop weeping, have a quick look round, goggle an instant and close forever. It's it you see and it alone, it's from it you set out to look for a face, to it you return having found nothing, nothing worth having, nothing but a kind of ashen smear, perhaps it's long grey hair, hanging in a tangle round the mouth, greasy with ancient tears, or the fringe of a mantle spread like a veil, or fingers opening and closing to try and shut out the world, or all together, fingers, hair and rags, mingled inextricably. Suppositions all equally vain, it's enough to enounce them to regret having spoken, familiar torment, a different past, it's often to be wished, different from yours, when you find out what it was. He is hairless and naked and his hands, laid flat on his knees once and for all, are in no danger of ever getting into mischief. And the face? Balls, all balls, I don't believe in the eye either, there's nothing here, nothing to see, nothing to see with, merciful coincidence, when you think what it would be, a world without spectator, and vice versa, brrr! No spectator then, and better still no spectacle, good riddance. If this noise would stop there'd be nothing more to say. I wonder what the chat is about at the moment. Worm presumably, Mahood being abandoned. And I await my turn. Yes indeed, I do not despair, all things considered, of drawing their attention to my case, some fine day. Not that it offers the least interest, hey, something wrong there, not that it is particularly interesting, I'll accept that, but it's my turn, I too have the right to be shown impossible. This will never end, there's no sense in fooling oneself, yes it will, they'll come round to it, after me it will be the end, they'll give up, saying, It's all a bubble, we've been told a lot of lies, he's been told a lot of lies, who he, the master, by whom, no one knows, the everlasting third party, he's the one to blame, for this state of affairs, the master's not to blame, neither are they, neither am I, least of all I, we were foolish to accuse one another, the master me, them, himself, they me, the master, themselves, I them, the master, myself, we are all innocent, enough. Innocent of what, no one knows, of wanting

to know, wanting to be able, of all this noise about nothing,
of this long sin against the silence that enfolds us, we won't
ask any more, what it covers, this innocence we have fallen
to, it covers everything, all faults, all questions, it puts an
end to questions. Then it will be over, thanks to me all will
be over, and they'll depart, one by one, or they'll drop,
they'll let themselves drop, where they stand, and never move
again, thanks to me, who could understand nothing, of all
they deemed it their duty to tell me, do nothing, of all they
deemed it their duty to tell me to do, and upon us all the
silence will fall again, and settle, like dust of sand, on the
arena, after the massacres. Bewitching prospect if ever there
was one, they are beginning to come round to my opinion,
after all it's possible I have one, they make me say, If only
this, if only that, but the idea is theirs, no, the idea is not theirs
either. As far as I personally am concerned there is every
likelihood of my being incapable of ever desiring or deploring
anything whatsoever. For it would seem difficult for someone, if I may so describe myself, to aspire towards a situation
of which, notwithstanding the enthusiastic descriptions lavished on him, he has not the remotest idea, or to desire with
a straight face the cessation of that other, equally unintelligible, assigned to him in the beginning and never modified.
This silence they are always talking about, from which supposedly he came, to which he will return when his act is
over, he doesn't know what it is, nor what he is meant to do,
in order to deserve it. That's the bright boy of the class speaking now, he's the one always called to the rescue when things
go badly, he talks all the time of merit and situations, he has
saved more than one, of suffering too, he knows how to stimulate the flagging spirit, stop the rot, with the simple use of this
mighty word alone, even if he has to add, a moment later.
But what suffering, since he has always suffered, which rather
damps the rejoicings. But he soon makes up for it, he puts
all to rights again, invoking the celebrated notions of quan-
tity, habit-formation, wear and tear, and others too numerous
for him to mention, and which he is thus in a position, in the
next belch, to declare inapplicable to the case before him, for
there is no end to his wits. But, see above, have they not
already bent over me till black and blue in the face, nay,
have they ever done anything else, during the past—no, no

dates for pity's sake, and another question, what am I doing
in Mahood's story, and in Worm's, or rather what are they
doing in mine, there are some irons in the fire to be going
on with, let them melt. Oh I know, I know, attention please,
this may mean something, I know, there's nothing new there,
it's all part of the same old irresistible boloney, namely, But
my dear man, come, be reasonable, look, this is you, look at
this photograph, and here's your file, no convictions, I assure
you, come now, make an effort, at your age, to have no identity, it's a scandal, I assure you, look at this photograph, what,
you see nothing, true for you, no matter, here, look at this
death's-head, you'll see, you'll be all right, it won't last
long, here, look, here's the record, insults to policemen,
indecent exposure, sins against holy ghost, contempt of
court, impertinence to superiors, impudence to inferiors,
deviations from reason, without battery, look, no battery,
it's nothing, you'll be all right, you'll see, I beg your
pardon, does he work, good God no, out of the question,
look, here's the medical report, spasmodic tabes, painless
ulcers, I repeat, painless, all is painless, multiple softenings,
manifold hardenings, insensitive to blows, sight failing,
chronic gripes, light diet, shit well tolerated, hearing
failing, heart irregular, sweet-tempered, smell failing, heavy
sleeper, no erections, would you like some more, commission
in the territorials, inoperable, untransportable, look, here's
the face, no no, the other end, I assure you, it's a bargain, I
beg your pardon, does he drink, good God yes, passionately,
I beg your pardon, father and mother, both dead, at seven
months interval, he at the conception, she at the nativity, I
assure you, you won't do better, at your age, no human shape,
the pity of it, look, here's the photograph, you'll see, you'll
be all right, what does it amount too, after all, a painful
moment, on the surface, then peace, underneath, it's the only
way, believe me, the only way out, I beg your pardon, have
I nothing else, why certainly, certainly, just a second, curious
you should mention it, I was wondering myself, just a second,
if you were not rather, just a second, here we are, this one
here, but I wanted to be sure, what, you don't understand,
neither do I, no matter, it's no time for levity, yes, I was right,
no doubt about it this time, it's you all over, look, here's the
photograph, take a look at that, dying on his feet, you'd

better hurry, it's a bargain, I assure you, and so on, till I'm
tempted, no, all lies, they know it well, I never understood, I
haven't stirred, all I've said, said I've done, said I've been, it's
they who said it, I've said nothing, I haven't stirred, they don't
understand, I can't stir, they think I don't want to, that their
conditions don't suit me, that they'll hit on others, in the
end, to my liking, then I'll stir, I'll be in the bag, that's how
I see it, I see nothing, they don't understand, I can't go to
them, they'll have to come and get me, if they want me,
Mahood won't get me out, nor Worm either, they set great
store on Worm, to coax me out, he was something new, different from all the others, meant to be, perhaps he was, to me
they're all the same, they don't understand, I can't stir, I'm
all right here, I'd be all right here, if they'd leave me,
let them come and get me, if they want me, they'll find
nothing, then they can depart, with an easy mind. And if
there is only one, like me, he can depart without fear of
remorse, having done all he could, and even more, to achieve
the impossible and so lost his life, or stay with me here, he
might do that, and be a like for me, that would be lovely,
my first like, that would be epoch-making, to know I had a
like, a congener, he wouldn't have to be like me, he couldn't
but be like me, he need only relax, he might believe what he
pleased, at the outset, that he was in hell, or that the place
was charming, he might even exclaim, I'll never stir again,
being used to announcing his decisions, at the top of his voice,
so as to get to know them better, he might even add, to cover
all risks, For the moment, it would be his last howler, he
need only relax, he'd disappear, he'd know nothing either,
there we'd be the two of us, unbeknown to ourselves, unbeknown to each other, that's a darling dream I've been having,
a broth of a dream. And it's not over. For here comes another,
to see what has happened to his pal, and get him out, and
back to his right mind, and back to his kin, with a flow of
threats and promises, and tales like this of wombs and cribs,
diapers bepissed and the first long trousers, love's young dream
and life's old lech, blood and tears and skin and bones and
tossing in the grave, and so coax him out, as he me, that's
right, pidgin bullskrit, and in the end, having lived his life,
no, before, but you've got my meaning, and there we are the
three of us, it's cosier, perpetual dream, you have merely to

sleep, not even that, it's like the old jingle, A dog crawled
into the kitchen and stole a crust of bread, then cook up with
I've forgotten what and walloped him till he was dead, second
verse, Then all the dogs came crawling and dug the dog a
tomb and wrote upon the tombstone for dogs and bitches to
come, third verse, as the first, fourth, as the second, fifth, as
the third, give us time, give us time and we'll be a multitude,
a thousand, ten thousand, there's no lack of room, adeste,
adeste, all ye living bastards, you'll be all right, you'll see,
you'll never be born again, what am I saying, you'll never have
been born, and bring your brats, our hell will be heaven to
them, after what you've done to them. But come to think of
it are we not already a goodly company, what right have I
to flatter myself I'm first, first in time I mean of course, there
we have a few more questions, please God they don't take the
fancy to answer them. What can they be hatching anyhow,
at this eleventh hour? Can it be they are resolved at last to
seize me by the horns? Looks like it. In that case tableau any
minute. Oyez, oyez, I was like them, before being like me, oh
the swine, that's one I won't get over in a hurry, no matter,
no matter, the charge is sounded, present arms, corpse, to
your guns, spermatozoon. I too, weary of pleading an incomprehensible cause, at six and eight the thousand flowers of
rhetoric, let myself drop among the contumacious, nice image
that, telescoping space, it must be the Pulitzer Prize, they
want to bore me to sleep, at long range, for fear I might
defend myself, they want to catch me alive, so as to be able
to kill me, thus I shall have lived, they think I'm alive, what
a business, were there but a cadaver it would smack of body-
snatching, not in a womb either, the slut has yet to menstruate
capable of whelping me, that should singularly narrow the
field of research, a sperm dying, of cold, in the sheets, feebly
wagging its little tail, perhaps I'm a drying sperm, in the sheets
of an innocent boy, even that takes time, no stone must be
left unturned, one mustn't be afraid of making a howler, how
can one know it is one before it's made, and one it most certainly is, now that it's irrevocable, for the good reason, here's
another, here comes another, unless it escapes them in time,
what a hope, the bright boy is there, for the excellent reason
that counts as living too, counts as murder, it's notorious, ah
you can't deny it, some people are lucky, born of a wet dream

and dead before morning, I must say I'm tempted, no, the
testis has yet to descend that would want any truck with me,
it's mutual, another gleam down the drain. And now one last
look at Mahood, at Worm, we'll never have another chance,
ah will they never learn sense, there's nothing to be got, there
was never anything to be got from those stories. I have mine,
somewhere, let them tell it to me, they'll see there's nothing
to be got from it either, nothing to be got from me, it will be
the end, of this hell of stories, you'd think I was cursing them,
always the same old trick, you'd be sorry for them, perhaps
I'll curse them yet, they'll know what it is to be a subject of
conversation, I'll impute words to them you wouldn't throw
to a dog, an ear, a mouth and in the middle a few rags of
mind, I'll get my own back, a few flitters of mind, they'll see
what it's like, I'll clap an eye at random in the thick of the
mess, on the off chance something might stray in front of it,
then I'll let down my trousers and shit stories on them, stories,
photographs, records, sites, lights, gods and fellow-creatures,
the daily round and common task, observing the while, Be
born, dear friends, be born, enter my arse, you'll just love my
colic pains, it won't take long, I've the bloody flux. They'll see
what it's like, that it's not so easy as it looks, that you must
have a taste for it, that you must be born alive, that it's not
something you can acquire, that will teach them perhaps, to
keep their nose out of my business. Yes, if I could, but I
can't, whatever it is, I can't any more, there was perhaps a
time I could, in the days when I was bursting my guts, as
per instructions, to bring back to the fold the dear lost lamb,
I'd been told he was dear, that he was dear to me, that I was
dear to him, that we were dear to each other, all my life I've
pelted him with twaddle, the dear departed, wondering what
he could possibly be like, wondering where we could possibly
have met, all my life, well, almost, damn the almost, all my
life, until I joined him, and now it's I am dear to them, now
it's they are dear to me, glad to hear it, they'll join us, one
by one, what a pity they are numberless, so are we, dear
charnel-house of renegades, this evening decidedly everything
is dear, no matter, the ancients hear nothing, and my old
quarry, there beside me, for him it's all over, beside me how
are you, underneath me, we're piled up in heaps, no, that
won't work either, no matter, it's a detail, for him it's all over,

him the second-last, and for me too, me the last, it will soon
be all over, I'll hear nothing more, I've nothing to do, simply
wait, it's a slow business, he'll come and lie on top of me,
lie beside me, my dear tormentor, his turn to suffer what he
made me suffer, mine to be at peace. How all comes right
in the end to be sure, it's thanks to patience, thanks to time,
it's thanks to the earth that revolves that the earth revolves
no more, that time ends its meal and pain comes to an end,
you have only to wait, without doing anything, it's no good
doing anything, and without understanding, there's no help
in understanding, and all comes right, nothing comes right,
nothing, nothing, this will never end, this voice will never
stop, I'm alone here, the first and the last, I never made anyone suffer, I never stopped anyone's sufferings, no one will
ever stop mine, they'll never depart, I'll never stir, I'll never
know peace, neither will they, but with this difference, that
they don't want it, they say they don't want it, they say I
don't want it either, don't want peace, after all perhaps they're
right, how could I want it, what is it, they say I suffer, perhaps they're right, and that I'd feel better if I did this, said
that, if my body stirred, if my head understood, if they went
silent and departed, perhaps they're right, how would I know
about these things, how would I understand what they're talking about, I'll never stir, never speak, they'll never go silent,
never depart, they'll never catch me, never stop trying, that's
that, I'm listening. Well I prefer that, I must say I prefer
that, that what, oh you know, who you, oh I suppose the
audience, well well, so there's an audience, it's a public show,
you buy your seat and you wait, perhaps it's free, a free show,
you take your seat and you wait for it to begin, or perhaps
it's compulsory, a compulsory show, you wait for the compulsory show to begin, it takes time, you hear a voice, perhaps
it's a recitation, that's the show, someone reciting, selected
passages, old favourites, a poetry matinée, or someone impro-
vising, you can barely hear him, that's the show, you can't
leave, you're afraid to leave, it might be worse elsewhere,
you make the best of it, you try and be reasonable, you came
too early, here we'd need latin, it's only beginning, it hasn't
begun, he's only preluding, clearing his throat, alone in his
dressing-room, he'll appear any moment, he'll begin any
moment, or it's the stage-manager, giving his instructions, his

last recommendations, before the curtain rises, that's the show, waiting for the show, to the sound of a murmur, you try and be reasonable, perhaps it's not a voice at all, perhaps it's the air, ascending, descending, flowing, eddying, seeking exit, finding none, and the spectators, where are they, you didn't notice, in the anguish of waiting, never noticed you were waiting alone, that's the show, waiting alone, in the restless air, for it to begin, for something to begin, for there to be something else but you, for the power to rise, the courage to leave, you try and be reasonable, perhaps you are blind, probably deaf, the show is over, all is over, but where then is the hand, the helping hand, or merely charitable, or the hired hand, it's a long time coming, to take yours and draw you away, that's the show, free, gratis and for nothing, waiting alone, blind, deaf, you don't know where, you don't know for what, for a hand to come and draw you away, somewhere else, where perhaps it's worse. And now for the it, I prefer that, I must say I prefer that, what a memory, real fly-paper, I don't know, I don't prefer it any more, that's all I know, so why bother about it, a thing you don't prefer, just think of that, bothering about that, perish the thought, one must wait, discover a preference, within one's bosom, then it will be time enough to institute an inquiry. Moreover, that's right, link, link, you never know, moreover their attitude towards me has not changed, I am deceived, they are deceived, they have tried to deceive me, saying their attitude towards me had changed, but they haven't deceived me, I didn't understand what they were trying to do to me, I say what I'm told to say, that's all there is to it, and yet I wonder, I don't know, I don't feel a mouth on me, I don't feel the jostle of words in my mouth, and when you say a poem you like, if you happen to like poetry, in the underground, or in bed, for yourself, the words are there, somewhere, without the least sound, I don't feel that either, words falling, you don't know where, you don't know whence, drops of silence through the silence, I don't feel it, I don't feel a mouth on me, nor a head, do I feel an ear, frankly now, do I feel an ear, well frankly now I don't, so much the worse, I don't feel an ear either, this is awful, make an effort, I must feel something, yes, I feel something, they say I feel something, I don't know what it is, I don't know what I feel, tell me what I feel and I'll tell you who I

am, they'll tell me who I am, I won't understand, but the thing
will be said, they'll have said who I am, and I'll have heard,
without an ear I'll have heard, and I'll have said it, without a
mouth I'll have said it, I'll have said it inside me, then in the
same breath outside me, perhaps that's what I feel, an outside and an inside and me in the middle, perhaps that's what
I am, the thing that divides the world in two, on the one
side the outside, on the other the inside, that can be as thin as
foil, I'm neither one side nor the other, I'm in the middle,
I'm the partition, I've two surfaces and no thickness, perhaps
that's what I feel, myself vibrating, I'm the tympanum, on the
one hand the mind, on the other the world, I don't belong to
either, it's not to me they're talking, it's not of me they're
talking, no, that's not it, I feel nothing of all that, try something else, herd of shites, say something else, for me to hear,
I don't know how, for me to say, I don't know how, what
clowns they are, to keep on saying the same thing when they
know it's not the right one, no, they know nothing either,
they forget, they think they change and they never change,
they'll be there saying the same thing till they die, then perhaps a little silence, till the next gang arrives on the site, I
alone am immortal, what can you expect, I can't get born,
perhaps that's their big idea, to keep on saying the same old
thing, generation after generation, till I go mad and begin to
scream, then they'll say, He's mewled, he'll rattle, it's mathe-
matical, let's get out to hell out of here, no point in waiting
for that, others need us, for him it's over, his troubles will
be over, he's saved, we've saved him, they're all the same,
they all let themselves be saved, they all let themselves be
born, he was a tough nut, he'll have a good time, a brilliant
career, in fury and remorse, he'll never forgive himself, and
so depart, thus communing, in Indian file, or two by two,
along the seashore, now it's the seashore, on the shingle, along
the sands, in the evening air, it's evening, that's all I know,
evening, shadows, somewhere, anywhere, on the earth. Go
mad, yes, but there it is, what would I go mad with, and evening isn't sure either, it needn't be evening, dawn too bestows
long shadows, on all that is still standing, that's all that
matters, only the shadows matter, with no life of their own,
no shape and no respite, perhaps it's dawn, evening of night,
it doesn't matter, and so depart, towards my brethren, no,

none of that, no brethren, that's right, take it back, they don't
know, they depart, not knowing whither, towards their master,
it's possible, make a note of that, it's just possible, to sue for
their freedom, for them it's the end, for me the beginning,
my end begins, they stop to listen to my screams, they'll never
stop again, yes, they'll stop, my screams will stop, from time
to time, I'll stop screaming, to listen and hear if anyone is
answering, to look and see if anyone is coming, then go, close
my eyes and go, screaming, to scream elsewhere. Yes, my
mouth, but there it is, I won't open it, I have no mouth, and
what about it, I'll grow one, a little hole at first, then wider and
wider, deeper and deeper, the air will gush into me, and out
a second later, howling. But is it not rather too much to ask,
to ask so much, of so little, is it really politic? And would it
not suffice, without any change in the structure of the thing
as it now stands, as it always stood, without a mouth being
opened at the place which even pain could never line, would
it not suffice to, to what, the thread is lost, no matter, here's
another, would not a little stir suffice, some tiny subsidence or
upheaval, that would start things off, the whole fabric would
be infected, the ball would start a-rolling, the disturbance
would spread to every part, locomotion itself would soon
appear, trips properly so called, business trips, pleasure trips,
research expeditions, sabbatical leaves, jaunts and rambles,
honeymoons at home and abroad and long sad solitary tramps
in the rain, I indicate the main trends, athletics, tossing in bed,
physical jerks, locomotor ataxy, death throes, rigor and rigor
mortis, emergal of the bony structure, that should suffice.
Unfortunately it's a question of words, of voices, one must
not forget that, one must try and not forget that completely,
of a statement to be made, by them, by me, some slight obscurity here, it might sometimes almost be wondered if all their
ballocks about life and death is not as foreign to their nature
as it is to mine. The fact is they no longer know where they've
got to in their affair, where they've got me to, I never knew,
I'm where I always was, wherever that is, and their affair, I
don't know what is meant by that, some process no doubt,
that I've got stuck in, or haven't yet come to, I've got nowhere,
in their affair, that's what galls them, they want me there
somewhere, anywhere, if only they'd stop committing reason,
on them, on me, on the purpose to be achieved, and simply

go on, with no illusion about having begun one day or ever being able to conclude, but it's too difficult, too difficult, for one
bereft of purpose, not to look forward to his end, and bereft
of all reason to exist, back to a time he did not. Difficult too
not to forget, in your thirst for something to do, in order to be
done with it, and have that much less to do, that there is
nothing to be done, nothing special to be done, nothing doable
to be done. No point either, in your thirst, your hunger, no,
no need of hunger, thirst is enough, no point in telling yourself stories, to pass the time, stories don't pass the time, nothing passes the time, that doesn't matter, that's how it is, you
tell yourself stories, then any old thing, saying, No more
stories from this day forth, and the stories go on, it's stories
still, or it was never stories, always any old thing, for as long
as you can remember, no, longer than that, any old thing, the
same old thing, to pass the time, then, as time didn't pass,
for no reason at all, in your thirst, trying to cease and never
ceasing, seeking the cause, the cause of talking and never
ceasing, finding the cause, losing it again, finding it again, not
finding it again, seeking no longer, seeking again, finding
again, losing again, finding nothing, finding at last, losing
again, talking without ceasing, thirstier than ever, seeking as
usual, losing as usual, blathering away, wondering what it's
all about, seeking what it can be you are seeking, exclaiming,
Ah yes, sighing. No no, crying, Enough, ejaculating, Not yet,
talking incessantly, any old thing, seeking once more, any
old thing, thirsting away, you don't know what for, ah yes,
something to do, no no, nothing to be done, and now enough
of that, unless perhaps, that's an idea, let's seek over there,
one last little effort, seek what, pertinent objection, let us try
and determine, before we seek, what it can be, before we seek
over there, over where, talking unceasingly, seeking incessantly, in yourself, outside yourself, cursing man, cursing
God, stopping cursing, past bearing it, going on bearing it,
seeking indefatigably, in the world of nature, the world of
man, where is nature, where is man, where are you, what are
you seeking, who is seeking, seeking who you are, supreme
aberration, where you are, what you're doing, what you've
done to them, what they've done to you, prattling along,
where are the others, who is talking, not I, where am I, where
is the place where I've always been, where are the others, it's

they are talking, talking to me, talking of me, I hear them, I'm mute, what do they want, what have I done to them, what have I done to God, what have they done to God, what has God done to us, nothing, and we've done nothing to him, you can't do anything to him, he can't do anything to us, we're innocent, he's innocent, it's nobody's fault, what's nobody's fault, this state of affairs, what state of affairs, so it is, so be it, don't fret, so it will be, how so, rattling on, dying of thirst, seeking determinedly, what they want, they want me to be, this, that, to howl, stir, crawl out of here, be born, die, listen, I'm listening, it's not enough, I must understand, I'm doing my best, I can't understand, I stop doing my best, I can't do my best, I can't go on, poor devil, neither can they, let them say what they want, give me something to do, something doable to do, poor devils, they can't, they don't know, they're like me, more and more, no more need of them, no more need of anyone, no one can do anything, it's I am talking, thirsting, starving, let it stand, in the ice and in the furnace, you feel nothing, strange, you don't feel a mouth on you, you don't feel your mouth any more, no need of a mouth, the words are everywhere, inside me, outside me, well well, a minute ago I had no thickness, I hear them, no need to hear them, no need of a head, impossible to stop them, impossible to stop, I'm in words, made of words, others' words, what others, the place too, the air, the walls, the floor, the ceiling, all words, the whole world is here with me, I'm the air, the walls, the walled-in one, everything yields, opens, ebbs, flows, like flakes, I'm all these flakes, meeting, mingling, falling asunder, wherever I go I find me, leave me, go towards me, come from me, nothing ever but me, a particle of me, retrieved, lost, gone astray, I'm all these words, all these strangers, this dust of words, with no ground for their settling, no sky for their dispersing, coming together to say, fleeing one another to say, that I am they, all of them, those that merge, those that part, those that never meet, and nothing else, yes, something else, that I'm something quite different, a quite different thing, a wordless thing in an empty place, a hard shut dry cold black place, where nothing stirs, nothing speaks, and that I listen, and that I seek, like a caged beast born of caged beasts born of caged beasts born of caged beasts born in a cage and dead in a cage, born and then dead, born in a cage

and then dead in a cage, in a word like a beast, in one
of their words, like such a beast, and that I seek, like
such a beast, with my little strength, such a beast, with
nothing of its species left but fear and fury, no, the fury
is past, nothing but fear, nothing of all its due but fear cen-
tupled, fear of its shadow, no, blind from birth, of sound
then, if you like, we'll have that, one must have something,
it's a pity, but there it is, fear of sound, fear of sounds, the
sounds of beasts, the sounds of men, sounds in the daytime
and sounds at night, that's enough, fear of sounds, all sounds,
more or less, more or less fear, all sounds, there's only one,
continuous, day and night, what is it, it's steps coming and
going, it's voices speaking for a moment, it's bodies groping
their way, it's the air, it's things, it's the air among the things,
that's enough, that I seek, like it, no, not like it, like me, in
my own way, what am I saying, after my fashion, that I seek,
what do I seek now, what it is, it must be that, it can only
be that, what it is, what it can be, what what can be, what I
seek, no, what I hear, now it comes back to me, all back to
me, they say I seek what it is I hear, I hear them, now it comes
back to me, what it can possibly be, and where it can possibly
come from, since all is silent here, and the walls thick, and
how I manage, without feeling an ear on me, or a head, or a
body, or a soul, how I manage, to do what, how I manage,
it's not clear, dear dear, you say it's not clear, something is
wanting to make it clear, I'll seek, what is wanting, to make
everything clear, I'm always seeking something, it's tiring in
the end, and it's only the beginning, how I manage, under such
conditions, to do what I'm doing, what am I doing, I must
find out what I'm doing, tell me what you're doing and I'll
ask you how it's possible, I hear, you say I hear, and that I
seek, it's a lie, I seek nothing, nothing any more, no matter,
let's leave it, no harking, and that I seek, listen to them now,
jogging my memory, seek what, firstly what it is, secondly
where it comes from, thirdly how I manage, that's it, now
we've got it, thirdly how I manage, to do it, seeing that this,
considering that that, inasmuch as God knows what, that's
clear now, how I manage to hear, and how I manage to understand, it's a lie, what would I understand with, that's what I'm
asking, how I manage to understand, oh not the half, nor the
hundredth, nor the five thousandth, let us go on dividing by

fifty, nor the quarter millionth, that's enough, but a little
nevertheless it's essential, it's preferable, it's a pity, but
there it is, just a little all the same, the least possible, it's
appreciable, it's enough, the rough meaning of one expression
in a thousand, in ten thousand, let us go on multiplying by ten,
nothing more restful than arithmetic, in a hundred thousand,
in a million, it's too much, too little, we've gone wrong somewhere, no matter, there is no great difference here between one
expression and the next, when you've grasped one you've
grasped them all, I am not in that fortunate position, all, how
you exaggerate, always out for the whole hog, the all of all
and the all of nothing, never in the happy golden, never,
always, it's too much, too little, often, seldom, let me now
sum up, after this digression, there is I, yes, I feel it, I confess,
I give in, there is I, it's essential, it's preferable, I wouldn't
have said so, I won't always say so, so let me hasten to take
advantage of being now obliged to say, in a manner of speaking, that there is I, on the one hand, and this noise on the
other, that I never doubted, no, let us be logical, there was
never any doubt about that, this noise, on the other, if it is
the other, that will very likely be the theme of our next deliberation, I sum up, now that I'm there it's I will do the sum-
ming up, it's I will say what is to be said and then say what
it was, that will be jolly, I sum up, I and this noise, I see nothing else for the moment, but I have only just taken over my
functions, I and this noise, and what about it, don't interrupt
me, I'm doing my best, I repeat, I and this noise, on
the subject of which, inverting the natural order, we would
seem to know for certain, among other things, what follows,
namely, on the one hand, with regard to the noise, that it has
not been possible up to date to determine with certainty, or
even approximately, what it is, in the way of noise, or how
it comes to me, or by what organ it is emitted, or by what
perceived, or by what intelligence apprehended, in its main
drift, and on the other, that is to say with regard to me, this
is going to take a little longer, with regard to me, nice time
we're going to have now, with regard to me, that it has not yet
been our good fortune to establish with any degree of accuracy
what I am, where I am, whether I am words among words, or
silence in the midst of silence, to recall only two of the hypotheses launched in this connexion, though silence to tell the

truth does not appear to have been very conspicuous up to
now, but appearances may sometimes be deceptive, I resume,
not yet our good fortune to establish, among other things,
what I am, no, sorry, already mentioned, what I'm doing, how
I manage, to hear, if I hear, if it's I who hear, and who can
doubt it, I don't know, doubt is present, in this connexion,
somewhere or other, I resume, how I manage to hear, if it's I
who hear, and how to understand, ellipse when possible, it
saves time, how to understand, same observation, and how it
happens, if it's I who speak, and it may be assumed it is, as
it may be suspected it is not, how it happens, if it's I who
speak, that I speak without ceasing, that I long to cease, that
I can't cease, I indicate the principal divisions, it's more syn-
optic, I resume, not the good fortune to establish, with regard
to me, if it's I who seek, what exactly it is I seek, find, lose,
find again, throw away, seek again, find again, throw away
again, no, I never threw anything away, never threw anything
away of all the things I found, never found anything that I
didn't lose, never lost anything that I mightn't as well have
thrown away, if it's I who seek, find, lose, find again, lose
again, seek in vain, seek no more, if it's I what it is, and if
it's not I who it is, and what it is, I see nothing else for the
moment, yes I do, I conclude, not the good fortune to establish, considering the futility of my telling myself even any old
thing, to pass the time, why I do it, if it's I who do it, as if
reasons were required for doing any old thing, to pass the
time, no matter, the question may be asked, off the record,
why time doesn't pass, doesn't pass from you, why it piles up
all about you, instant on instant, on all sides, deeper and
deeper, thicker and thicker, your time, others' time, the time
of the ancient dead and the dead yet unborn, why it buries
you grain by grain neither dead nor alive, with no memory of
anything, no hope of anything, no knowledge of anything, no
history and no prospects, buried under the seconds, saying
any old thing, your mouth full of sand, oh I know it's immaterial, time is one thing, I another, but the question may be
asked, why time doesn't pass, just like that, off the record,
en passant, to pass the time, I think that's all, for the moment,
I see nothing else, I see nothing whatever, for the time being.
But I really mustn't ask myself any more questions, if it's I,
I really must not. More resolutions, while we're at it, that's

right, resolutely, more resolutions. Make abundant use of the
principle of parsimony, as if it were familiar to me, it is not
too late. Assume notably henceforward that the thing said and
the thing heard have a common source, resisting for this purpose the temptation to call in question the possibility of assuming anything whatever. Situate this source in me, without
specifying where exactly, no finicking, anything is preferable
to the consciousness of third parties and, more generally
speaking, of an outer world. Carry if necessary this process
of compression to the point of abandoning all other postulates
than that of a deaf half-wit, hearing nothing of what he says
and understanding even less. Evoke at painful junctures, when
discouragement threatens to raise its head, the image of a vast
cretinous mouth, red, blubber and slobbering, in solitary con-
finement, extruding indefatigably, with a noise of wet kisses
and washing in a tub, the words that obstruct it. Set aside once
and for all, at the same time as the analogy with orthodox
damnation, all idea of beginning and end. Overcome, that
goes without saying, the fatal leaning towards expressiveness.
Equate me, without pity or scruple, with him who exists,
somehow, no matter how, no finicking, with him whose story
this story had the brief ambition to be. Better, ascribe to me
a body. Better still, arrogate to me a mind. Speak of a world
of my own, sometimes referred to as the inner, without choking. Doubt no more. Seek no more. Take advantage of the
brand-new soul and substantiality to abandon, with the only
possible abandon, deep down within. And finally, these and
other decisions having been taken, carry on cheerfully as before. Something has changed nevertheless. Not a word about
Mahood, or Worm, for the past—ah yes, I nearly forgot,
speak of time, without flinching, and what is more, it just occurs to me, by a natural association of ideas, treat of space
with the same easy grace, as if it were not bunged up on all
sides, a few inches away, after all that's something, a few
inches to be thankful for, it gives one air, room for the tongue
to loll, to have lolled, to loll on. When I think, that is to say,
no, let it stand, when I think of the time I've wasted with these
bran-dips, beginning with Murphy, who wasn't even the first,
when I had me, on the premises, within easy reach, tottering
under my own skin and bones, real ones, rotting with solitude
and neglect, till I doubted my own existence, and even still, to-

day, I have no faith in it, none, so that I have to say, when I speak, Who speaks, and seek, and so on and similarly for all the other things that happen to me and for which someone must be found, for things that happen must have someone to happen to, someone must stop them. But Murphy and the others, and last but not least the two old buffers here present, could not stop them, the things that happened to me, nothing could happen to them, of the things that happened to me, and nothing else either, there is nothing else, let us be lucid for once, nothing else but what happens to me, such as speaking, and such as seeking, and which cannot happen to me, which prowl round me, like bodies in torment, the torment of no abode, no repose, no, like hyenas, screeching and laughing, no, no better, no matter, I've shut my doors against them, I'm not at home to anything, my doors are shut against them, perhaps that's how I'll find silence, and peace at last, by opening my doors and letting myself be devoured, they'll stop howling, they'll start eating, the maws now howling. Open up, open up, you'll be all right, you'll see. What a joy it is, to turn and look astern, between two visits to the depths, scan in vain the horizon for a sail, it's a real pleasure, upon my word it is, to be unable to drown, under such conditions. Yes, but there it is, I am far from my doors, far from my walls, someone would have to wake the turnkey, there must be one somewhere, far from my subject too, let us get back to it, it's gone, no longer there where I thought I last saw it, strange this mixture of solid and liquid, where was I, ah yes, my subject, no longer there, or no longer the same, or I mistake the place, no, yes, it's the same, still there, in the same place, it's a pity, I would have liked to lose it, I would have liked to lose me, lose me the way I could long ago, when I still had some imagination, close my eyes and be in a wood, or on the seashore, or in a town where I don't know anyone, it's night, everyone has gone home, I walk the streets, I lash into them one after the other, it's the town of my youth, I'm looking for my mother to kill her, I should have thought of that a bit earlier, before being born, it's raining, I'm all right, I stride along on the crown of the street with great yaws to left and right, now that's all over, with closed eyes I see the same as with them open, namely, wait, I'll say it, I'll try and say it, I'm curious to know what it can possibly be that I see, with

closed eyes, with open eyes, nothing, I see nothing, well that
is a disappointment, I was hoping for something better than
that, is that what it is to be unable to lose yourself, I'm asking
myself a question, is that what it is, to see nothing, no matter
where I look, nor, eyeless, the little creature in his different
guises coming and going, now in shadow, now in light, doing
his best, seeking the means of staying among the living, of
getting off with his life, or shut up looking out of the window
at the ever-changing sky, is that it, to be unable to lose myself,
I don't know, what did I see in the old days, when I ventured a quick look, I don't know, I don't remember. There I
am in any case equipped with eyes, which I open and shut,
two, perhaps blue, knowing it avails nothing, for I have a head
now too, where all manner of things are known, can it be
of me I'm speaking, is it possible, of course not, that's
another thing I know, I'll speak of me when I speak no more.
In any case it's not a question of speaking of me, but of
speaking, of speaking no more, this slight confusion augurs well, now I'll have to find a name for this latest
surrogate, his head splitting with vile certainties and his
doll's eyes, later on, later on, first I must describe him
in greater detail, see what he's capable of, whence he
comes and whither he returns, in his head of course,
we don't intend to relapse into picaresque, with the stink
of Mahood and Worm still in our nostrils. Now it's I the
orator, the beleaguerers have departed, I am master on board,
after the rats, I no longer crawl between the thwarts, under
the moon, in the shadow of the lash, strange this mixture of
solid and liquid, a little air now is all we need to complete
the elements, no, I'm forgetting fire, unusual hell when you
come to think of it, perhaps it's paradise, perhaps it's the
earth, perhaps it's the shores of a lake beneath the earth, you
scarcely breathe, but you breathe, it's not certain, you see
nothing, hear nothing, you hear the long kiss of dead water
and mud, aloft at less than a score of fathoms men come and
go, you dream of them, in your long dream there's a place for
the waking, you wonder how you know all you know, you
even see grass, grass at dawn, glaucous with dew, not so blind
as all that my eyes, they're not mine, mine are done, they
don't even weep any more, they open and shut by the force
of habit, fifteen minutes exposure, fifteen minutes shutter,

like the owl cooped in the grotto in Battersea Park, ah misery, will I never stop wanting a life for myself? No no, no head either, anything you like, but not a head, in his head he doesn't go anywhere either, I've tried, lashed to the stake, blindfold, gagged to the gullet, you take the air, under the elms in se, murmuring Shelley, impervious to the shafts. Yes, a head, but solid, solid bone, and you embedded in it, like a fossil in the rock. Perhaps there go I after all. I can't go on in any case. But I must go on. So I'll go on. Air, air, I'll seek air, air in time, the air of time, and in space, in my head, that's how I'll go on. All very fine, but the voice is failing, it's the first time, no, I've been through that, it has even stopped, many a time, that's how it will end again, I'll go silent, for want of air, then the voice will come back and I'll begin again. My voice. The voice. I hardly hear it any more. I'm going silent. Hearing this voice no more, that's what I call going silent. That is to say I'll hear it still, if I listen hard. I'll listen hard. Listening hard, that what I call going silent. I'll hear it still, broken, faint, unintelligible, if I listen hard. Hearing it still, without hearing what it says, that's what I call going silent. Then it will flare up, like a kindling fire, a dying fire. Mahood explained that to me, and I'll emerge from silence. Hearing too little to be able to speak, that's my silence. That is to say I never stop speaking, but sometimes too low, too far away, too far within, to hear, no, I hear, to understand, not that I ever understand. It fades, it goes in, behind the door, I'm going silent, there's going to be silence, I'll listen, it's worse than speaking, no, no worse, no better. Unless this time it's the true silence, the one I'll never have to break any more, when I won't have to listen any more, when I can dribble in my corner, my head gone, my tongue dead, the one I have tried to earn, that I thought I could earn. I'm going to stop, that is to say I'm going to look as if I had, it will be like everything else. As if anyone were looking at me! As if it were I! It will be the same silence, the same as ever, murmurous with muted lamentation, panting and exhaling of impossible sorrow, like distant laughter, and brief spells of hush, as of one buried before his time. Long or short, the same silence. Then I resurrect and begin again. That's what I'll have got for all my pains. Unless this time it's the real silence at last. Perhaps I've said the thing that had to be said,

394   SAMUEL BECKETT

that gives me the right to be done with speech, done with
listening, done with hearing, without my knowing it. I'm
listening already, I'm going silent. The next time I won't go to
such pains, I'll tell one of Mahood's old tales, no matter
which, they are all alike, they won't tire me, I won't bother
any more about me, I'll know that no matter what I say the
result is the same, that I'll never be silent, never at peace.
Unless I try once more, just once more, one last time, to say
what has to be said, about me, I feel it's about me, perhaps
that's the mistake I make, perhaps that's my sin, so as to have
nothing more to say, nothing more to hear, till I die. It's
coming back. I'm glad. I'll try again, quick before it goes
again. Try what? I don't know. To continue. Now there is no
one left. That's a good continuation. No one left, it's embarrassing, if I had a memory it might tell me that this is the sign
of the end, this having no one left, no one to talk to, no one
to talk to you, so that you have to say, It's I who am doing this
to me, I who am talking to me about me. Then the breath
fails, the end begins, you go silent, it's the end, short-lived,
you begin again, you had forgotten, there's someone there,
someone talking to you, about you, about him, then a second,
then a third, then the second again, then all three together,
these figures just to give you an idea, talking to you, about
you, about them, all I have to do is listen, then they depart,
one by one, and the voice goes on, it's not theirs, they were
never there, there was never anyone but you, talking to you
about you, the breath fails, it's nearly the end, the breath
stops, it's the end, short-lived, I hear someone calling me,
it begins again, that must be how it goes, if I had a memory.
Even if there were things, a thing somewhere, a scrap of
nature, to talk about, you might be reconciled to having no
one left, to being yourself the talker, if only there were a thing
somewhere, to talk about, even though you couldn't see it,
or know what it was, simply feel it there, with you, you might
have the courage not to go silent, no, it's to go silent that
you need courage, for you'll be punished, punished for having
gone silent, and yet you can't do otherwise than go silent, than
be punished for having gone silent, than be punished for having been punished, since you begin again, the breath fails, if
only there were a thing, but there it is, there is not, they took
away things when they departed, they took away nature, there

was never anyone, anyone but me, anything but me, talking
to me of me, impossible to stop, impossible to go on, but I
must go on, I'll go on, without anyone, without anything, but
me, but my voice, that is to say I'll stop, I'll end, it's the end
already, short-lived, what is it, a little hole, you go down into
it, into the silence, it's worse than the noise, you listen, it's
worse than talking, no, not worse, no worse, you wait, in anguish, have they forgotten me, no, yes, no, someone calls me, I
crawl out again, what is it, a little hole, in the wilderness.
It's the end that is the worst, no, it's the beginning that is the
worst, then the middle, then the end, in the end it's the end
that is the worst, this voice that, I don't know, it's every second
that is the worst, it's a chronicle, the seconds pass, one after
another, jerkily, no flow, they don't pass, they arrive, bang,
bang, they bang into you, bounce off, fall and never move
again, when you have nothing left to say you talk of time, seconds of time, there are some people add them together to
make a life, I can't, each one is the first, no, the second, or the
third, I'm three seconds old, oh not every day of the week. I've
been away, done something, been in a hole, I've just crawled
out, perhaps I went silent, no, I say that in order to say something, in order to go on a little more, you must go on a little
more, you must go on a long time more, you must go on evermore, if I could remember what I have said I could repeat it, if
I could learn something by heart I'd be saved, I have to keep
on saying the same thing and each time it's an effort, the
seconds must be all alike and each one is infernal, what am
I saying now, I'm saying I wish I knew. And yet I have memories, I remember Worm, that is to say I have retained the
name, and the other, what is his name, what was his name, in
his jar, I can see him still, better than I can see me, I know
how he lived, now I remember, I alone saw him, but no one
sees me, nor him, I don't see him any more, Mahood, he
was called Mahood, I don't see him any more, I don't know
how he lived any more, he isn't there any more, he was never
there, in his jar, I never saw him, and yet I remember, I
remember having talked about him, I must have talked about
him, the same words recur and they are your memories. It is
I invented him, him and so many others, and the places where
they passed, the places where they stayed, in order to speak,
since I had to speak, without speaking of me, I couldn't speak

of me, I was never told I had to speak of me, I invented my
memories, not knowing what I was doing, not one is of me.
It is they asked me to speak of them, they wanted to know
what they were, how they lived, that suited me, I thought that
would suit me, since I had nothing to say and had to say something, I thought I was free to say any old thing, so long as I
didn't go silent. Then I said to myself that after all perhaps it
wasn't any old thing, the thing I was saying, that it might well
be the thing demanded of me, assuming something was being
demanded of me. No, I didn't think anything and I didn't
say anything to myself, I did what I could, a thing beyond
my strength, and often for exhaustion I gave up doing it, and
yet it went on being done, the voice being heard, the voice
which could not be mine, since I had none left, and yet which
could only be mine, since I could not go silent, and since I
was alone, in a place where no voice could reach me. Yes, in
my life, since we must call it so, there were three things, the
inability to speak, the inability to be silent, and solitude,
that's what I've had to make the best of. Yes, now I can
speak of my life, I'm too tired for niceties, but I don't know if
I, ever lived, I have really no opinion on the subject. However
that may be I think I'll soon go silent for good, in spite of
its being prohibited. Then, yes, phut, just like that, just like
one of the living, then I'll be dead, I think I'll soon be dead,
I hope I find it a change. I should have liked to go silent first,
there were moments I thought that would be my reward for
having spoken so long and so valiantly, to enter living into
silence, so as to be able to enjoy it, no, I don't know why, so
as to feel myself silent, one with all this quiet air shattered
unceasingly by my voice alone, no, it's not real air, I can't
say it, I can't say why I should have liked to be silent a little
before being dead, so as in the end to be a little as I always
was and never could be, without fear of worse to come peacefully in the place where I always was and could never rest in
peace, no, I don't know, it's simpler than that, I wanted myself, in my own land for a brief space, I didn't want to die
a stranger in the midst of strangers, a stranger in my own
midst, surrounded by invaders, no, I don't know what I
wanted, I don't know what I thought, I must have wanted so
many things, imagined so many things, while I was talking,
without knowing exactly what, enough to go blind, with long-

ings and visions, mingling and merging in one another, I'd
have been better employed minding what I was saying. But it
didn't happen like that, it happened like this, the way it's
happening now, that is to say, I don't know, you mustn't
believe what I'm saying, I don't know what I'm saying, I'm
doing as I always did, I'm going on as best I can. As to
believing I shall go silent for good and all, I don't believe it
particularly, I always believed it, as I always believed I would
never go silent, you can't call that believing, it's my walls.
But has nothing really changed, all this time? If instead
of having something to say I had something to do, with
my hands or feet, some little job, sorting things for example, or simply arranging things, suppose for the sake
of argument I had the job of moving things from one
place to another, then I'd know where I was, and how
far I had got, no, not necessarily, I can see it from here,
they would contrive things in such a way that I couldn't
suspect the two vessels, the one to be emptied and the
one to be filled, of being in reality one and the same,
it would be water, water, with my thimble I'd go and
draw it from one container and then I'd go and pour it
into another, or there would be four, or a hundred, half of
them to be filled, the other half to be emptied, numbered, the
even to be emptied, the uneven to be filled, no, it would be
more complicated, less symmetrical, no matter, to be emptied,
and filled, in a certain way, a certain order, in accordance with
certain homologies, the word is not too strong, so that I'd
have to think, tanks, communicating, communicating, connected by pipes under the floor, I can see it from here,
always showing the same level, no, that wouldn't work, too
hopeless, they'd arrange for me to have little attacks of hope
from time to time, yes, pipes and taps, I can see it from here,
so that I might fool myself from time to time, if I had that
to do, instead of this, some little job with fluids, filling and
emptying, always the same vessel, I'd be good at that, it would
be a better life than this, no, I mustn't start complaining, I'd
have a body, I wouldn't have to speak, I'd hear my steps,
almost without ceasing, and the noise of the water, and the
crying of the air trapped in the pipes, I don't understand,
I'd have bouts of zeal. I'd say to myself, the quicker I do
it the quicker it will be done, the things one has to listen to,

that's where hope would come in, it wouldn't be dark, impossible to do such work in the dark, that depends, yes, I must say I see no window, from here, whereas here that has no importance, that I see no window, here I needn't come and go, fortunately, I couldn't, nor be dexterous, for naturally the water would have great value and the least drop spilt on the way, or in the act of drawing, or in the act of pouring, would cost me dear, and how could you tell, in the dark, if a drop, what's this story, it's a story, now I've told another little story, about me, about the life that might have been mine for all the difference it would have made, which was perhaps mine, perhaps I went through that before being deemed worthy of going through this, who knows towards what high destiny I am heading, unless I am coming from it. But once again the fable must be of another, I see him so well, coming and going among his casks, trying to stop his hand from trembling, dropping his thimble, listening to it bouncing and rolling on the floor, scraping round for it with his foot, going down on his knees, going down on his belly, crawling, it stops there, it must have been I, but I never saw myself, so it can't have been I, I don't know, how can I recognize myself who never made my acquaintance, it stops there, that's all I know, I don't see him any more, I'll never see him again, yes I will, now he's there with the others, I won't name them again, you say that for something to say, you say anything for something to say, some do this, others that, he does as I said, I don't remember, he'll come back, to keep me company, only the wicked are solitary, I'll see him again, it's his fault, his fault for wanting to know what he was like, and how he lived, or he'll never come back, it's one or the other, they don't all come back, I mean there must be some I have only seen once, up to now, very true, it's only beginning, I feel the end at hand and the beginning likewise, to every man his orbit, that's obvious. But, and here I return to the charge, but has nothing really changed, all this mortal time, I'm speaking now of me, yes, henceforward I shall speak of none but me, that's decided, even though I should not succeed, there's no reason why I should succeed, so I need have no qualms. Nothing changed? I must be aging all the same, bah, I was always aged, always aging, and aging makes no difference, not to mention that all this

is not about me, hell, I've contradicted myself, no matter.
So long as one does not know what one is saying and can't
stop to inquire, in tranquillity, fortunately, fortunately, one
would like to stop, but unconditionally, I resume, so long as,
so long as, let me see, so long as one, so long as he, ah
fuck all that, so long as this, then that, agreed, that's good
enough, I nearly got stuck. Help, help, if I could only describe
this place, I who am so good at describing places, walls,
ceilings, floors, they are my speciality, doors, windows, what
haven't I imagined in the way of windows in the course of
my career, some opened on the sea, all you could see was
sea and sky, if I could put myself in a room, that would be
the end of the wordy-gurdy, even doorless, even windowless,
nothing but the four surfaces, the six surfaces, if I could
shut myself up, it would be a mine, it could be black dark,
I could be motionless and fixed, I'd find a way to explore
it, I'd listen to the echo, I'd get to know it, I'd get to remember it, I'd be home, I'd say what it's like, in my home,
instead of any old thing, this place, if I could describe this
place, portray it, I've tried, I feel no place, no place round
me, there's no end to me, I don't know what it is, it isn't
flesh, it doesn't end, it's like air, now I have it, you say
that, to say something, you won't say it long, like gas, balls,
balls, the place, then we'll see, first the place, then I'll find
me in it, I'll put me in it, a solid lump, in the middle, or
in a corner, well propped up on three sides, the place, if
only I could feel a place for me, I've tried, I'll try again,
none was ever mine, that sea under my window, higher than
the window, and the row-boat, do you remember, and the
river, and the bay, I knew I had memories, pity they are
not of me, and the stars, and the beacons, and the lights
of the buoys, and the mountain burning, it was the time
nothing was too good for me, the others benefited by it, they
died like flies, or the forest, a roof is not indispensable, an
interior, if I could be in a forest, caught in a thicket, or
wandering round in circles, it would be the end of this
blither, I'd describe the leaves, one by one, at the moment
of their growing, at the moment of their giving shade, at
the moment of their falling, those are good moments, for
one who has not to say, But it's not I, it's not I, where am
I, what am I doing, all this time, as if that mattered, but

there it is, that takes the heart out of you, your heart isn't
in it any more, your heart that was, among the brambles,
cradled by the shadows, you try the sea, you try the town,
you look for yourself in the mountains and the plains, it's
only natural, you want yourself, you want yourself in your
own little corner, it's not love, not curiosity, it's because
you're tired, you want to stop, travel no more, seek no more,
lie no more, speak no more, close your eyes, but your own,
in a word lay your hands on yourself, after that you'll make
short work of it. I notice one thing, the others have vanished,
completely, I don't like it. Notice, I notice nothing, I go on
as best I can, if it begins to mean something I can't help it,
I have passed by here, this has passed by me, thousands of
times, its turn has come again, it will pass on and something
else will be there, another instant of my old instant, there it is,
the old meaning that I'll give myself, that I won't be able to
give myself, there's a god for the damned, as on the first day,
today is the first day, it begins, I know it well, I'll remember
it as I go along, all adown it I'll be born and born, births for
nothing, and come to night without having been. Look at this
Tunis pink, it's dawn. If I could only shut myself up, quick,
I'll shut myself up, it won't be I, quick, I'll make a place, it
won't be mine, it doesn't matter, I don't feel any place for
me, perhaps that will come, I'll make it mine, I'll put myself
in it, I'll put someone in it, I'll find someone in it, I'll put myself in him, I'll say he's I, perhaps he'll keep me, perhaps the
place will keep us, me inside the other, the place all round us,
it will be over, all over, I won't have to try and move any
more, I'll close my eyes, all I'll have to do is talk, that will
be easy, I'll have things to say, about me, about my life, I'll
make it a good one, I'll know who's talking, and about what,
I'll know where I am, perhaps I'll be able to go silent, perhaps
that's all they're waiting for, there they are again, to pardon
me, waiting for me to reach home, to pardon me, it's the lie
they refuse to stop, I'll close my eyes, be happy at last, that's
the way it is this morning. Morning, I call that morning, that's
right, shilly-shally a little longer, I call that morning, I
haven't many words, I haven't much choice, I don't choose,
the word came, I should have avoided this bright stain, it's the
dayspring, but it doesn't last, I know it, I call that the dayspring, if, you could only see it. I'm off, you wouldn't think

so, perhaps it's my last gallop, I smell the stable, I always smelt the stable, it's I smell of the stable, there's no stable but me, for me. No, I won't do it, what won't I do, as if that depended on me, I won't seek my home any more, I don't know what I'll do, it would be occupied already, there would be someone there already, someone far gone, he wouldn't want me, I can understand him, I'd disturb him, what am I going to say now, I'm going to ask myself, I'm going to ask questions, that's a good stopgap, not that I'm in any danger of stopping, then why all this fuss, that's right, questions, I know millions, I must know millions, and then there are plans, when questions fail there are always plans, you say what you'll say and what you won't say, that doesn't commit you to anything and the evil moment passes, it drops stone dead, suddenly you hear yourself talking about God knows what as if you had done nothing else all your life, and neither have you, you come back from a far place, back to life, that's where you should be, where you are, far from here, far from everything, if only I could go there, if only I could describe it, I who am so good at topography, that's right, aspirations, when plans fail there are always aspirations, it's a knack, you must say it slowly, If only this, if only that, that gives you time, time for a cud of longing to rise up in the back of your gullet, nothing remains but to look as if you enjoyed chewing it, there's no knowing where that may lead you, on tracks as beaten as the day is long, often you pass yourself by, someone passes himself by, if only you knew, that's right, aspirations, you turn and look behind you, so does the other, you weep for him, he weeps for you, it's screamingly sad, anything rather than laughter. What else, opinions, comparisons, anything rather than laughter, all helps, can't help helping, to get you over the pretty pass, the things you have to listen to, what pretty pass, it's not I speaking, it's not I hearing, let us not go into that, let us go on as if I were the only one in the world, whereas I'm the only one absent from it, or with others, what difference does it make, others present, others absent, they are not obliged to make themselves manifest, all that is needed is to wander and let wander, be this slow boundless whirlwind and every particle of its dust, it's impossible. Someone speaks, someone hears, no need to go any further, it is not he, it's I, or another, or others, what does it matter, the case is clear,

it is not he, he who I know I am, that's all I know, who I
cannot say I am, I can't say anything, I've tried, I'm trying, he
knows nothing, knows of nothing, neither what it is to speak,
nor what it is to hear, to know nothing, to be capable of
nothing, and to have to try, you don't try any more, no need
to try, it goes on by itself, it drags on by itself, from word to
word, a labouring whirl, you are in it somewhere, everywhere,
not he, if only I could forget him, have one second of this
noise that carries me away, without having to say, I don't, I
haven't time, It's not I, I am he, after all, why not, why not
say it, I must have said it, as well that as anything else, it's not
I, not I, I can't say it, it came like that, it comes like that, it's
not I, if only it could be about him, if only it could come
about him, I'd deny him, with pleasure, if that could help, it's
I, here it's I, speak to me of him, let me speak of him, that's
all I ask, I never asked for anything, make me speak of him,
what a mess, now there is no one left, long may it last. In
the end it comes to that, to the survival of that alone, then the
words come back, someone says I, unbelieving. If only I could
make an effort, an effort of attention, to try and discover
what's happening, what's happening to me, what then, I don't
know, I've forgotten my apodosis, but I can't, I don't hear any
more, I'm sleeping, they call that sleeping, there they are
again, we'll have to start killing them again, I hear this horrible
noise, coming back takes time, I don't know where from,
I was nearly there, I was nearly sleeping, I call that sleeping,
there is no one but me, there was never anyone but me, here
I mean, elsewhere is another matter, I was never elsewhere,
here is my only elsewhere, it's I who do this thing and I who
suffer it, it's not possible otherwise, it's not possible so, it's not
my fault, all I can say is that it's not my fault, it's not anyone's
fault, since there isn't anyone it can't be anyone's fault, since
there isn't anyone but me it can't be mine, sometimes you'd
think I was reasoning, I've no objection, they must have taught
me reasoning too, they must have begun teaching me, before
they deserted me, I don't remember that period, but it must
have marked me, I don't remember having been deserted, perhaps I received a shock. Strange, these phrases that die for
no reason, strange, what's strange about it, here all is strange,
all is strange when you come to think of it, no, it's coming
to think of it that is strange, am I to suppose I am inhabited,

I can't suppose anything, I have to go on, that's what I'm
doing, let others suppose, there must be others in other else-
wheres, each one in his little elsewhere, this word that keeps
coming back, each one saying to himself, when the moment
comes, the moment to say it, Let others suppose, and so on,
so on, let others do this, others do that, if there are any, that
helps you on, that helps you forward, I believe in progress,
I know how to believe too, they must have taught me believing
too, no, no one ever taught me anything, I never learnt anything, I've always been here, here there was never anyone
but me, never, always, me, no one, old slush to be churned
everlastingly, now it's slush, a minute ago it was dust, it must
have rained. He must have travelled, he whose voice it is,
he must have seen, with his eyes, a man or two, a thing or
two, been aloft, in the light, or else heard tales, travellers
found him and told him tales, that proves my innocence, who
says, That proves my innocence, he says it, or they say it, yes,
they who reason, they who believe, no, in the singular, he
who lived, or saw some who had, he speaks of me, as if I were
not he, as if I were not he, both, and as if I were others, one
after another, he is the afflicted, I am far, do you hear him,
he says I'm far, as if I were he, no, as if I were not he, for
he is not far, he is here, it's he who speaks, he says it's I, then
he says it's not, I am far, do you hear him, he seeks me I
don't know why, he doesn't know why, he calls me, he wants
me to come out, he thinks I can come out, he wants me to be
he, or another, let us be fair, he wants me to rise up, up into
him, or up into another, let us be impartial, he thinks he's
caught me, he feels me in him, then he says I, as if I were he,
or in another, let us be just, then he says Murphy, or Molloy,
I forget, as if I were Malone, but their day is done, he wants
none but himself, for me, he thinks it's his last chance, he
thinks that, they taught him thinking, it's always he who
speaks, Mercier never spoke, Moran never spoke, I never
spoke, I seem to speak, that's because he says I as if he were
I, I nearly believed him, do you hear him, as if he were I, I
who am far, who can't move, can't be found, but neither can
he, he can only talk, if that much, perhaps it's not he, perhaps
it's a multitude, one after another, what confusion, someone mentions confusion, is it a sin, all here is sin, you don't
know why, you don't know whose, you don't know against

whom, someone says you, it's the fault of the pronouns, there
is no name for me, no pronoun for me, all the trouble comes
from that, that, it's a kind of pronoun too, it isn't that either,
I'm not that either, let us leave all that, forget about all that,
it's not difficult, our concern is with someone, or our concern
is with something, now we're getting it, someone or something
that is not there, or that is not anywhere, or that is there,
here, why not, after all, and our concern is with speaking of
that, now we've got it, you don't know why, why you must
speak of that, but there it is, you can't speak of that, no one
can speak of that, you speak of yourself, someone speaks of
himself, that's it, in the singular, a single one, the man on
duty, he, I, no matter, the man on duty speaks of himself, it's
not that, of others, it's not that either, he doesn't know, how
could he know, whether he has spoken of that or not, when
speaking of himself, when speaking of others, when speaking of things, how can I know, I can't know, if I've spoken
of him, I can only speak of me, no, I can't speak of anything,
and yet I speak, perhaps it's of him, I'll never know, how
could I know, who could know, who knowing could tell me,
I don't know who it's all about, that's all I know, no, I must
know something else, they must have taught me something,
it's about him who knows nothing, wants nothing, can do
nothing, if it's possible you can do nothing when you want
nothing, who cannot hear, cannot speak, who is I, who cannot
be I, of whom I can't speak, of whom I must speak, that's all
hypotheses, I said nothing, someone said nothing, it's not a
question of hypotheses, it's a question of going on, it goes on,
hypotheses are like everything else, they help you on, as if
there were need of help, that's right, impersonal, as if there
were any need of help to go on with a thing that can't stop,
and yet it will, it will stop, do you hear, the voice says it
will stop, some day, it says it will stop and it says it will never
stop, fortunately I have no opinion, what would I have an
opinion with, with my mouth perhaps, if it's mine, I don't
feel a mouth on me, that means nothing, if only I could feel
a mouth on me, if only I could feel something on me, I'll try,
if I can, I know it's not I, that's all I know, I say I, knowing
it's not I, I am far, far, what does that mean, far, no need to
be far, perhaps he's here, in my arms, I don't feel any arms
on me, if only I could feel something on me, it would be a

starting-point, a starting-point, ah if I could laugh, I know
what it is, they must have told me what it is, but I can't do
it, they can't have shown me how to do it, perhaps it's one of
those gifts that can't be acquired. The silence, a word on the
silence, in the silence, that's the worst, to speak of silence,
then lock me up, lock someone up, that is to say, what is that
to say calm, calm, I'm calm, I'm locked up, I'm in something,
it's not I, that's all I know, no more about that, that is to say,
make a place, a little world, it will be round, this time it will
be round, it's not certain, low of ceiling, thick of wall, why
low, why thick, I don't know, it isn't certain, it remains to be
seen, all remains to be seen, a little world, try and find out
what it's like, try and guess, put someone in it, seek someone
in it, and what he's like, and how he manages, it won't be I,
no matter, perhaps it will, perhaps it will be my world, possible
coincidence, there won't be windows, we're done with windows, the sea refused me, the sky didn't see me, I wasn't
there, and the summer evening air weighing on my eyelids, we must have eyelids, we must have eyeballs, it's
preferable, they must have explained to me, someone
must have explained to me, what it's like, an eye, at the
window, before the sea, before the earth, before the sky,
at the window, against the air, opening, shutting, grey,
black, grey, black, I must have understood, I must have
wanted it, wanted the eye, for my own, I must have tried, all
the things they've told me, all the things I've tried, they come
in useful still, when I think of them, that too, you must go
on thinking too, the old thoughts, they call that thinking, it's
visions, shreds of old visions, that's all you can see, a few old
pictures, a window, what need had they to show me a window,
saying, no, I forget, it doesn't come back to me, a window,
saying, There are others, even more beautiful, and the rest,
walls, sky, man, like Mahood, a little nature, too long to go
over, too forgotten, too little forgotten, was it necessary, but
was that how it happened, who can have come here, the devil
perhaps, I can think of no one else, it's he showed me everything, here, in the dark, and how to speak, and what to say,
and a little nature, and a few names, and the outside of men,
those in my image, whom I might resemble, and their way of
living, in rooms, in sheds, in caverns, in woods, or coming and
going, I forget, and who went away and left me, knowing I

was tempted, knowing I was lost, whether I succumbed or not,
have I succumbed or not, I don't know, it's not I, that's all I
know, since that day it's not I any more, since that day there
is no one any more, I must have succumbed. That's all hypotheses, that helps you forward, I believe in progress, I believe in silence, ah yes, a few words on the silence, then the
little world, that will be enough, for the rest of eternity, you'd
think it was I, I speaking, I hearing, I making plans, for the
passing hour, for the rest of eternity, whereas I'm far, or in
my arms somewhere, or stowed away somewhere, behind
walls, a few words on the silence, then just one thing more,
just one space and someone within, perhaps, until the end, I
believe it, it's evening already, I call that evening, I wish you
could see it, I believe it this evening, it's announced and I believe it, you announce, then you renounce, so it is, that
helps you on, that helps the end to come, evenings when
there is an end, I speak of evening, someone speaks of evening, perhaps it's still morning, perhaps it's still night, personally I have no opinion. They love each other, marry, in
order to love each other better, more conveniently, he goes
to the wars, he dies at the wars, she weeps, with emotion, at
having loved him, at having lost him, yep, marries again, in
order to love again, more conveniently again, they love each
other, you love as many times as necessary, as necessary in
order to be happy, he comes back, the other comes back, from
the wars, he didn't die at the wars after all, she goes to the
station, to meet him, he dies in the train, of emotion, at
the thought of seeing her again, having her again, she weeps,
weeps again, with emotion again, at having lost him again,
yep, goes back to the house, he's dead, the other is dead, the
mother-in-law takes him down, he hanged himself, with
emotion, at the thought of losing her, she weeps, weeps louder,
at having loved him, at having lost him, there's a story for
you, that was to teach me the nature of emotion, that's called
emotion, what emotion can do, given favourable conditions,
what love can do, well well, so that's emotion, that's love,
and trains, the nature of trains, and the meaning of your back
to the engine, and guards, stations, platforms, wars, love,
heart-rending cries, that must be the mother-in-law, her cries
rend the heart as she takes down her son, or her son-in-law,
I don't know, it must be her son, since she cries, and the door,

the house-door is bolted, when she got back from the station
she found the house-door bolted, who bolted it, he the better
to hang himself, or the mother-in-law the better to take him
down, or to prevent her daughter-in-law from re-entering the
premises, there's a story for you, it must be the daughter-in-
law, it isn't the son-in-law and the daughter, it's the daughter-
in-law and the son, how I reason to be sure this evening, it
was to teach me how to reason, it was to tempt me to go, to
the place where you can come to an end, I must have been
a good pupil up to a point, I couldn't get beyond a certain
point, I can understand their annoyance, this evening I begin
to understand, oh there's no danger, it's not I, it wasn't
I, the door, it's the door interests me, a wooden door,
who bolted the door, and for what purpose, I'll never know,
there's a story for you, I thought they were over, perhaps it's
a new one, lepping fresh, is it the return to the world of fable,
no, just a reminder, to make me regret what I have lost, long
to be again in the place I was banished from, unfortunately
it doesn't remind me of anything. The silence, speak of the
silence before going into it, was I there already, I don't know,
at every instant I'm there, listen to me speaking of it, I knew
it would come, I emerge from it to speak of it, I stay in it
to speak of it, if it's I who speak, and it's not, I act as if it
were, sometimes I act as if it were, but at length, was I ever
there at length, a long stay, I understand nothing about duration, I can't speak of it, oh I know I speak of it, I say never
and ever, I speak of the four seasons and the different parts
of the day and night, the night has no parts, that's because you
are asleep, the seasons must be very similar, perhaps it's
springtime now, that's all words they taught me, without making their meaning clear to me, that's how I learnt to reason,
I use them all, all the words they showed me, there were
columns of them, oh the strange glow all of a sudden, they
were on lists, with images opposite, I must have forgotten
them, I must have mixed them up, these nameless images I
have, these imageless names, these windows I should perhaps
rather call doors, at least by some other name, and this word
man which is perhaps not the right one for the thing I see
when I hear it, but an instant, an hour, and so on, how can
they be represented, a life, how could that be made clear to
me, here, in the dark, I call that the dark, perhaps it's azure,

blank words, but I use them, they keep coming back, all those they showed me, all those I remember, I need them all, to be able to go on, it's a lie, a score would be plenty, tried and trusty, unforgettable, nicely varied, that would be palette enough, I'd mix them, I'd vary them, that would be gamut enough, all the things I'd do if I could, if I wished, if I could wish, no need to wish, that's how it will end, in heart-rending cries, inarticulate murmurs, to be invented, as I go along, improvised, as I groan along, I'll laugh, that's how it will end, in a chuckle, chuck chuck, ow, ha, pa, I'll practise, nyum, hoo, plop, psss, nothing but emotion, bing bang, that's blows, ugh, pooh, what else, oooh, aaah, that's love, enough, it's tiring, hee hee, that's the Abderite, no, the other, in the end, it's the end, the ending end, it's the silence, a few gurgles on the silence, the real silence, not the one where I macerate up to the mouth, up to the ear, that covers me, uncovers me, breathes with me, like a cat with a mouse, that of the drowned, I've drowned, more than once, it wasn't I, suffo-cated, set fire to me, thumped on my head with wood and iron, it wasn't I, there yas no head, no wood, no iron, I didn't do anything to me, I didn't do anything to anyone, no one did anything to me, there is no one, I've looked, no one but me, no, not me either, I've looked everywhere, there must be someone, the voice must belong to someone, I've no objec-tion, what it wants I want, I am it, I've said so, it says so, from time to time it says so, then it says not, I've no objec-tion, I want it to go silent, it wants to go silent, it can't, it does for a second, then it starts again, that's not the real silence, it says that's not the real silence, what can be said of the real silence, I don't know, that I don't know what it is, that there is no such thing, that perhaps there is such a thing, yes, that perhaps there is, somewhere, I'll never know. But when it falters and when it stops, but it falters every instant, it stops every instant, yes, but when it stops for a good few moments, a good few moments, what are a good few moments, what then, murmurs, then it must be murmurs, and listening, someone listening, no need of an ear, no need of a mouth, the voice listens, as when it speaks, listens to its silence, that makes a murmur, that makes a voice, a small voice, the same voice only small, it sticks in the throat, there's the throat again, there's the mouth again, it fills the ear, there's the ear again, then I vomit, someone vomits, someone starts vomiting again, that must be how it happens, I have no explanations to offer, none to demand, the comma will come where I'll drown for good, then the silence, I believe it this evening, still this evening, how it drags on, I've no objection, perhaps it's springtime, violets, no, that's autumn, there's a time for everything, for the things that pass, the things that end, they could never get me to understand that, the things that stir, depart, return, a light changing, they could never get me to see that, and death into the bargain, a voice dying, that's a good one, silence at last, not a murmur, no air, no one listening, not for the likes of me, amen, on we go. Enormous prison, like a hundred thousand cathedrals, never anything else any more, from this time forth, and in it, somewhere, perhaps, riveted, tiny, the prisoner, how can he be found, how false this space is, what falseness instantly, to want to draw that round you, to want to put a being there, a cell would be plenty, if I gave up, if only I could give up, before beginning, before beginning again, what breathlessness, that's right, ejaculations, that helps you on, that puts off the fatal hour, no, the reverse, I don't know, start again, in this immensity, this obscurity, go through the motions of starting again, you who can't stir, you who never started, you the who, go through the motions, what motions, you can't stir, you launch your voice, it dies away in the vault, it calls that a vault, perhaps it's the abyss, those are words, it speaks of a prison, I've no objection, vast enough for a whole people, for me alone, or waiting for me, I'll go there now, I'll try and go there now, I can't stir, I'm there already, I must be there already, perhaps I'm not alone, perhaps a whole people is here, and the voice its voice, coming to me fitfully, we would have lived, been free a moment, now we talk about it, each one to himself, each one out loud for himself, and we listen, a whole people, talking and listening, all together, that would ex, no, I'm alone, perhaps the first, or perhaps the last, talking alone, listening alone, alone alone, the others are gone, they have been stilled, their voices stilled, their listening stilled, one by one, at each new-coming, another will come, I won't be the last, I'll be with the others, I'll be as gone, in the silence, it won't be I, it's not I, I'm not there yet, I'll go there now, I'll try and go there now, no use trying, I wait for my turn, my turn to go there, my turn to talk

there, my turn to listen there, my turn to wait there for my
turn to go, to be as gone, it's unending, it will be unending,
gone where, where do you go from there, you must go somewhere else, wait somewhere else, for your turn to go again,
and so on, a whole people, or I alone, and come back, and
begin again, no, go on, go on again, it's a circuit, a long
circuit, I know it well, I must know it well, it's a lie, I can't
stir, I haven't stirred, I launch the voice, I hear a voice, there
is nowhere but here, there are not two places, there are not
two prisons, it's my parlour, it's a parlour, where I wait for
nothing, I don't know where it is, I don't know what it's like,
that's no business of mine, I don't know if it's big, or if it's
small, or if it's closed, or if it's open, that's right, reiterate,
that helps you on, open on what, there is nothing else, only
it, open on the void, open on the nothing, I've no objection,
those are words, open on the silence, looking out on the
silence, straight out, why not, all this time on the brink of
silence, I knew it, on a rock, lashed to a rock, in the midst
of silence, its great swell rears towards me, I'm streaming with
it, it's an image, those are words, it's a body, it's not I, I
knew it wouldn't be I, I'm not outside, I'm inside, I'm in
something, I'm shut up, the silence is outside, outside, inside,
there is nothing but here, and the silence outside, nothing but
this voice and the silence all round, no need of walls, yes, we
must have walls, I need walls, good and thick, I need a prison,
I was right, for me alone, I'll go there now, I'll put me in it,
I'm there already, I'll start looking for me now, I'm there
somewhere, it won't be I, no matter, I'll say it's I, perhaps it
will be I, perhaps that's all they're waiting for, there they are
again, to give me quittance, waiting for me to say I'm someone, to say I'm somewhere, to put me out, into the silence, I see
nothing, it's because there is nothing, or it's because I have no
eyes, or both, that makes three possibilities, to choose from,
but do I really see nothing, it's not the moment to tell a lie,
but how can you not tell a lie, what an idea, a voice like this,
who can check it, it tries everything, it's blind, it seeks me
blindly, in the dark, it seeks a mouth, to enter into, who can
query it, there is no other, you'd need a head, you'd need
things, I don't know, I look too often as if I knew, it's the
voice does that, it goes all knowing, to make me think I know,
to make me think it's mine, it has no interest in eyes, it says

I have none, or that they are no use to me, then it speaks of
tears, then it speaks of gleams, it is truly at a loss, gleams,
yes, far, or near, distances, you know, measurements, enough
said, gleams, as at dawn, then dying, as at evening, or flaring
up, they do that too, blaze up more dazzling than snow, for
a second, that's short, then fizzle out, that's true enough, if
you like, one forgets, I forget, I say I see nothing, or I say
it's all in my head, as if I felt a head on me, that's all hypotheses, lies, these gleams too, they were to save me, they
were to devour me, that came to nothing, I see nothing, either
because of this or else on account of that, and these images
at which they watered me, like a camel, before the desert,
I don't know, more lies, just for the fun of it, fun, what fun
we've had, what fun of it, all lies, that's soon said, you must
say soon, it's the regulations. The place, I'll make it all the
same, I'll make it in my head, I'll draw it out of my memory,
I'll gather it all about me, I'll make myself a head, I'll make
myself a memory, I have only to listen, the voice will tell me
everything, tell it to me again, everything I need, in dribs and
drabs, breathless, it's like a confession, a last confession, you
think it's finished, then it starts off again, there were so many
sins, the memory is so bad, the words don't come, the words
fail, the breath fails, no it's something else, it's an indictment,
a dying voice accusing, accusing me, you must accuse someone, a culprit is indispensable, it speaks of my sins, it speaks
of my head, it says it's mine, it says that I repent, that I
want to be punished, better than I am, that I want to go, give
myself up, a victim is essential, I have only to listen, it will
show me my hiding-place, what it's like, where the door is,
if there's a door, and whereabouts I am in it, and what lies
between us, how the land lies, what kind of country, whether
it's sea, or whether it's mountain, and the way to take, so that
I may go, make my escape, give myself up, come to the place
where the axe falls, without further ceremony, on all who
come from here, I'm not the first, I won't be the first, it will
best me in the end, it has bested better than me, it will
tell me what to do, in order to rise, move, act like a body
endowed with despair, that's how I reason, that's how
I hear myself reasoning, all lies, it's not me they're
calling, not me they're talking about, it's not yet my turn, it's
someone else's turn, that's why I can't stir, that's why I don't

feel a body on me, I'm not suffering enough yet, it's
not yet my turn, not suffering enough to be able to stir,
to have a body, complete with head, to be able to understand,
to have eyes to light the way, I merely hear, without understanding, without being able to profit by it, by what I hear,
to do what, to rise and go and be done with hearing, I don't
hear everything, that must be it, the important things escape
me, it's not my turn, the topographical and anatomical information in particular is lost on me, no, I hear everything, what
difference does it make, the moment it's not my turn, my turn
to understand, my turn to live, my turn of the lifescrew, it
calls that living, the space of the way from here to the door,
it's all there, in what I hear, somewhere, if all has been said,
all this long time, all must have been said, but it's not my
turn to know what, to know what I am, where I am, and what
I should do to stop being it, to stop being there, that's cohe-
rent, so as to be another, no, the same, I don't know, depart
into life, travel the road, find the door, find the axe, perhaps
it's a cord, for the neck, for the throat, for the cords, or
fingers, I'll have eyes, I'll see fingers, it will be the silence,
perhaps it's a drop, find the door, open the door, drop, into
the silence, it won't be I, I'll stay here, or there, more likely
there, it will never be I, that's all I know, it's all been done
already, said and said again, the departure, the body that rises,
the way, in colour, the arrival, the door that opens, closes
again, it was never I, I've never stirred, I've listened, I must
have spoken, why deny it, why not admit it, after all, I deny
nothing, I admit nothing, I say what I hear, I hear what I
say, I don't know, one or the other, or both, that makes three
possibilities, pick your fancy, all these stories about travellers,
these stories about paralytics, all are mine, I must be extremely
old, or it's memory playing tricks, if only I knew if I've lived,
if I live, if I'll live, that would simplify everything, impossible
to find out, that's where you're buggered, I haven't stirred,
that's all I know, no, I know something else, it's not I, I
always forget that, I resume, you must resume, never stirred
from here, never stopped telling stories, to myself, hardly
hearing them, hearing something else, listening for something
else, wondering now and then where I got them from, was I
in the land of the living, were they in mine, and where, where
do I store them, in my head, I don't feel a head on me, and

what do I tell them with, with my mouth, same remark, and what do I hear them with, and so on, the old rigmarole, it can't be I, or it's because I pay no heed, it's such an old habit, I do it without heeding, or as if I were somewhere else, there I am far again, there I am the absentee again, it's his turn again now, he who neither speaks nor listens, who has neither body nor soul, it's something else he has, he must have something, he must be somewhere, he is made of silence, there's a pretty analysis, he's in the silence, he's the one to be sought, the one to be, the one to be spoken of, the one to speak, but he can't speak, then I could stop, I'd be he, I'd be the silence, I'd be back in the silence, we'd be reunited, his story the story to be told, but he has no story, he hasn't been in story, it's not certain, he's in his own story, unimaginable, unspeakable, that doesn't matter, the attempt must be made, in the old stories incomprehensibly mine, to find his, it must be there somewhere, it must have been mine, before being his, I'll recognize it, in the end I'll recognize it, the story of the silence that he never left, that I should never have left, that I may never find again, that I may find again, then it will be he, it will be I, it will be the place, the silence, the end, the beginning, the beginning again, how can I say it, that's all words, they're all I have, and not many of them, the words fail, the voice fails, so be it, I know that well, it will be the silence, full of murmurs, distant cries, the usual silence, spent listening, spent waiting, waiting for the voice, the cries abate, like all cries, that is to say they stop, the murmurs cease, they give up, the voice begins again, it begins trying again, quick now before there is none left, no voice left, nothing left but the core of murmurs, distant cries, quick now and try again, with the words that remain, try what, I don't know, I've forgotten, it doesn't matter, I never knew, to have them carry me into my story, the words that remain, my old story, which I've forgotten, far from here, through the noise, through the door, into the silence, that must be it, it's too late, perhaps it's too late, perhaps they have, how would I know, in the silence you don't know, perhaps it's the door, perhaps I'm at the door, that would surprise me, perhaps it's I, perhaps somewhere or other it was I, I can depart, all this time I've journeyed without knowing it, it's I now at the door, what door, what's a door doing here, it's the last words, the true last, or it's the murmurs, the murmurs are coming, I know that well, no, not even that, you talk of murmurs, distant cries, as long as you can talk, you talk of them before and you talk of them after, more lies, it will be the silence, the one that doesn't last, spent listening, spent waiting, for it to be broken, for the voice to break it, perhaps there's no other, I don't know, it's not worth having, that's all I know, it's not I, that's all I know, it's not mine, it's the only one I ever had, that's a lie, I must have had the other, the one that lasts, but it didn't last, I don't understand, that is to say it did, it still lasts, I'm still in it, I left myself behind in it, I'm waiting for me there, no, there you don't wait, you don't listen, I don't know, perhaps it's a dream, all a dream, that would surprise me, I'll wake, in the silence, and never sleep again, it will be I, or dream, dream again, dream of a silence, a dream silence, full of murmurs, I don't know, that's all words, never wake, all words, there's nothing else, you must go on, that's all I know, they're going to stop, I know that well, I can feel it, they're going to abandon me, it will be the silence, for a moment, a good few moments, or it will be mine, the lasting one, that didn't last, that still lasts, it will be I, you must go on, I can't go on, you must go on, I'll go on, you must say words, as long as there are any, until they find me, until they say me, strange pain, strange sin, you must go on, perhaps it's done already, perhaps they have said me already, perhaps they have carried me to the threshold of my story, before the door that opens on my story, that would surprise me, if it opens, it will be I, it will be the silence, where I am, I don't know, I'll never know, in the silence you don't know, you must go on, I can't go on, I'll go on.